Bird, Horse, and Muffin

A novel

By Susan D. Hill

To the children of Uganda...

How Much Love

How graceful is your grace?
How much lovingkindness is forever?

How much mercy is there,
When it comes new every morning?

How much love is there, when blood is the only cure?
How much fire of desire must be in my Lord?
How much anger is the wrath on injustice?
How much fear will come on the wicked man?

How much shouting will be done,
When a white horse comes through the clouds in splendor?

How much love does it take to save a man?

It takes it all, it takes it all, it takes it all.
Every bit, it takes it all.

Nothing held back, nothing kept in reserve,
Nothing kept for another day.
Nothing spent on something else that we don't know about,
It's all been spent, and it was spent in a day.

It's all been done, it's all been said, it's all been spent...
And it was finished,
Yes it was finished in a day.

A spontaneous song, performed by Don Potter in Holland

I AM NOT OLD, but I'm no longer a child. Sometimes I'm brave enough to think about those days—days of suffocating fear and weeks when sadness had no end, and I lived with many questions tapping on my brain like a relentless woodpecker. Each new bend in the road of twists and turns thrust me into the unknown like a wild mustang ride—snorting, rearing, and trampling my simple world. And when the quiet came at night, my heart seemed as cold as the bottom of the great lake.

Yet Nana's gentle hand on my arm, or the look in Skeets' kind eyes, well, they kept something *muffin* alive in me. They made me believe a greater thing could happen, something I've never quite been able to explain—that calm knowing inside, the surge of boldness I felt, and the certainty of where it was from. I sometimes wonder at how easily I could have ignored it. I could've been distracted and missed it.

But I didn't. Somehow, I didn't.

Chapter 1

How graceful is your grace?

THE FIRST TIME I heard God speak was in a school parking lot. I was ten years old.

My heart flipped violently. The words were unmistakable, as if He stood right behind me and whispered in my left ear. I twirled a complete circle but found no one.

Chills rippled across my skin like electric current. I sank to my knees. God sounded calm. Still I gasped, because Mama said He didn't lie. A perfect summer day had become a muted fuzzy dream.

The morning had started with warm rays through my bedroom window and the fresh earth smell that follows a summer rain. I bounded down the stairs like a cat that smells tuna in the air, but I stopped short on the landing.

Our only happy-family picture hung on the wall, slightly askew. I tilted my head. There, in black and white, we huddled on our sailboat with the mainsail for a backdrop. The wind had played with our hair, and we were all smiles. Grace, or Mama as we called her, held my little brother Tuck on her hip. My older brother Wyeth posed behind me. He made bunny-ears at the back of my head, which he later claimed was just a peace sign. Being the only girl, I remained an easy target. Our father, Hank, looked rather handsome but towered over us with a firm grip on the tiller. Somehow, his smile didn't belong to his face.

1

My chest tightened. I turned away.

The sound of running water in the kitchen sink spread uneasiness through my body. I always calmed myself down before entering the kitchen, because it was Father's Command Central in the mornings. He had a set routine—making his coffee just so, arranging his spoon, sugar bowl, and Cleveland Indians mug in a line on the counter. He'd lay *The Plain Dealer* on the table with a freshly sharpened pencil for the crossword puzzle. I swore acid rain came out his pores if that pencil went missing.

Mornings were not a time to be boisterous. Noise or commotion made him grouchy. I had learned that the hard way one time, when Wyeth gave my knee a horse-bite at breakfast. The tablecloth concealed the fact that he started it. Father shouted at me for kicking and shrieking, while my brother got off scot-free, the weasel.

But none of that mattered now. Two weeks ago, Father had left us.

I peeked around the wall. "Bird-brain," I chided myself. No need to act all grownup-like. After a few deep breaths, I settled quietly into my place at the breakfast table.

Mama stood basking in sunlight by the kitchen sink. Her slender body leaned against the counter. Hot water from the faucet formed a swirling mist that fogged up the window. Wasting hot water in our household was a mortal sin, but she seemed unconcerned and lost in thought. I stared at her beautiful silhouette.

Extending her right leg with pointed toes, she lifted her opposing arm with ballet gracefulness and stretched to her limit, as if offering God an invisible gift. After a moment, her arm descended gently back to her side, with hand and fingers floating down like a dove. The sweep of her arm completed a circle.

Then, with one knee raised, she made a slow pirouette like the tiny ballerina that revolved in my jewelry box. Steam billowed around her in the light. Her eyes were closed, her cheeks pink and glistening. She appeared to be dancing in some imaginary place.

I watched, leaning toward her in my seat, wanting to be wherever she was. Then her eyes caught mine. Her poise deflated. She turned and shut off the water. "There you are." She blinked over and over and appeared embarrassed. The skin below her eyes was shiny and wet.

My cheeks felt hot. It seemed as though I'd interrupted a

2

private moment. I stirred Tang into the cold water in my favorite Flintstones glass and splashed some milk on my cereal. "Where are the boys?" I asked, trying to sound normal.

"Wy had to walk Tuck to Indian Guides." She meant in Father's place, but didn't say so.

The lights flickered. Usually that happened right before a power outage.

"Iris." Mama squeezed my shoulder as she opened the fridge. "You can't wear those thongs, *remember?*"

Father had said all sandals were "inapt" for school, and Mama had to back him up. I'd look up the word later, but I knew it meant a big fat "no." Summer school should be different, especially on the very last day. Wearing flip-flops was part of summertime itself and second only to going barefoot. Father seemed to have rules about every doggone thing, and sometimes the twinge of defiance felt better than a joyless life.

"But, Mama..." I pleaded, "He's gone, so why not?"

She gave me the ain't-no-way look. "Besides," she added, "It's cool and wet from the storm last night."

I slumped my shoulders.

"Go on now. Grab those new sneakers that your..." Her voice trailed off. She probably didn't want to mention my father's name.

I stood after spooning my last bite, glaring at her. With a sad smile, she tenderly reeled my stiff body into the sanctuary of her soft chest. I surrendered, though anger rumbled inside. My eyes watered. I shut them hard, wishing Mama and I could both twirl with the lightheartedness of dancers. Pressing my nose into her blouse, I lingered there, soothed by her clean sheet smell.

"I'm sorry Rissy," she whispered.

Defying my father had consequences. We didn't talk about it. I glanced at our embrace in the hall mirror. Tears spilled over her lower lids. She nuzzled my head.

After a minute, I pulled away and stuffed the dumb white Keds into my backpack. I let the screen door slam extra loud and clomped down the front steps. At the end of the driveway, I looked over my shoulder. Mama stood silently in the doorway, tying her apron. She raised a hand and fluttered her fingers. I ducked my chin, pretending not to see.

IT WAS THE SUMMER of 1979 in Beaconsfield, Ohio. Wyeth and his friends were obsessed with "Rocky," while girls my age were singing Bee Gees songs and watching *Happy Days* on TV.

I loved our small town on the western shore of Lake Erie. Smack dab through the center of the township lay a wide and wooded area that separated rows of houses on either side. We called it the Middle Strip. I considered it my own personal forest, complete with dark scary places where I was quite sure a porcupine lived.

Most girls, especially the prissy ones, avoided the Strip on their way to school, because there wasn't any clear path. I knew where to pick it up. Beyond the chokecherry patch, a certain cluster of weeping willows formed a concealing curtain. Pulling the branches aside, made the path magically appear. It flowed like a stream around the trees. Each curve and every exposed root was familiar.

I scrambled up the steep place. At the top, a rope lay fastened to the trunk of a thick oak tree. Holding the cord, I rappelled down the slope on the other side, releasing the rope's stubby end to jump the last part of my descent.

After that, the trail veered right toward a swampy area teeming with new batches of mosquitoes. I always outran them, flapping my arms like a great blue heron. A shadowy, deep ravine yawned to the left, promising adventure for another day. Instead I followed the brightness overhead to a fragrant meadow where the Middle Strip ended near town. That morning, I stopped to put on my shoes.

My wet feet looked horribly white for early July. It was downright humiliating. I could've convinced Mama on the flip-flop thing had I really pressed her. Father wouldn't even know. But then there was my teacher. Nothing got by her. Yesterday, my classmate Billy actually thought he could get away with keeping his frog, One-Eyed Jack, inside his desk. He needed to think again.

Tying the laces, I glanced back at my woods. How many times I had traveled through them on my way to Kensington School. *Kindergarten, first, second, third, fourth, fifth and six...*seven years added up. Over a thousand days worth.

And now summer school. I huffed and squinted. I wanted to be down at the park with the other kids watching city workers set up the fireworks. Instead I would be trapped in Reading Lab, where I wasn't allowed to read one word at a time anymore. My eyes had to keep up with the moving red dot as it passed over sentences on a screen.

"Reeeeding Lab," I said with deliberate irritation, in my best nasally tone. Tipping my head back, I looked at the great expanse of sky over the lake. Horsetail cloud wisps stretched across the blue heaven.

God, please help me pass the test. I'll try to focus, I promise.

A knot tightened in my gut. If I didn't pass, I might have to face one of Father's lectures. He could return any moment. His stiff lips and clenched teeth made him seem like Sarge who was always angry with Beetle Bailey. If I failed, he'd probably lock me in my room and feed me liver and spinach until I finished the summer reading list. He'd remind me that girls who fall behind in school end up as hospital aides, cleaning up stinky old bedpans. A bubble of nausea rose in my throat.

Realizing the time, I jumped up to run the rest of the way. The safety guard had already left his post. Not a good sign. I passed Mike's Delicatessen. No time for penny candy. At the red light, I crossed Lake Road, still sprinting.

As I mounted two steps at a time, my thighs started burning like the time I beat the three fastest boys at the hundred-yard dash. But it didn't feel thrilling today. I slowed only to make a silly face at Anna Rae, who was imprisoned in remedial math class.

At the Reading Lab entrance, I stopped abruptly. My heart pounded in my ears. The mottled glass window in the door kept other students from spying on us. It didn't really help. No matter how stealthily I entered or left the Lab, some kids knew everything and told everyone. They called us "Polka Dots" and referred to Reading Lab as the Dancing Dot Club.

Once, two pretty girls cornered Billy and me by the drinking fountain. "How brainless do you have to be to join the *Club*?" they tittered. They weren't pretty on the inside. Their words smarted and made my eyes sting. After today, all that would end, and I'd disappear into the sea of students at junior high—that is, *if* I passed the test.

"Iris? Is that you?' My teacher's shrill voice nailed me as I turned the black-enameled knob. "You're late!"

"I'm sorry." The door clicked behind me. The other students looked up in unison like a blob creature with twenty-eyes.

"*Sorry?*" Her voice rose another octave. "This is the *third* time this week!"

I didn't dare make eye contact. Without meaning to, I focused on her red gummy-worm lips. In fact, I usually looked at peoples' mouths when they spoke and often missed what they said. Each mouth was unique, and a smile either made someone more attractive or just plain creepy.

Some people had beautiful teeth like white corn kernels lined up in a row. Their smiles made me feel warm all over. On the other hand, I'd seen more than one mouth with pointy vampire canines. Old people had teeth like porcelain sinks with hard water stains. And then there was poor Billy. His buckteeth were worse than any I knew. Father once said, "That boy could eat a peach through a picket fence." I guess I noticed these things more than most, because my father was an orthodontist.

"Have you heard a single word I've said, young lady?" She stood too close to me.

I nodded.

"I rang your mother. She said you left in plenty of time." My teacher had accidentally swiped some lipstick on her upper teeth. "What happens to you on the way to school?"

I swallowed hard, resisting the urge to laugh at her red teeth. My gut churned until I glanced at Billy. He slowly pointed to a white plastic container with holes poked in the lid. The humor of the moment vanished. One-Eyed Jack had been discovered.

"Are you daydreaming, Miss Somerset?"

"It won't happen again," I said, batting my eyelashes in earnest.

The more upset she became, the less chance I had of passing. I held my breath. She searched my face for insincerity with her built-in lie detector. One of her painted-on eyebrows rose higher than the other. Finally she turned tail and strutted back to her desk.

"Miss Iris...today is your last chance to finish up before the holiday. If you don't pass the exam this time, you'll be back for second session after the Fourth. Now, wouldn't you rather be swimming like, say, Mister One-Eye here?" She glanced at the frog containment bucket.

"Yes ma'am."

Muffled laughter circulated the room. Billy quickly curved his face away, straining his lips to cover his teeth.

"Well, get to it then." She handed me the final exam.

I scurried to my desk. Reading comprehension was not my weakness. I even collected big, sophisticated words. My problem was speed. So I skimmed and wrote my answers like a maniac, glancing at the clock every few minutes. I could feel her eyes watching me. She always caught the cheaters. My right foot tapped impulsively, and I nearly slipped off my chair when the timer buzzed. She snatched our papers straight away.

The long silence of waiting for her to grade them was the worst part. Sunlight moved from my desk to Billy's. He dozed, resting his head on his folded arms. A small line of drool trickled from his mouth and looked like melted gold in the sunshine.

I cracked all my knuckles twice. Then I counted hooks by the coatroom. I looked over. My teacher was still grading. On my fingers, I calculated the number of words in the *Star-Spangled Banner*, but got stuck on "perilous night," trying to determine if "peril us" was one word or two.

"Iris Somerset?" My teacher rose from her squeaky chair and walked to my desk. "It's a small miracle, but you have passed."

Leaping out of my seat, I threw my arms around her thick waist. It felt like the moment I knew I could swim underwater and not drown. She promptly handed me the summer reading list. I hoisted my backpack over my shoulder and charged out of the room. I couldn't wait to tell Anna Rae my big news.

The bell sounded. I planted my feet by her classroom door, shifting my weight left and right. Anna raised a wait-a-minute finger. Perturbed, I strolled outside by the parking lot to linger in the shade of an apple tree. I kicked off my new shoes and stretched out my toes in the cool grass. Hanging on a low branch, I looked around the schoolyard and started my farewells.

"Goodbye merry-go-round. Goodbye jungle-gym." I felt happy and sad about it. "Goodbye swings and tether ball. See you later, bike rack." What a strange feeling to leave everything I knew so well. I'd miss Bike Safety Week, when we all decorated our bikes with streamers and balloons and wore outlandish hats.

"Outlaaandish." I let the fabulous word roll off my tongue.

"Goodbye tall slide and swinging bridge." Anna Rae still hadn't come.

I looked at the open area on the playground and remembered the school carnival, especially the Cake Walk. My father said it was too easy, hence the name. I wasn't sure what *hence* meant. All I knew was if the carousel music started up and you stepped from one square to the next long enough, they handed you a pan of brownies or a blueberry pie just like that! Billy had to spend nineteen tickets one year, but refused to go home without some kind of baked goods.

Warm air wafted from the sizzling asphalt. Most of the summer school students were well on their way home now. The playground seemed unusually quiet. A light wind toyed with the swings.

A tiny white butterfly hopscotched from leaf to leaf on the young apple tree. I extended my fingers, but it darted out of reach. With feathery wings, it floated off in a puff of air. I'd remember it clearly, like a recurring dream, because it happened on the last day of my childhood.

Your mom is dead, I heard in my mind. It was a clear, calm voice. *But she's okay.*

Chapter 2

THE EXIT DOOR burst open. Anna Rae skipped across the playground.

"I'm done now, forrrevver!" she shouted, swaying her arms over her head. She beelined toward me but slowed as she neared. "What happened to you?" She waved the air overhead. "*Don't* tell me you gotta come back for second session?"

Questions swirled like dust devils inside my head.

"I'm done now...*forever.*" My echo of her phrase came in slow motion. I wasn't sure if I said the words or only thought them. My face tingled.

"Well, don't sound so excited about it." Anna Rae threw her backpack by the tree and flopped down. "Ahh, summertime." She stretched out and gazed at the sky before looking at me. "Rissy. You're creeping me out. What's the problem?"

"It's all...*wrecked* now." I heard my voice's monotone. It sounded strange.

"Wrecked? What on earth?"

"Mama's dead." The words left my mouth but stayed in my mind. My lips trembled. Haunting whispers pushed me where I didn't want to go. I covered my face, but Anna Rae would not relent.

"What are you talking about, you crazy goat!" She rolled over to face me.

I didn't respond. She sat up.

9

I clutched my knees, closed my eyes, desperate to stop the rising dread.

A memory surfaced like a vision. Mama's face gradually became clear, emerging into daylight from a deep blue pool.

"An iris is a purple-blue flower," she said with a little laugh. *"It's also the colored part of your eyes that lets in the light."* Her eyes studied mine. *"Yours are such an iridescent blue."* Her smooth hands caressed the sides of my face. *"And in old stories, Iris means messenger of God."* Light shone all around her, growing brighter. *"You already see beyond your years, my darling. God will show you things."*

"Rissy! You hear me?"

It didn't sound like Mama anymore. Anna Rae's voice pulled me back to reality.

I exhaled a long slow breath. "I don't know." I glanced up at her.

"What do you mean? And *why* are you whispering?" She waited without blinking.

At first, I didn't have any words to describe it. "I was alone, here, by this tree."

The wind stirred the leaves overhead.

"Go on." Anna Rae leaned in closer.

"I was waiting for you." My body began to shake uncontrollably. Shivers crossed my chest and rolled down my legs.

Anna stared at me.

"Then I heard..." My voice sounded small like Alice, shrinking in Wonderland.

"What did you hear?" Anna glanced at the school.

I shook my head. "I, I think...it was God." Tears filled my eyes.

She pursed her lips and studied me.

"It had to be God," I said.

Anna Rae's lips parted. Her eyes grew big. She put her hands on my shoulders. "God said your mom is—*dead?*" Even she could barely utter the word.

I nodded, wiping tears on the back of my hand. I didn't want to talk. I had too many questions. My mind crawled with dark thoughts.

Anna Rae grew quiet and turned to sit cross-legged. Together we stared in silence at the empty playground while a crow pestered a small sparrow over a crust of bread.

Moments later, a Pontiac Sunbird pulled into the parking lot with a short screech. My neighbor, Mrs. Peate, swung her legs out of the car and simultaneously dumped her entire purse on the black-top. I heard her moan as she reached for a tube of lipstick that had rolled under the adjacent car. She pulled herself together and scanned the playground. Red splotches covered her neck. She saw us and hurried over. I knew she'd be the one to come.

"Iris, honey," she said, twisting her watch. "You need to get in the car. You too, Anna Rae. I'll take you by your place."

Moving as in a trance, we gathered our things and climbed in the backseat. I put on my seatbelt, pulling it tight out of habit.

"Be right back," Mrs. Peate said, finger-combing her short tuffs of red hair. She headed toward the principal's office.

Anna Rae turned to me. "Has Mrs. Peate *ever* picked you up from school before?"

"Once."

"When?"

"When my dad was in the hospital."

"Did your teacher say she'd be coming today?"

"No."

I studied the rubber mat on the floor. A big box of Kleenex crowded the space by my feet. I felt stuck in a time warp, obsessed with every detail of the car's interior—crusty mud flecks on the car-pet, dried bug splats on the windshield, a few tissues wadded up on the dash. The odometer said 139100 and the car keys dangled down, still swinging slightly. A fly buzzed along the window, but other-wise everything was still. Anna Rae sat hugging her knees. Strands of hair hid her face.

The door opened. The car rocked slightly as Mrs. Peate settled in. She started the engine and slowly pulled onto Lake Road. We were at least a mile from school when she finally spoke. "Iris." Her voice sounded weak.

I knew it would be hard for her. After a long pause, she inhaled and tried again. "There's something I need to tell you..." Her voice started to break up. "Your mom..."

"She's dead," I interrupted. I could hear my voice inside my head and outside my body at the same time. What was happening to me?

Mrs. Peate stifled a gasp and remained speechless for the duration of the ride. She dabbed her eyes with tissues. Anna Rae pulled the neck hole of her t-shirt up over her face and quietly sobbed.

Through steady tears, I watched a rolling mural of happy scenes out the window. People crowded around a fireworks stand. Several children jumped up and down while their dad reached for his wallet. A woman jogged in the park with two poodles on leashes. Sunlight shimmered like tiny diamonds across the water, and a few sailboats had spinnakers ballooning out over their bows. A steady south wind. Perfect for a race.

It was all someone else's life now.

We came to a stop and the door opened. Anna Rae touched my hand. Then the door closed. The car continued on. My eyelids were heavy, my throat dry. I slumped over until the car rocked through the pothole at the end of our driveway.

Two squad cars and an ambulance with flashing lights crowded the space where we usually parked. Mrs. Peate slowed to a stop on the grass. Father would have been ticked about that. Mr. Redinger, who lived two doors down, once said Father was "meticulous" about his lawn. It meant fussy, but I preferred the clicking sound of his word.

"Come on, sweetheart." Mrs. Peate gently held my upper arm and helped me wiggle out. My legs felt clumsy, as if the lawn was made of mattresses. A man with greasy black hair took snapshots of the house with a boxy camera. He pulled a small notebook from his back pocket as we passed by. I could feel his x-ray eyes scanning me.

Mrs. Peate navigated through the crowd. I trailed on her heels like an obedient dog, following her to the porch where other neighbors stood murmuring to one another. Some turned to stare, but no one said anything. The screen door moaned as she pushed it open, and everything seemed normal for a cruel, fleeting second.

An empty pie tin sat on the counter. A bit of crust and a few glazed pecans were left. That was strange. Mama always made lemon meringue pie for the Fourth of July, though pecan was her favorite.

My grandparents, Nana and Pops, huddled in the living room, talking to a policeman in low tones. Tear lines streaked down Nana's powdered cheeks. Pops' face appeared pale, and his hand trembled as he gestured. They didn't see me through the forest of adults. Hopefully, Father was still away.

The police had already blocked off my parents' bedroom door from the living room. How strange to be denied access around my own house. I suddenly thought of Mama's diary in the drawer of her bedside table. I had to get it. I needed it. The cops probably didn't know about the back entry to the bedroom through the kitchen. I headed that way.

Passing the pantry, I heard a faint whimper. At first it sounded like Mr. Kibbs, our orange tabby. He often got stuck in the dirty rag hamper, because he'd become such a fat Twinkie and didn't have front claws. I pried the pantry door open. It was a pocket door with whiney wheels that rolled on a track. No kitty in sight.

Crouched next to the flour bin on the floor sat my little brother, Tuck. He was small for a four-year-old. I ran my fingers through his soft brown curls. He looked up with puffy eyes. My heart pained for him and all that he wouldn't understand. I squished in beside his small body. A large sack of dried beans didn't leave much room, and the lower shelf with cracker tins forced me to bow my head. I rested my cheek on my knees.

Thirteen nights ago, I had hidden in the very same spot. Fortunately, Tuck had fallen asleep in his room upstairs with a window fan drowning out all sounds. Late that evening, Wyeth was in serious trouble. Father had called him up short on a white lie. I had watched nervously through the narrow opening of the pantry door. Nearly a teenager, my brother got testy with Father.

My parents and Wyeth stood facing each other in the kitchen.

"He's a liar through and through, Mother!" Father had said, pounding a thick phonebook on the counter.

Wyeth took a step back and glowered at Father. You'd have thought an arrow had just struck Wy's chest dead-on.

"Be quiet, Hank!" Mama sounded furious. "He didn't mean any trouble by it." She moved closer to Wyeth.

"What in the Sam Hill did you say?" Father bellowed at her, his face turning bright red.

She didn't answer, but pressed her lips into a line.

"Don't get mouthy with me, woman! He's hiding something, the stubborn mule!" He spoke as if my brother wasn't even there.

I could see the full circles of Wy's brown eyes. Pressure mounted. He gripped the edge of the stove. Then, as I feared, my brother erupted. "What's a *little* white lie when *bigger* lies are going on anyways!" He spit a few forbidden words at Father.

I cringed inside.

Father lunged at him, but my brother tore out the backdoor.

"I'm done with all of you!" Wyeth screamed, causing his voice to crack.

Mama burst into tears and ran to the bedroom.

Father switched directions and stomped toward her, knocking a chair out of the way. "Don't you turn your back on me! You're part of this!" He took big thundering steps, pursuing her like a mouse he intended to crush. The bedroom door slammed behind him.

All air got sucked from my lungs.

Wyeth's outburst sparked the worst fight ever between our parents. I'd never heard so much yelling and crying, and Mama did all the crying. From inside the pantry, their argument sounded muffled. I scarcely made out their words, though I strained to hear. I pictured them shouting face-to-face. A loud crash made me wonder if he was smacking her around.

I had made up my mind then and there to throw myself between them. My stomach muscles tightened with urgency. I squatted in the shadowy cupboard ready to charge. But then, it got strangely quiet. My breathing became labored.

Unexpectedly, Father stormed out of the bedroom. His angry footsteps passed inches from me, vibrating the floor. I heard the tinkling of keys before the front door closed with a bang. He pealed off in our old yellow Buick. The muffler rumbled, and then it backfired.

My lungs heaved from lack of air.

Mama would've been upset with my eavesdropping that dreadful night, but I had to know if she was all right. Painstakingly, I opened the pantry door, inch by inch, rubbing Crisco on the wheels and track to keep them from squeaking. At last, I slipped out the narrow opening.

Their bedroom door stood slightly ajar. Mama knelt beside the bed, her face hidden by the comforter. With outstretched arms on the bed, she clasped her hands, praying between sobs. Something had gone terribly wrong. My whole body ached to go in and wrap myself around her waist.

I blinked hot tears, remembering that horrible scene.

Mama could always smooth things over when it came to our father. But that night was different. She looked broken in pieces and would've been all the more crushed knowing I had witnessed their fight. So I kept silent, but decided to stay near in case Father returned. Squeezing back into the pantry, I rolled the door shut and cried myself to sleep, using a bag of marshmallows for a pillow.

As it turned out, Wyeth only ran away to the backyard and spent the night in the old Chevy truck by the sycamore tree. The morning after, he appeared without apology, but Father did not return. Thirteen days had come and gone.

Now Mama was dead.

I eyed Tuck. One knee had a nasty scrape, red with inflammation. "Don't pick your scab, buddy," I said. "Let it come off on its own."

His bottom lip jutted out. He flashed his angry face at me, but I kissed his forehead before climbing out of the cramped space.

No one seemed to notice me. I tiptoed to the back entry of my parents' bedroom to open the door a crack. I started to tremble again. A white sheet concealed a lumpy object on the floor. I shifted my weight to get a better view. The cloth had not covered a pale arm, and the exposed hand held a phone receiver.

My legs went limp. I slid down the wall in the dim hallway, growing faint and queasy. The floor spun in slow motion. I didn't feel attached to the ground. Was I dying too? Would I float away? I grabbed the heating grate to get my bearings and curled up, making myself as small as possible. A cold sweat came over me. Stomach acid stung my throat. I don't know how long I stayed there.

Eventually a commotion stirred in the bedroom. I slowly emerged to peek in on the scene. Official-looking people had entered the bedroom through the other door. A woman pulled the sheet aside.

I couldn't breathe.

Next, two men grunted as they lifted Mama's flaccid body to a cot on wheels. Her face looked mannequin-like. The woman zipped up the black plastic over her face, as if they were shipping our Mama off in a large duffle bag. Footsteps now, the only sound as they rolled her away.

My body felt entombed in concrete. Darkness hung on my shoulders. I shuddered. For the first time in my life, I was afraid of something other than Father. I had never imagined life without Mama.

After what seemed like a long time, the heaviness lifted. I went in the empty bedroom. Someone had drawn the curtains, but the windows were wide open. Summer breezes swung the drapes around like tall gray ghosts. I slid into Mama's side of the bed, cocooning inside her sage green comforter. Face down in her pillow, I smelled a hint of lavender.

Then someone closed the front door forcefully, rattling the windows like a sonic boom. "Get out! Get the hell out of our house!" It was Wyeth. "Who do you think you are? We're not a freak show!" He raged. "Get out now!"

"Wyeth, *Wyeth.*" Pops tried calming him.

"No! Leave me alone! No one cares about us!"

A policeman spoke. "Sir, please *do* ask everyone to go home. We need to finish up without an audience."

Pops repeated the officer's request to the neighbors who stood on the porch.

The backdoor closed with another bang, and something in the kitchen crashed to the floor. I popped up, trying to untwist my legs from the comforter. One foot stayed tangled, and I plummeted off the bed.

"Oww!" My chin hit the sideboard as I landed hard on my right shoulder. I shook my head and touched my jaw. No blood. All at once, I remembered the diary. The bedside table drawer was partly open. I searched around. It had to be under all those old Reader's Digests and half-squeezed tubes of lotion.

My fingers found a smooth leather surface. I grabbed the book and jiggled it loose. The police could return any second. Stuffing it into my shorts, I pulled my shirt over the top corners and escaped out the only bedroom window missing a screen—the place where Mama let Kibbs in at night.

The wind gusted harder now. Heavy clouds were already dropping sheets of rain to the west.

Years ago, I'd told Mama those kinds of rain clouds were "ruined."

"Ruined? What do you mean?" she had asked.

I was only four or five then, but I loved new words. "You know, when the mean sisters *ruined* Cinderella's dress for the ball."

"Oh yes, her pretty gown—all torn up. I remember now."

"See Mama." I pointed to the sky. "The clouds look like that."

16

She searched the sky and gave me a glowing smile.

But now, I knew that *ruined* had a far different meaning.

Father was gone, and Mama was dead.

I squeezed through the space in the raspberry hedge. The thorns tore my skin. Thin red lines of blood formed on my upper arm. I didn't care. I headed toward the large sycamore. Other than the pantry, the tree had become a place to be alone, the place where I whispered things to God.

As I rounded the corner of the shed, I stopped abruptly. Wyeth ranted like a wild savage, ripping bark slabs off the tree's trunk, hurling one after another at Father's broken-down truck.

Chapter 3

WIND WHIPPED AROUND the corner, blowing dust in Wyeth's face. A large raindrop pelted his cheek. He squinted but didn't slow down. Having stripped all the loose bark, he reached for firewood and hurled a hefty log at the truck's windshield. Spiderweb fractures spread across the window. The sound of splintering glass snapped me out of a stupor. I ran up to block his aim.

"Stop it, Wyeth! Stop it! Father's gonna kill you!"

"Where *was* he? Mama *needed* him!" He kicked the air with force. "You think he gives a rat's ass about his truck?" His voice had gone hoarse.

"I don't know! You're making it worse!"

"Why should I care?" Wy hoisted another piece of wood. "He hates me!"

"No! Stop it!"

"Out of my way!"

I jumped up and grabbed the log he held above his head. Though skinny for my age, I was scrappy and I refused to let go. Still, he outmaneuvered me, yanking the wood from my grasp. All at once, the piece came down squarely on my head.

I lost all strength. Whirling in dizziness, I scraped my arm on the wood stack and fell facedown in a bed of dandelions. The world went gray except for floating sparkles. Dazed but conscious, I lay at his feet. My head throbbed.

The clouds burst overhead. Big drops of rain fell like staccato notes.

Wyeth groaned and dropped to his knees. It wasn't a fight he wanted to win—I just got in the way. Bowing down, he rested his head on my limp body. He seemed perfectly calm, but not for long. Soon his chest swelled with great sobs.

"You—just—don't—get it." His lungs heaved again. "He *particularly* hates me."

Particularly? I was too foggy to think about a big word like that.

He exhaled deeply. "And now...he's in charge." More moaning followed. "We're screwed."

After a few minutes, the storm's thrust moved through. A gentle drizzle trailed behind the front. Wyeth's breath felt warm through my shirt. He put his right arm over me, and we lay entwined on the ground. Tears mixed with rain, and time paused.

"Rissy?" he said, finally.

"Hmm?"

"Sorry about your head." His voice was scratchy, but he'd calmed down.

"Mmm." I felt a chill coming on.

"If Father comes back, don't tell." His voice quivered a little.

"Mmm-hmm." I murmured. *If he comes back.*

After awhile, Wyeth sat up and shook raindrops off a dandelion bloom. He studied it intently. "Why do people mow these down or poison them? Who decides what's a weed or a flower anyway?"

My brother got bothered about the weirdest things. Simple answers didn't satisfy him. He obsessed on anything that seemed unfair. Such causes became his special burden—a reason to shake his fist at parents, police, teachers and even God.

I thought about dandelions. They were strong, returning year after year cheerful and bold, their color more vibrant than roses.

"Nobody'll arrest you if you wanna call them flowers," I offered.

Wyeth flicked the weed away. "What if we got it all wrong? Maybe in Africa, dandelions cure diseases, and we just believed some grownup here who told us that they're worthless."

I shivered, unable to hold still.

"Hey, you're shakin' like crazy." He turned me over.

"My head!" The pain felt like heavy marbles rolling inside my skull.

He examined my hair for blood. "Got a nice ol' goose egg up here." A smirky little smile streaked across his face. He had no appreciation of my mouth-watering abilities.

"It's not funny, Wyeth."

"Who's laughing?" He squatted and checked my right forearm. "Don't worry. You're gonna be okay."

"Ouch, ouch, ouch...*don't!*" My arm felt raw. Sharp pain flared.

"Look at it this way. At least you're not brain dead from the log." He brushed debris off the oozing cut on my arm, and I let loose a high-pitched scream. "Okay already! Don't go crazy on me. Let's show Nana." He ducked his head under my other arm to leverage my weight. "C'mon now. Grab me."

I clutched his neck. He pulled me upright, wrapping his right arm around my waist. I was wobbly at best, but we ambled toward the house. That's when he noticed the diary.

"What's this?"

My damp shirt clung to my body, revealing the edge of the journal. "Nothing. Go slower."

"What are you hiding?"

I lowered my chin and looked at him shyly. "It's Mama's diary. They might take her stuff, and..." I rarely told him my inner thoughts and desires.

"And, what?" he said.

"I want it."

His eyes softened.

He steered me toward the garage. Once inside, I pulled out the leather book.

"Where'd you get it?" He looked it over, flipping a few pages.

"In Mama's bedside table. You didn't know?"

"Nope." He slid it inside a folded tarp on the garage shelf. "Now don't be a dingbat and forget where it is."

We staggered up the backdoor steps. Nana appeared quickly and ushered me to a chair at the breakfast table. Wyeth bolted upstairs to change, while Nana searched for the first aid kit. Blood dripped down my arm, making a small red pool on a paper napkin.

"What happened here, young lady?" A booming voice came from behind. I jumped in my seat. He walked into view. "Didn't mean to startle you. I'm Jack Roberts." He smiled slightly without showing his teeth. His eyes looked tired. A pale scar on the side of his neck stretched up behind his right ear. "Older brother beatin' on you again?"

The question worried me. He had to be a cop though he wore a coat and tie. All policemen might be like my father. I'd need to word things carefully. Clearing my throat I said, "It was—an accident."

"I see." He peered over his glasses. "You must be Iris?"

"Yes sir."

Another cop entered the kitchen, motioning for him to come.

"Excuse me, Miss Somerset," Roberts said. "I'm the detective."

I gave him a slight nod.

They turned away to speak in low tones, but I could hear nearly all they said.

"Carbon monoxide poisoning, most likely," said the cop in uniform. They peered into the garage from the kitchen door, while he described to Roberts how it might've happened. They discussed the scene like it was some kind of a science project.

The night before, a cold front had brought heavy rains. The police found all the windows in the house tightly shut. The wrap around porch shaded the first floor, and damp air made the house chilly. The power went off at some point, and my mother probably started a small generator in the garage to warm the kitchen. A portable electric heater remained plugged into it with an extension cord and was still droning when they found her. The door between the garage and the kitchen had been left wide open, allowing the fumes in. Odds were, she didn't realize the generator fumes needed ventilation.

"It was the kind of thing a man would know," said the cop.

"Or a husband," Roberts noted.

"Mr. Peate said his car was in the driveway this morning."

"Yes." The detective glanced my way. "It's troubling."

He'd been here? This morning? Just the mention of Father sent chills up my backbone.

Wyeth had returned in dry clothes and was listening to their conversation as well. He slithered around the corner in secret-agent fashion. After the two officers left the room, he tiptoed out to the garage.

The bloodspot had doubled its stain when Nana returned with the medicine kit.

"So, what happened here?" She pointed to my arm.

"I guess I hit the log pile."

"On purpose?"

"No, no. I fell. Then Wyeth wiped the dirt out of the cut, and I screamed. Why do boys do that?"

"They're wired differently. They *like* blood."

Nana put pressure on the wound. I thought about Wyeth lifting me up, steadying my balance. He acted strong and caring. I longed for that version of my brother, but somehow we stayed mildly irritated with each other.

"You're soaked to the bone, child. What were you two doing out in that storm?"

I closed my eyes. The fight flashed through my mind.

"We had to have it out." I wanted to be honest but didn't want to blab everything.

Nana opened the box of antiseptics, ointments and assorted supplies. "Have it out? What's that s'pose to mean?" She patted the scrape with a cottonball soaked in peroxide.

I flinched. The solution fizzed on my skin. "I dunno. He's upset all the time now, and I was dumb enough to get in the middle of it." A lump formed in my throat. "I just want him to be okay." I swallowed hard.

Tears filled her lower lids. She didn't look up.

"He's mad about the neighbors gawking at us. He's annoyed with Tuck. He hates Father and picks fights with me, and then cries his eyes out. It's like living next to a stick of dynamite."

She nodded silently and wiped her eyes with a paper napkin.

Fortunately the Merthiolate bottle was empty. I dreaded the stinging neon-orange stuff. My thoughts turned to Wyeth's wild words. "Nana, what does 'particularly' mean?"

"Particularly? It's like something specific or special."

"So, what if someone was particularly—well, let's say loved."

"Well, *you are* particularly loved, honey. It means you're especially cared for, loved more than others. Singled out." Nana glanced up at me to see if I'd explain.

"I see." I avoided her eyes. "It's just a new word. That's all."

She closed up the kit.

"What about my head?" I pointed.

"Oh. I didn't know." She parted my hair with her fingers in several places. "No blood. A good-sized bump, though. We'll ice it."

My shivers returned.

"Let's get you warmed up first." She took my hand, and we headed upstairs to start a bath. Soon hot water steamed the room, making a soft cloud.

I worked my way into the tub, feet first, then knees. "Ouch, ouch, ouch!" The hot water pricked my chilled skin. I finally eased back, submerging with my injured arm up like a submarine scope.

Mama had loved baths. She'd tie her thick brown hair in a ponytail. Her curls were natural. She often wore her hair in an up-do like that on special occasions. When Mama dressed up, a little mascara, powder, and red lipstick transformed her into the most beautiful woman in the world.

A week ago, she'd bought fancy white sandals with pointy heels. They could've passed for glass slippers. I intended to borrow them for a play. But now, she wouldn't get to wear them—ever.

Did people have shoes in heaven? It was a silly thought. I scolded myself. "*Ludicrous!*" I used the raspy word whenever possible.

My body felt light in the water. Did the dead feel weightless? What happened when people left their bodies? Was Mama hovering somewhere? Was she alone or scared? A small tear trickled down into the water, making the faintest ripple.

Soon, I felt thoroughly cooked. I dried off and dressed. Nana had set fresh clothes inside the door. Balancing on the bathroom stool, I elbowed the fog off the mirror. My face was bright pink, making my eyes bluer than blue. I brushed out my light brown hair until it was pencil straight again. Wy called me a dirty blond, which felt like an insult. Only Tuck had inherited Mama's beautiful brown curls.

Sliding into my moccasins, I headed downstairs, intent on finding the new white sandals. Her closet was the likely place. I paused to wrap myself in her hanging bathrobe. It smelled like her. Under the rack of blouses, I found penny loafers, some old slippers, and assorted tennis shoes. The trunk was full of sweaters and blankets. No sandals. Even the pink and white shoebox they came in was gone.

I opened Father's closet door and sighed. It was annoyingly neat. I checked Father's side of the bed, lifting the comforter to check underneath. A chewed up catnip mouse and one lonely sock hid in the dim light. I crawled under to get a better look, when the lump on my head brushed against something hard.

"Oww!" Rolling over, I looked up. Duck-taped to the bed frame, inches from my face, hung a pistol.

My heart froze. I'd never seen a real gun.

At that very moment, someone entered the room. I stopped breathing as if the bed had dropped on my chest. My legs were visible. Luckily, the person went to Mama's side of the bed.

Dark leather shoes pressed into the carpeting. Strong hands appeared, turning a tape measure one way, then another. He crouched there for the longest time, while I was suffocating. After pawing through the drawer where the diary had been, he finally stood up.

A slight wheeze came out of my nose. Silence filled the room. My heart pounded a deafening noise in my ears. I shut my eyes, fearing his face would soon appear under the bed. If he saw me, he was sure to see the gun.

"Detective?" Pops called.

"Coming!" Roberts shouted back.

His feet turned toward the door. The floor pulsed with his stride. I remained perfectly still, recovering with short, controlled breaths.

Straightening my neck, I took a second look at the gun. I touched the barrel. The hard smooth metal felt cold against my fingers. It made me queasy inside.

What if Father was a bad man?

Chapter 4

How much lovingkindness is forever?

ATHER OWNED A GUN—a genuine, bona fide gun. The thought rattled my bones. What would become of us? It hung inches from my face—a cold steely pistol, capable of taking life instantly.

My father's secrets had already created as much distance between us as his toxic personality. It had been a long time since I'd called him Daddy. In the last year, he rarely offered a smile, his mouth a straight tight line. Sometimes he'd stare right through me or walk by without saying a word. I apologized for everything and nothing, hoping to fix something that seemed broken. It didn't help.

I rolled out from under my parents' bed. As I brushed carpet lint from my shirt, a dream came to mind. In it, my father told me to go to bed. His voice sounded stern. I walked down a narrow hall through an unfamiliar house. Many soft beds filled my bedroom, but I curled up on a small tiled counter under some cupboards. No pillow, no covers, no comfort of any kind, as if I already took up too much space. Shivering and alone, I laid there soundlessly. At the end of the dream, my father stood at the doorway, checking on me.

I shook off the memory and entered the living room like a sleepwalker. It was dinnertime. The day had passed in a way that didn't mark time. I hadn't eaten anything since breakfast and felt light-headed. Tuck was balled up on the couch, wrapped in a plaid

blanket we used at football games. Apparently someone had discovered him in the pantry. His red eyes and furrowed brow said it
all.

I sank down and encircled him with my body. A young child
should be upset over a broken toy or a missing kitty—not losing a
mama. It was too much to bear.

Pops stood in the hall talking to Roberts when the front door
opened. Mrs. Peate entered the house carrying a steaming Dutch
oven. The smell of onions and browned beef came in her wake. Mr.
Peate followed with a saucepan in each hand, working the screen
door with his elbow so it wouldn't slam.

Mama used to say, "Onions are God's gift to tired housewives."
She'd melt butter and fry onions in a deep cast iron pan, which she
called "the original crock pot." Immediately the smell would per-
meate the house, assuring us that dinner was underway. It worked
like magic on Father. He'd wait patiently for dinner and watch Mr.
Cronkite sum up the day. However, if nothing was started, he'd
hover her in the kitchen all cranky and imposing until supper was
ready.

The smell of Mrs. Peate's roasted meat mysteriously summoned
all the men in the house. Two policemen came up from the basement. Their boots sounded like a small herd of cows on the wooden
steps. Pops motioned them to join in. Even Wyeth emerged from the
garage.

"There's enough for everyone," Mrs. Peate announced.

"Thank you ma'am, but we're done for now." Roberts spoke for
the other cops. He looked at Pops and opened his hand toward
Nana. "Could I speak with you both before we leave?"

"Of course," Pops said. "You kids stay at the table. Mrs. Peate
will serve up your dinner." Though Pops said it kindly, his tone carried authority. He was a moody old soul, but not like Father. If he
woke up all "trollish," as Nana would say, he'd tell others to have a
good day anyway. No one took it personally.

Mr. Peate pulled me to my feet. Then he scooped up Tuck,
blanket and all, to nest him in a chair with arms. Wyeth lifted the lid
of the Dutch oven to take a whiff. Hot gravy still bubbled around
the pot roast.

As soon as my grandparents joined Roberts on the front porch,
I slipped away, saying I needed to use the bathroom. I had to know

what they were saying. I hid behind the open front door. They stood on the other side of the screen.

"Folks, I'm afraid I don't have good news. We're inconclusive about what happened here, so there'll be an investigation. Apparently Hank showed up here this morning after being gone for nearly two weeks. He left again, but we're not sure if he came before or after Grace died. Do you know how to contact your son-in-law?"

"It's sketchy at best," said Pops. "We think he's staying at a small hotel in downtown Cleveland."

"What else can you tell me? Sounds like some trouble going on."

Pops hesitated.

Nana cleared her throat and nodded. "Our daughter was deeply discouraged. And a little scared. They were fighting a lot, and sometimes he'd threaten the..." Her voice choked.

The detective touched her arm gently. "It's been a tough day ma'am."

After a few moments, she blew her nose and continued. "He'd threaten the kids. Especially Wyeth," she whispered.

"Are we talking about physical abuse?" Roberts said in a hushed tone.

Silence followed.

"Okay." Roberts jotted a note on his pad. "I'll cover more details later. We'll leave now so you can be with your family."

With that, I stepped away from the entrance, tiptoed to the bathroom, and promptly flushed the toilet. Returning to the table, I ate several bites, but then just pushed food around my plate with a fork. What did Roberts mean by the word—*inconclusive*?

It was past eight by the time Mrs. Peate cleared the last plate from the table. Nana encouraged us to get ready for bed and handed me a bag of frozen peas for the bump on my head. Wyeth was unusually quiet as he headed to his room.

I forgot my usual round of hugs until Pops intercepted me at the bottom of the stairs. His neatly trimmed gray beard was the only thing that made him look old. He didn't wear glasses and still had a full head of hair. His outstretched hands were rough and strong from working with wood.

"Hey girl." His voice sounded tender.

I felt numb and empty, but dutifully put my arms around my grandfather.

"Say now—you're stiff as an ironing board," he teased. "Give me a *real* hug."

I softened a little and returned his embrace. My eyes filled with tears. A deep ache for my father's love flickered like an old flashlight with a weak battery. I didn't want to feel that way about him, but the longing was as desperate as thirst.

Once at an Indians' baseball game, Father suddenly pulled me close when a foul ball zinged off the bat heading straight for us. He held me tight, ready to fend off the ball. Surprised to find myself in his arms, I wanted to stay there. But he pulled away when the danger passed. The memory brought a sharp pain in my chest.

I let go of my grandfather. "I'm okay, Poppy," I said, giving him a sideways glance as I went up the stairs.

He stood at the bottom step and watched me go. I was a bad liar.

In my dress-up box, I found one of Mama's slips to wear as a nightgown. It felt cool and soft as I pulled it over my sore head and bandaged arm. I tied the straps in a knot behind my neck. Relieved to be alone, I climbed under the covers with my big blue Webster's and steadied the frozen pea pack on the top of my head.

The dictionary was one of my favorite books. You could tell by the ruffled pages that it was well used. I had an undeniable love affair with words.

One time, Wyeth had asked me what I saved for keeps. I stalled a minute. Wyeth collected snakeskins, foreign coins and arrowheads. Tuck was all about fireflies and fool's gold. I didn't really save anything. Then it occurred to me.

"I collect ostentatious jargon."

He stared at me. "What?"

"You know...grandiose terminology."

Wyeth rolled his eyes. "Right, Iris. You're *so* weird."

I smiled thinking about how I flashed him a big toothy grin and looked down my nose at him just the same.

As member of the Somerset family, we had to be careful with words in general. Any sort of name-calling was a grievous sin. You had to pay a whole dollar on the spot if you called anyone a jerk or an idiot, though I got away with some words like "scatterbrain." Mama bailed me out with Father, saying the term was "a descriptive adjective for a person who had a lot on his mind—and not necessarily derogatory."

Of course there were worse ways to say things, but those words cost ten dollars. So Wyeth and I composed our own language of name-calling. Speaking in code, only we knew the degree of insult.

For example, if you were slightly annoyed with a certain someone, you'd call him a "Bird Barn." If he seriously irritated you, the term was "Big Pony," or something pertaining to horses, donkeys or mules, in that order. But if you were downright exasperated, then "Bone Cat," was the worst name of all. But often, we'd make up new expressions to fit the moment.

Inventing new words and meanings was like being in a secret club. We'd say, "Who *booned* in here?" when referring to bathroom humor. "Farn" meant darn, which originally meant damn, a ten-dollar word. "Poonie" signaled that you were really, truly, cross-your-heart-and-hoped-to-die telling the truth.

But our favorite term was "chauney"—a mysterious word Wy and I made up.

The whole chauney thing started when Nana told us that she understood people based on whether they were *bird, horse* or *muffin*. At first we wondered if our grandma had taken crazy pills, or mixed whiskey in her lemonade. She wouldn't explain these categories to us, but we gradually understood as she practiced her bizarre form of people watching.

"Most children are *muffins*," she'd say, "But occasionally you'll see a hint of *bird* or *horse*." Another clue she handed down was the fact that people were usually a combination of two, but rarely *bird* and *horse* together. There seemed to be something especially negative about that. Wyeth and I both nodded but looked at each other with great big eyes.

Then one time, Nana and I stood in the grocery store checkout line waiting on a man who couldn't make up his mind about which carton of cigarettes he wanted. He scanned the stocked shelves with quick movements of his head—up and down, then side to side. He had big fidgety hands and didn't blink as he rummaged around. Turned out, he was searching for Silva Thins, a brand the store didn't carry.

"*Bird.* Definitely *bird.*" Nana spoke with certainty. I looked up at her, not making the connection right away. A second later, I understood. It had something to do with the way people looked or the manner in which they moved or even their personality quirks.

"Yes, you're probably right," I said in an uppity tone.

She nodded. A tiny smile appeared in the corner of her mouth. She knew I was catching on. After that, coded language became my favorite pastime, and I seized the game with great enthusiasm.

"Chauney," pronounced *chawn-knee*, became the ultimate coded word because it was complicated, and only Wyeth and I really understood its meaning. It had to do with people's peculiar little habits that were quaint, odd and specific to them. Usually the person acting chauney didn't know it. But not everything in that broad definition was chauney.

I laid back on my pillow, thinking about how much language meant to me and how even made-up words shaped the way I viewed life itself. In the early days of chauney usage, Nana personified the word. Her *bird-horse-muffin* game was unique for starters, but other examples of chauneyness abounded. For instance, Nana was a beautiful woman in her old age, but whenever she tried to open a jar with a tight lid or lift a heavy box, she grimaced something awful. Before our eyes, her expression changed into the face of a lunatic. We thought it the strangest thing and described it as chauney. We'd give her a dumb-deer stare if she asked what chauney meant, but later agreed it was a bit chauney of her to ask the question.

Over time I filled a little notebook with interesting or unusual words that I had discovered or made up. Sometimes, I used big words in ways that didn't fit the context. Mama would explain, but Wyeth would mouth the word "chauney" and giggle to himself. I insisted that since we made up the word, neither one of us could *be* chauney. Wyeth claimed it was a phenomenon of the feminine species as they grew from girls to women. Older females were particularly plagued with chauneyness.

I told him he was a Bone Cat.

But my interest in words also gave me access to the adult world. I made an effort to understand their conversations, though they probably thought otherwise. The devastating part was discovering the world wasn't as simple or as nice as I thought it was.

The night of my mother's death, I had one word on my mind. The detective had said the situation was *enkonklusif.* I searched through "E" words for a while. Maybe it was police terminology, or worse, Russian. It took awhile, but I switched to the "I" section and finally found it.

Inconclusive...leading to no definite result. I flipped back to see what the opposite meant, a trick I learned from Nana. *Conclusive... leaving no questions. Final.*

I thought about the detective's comment. What exactly was the question? Mama was dead. That seemed pretty final. Flashbacks from the day crossed my mind. Then a single idea surfaced.

Detectives come when there's been a murder.

My heart seized up. The word was unspeakable, unimaginable. I shielded myself with the dictionary but like a sniper's bullet, the thought had already shattered any sense of security. Lying back, I stared at a small spider on the ceiling until fatigue pulled me off to sleep.

At some point in the night, I rolled over. The dictionary made a falling-body thud when it hit the floor. The noise startled me. Urgent questions took on a life all their own in my half-awake mind. The cold pistol, the scarred neck of Detective Roberts, Mama's lifeless body, and the sound of Father yelling swirled around me like Dorothy's tornado on her way to Oz. I took slow deep breaths until the worst of it passed. My fears ebbed and flowed until sleep finally carried me off to a restful place, away from all the clamor and sadness.

Gradually, a soothing dream formed, bringing warmth and light across my mind. Happy sounds of music and faint laughter filled the atmosphere. A beautiful garden scene took shape, though it was unclear at first.

Then my mother appeared, front and center, in startling definition. She looked young and vibrant, her brown eyes gleaming with life. Her cheeks were aflame with the blush of a sun-kissed peach, and her smile filled the air with irresistible happiness. She wore a lavish white gown, and her hair was styled up. Curls tumbled down the right side of her neck. The light around her radiated out, touching every part of my being.

I felt afraid to speak or move, believing it would all vanish. I wanted to stay with her as long as possible. Her luminous presence made me lost to the world.

Mama turned her gaze and looked straight at me, as if she knew something. She peered into my eyes and spoke slowly, with great care.

"Iris..."

Oh Mama! Pressure rose up through my body into my throat. My mouth tried to form words, but my tongue was thick. I couldn't answer her.

She smiled. "Jesus says...it's okay about the shoes."

At first I was confused. *The flip-flops?* No. Maybe not.

Then it hit me. Her new sandals were missing! They'd go perfectly with her heavenly dress. I wanted to tell her, but felt mute in the sheer glory of the scene. I may have just nodded.

With sparkling eyes, she twirled in her long flowing gown with ballerina loveliness and perfect freedom. I could scarcely take it in.

Eventually, I looked down to the edge of her translucent dress. Mama's feet were bare. In heaven, it seemed, you were allowed to go barefoot.

Chapter 5

"OUCH, KIBBS! Go away!"

I'd been reaching for my mother, leaning forward. I longed for her touch, her smell, her voice, but the heavenly vision vanished when the cat landed on my face. I squinted in the bright morning light, searching the room. Only specks of dust whirled aimlessly.

"Oh Mama!" I turned, bawling into my pillow.

Mr. Kibbs returned and sat like a nurse, waiting to see what would become of me. I could feel his purring body but shooed him away. He sauntered off with his tail straight up and hooked at the top like a question mark. The sound of lawnmowers hummed in the neighborhood.

Beaconsfield had been a perfect place for our family. The pace of life was slow in our little town. People left keys in their cars and their front doors unlocked during the day. You could have a charge account at the local grocery or drugstore. Anyone could borrow his neighbor's snow shovel without asking. We even walked to school.

Billy's family, the Stebbins, flooded their backyard in the winter to provide a homemade ice rink. Mr. Stebbins fired up a pot-bellied woodstove in a little shack so we could warm our feet. Without it, thawing frozen toes was pure agony. On really cold days, Mrs. Stebbins brought a bowl of hot fries with ketchup out to the warming shed. I remembered savoring each salty strip like it was my last meal and thought about the strangeness of eating potatoes and tomatoes together.

When snow melted off in early spring, Wyeth and I played *Waterbaby* on the way to school. Some of the slate sidewalks had a "W" carved along the edge and the game involved avoiding Ws by jumping over them. If you stepped on any section with the dreaded mark, you were penalized with a letter. If it spelled out "W-A-T-E-R-B-A-B-Y," you lost.

When school got out in June, Anna Rae and I spent hours roller-skating down the sidewalks, including a few paved driveways. After dinner, sprinklers came on with great sprays of water slowly rotating back and forth like giant liquid rakes. We timed our skating speeds to get as wet as possible on hot summer evenings when the sun didn't set till after ten. The first nine years of my childhood had been joyfully uncomplicated.

I wanted that life back.

Fat chance. Mama's friendliness had shown our neighbors that we were a normal family. She'd feed the scary dog next door and water plants for older folks on the block. Father, on the other hand, could spoil everything. He had changed so much in the last year. Other kids saw him as the weird, grumpy dad who avoided people in general. He'd point and frown when kids rode their bikes on the edge of our lawn. "Look out, *you!*" he'd say, as if he didn't know their names. If he came back, it'd be easier to start over in a town where no one knew us.

I pushed back the bedcovers, leaning forward to sit up. Pain shot through my head. The frozen pea pack had become soggy and warm.

Half asleep, I stumbled toward the bathroom. I didn't recognize myself in the mirror. My eyes were nearly swollen shut from crying. I had morphed into an alien being from one of my brother's sci-fi books. Cold water felt good on my face. I pressed a wet washcloth in around my eyes.

Returning to my bed, I tried to conjure up the dream. It wasn't hard. The scene had been so clear—Mama's glowing face, her serene eyes, and the sunburst of her smile. If anyone thought she was beautiful in life, they should've seen her in my dream.

The house seemed terribly quiet and empty. Nana and Pops were probably still asleep. I expected to hear the clatter of pans, or the sound of cupboard doors opening and closing in the kitchen. Where was the syrupy voice of the morning radio host? Or the churning sound of the washing machine? Or the sizzle and pop of a frying egg? Mama sounds. I would gladly eat liver and spinach if she had been down there making it for breakfast.

Tossing the wet cloth in the sink, I headed downstairs and ambled into the kitchen. The clean pie tin leaned upside down in the dish drainer. No lemon-meringue pie today. No parade or marching band. No barbequed ribs, corn-on-the-cob, or dodge ball games either. No reasons to roll down grassy hills by the lake. How could I watch fireworks in the park without sitting with my mother, leaning back on her soft chest? My mother had been a moving, living, breathing person just yesterday morning.

Mama's love was a magical force like gravity, grounding me to earth. Her kindness held the power of sunlight, giving life to a seed or the invisible pull of the moon on ocean tides. I learned about these mysterious forces in school, but what did it matter? The sun and the moon didn't care about me. Sliding into my chair, I lowered my head to the breakfast table, wilted as an unwatered flower.

Nana shuffled into the kitchen, pulling on her bathrobe. I couldn't think of a single thing to say. Normal greetings like "Good morning" or "How'd you sleep?" seemed pointless. She touched my head in passing as she went to start the coffee.

Eventually the pot steamed and sputtered, drawing up the last bit of water. Coffee had a strong smell—a mix of roasted nuts, molasses and wood fire. Its aroma floated in the room. I lifted my head when she sat down with a fresh cup.

"Want some?" she asked.

I shrugged.

"You might like it if I doctor it up." She made a little wink.

"Hmm?"

"You know, milk and sugar? Maybe a little cocoa powder."

"Okay." I didn't feel enthused but sat up straighter.

Nana mixed her coffee potion for me and handed me a spoon.

I watched the steam rise. "Nana?" I laid my spoon in the saucer.

"Hmm?" She took a few sips and then cleared her throat.

"Do you think dreams are real?

"Sure, I have loads of them."

"No, what I mean is..." I cupped the side of my mouth, in case Wyeth was in earshot. "Are they *something more*?"

"More?" She put her cup back in its saucer.

"Like a bit of heaven coming to earth." I squinted, waiting for her reply.

"Well yes, in a sense." She studied my face and continued. "God talked to people through dreams in the Bible a whole bunch. I think He still does."

"Has it ever happened to you?"

She smiled. "Surely you remember the adoption dream?"

"Oh yeah." I held my cup with my pinky extended. "Tell me again."

She leaned back and covered her eyes with one hand, rubbing her temples. It had been awhile since I heard Nana's version. She started with her wedding day.

"Well, believe it or not, I was once a young woman with wavy auburn hair. I had a figure back then. Pops stood at the altar, looking very debonair with a nice haircut and a new suit. His thick hair used to be jet black, because he's one-sixteenth Indian, you know." She poured a little more milk into her coffee.

"What does that mean?"

"It means his great-great grandmother was full-blooded Cherokee."

"No, no, I mean *debonair*. And how do you spell it?"

"D-e-b-o-n-a-i-r."

I wrote with one of Father's sharp pencils on my napkin.

"Do you know what charming means?" she continued.

"Sorta. Mama could charm Moose."

"Who's Moose?"

"That cranky old basset hound next door. She'd sing to him. Then he'd get all friendly, wagging his tail under his belly, as if to say sorry for being such a grouch."

Nana straightened her posture. "Yes, that's the idea. Pops had that kind of effect on me. Still does."

Pops was Nana's match. They enjoyed the same things like Neapolitan ice cream, fried baloney sandwiches, baseball games, and dancing to Ella Fitzgerald songs. She said they agreed on all important matters—like God, and family, and how many kids they wanted.

"How many kids *did* you want?" I asked.

"Well see, that's just it. We wanted a houseful, but your Uncle Skeets was the only one for five years." She stood to pour a second cup.

"Were you and Pops mad at each other or something?" I had a general idea of how babies were made. My cheeks became warm.

"No, no darling. It's called infertility. Means your baby house isn't working properly."

I really didn't want all the messy details about body organs and pressed on. "So what about the dream?" I tapped my pencil on the table.

"Yes, I'm getting to that. When Skeets turned two, we asked God to let us adopt a little girl. We prayed and prayed and prayed...for three years." She returned to her seat.

"Was God busy or something?"

"No, it's not like that. God just sees and knows things we can't understand. Sometimes timing is everything." She nodded in a knowing kind of way.

My mind darted back and forth. *Timing is everything?* Mama's time was cut short, and I certainly didn't feel *ready* to lose her.

"Iris. You have that faraway look."

"Just thinking." I swung my feet back and forth under my chair.

"I see." She continued. "Well, after praying and waiting, I went to bed one night and had a dream. In the dream, I stood at the entrance to Jeremiah House, the city mission on Superior Avenue. You know the one." She studied me again.

"Sure." I had been there with Father to help at the soup kitchen.

Nana continued. "I entered the building and climbed a giant staircase, like a stairway to heaven. When I reached the top, a nurse led me down a hall to a nursery. As we entered, I saw her—a beautiful baby girl asleep in a white wicker cradle, shrouded by a sheer veil. I pulled the covering away. She had soft brown curls, creamy pink cheeks, and a tiny rosebud mouth. Then the nurse said, 'Her name is Grace.'"

"Now comes the *best* part." I set my cup in the saucer and waited.

"The very next day in real life, I called Jeremiah House. A newborn girl had just arrived and fit our request! We drove downtown to see her, *and...*" she paused for dramatic effect. "The real baby looked exactly like the one in my dream."

"And *that baby* was my mom!" My heart lifted a little.

Nana looked at me. Her eyes were sad, but her mouth smiled. Every wrinkle across her cheeks and forehead joined the smile, but tears rolled down over each crease. It was a most curious expression.

"I don't understand, Nanny. Were you happy or sad?"

"Happy then...sad now."

I hopped up to get several tissues while she covered her eyes and wept. When I returned, I hugged her from behind, lacing my arms around her shoulders and neck. Her body, hidden by her robe, seemed frailer than I remembered. A disease called M.S. had robbed some of her strength, but she rarely complained. After a few minutes, she wiped her nose and sighed.

"I'm okay, honey. It's just that God said something to me."

"Was it a man's voice?" I glanced around the room. "Was it right behind you?"

"Well, no, not exactly." She lifted a fresh Kleenex to her eyes.

Disappointment settled on me. "Well, what did He say?"

Nana sighed and stared at the cracked ceiling. I looked up too, just in case. "He said, 'Let...the children...come to Me.'"

"I don't get it...*what* children?" I knelt next to her on my knees.

"I read it this morning. Matthew, I think it was."

"Matthew who?"

"The book of Matthew." She slowly shook her head. "All those years ago, God gave me a gift named Grace, and we got to have her for a time." She paused to compose herself. "But now, He's saying, 'Let her come back to Me.'"

That made no sense at all. Why would God take away a perfectly good Mama? God was too good for that to be true. Something *happened* to Mama. My gut tightened.

I sprang to my feet. "Nana, did someone murder our Mama?"

"Heavens, child! What gave you that idea?" She flashed a big-eyed look at me.

"Why else would a detective come to our house?" I started pacing. "He said the situation was inconclusive. I *know* what that means. I looked it up."

She flattened her hands on the table. "Don't trouble yourself with those thoughts."

Wyeth entered the kitchen. "But we have a right to know." His voice cracked as he opened the fridge. Obviously, he'd heard my question.

"Listen kids, we must let the police do their job," said Nana.

"But they don't *know* everything." Wyeth sounded on the verge of tears.

"What do you mean?" I asked, returning to my seat.

He placed a tall glass and the carton of milk on the table. Leaning on his elbows, he balled his fists over his eyes. We waited for him to speak. The air felt thick, like the next thing he said would change everything.

"Mom baked a pecan pie yesterday—her favorite. But she always makes lemon meringue on the Fourth." He looked at us, bobbing his head, like we should understand.

I didn't follow.

He rolled his eyes and continued. "She ate the whole pie! There was only one plate and one fork in the sink!"

"What does that have to do with anything?" Now I was frustrated.

"Don't you get it?" He slammed the table with his fist. "She always worried about getting fat!" His chin started quivering.

"What are you saying, Wyeth?" Nana pursed her lips and blinked hard.

He held his palms out and blurted, "People do things they've always wanted to do, when they know they're going to die!" He emptied his lungs with a great moan, fighting back his emotions. He swallowed hard and then bowed his head. His sandy-colored bangs partially covered his eyes.

Nana touched Wyeth's arm. Surprisingly, he didn't pull away. Her tone was gentle. "Wyeth, your mother wasn't sick, and there was no indication that she was about to die. What makes you think that?"

He buried his face in his crossed arms on the table. "She...didn't want... to be here...anymore." His thoughts sputtered out. "Dad left her...Tuck whines and cries...and me! It's me! I'm such a jerk!"

"Wyeth..." Nana rubbed his arm.

Finally, he lifted his face. His eyes were red. "Last night, I read the last page, in her book, you know—her diary." He looked directly at Nana as he pulled the diary from his back pocket and laid it open on the table. "Right here, July 3, 1979." He pointed to her last entry. "She wrote, 'Today is *my* independence day.'"

Nana's mouth fell open. "Wyeth...don't!"

He shook his head. "No, no, listen to me! It wasn't an accident! And nobody killed her." He started to sob. "Don't you see? She *wanted* to die!"

Chapter 6

THE NEXT THREE days were a blur of activity, decisions, and roller coaster feelings. My head still throbbed when I stood up or leaned over. My arm had purple-yellow bruises around the scabs, and every day they got uglier.

Mrs. Stebbins and Mrs. Peate organized food offerings, while Pops worked on funeral arrangements with Nana's help. Cards and flowers arrived on the front porch or were left inside the screen door, and at any given moment someone was weeping.

Wyeth displayed none of his snotty-nose attitude and stared at nothing with dead shark eyes. Nana told him his face looked ashen and encouraged him to eat. I added "ashen" to my word collection.

The phone rang constantly. My job was to be polite and say, "Somerset residence, Iris speaking." But after sixty-seven calls, I just uttered one-word greetings like, "Hey" or "What?" All I could think about was how and why our Mama died.

The police returned to scour our house for any trace of evidence. Detective Roberts interviewed every family member except Tuck, who'd been farmed out to the Peates. Nana and Pops sat with me when my turn came.

I had to explain the ridiculous fight over my thongs and other details of that dreadful morning. Roberts pressed me about what my mother said as I left for summer school. I couldn't remember. My face got hot. I didn't know those moments with her were a final goodbye.

He also asked me if anything unusual had happened in the last few months. I told how Wyeth forgot to take out the garbage on a sweltering day in June. The garage stunk like a dead chicken in the undying heat of summer. Of course the odor drifted into the kitchen, because the garage was attached to the house. To fix the situation Wyeth had lifted the garage door a foot, hoping to draw out the stench, but a pregnant skunk snuck in and made a nest in the spare tire behind the wheelbarrow. Each day the trash smelled worse, so none of us went in there. As soon as the garbage collector rescued us, Wyeth closed the door, not realizing he had separated the mother skunk from her babies.

"Oh my," said Roberts, his eyes grew big with anticipation. "So then what?"

"Tuck found the little fur balls and kept them in the basement utility sink, giving them their own bowl of Cheerios with milk. Father had been away at an orthodontic conference. Everything went along swell until Kibbs discovered them and began screeching like a wild animal."

"I see." The detective fingered his pen, trying hard not to smile. "Did Tuck get in trouble?" I could see his lips tightening.

"No, no. When Father returned, he automatically blamed Wyeth and ordered him to clean up the mess."

"Automatically, you say?"

"Yes, Wyeth's usually the one. He back-talked Father, insisting the baby skunk part wasn't his fault. That didn't fly. He got grounded for two weeks. Still, Tuck had to help Mama clean up the poop in the sink. It was hard to say which was worse."

"Mm-hmm." Detective Roberts smiled with pursed lips and made a few notes. I could tell he liked my story.

Soon his smile faded. "Iris, how do you feel around your father?"

I felt a twinge in my armpits. To speak openly felt like stepping outside naked.

"Honey, is something wrong?" Nana could read me.

"No, just thinking."

Pops leaned forward. "It's okay, Rissy. Just be honest."

I pulled my knees to my chin. A sudden urge to hide in the closet possessed me. "Going to the mission house with him was okay. He liked serving soup." I stalled, hoping to come across upbeat, but my voice sounded flat.

No one moved. The silence grew awkward.

"And he seems happier when we go sailing," I added.

Roberts gave me plenty of room to say anything I wanted. "I'm not asking about him, Iris. What is it like for you?" He lightly touched my arm.

Roberts, Nana, Pops and I sat in a circle. It felt like our legs were touching. I tried to scoot back my chair.

"Sometimes...I'm a little scared...because he wants everything *just so*." I fingered the fringed edge of my cutoffs.

"Tell me more," said the detective.

"He has places for everything. The kitchen scissors go in the front right corner of the drawer beside the stove."

The detective became very *bird*. He made quick little notes, his pen pecking at the page.

"And his bathroom..." I continued. "I can't use it. I can't park my bike on the front walk. I can't wear flips flops to summer school." My list was longer, but his next question stopped me cold.

"Do you ever think your father isn't the person you thought he was? I mean—does he have any secrets?"

I looked down. The hidden gun came to mind. *I will not tell him. I will not.* I squeezed my eyelids tight and diverted him with a different story.

"Well...on my tenth birthday I had my first slumber party. In the night I got thirsty. Mama kept a few sodas under the kitchen sink for special occasions, so I grabbed a small bottle in the dark, thinking it was ginger ale. I downed the whole thing in one swoop. The bitter taste surprised me. I was sure it was liquor."

The detective seemed intent on his notes.

"I barged into my parents' bedroom to tell them I was drunk. I thought it best to fess up right away."

"Indeed," he murmured.

"Father hauled me by the arm to the kitchen and started yelling until Mama entered. She lifted the empty bottle and said, 'Iris, is *this* what you drank?' I nodded, wondering how soon I'd pass out. Turns out it was just tonic water."

As I remembered the scene, my parents' faces emerged in my mind. Mama had tilted her head back and laughed like crazy. Father's face grew beet red. At the time, I was confused by their different reactions. But later, I understood.

"See," I continued, "he was miffed because first, I didn't knock.

Then, I disturbed his sleep for nothing, and when Mama interrupted him and then *laughed*—well, you don't *ever* do that."

"Was he physically rough with you?" Roberts asked.

"A little. It was the first time he didn't seem like my dad. And since then, he's had a Bone Cat temper with all of us."

"A what?"

"He gets hopping mad and shouts in your face. I didn't do anything wrong that night, but he made me feel like I'd go to hell if I ever drank alcohol."

"Now, now, Rissy." Pops shook his head slightly.

Roberts leaned back in his chair, shifting his weight. "Tell me Iris. Does your Father drink alcohol? Have you ever seen him drunk?"

"No sir. I don't think we have any in the house."

"What can you tell me about the night your father left?"

"As usual, it started with Wyeth. He got caught lying and my parents had a huge spat over it. I hid in the pantry. Mama cried real hard, and Father shouted, 'White lies are still lies!' He sounded like he might explode like a bomb on Wyeth. I thought he'd even hit Mama. Instead, he marched out of the house and drove off. That's all I know."

Nana shuddered and clasped her hands. "My God!"

"What was the white lie?" asked Roberts.

I raised my shoulders and shook my head.

Then he bent forward to speak in my ear. "Has your father ever hit you or hurt you in some way?"

I lowered my chin, letting my hair veil my face. A familiar, sickening emotion coiled in my gut. "Not with his fists." My voice trembled. "It's his eyes...they're so cold." My chin quivered as I fought back tears.

How could I explain? There'd been trouble on and off between my parents since last fall. Mama tried casting a hopeful glow on things—but it didn't fool me. The minute Father's car rolled into the driveway each night, I stiffened right up and wondered if the pressure in my chest would ever go away.

My parents rarely argued in front of us, but heated words were hurled back and forth behind closed doors. If that wasn't bad enough, their silence was worse. It made us all ill at ease, especially at suppertime. I remembered feeling like heavy weights were strapped to my legs and arms as I cleared the table.

Roberts watched me, waiting patiently. "Anything more you

44

want to tell me?" he asked, gently.

My hands felt clammy on my knees. "I know what kind of day it's gonna be..." I said in a slow deliberate way. "...By the way he combs his hair in front of the mirror."

Roberts laid down his pen. I returned to my post by the phone.

Later, Wyeth was called in. He mentioned the last entry in Mama's diary and his idea about it. As I feared, the detective asked for her journal. Wyeth also talked about Mama's unhappiness and used the word "cruel" when talking about Father. I missed the white lie explanation, because the church secretary called. Towards the end, Roberts asked Wyeth if he felt picked on. My brother's cheeks were flushed with color. He couldn't speak. I guess his tears answered for him.

The phone wasn't quite as busy when Nana and Pops were interviewed.

"Hank seemed like such a nice young man when we first met him. We felt happy for our daughter. He had pleasant manners, went to church and had a good job." Nana sighed. "But something changed."

"Can you be more specific, ma'am?" asked Roberts.

"Sometimes you just sense things." Nana's lips tightened.

"I agree, Ma'am. But we need facts, not opinions."

Pops chimed in. "Hank became very religious this past year, but not in a good way."

"A bit fanatical." Nana explained. "He acted all uppity with our pastor, like he had a direct connection with God."

"How'd this affect the family?" Roberts opened a fresh page in his notepad.

"He's very controlling and legalistic," said Nana, straightening her back.

"Specifically?"

"He became ridiculous about money, controlling every penny. He questioned Grace's comings and goings." She exhaled.

"One minute, you think he's an agreeable fellow, and then..." Pops snapped his fingers. "...the tiniest thing would set him off."

Roberts lowered his voice. "Any instances with the children?"

"The kids were punished for being late for church or if they didn't memorize their verses word-for-word. Absurd violations, if you ask me," said Pops. "Where's the love of God in that?"

Roberts pushed his glasses up his nose and glanced around the room to see who was in earshot. I turned away, pretending to talk on the phone.

"Was Hank angry enough to harm Grace?" he asked.

Nana and Pops made no sound, but their faces lost all expression. Fear dropped into my stomach like a rock.

Roberts gathered his papers, shook hands with my grandparents and left. Mama's diary went with him. Tears formed in the corners of my eyes. I buried my head under the couch pillows. We were going to be orphans for sure.

Wyeth stayed locked in his room the rest of that day. He taped a small note by the doorknob, saying "GO AWAY! I *mean* it."

The last time he posted such a warning, it was a trap. He had rigged some fishing line from the doorframe through an eye-screw anchored in the door. At the other end of the line, he attached a fake furry mouse, made with a rabbit's foot. When I opened his door, the effect was a rodent scuttling straight toward me. I gave him an honest-to-goodness scream, which was exactly what he wanted, the sly fox.

But today, things were different. I didn't go in.

Anna Rae came by to see me but didn't act like herself. We sat on the porch swing, dangling our "green bean legs" as Pops called them. We'd either start to say something at the same time or sit in tongue-tied silence, careful to not look at each other. Normally, this would have been funny, but now it was just strange. I gave her a stick of Juicy Fruit. She left when the flavor ran out.

It was just as well. I couldn't talk about the sadness I felt. My own voice sounded strange. Tuck easily set me off with his sobbing. His pain unraveled all the brave composure I worked so hard to muster.

Looking through the wrong end of Tuck's toy binoculars, I surveyed the neighborhood. The lens made everything appear far away, out of reach with miniature houses, neatly cut lawns, gumdrop-sized shrubs and tiny fire hydrants.

THE DAY OF the funeral finally arrived, but the limousine service wouldn't come until noon. It was a sultry morning, the kind that makes you want to nurse a popsicle. I grabbed one and went to sit in the shade of the sycamore tree. The poor tree looked buck-naked from Wyeth's attack. I put my arm around its trunk and circled it while licking my frozen treat. An hour felt like a whole day, and yet, waiting was all we could do. Overhead, gray clouds like patchwork covered the sky, allowing an occasional splash of sun. They teased me with a few raindrops, but a cooling downpour never came.

I wandered upstairs. Nana had laid out formal clothes for Wyeth and Tuck. I elbowed my way through the closet, searching for my frilliest white dress. When I announced I was going barefoot like Mama, Nana pulled out my black patent leather shoes.

During that wait, Wyeth gave the word "sulk" new meaning. My dictionary said it meant angry silence. Meanwhile, my grandparents coped, I fretted, and Tuck clung to an idea that Mama was just gone for a little while. The endless tick-tock of the hall clock, the dull sky and the stifling heat all continued without end. I wandered about like a puzzle piece that didn't seem to fit anywhere, useless and without any purpose.

Finally, a shiny black car pulled into our driveway. It was time. Pops discovered several bouquets of flowers by the front door. They'd been placed on the porch since he'd returned with the paper. I heard the rhythm of his breathing change. He took off his glasses to wipe his eyes.

When the family gathered downstairs to file out, the phone rang. Nana waved her hand as if to say, "Let it go," but I'd already grabbed the receiver out of habit.

"Somersets. Can we call you back?"

"Iris."

I dropped to the kitchen stool, grabbing the counter for balance.

"Father?" I whispered, straining to stay calm.

"It's me." His words were solemn. A terrible empty pause followed.

"Rissy! The fancy car is here!" Tuck shouted from the hallway. The screen door slammed after him.

"Coming!" I hollered, covering the receiver with my palm. Then I spoke quietly. "Do you *know*?" I mumbled. My throat felt parched.

"Yesss, I know. I'll be at the fune-ral." His voice sounded sloppy. "Don't worry. Everythin'ill be fine." He didn't sound convincing.

"I gotta go. The family's waiting for—"

He hung up on me. Abruptly. I didn't get to finish my sentence. The familiar tension returned like poison seeping into my chest. I put the receiver in place and ambled toward the door on weak legs.

Chapter 7

H E *DISCONNECTED.*

The word fit, considering he'd gone missing. Did he even care about our shipwrecked lives? My stomach felt all twisted up. We rode silently in the limo following the hearse, but there was nothing silent about my mind. I didn't have the nerve to tell the family. Especially Wyeth. His anger and pain seemed quieted now, but only like a sleeping monster.

"Who was it?" asked Nana.

"Just someone about the funeral...caller number eighty-nine." A chill of perspiration formed on my neck. It wasn't really a lie.

Nana gazed out the window. The lake looked gray-blue and choppy. Each of us steadied a vase of flowers on our laps. The fragrance of roses and peonies filled the air.

I closed my eyes. What now? What if Father came home? Of course he would. He was our only parent. Without Mama though, everything would be different. Different like couches without cushions, food without flavor.

By Kensington School, the driver switched lanes before the light. We crossed the bridge over Rocky Cliffs River, and I gazed down at the slow-moving water. Last February a man had fallen through the ice in the channel below. Plunging into frigid water, he grabbed the broken edge and yelled for help. Not a soul in sight. Mama had read us the story from the *Cleveland Plain Deal-*

er, and I remembered feeling stricken for the guy.

In complete panic, the man believed swimming under the frozen surface to the shore was his only chance. But all at once he heard a voice say, "Don't do it!"

"Was it odd, or was it God?" Mama loved to ask.

The man fought his instincts and waited for help, but his limbs were freezing fast. His body grew rigid, and soon he slipped under. It was over.

Then, a miracle happened. After a minute, he suddenly realized he could move his arms again and frantically surfaced for air. When he opened his eyes, an orange life preserver floated within reach.

Mama read on. Even Wyeth had been spellbound.

The newspaper reported an amazing series of coincidences. A taxi driver crossing the bridge glanced down at the exact moment the man broke through the ice. He radioed his dispatcher, who contacted the police. A squad car happened to be moments away. A girl walking in the area heard the man's shout for help and rallied some neighbors. They crept out on the ice and threw him the life preserver. When the man surfaced, he managed to get his arm through the hole, buying time, but eventually his grip failed. Meanwhile, the police found a dinghy nearby and pushed it out to the hole. The man inexplicably came up for air two more times, but was completely out of sight when police got to the broken ice. One cop reached down as far as he could in the water. To his surprise, he grabbed the collar of the man's jacket and pulled him up, nearly capsizing the boat. All that had happened in eleven minutes.

The man fully recovered and spoke at our church several months later. He talked about the peace he felt underwater. Being a thin and muscular man, he should've sunk straight to the bottom. The current could've carried him away under the solid ice. He said the mysteries and coincidences that saved his life had to be God. I felt awed back then, but now the memory shredded me. Did God forget Mama? Did He blink when she was in danger? Anger burned in my lungs like hot coals.

Nana's voice jarred me out of my dark thoughts. "Skeets' plane should have landed a half an hour ago." She looked directly at Pops. "I thought for sure the phone call was him."

"Don't worry, Love. He's taking a taxi from the airport. He'll get there in time."

Nana nodded, but her lips stayed pursed. Within several blocks of the church, cars lined the curbs in every direction. She pressed a few Kleenexes into my palm as we pulled up to the side door. Ivy covered the brick walls surrounding the entrance.

The funeral director took our flower arrangements and spoke in a sickeningly nice voice. "If you please, a reception room for family of the deceased is upstairs to the left."

I hated the word *deceased*. It sounded like "disease" and reminded me of pictures in *National Geographic*. We piled out.

Tuck and I did as we were told and climbed the stairs to the second floor. We entered the reception hall where several dozen extended relatives lingered. They came mostly from Mama's family. A few of my father's cousins stood in the room. They were from Cincinnati. I'd met some of them before, but by and large, they were strangers.

I glanced around. Crystal chandeliers hung from the high ceilings. Towards the back of the room, large glass windows glowed with sunbeams. The light whitewashed the room making silhouettes of everyone. A man worked his way though the crowd, heading my way. He strode with such purpose that others stepped aside. I squinted to make out his face. It was my uncle! Everyone called him Skeets.

Before I said a word, he scooped me up and kissed my forehead. He smelled like cinnamon gum and Old Spice. My cheek pressed against his warm neck. The dull ache of longing swept over me. I knew the feeling from Girl Scout camp. I was homesick.

"Rissy, my girl," he said. "You pretty little thing! I can hardly believe you're ten already, yeah?"

"Ten and a half," I corrected him. Half years were terribly important when keeping up with a slightly older brother.

He set me down, searching my eyes. It had been six long months since I'd seen him. Africa was oceans away. His hair was longer and curlier than before, and his whiskers looked like sandpaper in the sunlight. I studied his beautiful teeth.

Tuck body-slammed our uncle from the side. Skeets dropped to a knee with staged exaggeration.

"Bang! What hit me? Why, it's Tucker James!"

Tuck clung to Skeets as if he were a lifebuoy.

"Hey, where's Wyeth and Pops?" my uncle asked.

"Tall-carriers," I said like a know-it-all.

"I think you mean "pallbearers." He kept his face serious, even though I had flubbed.

It was new word. I hated not getting it right. "Yes, pallbearers. That's what I meant."

Nana entered our circle of arms, and Skeets turned to her.

"Oh, Mother...I'm so, so sorry."

Nana burst into a mess of tears, so I handed her my Kleenex. Skeets' eyes welled up too. Tuck and I looked at each other, lost again in the fog of grief. Yet my sadness faded in the pure joy of my uncle's presence. When Nana calmed down, we all walked hand-in-hand into the sanctuary.

My skin tingled with a thousand pinpricks when I saw Father's familiar profile. He stood near the rear of the room and wore a tidy black suit that seemed too big for him. He looked awful, like someone with the flu. He glanced at me with weary eyes.

Nana and Skeets remained focused on each other.

"Skeets, we didn't give you much lead time, but would you say a few words in the service?"

"Sure." Skeets put his arm around her back and pulled her close. "Where's Hank?"

She wiped her nose. "He's all but disappeared."

We took our places in the front row. I peered over my shoulder to see Father again. He had lowered his face.

Families crammed into the pews, and numerous people stood in the spaces along the side. Others pressed in the back by the foyer. Many used their paper programs as fans. The humidity combined with body heat felt overwhelming, and I wondered if a small cloud would form in the ceiling. The Bible talked about a cloud filling the temple. Without air conditioning, it was entirely possible.

A wide assortment of flower arrangements filled the staging area. After the casket had been placed in front, Wyeth and Pops joined us. The ceremony began with a few hymns about heaven and how *death has no sting.*

I leaned over and whispered to Skeets. "You know, they're inconclusive."

"Inconclusive?" His eyebrows lifted.

"About how and why Mama died."

"I know. It's upsetting." Skeets took my hand. "Don't worry. Truth will come."

"I'm inconclusive too."

"What do you mean?" Our eyes met.

"About God." My voice faltered. "Death stings."

He pressed his lips together and gave an understanding nod.

The organist started to play the lead-in for *How Great Thou Art.* I couldn't bear to sing it. I didn't want to make a spectacle of myself, because you're not allowed to be mad at God, especially in church.

When I was little, I thought God lived in the church building, and heaven was on the third floor. I assumed that when people died, the funeral staff took them upstairs and put all the grandmas in one pile. The grandpas were placed in another area, and who knew what they did with you, if you died before you were old. I remembered asking Mama if I'd see Grandma Somerset in heaven because of the different stacks. I was serious. These were important questions, yet Mama couldn't help but laugh.

I knew more now that I was ten and a half. God didn't live at the church, and shortly, Mama would be in the ground. Church was just a place where everyone watched everyone else so they'd have something to talk about on Sunday afternoons when the football games were over.

I felt watched. Someone might notice I wasn't singing. If I bowed my head, maybe they'd think I was praying. I concentrated on happy things—picking raspberries, campfires, convertible Mustangs, clean sheets, twirling on ice skates...but my attempts at distraction didn't work. Sorrow and anger had an ongoing tug-of-war inside my chest.

I had to stop thinking or soon I'd be blubbering, and as sure as ants at a picnic, they'd come—women with bright red lipstick and too much perfume...men with bushy eyebrows and yellow teeth. They'd press in and fawn all over me with nauseating pity. I'd just boil over. I was certain of it.

The minister called Skeets to the front. I came out of my daze as he stood up to go.

He pulled on my pinky finger. "Had a dream last night," he whispered. "And you were in it."

Chapter 8

S KEETS CALLED OUR mama "Gracie." His face gleamed as he told stories about her from the pulpit. I watched his eyes and the corners of his mouth. But I only half-listened. My feet itched like crazy. I wanted to kick off my patent leather shoes.

"I don't know how to make it better—except for this..." Skeets moved closer to the microphone. "Find comfort in the greater story, the one that God's telling." He stepped down, and the organist revved up the pipes for a resounding victory song—*A Mighty Fortress is Our God.*

One lit-tle word shall fell-el-el him! What exactly *was* that word? The lyrics seemed scary to begin with, talking about "ancient foes" and "cruel hate." The one and only word seemed all-important. Was it in my vocabulary? I had to know.

After the closing prayer, my main concern became dodging the crowd. I hated the attention of others. You know, poor little girl...daddy on the run...mama dead and gone. It felt like standing around with a stake through your heart. When Grandma Somerset died a few years ago, people I barely knew patted me on the head, pinched my cheeks, and even kissed my forehead. They moved closer every time I backed up.

Fortunately, the ushers let our family exit first. We shuffled along as a unit in the center aisle. I held Skeets' hand and looked down to avoid the kaleidoscope of sad faces.

Father should have sat with us. It didn't feel right. Near the back, I glanced in his direction, but a maze of bodies separated us. Long-faced people whispered and clasped hands. He had to know we were passing by. Still, he didn't lift his head.

Nana and Pops stoically greeted guests in the foyer, while Skeets guided Tuck and me through a back hallway toward the limo. He grabbed his backpack and a large duffle bag that he'd stashed under a rack of choir robes. We climbed inside the shiny car while Skeets asked the driver to pop the trunk. After loading his bag, he joined us.

Skeets was truly my favorite uncle, even though he was the only one. For starters, he had stunning green eyes. I'd never known anyone with green eyes, but it was more than that. Some unseen energy swirled all around him. Yet it also came from inside him and especially flowed out from his face. You could feel it with your eyes closed. The only word I'd found in the dictionary that even came close to describing it was *gusto*.

For instance, when he played the piano, you'd have thought he was using the musical score for an entire orchestra. The fullness of sound ranged from thunderous storms to delicate lullabies.

He went out for numerous sports from golfing to lacrosse. He traveled to Timbuktu-places, read hundreds of books, and sampled every kind of weird food you could imagine, including squid. He seemed like a dozen souls wrapped into one human being.

Mama had been all smiles recounting their childhood together in Akron, Ohio. In grade school, my uncle was small for his age and often badgered by other kids. Some of the boys nicknamed him "Skeeter"—short for mosquito. They easily conquered him in their king-of-the-mountain games.

Later, the same bunch showed more respect when he became the champion Jacks player for three whole years. In kid-time, that's forever. His quick-handed coordination left everyone dumbfounded. The boys eagerly cheered him on, because various girls had previously sewn up the title. Mama said on his third win, two sixth graders carried him on their shoulders like a mascot. "Skeeter," was shortened to "Skeets," and the nickname stuck.

As a young teen, he rode bareback on the family mare and "broke" a heifer, so Mama would have something to ride. The "cow and pony show" drew some stares along the road. I pictured Skeets on the horse, trotting in circles around her slow swaggering cow, as they headed down to the Little Cuyahoga River. The mare had a nicer gait but was too high strung for Mama's taste. By the end of the day, when the horse had "burned off its vinegar," Mama would join her brother on the mare. With the cow in tow, they'd trail on home, singing old songs like *Green Grow the Rushes O*. Skeets and Gracie melded together like warm butter and succotash.

Shrouded by tinted windows, Tuck and I hid with our uncle in the funeral car. He made every effort to be merry, though his eyes looked glossy.

"Ah, here we go. You two might enjoy browsing through this," he said, pulling an inflight magazine from his backpack. "*Specially* the pictures," he added rather coyly.

We needed a break from all the glumness. Tuck and I beamed at each other. We knew exactly what to look for. To our delight, every single photo of any smiling person had several teeth "missing." Skeets had blackened them out.

Of course, magazines featured beautiful and sophisticated people, which made their goofy expressions all the more hilarious. Eventually we came to a full-page ad where the tagline promised, "A lovely smile in just ten days." The picture showed an enthusiastic dentist standing behind his happy patient. Both were missing the same three teeth. Tuck and I doubled over with laughter.

Skeets chuckled too as he took a greasy paper bag out of a zipped pocket on his backpack. He'd brought a treat from Africa and made us promise to try something new. We were likely risking our very lives, but curiosity prevailed.

"It's *nsenene*." Skeets placed a fried grasshopper in each of our hands. I shrieked and immediately dropped mine. Tuck took a sniff and popped it in his mouth. He chomped for a while, trying hard to grin through a contorted face.

"It's goood Rissy. Reaally." Tuck would do just about anything for Skeets.

"Don't talk with your mouth full, Tucker." I said in my Boss-Hogg voice. Wyeth had bestowed the title, saying Tuck was my poor little shoat.

"C'mon, Junebutter. You have to try 'em." Skeets pulled my arm, gently goading me. "They're a delicacy in Uganda." Skeets invented nicknames for me, combining two words in weird and wonderful ways—Jollyhopper, Pupcake, or Junebutter. But I really loved it when he called me Wild Iris Rose.

I closed my eyes and pretended the grasshopper was a different kind of french fry. Dreaming of ketchup, I chewed the crunchy thing for a few seconds, but mostly swallowed it whole. It's how I handled asparagus—gulping down bites like enormous green pills with a large glass of milk. I offered a weak smile. He kissed my head.

"You said you had a dream about me," I reminded him.

"Right." He cracked open the limo door to let in some air while we waited for my grandparents. "It started when two African friends of mine died a couple months ago. One had a wasting disease. The other hit a large goat with his motorbike and wrecked. Both were too young to die."

Tuck reached for more nsenene, dangling one by its leg before dropping the spindly insect into his baby-bird mouth.

"So was it about them?" I asked. "I mean, the dream."

"Well, not exactly. Their lives ended about the same time. One had a long agonizing death, and the other, instant." He rubbed his forehead. "I was deeply troubled about it and laid in bed one night arguing with God."

His honesty astonished me. Adults didn't talk like that.

He cleared his throat. "So in the dream, you and I were seated with several others at a great round table in a forest clearing. Giant sequoia trees surrounded us like a natural cathedral—a place where heaven seemed closer to earth."

"Who were the others?" I asked.

"Don't really know, but we were all brainstorming about how to help the two families left behind." He raised a finger. "And you took notes on a yellow lined pad, writing down words and phrases like you always do.

"Did we have any brainy ideas?" I asked.

"Not really. Can't fix heartache very easily."

"Hmm." I folded my hands.

He touched my knee. "Here's the thing. Suddenly the heavens opened like a window above us, and God's enormous right arm swung down gradually..." Skeets demonstrated with his arm. "It stopped exactly over our table. I'm tellin' you, it was taller than any skyscraper."

"Scary!" I said, wiping my forehead.

"Yeah. It felt that way. No one moved." He turned to look in my eyes. "His index finger pointed at your pad of paper, Rissy."

"What?" My gut tightened.

"Then, God spoke."

My eyes bulged with expectation.

"I gotta tell you, girl—it was absolutely the *kindest* voice I've ever heard. In fact that's what I remember the most."

God had sounded kind on the school playground, though He'd given me dreadful news. Tears formed on my lower lids. "Well what did he say? You're killin' me."

Skeets' eyes softened. He took my hands.

"He said, 'It's *not—about—this—life.*'" Skeets accented each word, and then brushed my bangs to one side. "And to you, God said, 'Take note of that.'"

I leaned back in silence. Life did seem like a matter of days, months and years—a wink of eternal time. We amounted to a speck on the earth. Our planet hung in the sky like a small pea in an unending universe. And beyond that, there were countless solar systems and galaxies. What was it all for? My teacher said we'd simply vaporize if the sun were just a tiny bit hotter. It was a miracle that we existed at all. Yet this was all I knew. I shifted in my seat.

"Then why do we have to go through all this?" My voice broke up with emotion.

Tuck groaned beside me. He dropped a handful of fried bugs back in the bag and slumped over. His face looked pasty.

"Well, that's a big ol' question," Skeets said, releasing a great sigh. "And I s'pose God will have to answer that one. But He means it isn't *only* about this life."

I turned away and looked out the window, biting the inside of my lip.

His warm hand rested over mine. "But I can tell you this much, Rissy..."

I slowly glanced over my shoulder to check his expression and see his eyes.

"He has the happy ending in hand."

Soon the rest of the family loaded into the limo for a somber ride to the graveyard. Inside the cemetery gates, car doors opened and closed. Soundlessly, people strolled across neatly cut grass to the gravesite. No one said a word except the minister, who made a short speech. While he made lofty promises, Tuck vomited behind a large gravestone engraved with the name, BLISS. Too many grasshoppers. Young oak trees waved their leaves in the afternoon breeze as Mama's coffin was lowered into a deep earthen hole. My heart wanted to fly out of my chest in a burst of sorrow. And, as far as I knew, Father never came.

Skeets brought my little brother to the car. Tuck fell asleep on Pops' lap for the drive home. The long car rolled into our driveway, missing the pothole. Everyone quietly gathered his or her things. Pops asked Wy to get my uncle's duffle bag, while Skeets carried my baby brother inside.

I walked to the end of the driveway in my lacy white dress. The crunch of tires on gravel told me to move to one side so the black funeral car could pass. I saw my ghostlike reflection as it went by. The car drove away, shrinking to a tiny dot before turning the corner.

I slipped off my fancy shoes. The earth felt cool under my feet. A gentle wind lifted the edge of my dress. I was still alive, but the ache in my heart would not go away. I felt too young to not have a mama. A single tear rolled down my hot cheek, and I stood there until it dried into a salty line.

Chapter 9

How much mercy is there, when it comes new every morning?

W HEN I FINALLY mounted the front steps, Wyeth threw my
cutoffs out the bedroom window with perfect aim. They
landed on my head like a clumsy bird.

"Hey!" I hated his ambushes.

"Change your clothes, girl!" he yelled. "Skeets and I are waitin'
on you."

It felt good to get into play clothes. I left my lacey dress in a
heap. Nana handed me a bag of snacks with three cans of Fresca as I
slipped out the door.

Skeets, Wy and I headed down the path toward Rocky Cliffs
River. I skipped now and then to keep up with my uncle. Wyeth
stopped to heave big flat rocks into the river. When they landed in
deeper spots, they made a heavy "doink" sound.

Eyeing the water ahead, Skeets abruptly bolted and threw his
backpack in the bushes. He dove in frog-leg style and yelped upon
surfacing. The water must have felt cold. He swam against the current towards a long shallow shoreline. The hunt for crawdads was
on. His feet waved in the air.

Wyeth followed without hesitation, but forgot to kick off his
flip-flops and had to chase them downstream. Eventually, he
worked his way back to us. The guys placed the wiggly creatures in

a plastic bread bag while I waded in slower current, looking for heart-shaped rocks.

I lifted a small black stone from the current. It was almost a perfect oval but flat and polished, smooth as marble. I stuck it in my pocket. I would keep it to remember the day.

There was something captivating about rivers. In summertime, the sound and feel of a moving stream was the best kind of respite. I often wondered where all the water came from, especially during hot dry spells. Its constant flow didn't seem logical, but you could count on it being there.

After a bit, Skeets and Wy built a crackling fire by the river's edge. I gathered sticks of driftwood to help. My uncle pulled out an old aluminum saucepan from his pack. He said boiling the critters gave them a merciful end. I was not convinced that anything with pincers was edible, especially after Tuck's bellyache from the *nsenene.*

"They're like bitty little shrimp. Eat one, you Big Pony," Wyeth said, acting all superior.

"Not hungry enough."

"Bummer. Chicks are always chicken," Wyeth said, laughing at his own stupid joke. "Maybe that's where the word came from. You ought to know."

I sneered. It felt weird to be our normal snippy selves on the day we buried Mama.

I opened the bag of food and found little boxes of raisins, a few apples, and a bag of Fritos. I snapped the metal tab on a soda and took a long drink. It fizzed up into my sinuses.

Skeets rinsed out the pan in the river and filled it full to put out the fire. Wyeth and I warmed our bodies in the late afternoon sun to dry. Soon Skeets stretched out next to us.

With closed eyes, I replayed the memorial service in my mind.

"Skeets?" I said. "What *is* that "one little word"? You know, the one in the 'Mighty Fortress' song?

My uncle rolled to one side. "I see. You want it for your collection, yeah?" He broke into a wide grin.

"Well, it seemed pretty important."

"Mmm." He sat up, rubbing his mouth with the back of his hand. "You know, sometimes the best things from God are slightly hidden."

I sat up and crossed my legs. "Can't you just tell me?"

Skeets tipped his head as if reconsidering. "Tell you what. Here's a clue." He opened the last Fresca and took a swig. "In Masaka, the town near my orphan home, there was this crazy, demon-possessed guy. He'd tear around half-naked screaming at people."

Wyeth opened his eyes. "What the heck?"

"I'm not making it up. The locals called him a 'night dancer' because he'd strip down nude at night and cavort around. One day, he came out by the orphanage and railed on our gate. I reached out saying, 'Brother, let me pray for you,' but he only growled at me."

"That's downright creepy!" I said. It felt unsettling to think about stuff like that.

Skeets continued. "So I just sang a song—*Jesus Loves Me.* You know it, right?"

I nodded and glanced over at Wyeth. He was bug-eyed.

"And that guy cleared outta there jackrabbit-fast!" Skeets raised his eyebrows and laughed.

"No way!" said Wy.

"But I still don't know the one little word." I puckered my lips.

"You think on that and let God tell you. And when He does, it'll stay with you your whole life."

A light breeze swept across my body, blowing my hair away from my face. It felt like Mama pulling my locks back for a ponytail. The mood was shifting. It wasn't just any old happy-go-lucky day.

"Skeets?" Wyeth had no spunk in his voice.

"Yes sir," he answered with playful formality.

"What's going to happen to us?" The gurgling river sounded so merry compared to his sudden weighty question.

Skeets scanned the ground and released a deep sigh. "I don't know exactly. But I plan to get some idea from Detective Roberts tonight. He's a school buddy of mine."

"Is Father in trouble?" I winced, waiting for the answer.

"Your father left on bad terms, but that doesn't mean he's done anything wrong. And he's *still* your father."

"Yeah." Wyeth scoffed. "But I'm not stoked for him to come home."

"Don't get stirred up, my man. Let's see how it all works out. I know Nana is weaker every time I return. It'd be too much for them to have you."

We returned to silence. The pause felt heavy. I'd seen Father's gun. They hadn't. Wyeth had blurted something the night of our parents' big fight. Something about "other lies," regarding our dad. I wondered what Skeets knew.

The sun drifted down in the sky. A blue heron coasted soundlessly over the water towards the other bank where the cliffs rose up. We gathered ourselves and began the hike home. Wyeth lingered behind, skipping rocks. Skeets and I walked hand-in-hand.

When we arrived home, the kitchen counters were crammed with casseroles and baked goods from neighbors. I sampled a few and then settled in the hammock to watch the sunset. Tuck had revived after a good nap and rolled in with me.

We often imagined our hammock was a pirate ship. I composed songs about two infamous cats that lived on the boat named Rickets and Scurvy. I used melodies like, *Bingo*, or *I've Been Working on the Railroad*, with different lyrics.

The musical sagas told how the captain's talking parrot—a measly little tattletale—persecuted the cheeky felines. The bird squawked, "Stealers! Stealers!" if the cats nibbled on the crew's leftover sardines. Never mind the kitties were starving. They also survived being hurled overboard, because they had nine lives...but who was counting. They'd live forever in our song.

Skeets came out to swing with us. He tied my jump rope to a nearby tree. By tugging on it, he kept us moving in time with my song. We pretended to be in a perilous storm, rocking high and low. Tuck flailed his arms, squealing with delight. But I felt a little seasick. Skeets finally brought our swinging ship back to safe harbor.

"Skeets?" I said.

"Yes darlin'."

"Is *perilous* one word or two?"

He grinned at first. "It's actually one. But 'peril us' kind of means the same thing."

"Well it doesn't work with *generous* or *cantankerous*."

"Right-tee-oh." He chuckled. "It's *mysteeerious*. There will always be some mystery-for-us," he said, walking his fingers up my arm like a spider.

I crunched my shoulders and leaned against his strong body.

"But mystery is better than peril." He whispered, as if talking to himself.

The moon rose in the east. It was only a sliver that night, though I knew the rest of its roundness was hidden in the dark. Fireflies started lighting up the yard like earth-bound stars, as the sun gracefully slipped off to bed. We rested in our uncle's arms, suspended in a moment of comfort. Perhaps we'd feel this way tomorrow, or maybe the day after that, but I knew it wouldn't last.

Chapter 10

How much love is there, when blood is the only cure?

O UR HAMMOCK BOAT swayed peacefully until Nana hollered out the backdoor.

"Skeeeeeets!" She sounded screechy. Pops dubbed it her "fishwife call," but in our world it was simply chauney.

"Comin!" my uncle answered. Then he turned to us. "Jack Roberts is here."

Together, we tumbled out of the hammock. Pops met us at the door, saying it was way past bedtime. Tuck immediately unraveled with an ear-piercing whine that turned into a Big Pony tantrum. He twisted his shoulders back and forth like a washing machine so no one would touch him. Then he glared at Pops before crumpling to the floor. Skeets promised there'd be a new adventure tomorrow, and finally calmed him down. Tuck wiped his eyes and slowly hopped up the steps, one at a time, holding my grandfather's hand.

Tuck missed Mama most at bedtime. He'd been having meltdowns all week without her. It wasn't just the routine of bath and bedtime stories. The best part happened after he settled in bed and she folded the sheet's edge over the blanket. That's when she hummed. Sometimes she would sing softly, but mostly her low-pitch humming was the thing. It soothed all the skinned-knee, loose-tooth, broken-toy kinds of trouble. I knew what he was missing. Wyeth probably did too.

I scurried to my room and slipped on my nightgown. My hands trembled as I washed my face. Roberts made me nervous. He reminded me of the school principal who Nana said was an angry-nice man, whatever that meant. His neck scar bothered me, and the fact that he asked a lot of nosy questions. Still, he might know if Father was coming home.

Pops summoned Nana to read Tuck a chapter in *The Tale of Peter Rabbit*, while he checked on Wyeth. In the hallway, I kissed my grandparents goodnight and shut my door. I listened for a few seconds and then climbed out my bedroom window, using the clematis trellis as a ladder. I had to eavesdrop.

Through the windows, I saw Skeets and Roberts standing by the breakfast table. *Rats!* My pantry hideout wouldn't work. I dashed around to the front door and slipped inside the front hall closet. As I guessed, the two men eventually moved to the living room where I could listen and watch through the door's slit. My uncle sat with his back to me, but I could make out the detective's face from the side.

"You sly ol' coot!" he said to Skeets. "How did you get these bugs through Customs?"

"They didn't ask, and I didn't tell. Besides, they're roasted, so what's the problem?"

"A strange snack." He swallowed. "But tasty, I admit."

The paper bag rustled.

"Skeets...I'm sorry about your sister."

My uncle lowered his head. A moment of stillness followed.

Kibbs wove his fat body around the chairs, rubbing his face on their legs. I knew his motor was running because his nose squeaked when he purred.

"What can you tell me about Hank?" asked Skeets. He sounded stern. It startled me. I didn't know that voice.

"So far, not much. He left Grace about three weeks ago. Some kind of big fight over Wyeth."

"Yeah. Mother told me that much."

"Man, he's an odd duck," Roberts said in hushed tones.

"Meaning?"

"*I* have to tell *you*?" He set the paper bag on the side table.

"I guess I've been away too long," Skeets said with palms turned up.

"Well, he's a loner...drives a shabby lookin' Buick, yet he's a perfectionist and really antagonizes Wyeth. And according to your folks, he's super religious. How does all that square? It's messed up, if you ask me."

"Religiosity has an ugly side," Skeets added. "What about abuse? Do you think he took things out on my sister and the kids?"

"Not physically. Maybe emotionally or psychologically."

Skeets rested his head on one hand. "Hank wasn't always like that, you know. Something changed." My uncle always believed the best about people.

"Well, we found him at a dive hotel in Lakewood," said Roberts. "He said he came to get a few things on the day Grace died—nothing more. No marks of a scuffle on her body or his. Frankly, he's as freaked out as anybody."

"Why didn't he come for the kids right away...or sit with us at the funeral?"

"Look, when life gets complicated, some men just dump their families." Roberts exhaled. "I see it all the time."

"Yeah, yeah..." Skeets didn't sound convinced.

"Hell, I can't arrest a guy for having a fight with his wife."

"Jack, these kids mean the world to me." My uncle's voice broke up a little.

Roberts nodded. "Wyeth's a loaded pistol, you know."

Just the mention of a gun made it hard for me to swallow.

"Yeah, I know." Skeets cleared his throat. "So what'll happen next?"

"Hank has custody, and he owns the house. Most likely he'll move back in. We really don't have a case unless the court orders a psychological evaluation based on the kids' stories."

My mind darted ahead. Roberts knew I was scared of my father. Would that make my dad a bad parent? As hard as things had been, I didn't want to be an orphan.

"And that's it?" Skeet sounded irritated.

"Fraid so. Don't worry, man," said Roberts. "We'll get some eyes in the neighborhood. Those folks across the street..." He pointed toward the front door. "The Peates? They'll watch."

It got really quiet. My uncle appeared deep in thought.

"But there's something else." Roberts paused. He leaned forward as if he was going to whisper. "We've ruled out homicide, but not suicide."

"What the...?" Skeets shook his head. "You don't know my sister," he said with intensity.

A shudder passed through my body.

Roberts pulled out the diary and read Mama's final entry. He looked at Skeets with sad eyes, like he should've taken back every word. My uncle tipped his head back against the leather chair. The air felt thick. A sharp pain passed through my shoulders.

"Her 'independence day' was about freedom." Skeets straightened his hunched shoulders. "Freedom from fear, because—well, let's just say life with Hank 'weren't no picnic.'" He shook his head, as if chasing away gloomy thoughts.

Roberts waited, like he didn't know how to respond.

Skeets completed his thought. "Her words mean something else, Jack. She'd *never* take her own life."

"Well my conclusion is the whole damn thing was a tragic accident." He slapped his knee. It's a crying shame."

"Yeah, I know that too in my spirit," said Skeets.

"Interesting. So now you're a psychic?" Roberts said with an uneasy laugh. "I could use your cosmic powers." Maybe he was trying to change the subject.

"It's cosmic all right, but not from the dark side," said Skeets.

They looked at each other for a moment.

"What exactly do you mean?" asked Roberts.

"It's God, Jack. He finds ways to tell me stuff."

"You're kidding, right?" Roberts slumped back in his chair.

"No."

"So, you're—*special*?" He winked at my uncle.

"Not at all. God will talk to anyone. A lot of churchgoers don't believe that though. You know...that God is accessible," said Skeets. "It's against their religion."

"Very funny. But, I wouldn't know," Roberts stated. "I'm wary of all things religious."

"Ahh, you've been cornered by some well-meaning believers?"

"Maybe," said Roberts. "But, c'mon man. Tell me you're not one of those nuts who say, "God *told* me.'"

"I understand what you're saying," Skeets said.

"Okay, humor me. How do you really know when God is talking?" asked Roberts.

My uncle scratched his chin and thought for a minute. "Well, for me it started with dreams."

"Dreams? Oh sure. Here we go."

"No really, man. Then other things happened—like coincidences, except they weren't. Or at a crucial moment, an idea would come outta nowhere, like an interruption to my thoughts. I started to notice things."

"For instance?" Roberts taunted him.

"Let me think." Skeets kicked off his loafers and shifted his weight. The detective didn't budge. Kibbs traipsed down the hall, heading my way.

"Okay. Here's one," said my uncle. "Recently, I had a dream about the Pope. Don't know why. But it was the new guy—John Paul."

Roberts nodded.

"So, in the dream, I was standing on a curb surrounded by a huge crowd. We're all watching for the Pope, thinking he'd pass by in his white car. I just wanted a look at him."

Kibbs planted himself right by the closet opening, pestering me with one paw as if I were giant mouse.

"Go away! Shoo!" I whisper-yelled, swatting the air. It didn't help. The more I batted at him, the more he wanted to play. I pretended to sleep. He was about to blow my cover.

"I scanned the crowd to my left." Skeets continued. "Thousands upon thousands of people."

The detective listened with arms crossed.

"Then glancing to my right, I jumped back completely stunned. The Pope was only twenty feet away! He walked along, shaking hands with people like an ordinary guy."

"What'd you expect?"

"I don't know—more security, I guess."

"So what happened?" Roberts jiggled his right leg on the ball of his foot.

"Here's the shocker. When my turn came, the Pope strolled right up to me, took my head in his hands, and kissed my forehead like I was his favorite nephew. Then I woke up."

"So *that* was God talking to you?"

"Yeah, but I had no memory of the dream by morning."

"What?"

"Hold on. I got out of bed, made some coffee and flipped on the TV. Guess what came on the screen?" He paused, but Roberts didn't answer. "The Pope—doing Mass! Yeah, the whole dream came back in an instant, right there in my kitchen. This time I wrote it down."

"Okay, weirdo," Roberts said in a smart-alecky way. "I suppose he also came to your front door."

If one of my schoolmates had spoken to me like that, I would've quit right then. I knew what it felt like to be teased. But Skeets ignored the sarcasm.

"Well, it gets weirder. At the same time in real life, some wealthy people from New York invited me to speak about my work in Africa. A college friend arranged the gathering. I got there late because of traffic. People were already arriving. My friend pulled me into the kitchen to meet the host." Skeets leaned forward. "The guy must've only been fifty, but he had all white hair and was a dead ringer for the Pope."

"Ha!" Roberts' short laugh ended as quickly as it started.

"Well, the meeting began, and I gave my little speech. When I finished, the host walked right up to me, took my head in his hands, and kissed my forehead!"

"No way!" The detective's lower lip jutted out. I saw his Adam's apple rise and fall several times. "What the hell does that mean?"

"It's pretty simple really. Many people are looking for God, and if we get a glimpse of Him, well, that's probably as good as it gets," offered Skeets.

"But the Pope isn't God."

"Right. You could say he's a man delivering His message."

"But he didn't say a damn thing."

Skeets paused, collecting his thoughts.

"No. But, he came in close to give a kiss of affection—because *that's* how God really feels about us."

When Skeets said that, it looked as though an angel had appeared to Roberts. I swear it. His unblinking eyes grew wide. But suddenly, he scoffed.

"Maybe that's how God feels about you," Roberts said in a barely audible voice. He began tapping his fingers on the arm of the couch, lightly at first, then hard enough to make a sound. His expression darkened like a building thunderstorm. Wrinkles formed across his forehead. His lips thinned. Finally, he stood up and began to pace.

I scooted back to remain hidden.

"Okay. Here's what I want to know." Roberts sounded like he wanted to pick a fight. "When I returned from Vietnam, I took this job and I've put a lot of bad guys on death row."

Skeets just listened.

"The worst case so far involved a little girl who was lured from the Westgate Mall by a man she knew. The guy was the son of her old babysitter. The jerk took the girl out in the countryside and beat her to death with a flipping shovel."

I gasped. Both men looked around the room. I pinched Kibbs and he ran off.

"It's the cat. Go on," said Skeets.

"Well, after the girl was dead, he raped her."

My heart pumped hard. Rape was something bad, though I wasn't sure what it meant. I half-covered my ears and balled up, hugging my knees.

"That's horrific," said Skeets.

"Yeah, and in my experience, the reverse order of that is significant. A guy usually kills afterwards to clean up his mess. Turns out the sicko had been a warlock, deep into all kinds of occult crap."

"Did you get him?"

"Yeah. But here's what really eats me. During the trial, I got to know the girl's parents. Over the months and years that followed, they *never ever* got over it. First the mom died, and a year later, the dad keeled over." Roberts lifted his arms with exasperation. "They weren't even forty years old!"

Skeets shook his head in disbelief.

Roberts stopped pacing and raised his index finger as if to scold.

"And I'm telling you, they were *God—fearing—people!*"

His anger pinned me to the back wall of the closet. Roberts continued his rant, marching back and forth.

"So then, the Supreme Court ruled the death penalty unconstitutional, which changed 120 sentences to life imprisonment here in Ohio. Basically, the guy who destroyed this little family gets to live indefinitely, and on our dime. Damn, if that didn't beat all! I punched a hole through the drywall in my office!"

Skeets still listened without comment.

"After a while, this scumbag decided to write me, and one day I got a long letter from him." Roberts stood by Skeets now, facing him dead-on. "He wrote all kinds of religious mumbo-jumbo. And at the end, he said he'd *'found Jeeeesus.'*" The detective grimaced in an insulting way, as if he didn't believe in the killer's sincerity. With squinty eyes and a strained voice, he stabbed Skeets with his question: "Now tell me—what does *your God* have to say about *that?*"

I felt gut-punched.

Skeets shut his eyes, as if waiting for an answer from heaven. He would need one. The situation grew tenser with each tick of the hall clock. Finally, my uncle responded with surprising tenderness.

"Well, I don't know everything, Jack." He looked up at Roberts. "But Jesus, who said He was God, was also brutally murdered. And He was as innocent as that girl."

Roberts wilted and sank down on the sofa.

Skeets continued. "And as He hung there dying—all beaten and bloody—He said, 'Father, forgive them...'" My uncle's voice broke off.

Roberts finished the sentence. "Because they *don't know* what they're doing." He knew the verse, but looked surprised as he said it.

My uncle nodded. "Yeah. You know this. And two criminals died next to Jesus, remember? The first one cursed Him. But the other guy humbled himself." Skeets' voice cracked. "And Jesus told him, he'd be in paradise that very day."

Roberts' cheeks glistened with moisture. The creases around his eyes softened as anger drained from his face.

"It's not like God is surprised by what goes on down here." Skeets made a sweeping gesture with his arm. "Believe me, He knows all about it. But here's the thing, Jack." He put his hand on Roberts' knee. "He's far more interested in a change of heart."

The detective blinked hard and lowered his head.

Skeets waited. A minute went by. "This isn't about that guy on death row, is it?"

Roberts looked up, his eyes all shiny and red. He shook his head no. "Vietnam," he said in a broken voice.

Skeets moved off his chair to kneel before his friend, placing an arm around his shoulders.

Nothing more was said for what felt like a very long time.

I rested my head against the wall and closed my eyes. The very atmosphere in the house had shifted somehow. Warm tears slid down my cheeks, but I wasn't sad. Rather buoyed up, even held by something.

"Glory," I murmured. "The splendor of heaven." It was the only word I could think of at the moment. Now it was more than black letters on a white page in my notebook. Something alive, something beautiful and even supernatural swelled in the room. You couldn't see it with your eyes, but it was just as real. It came in waves, the big rolling kind that well under the stern of your boat when the wind is behind you. And with a mighty surge, it can carry you forward to a new place.

The men rustled to their feet, and I snapped into the present.

"Thanks." Roberts extended his arm. His voice sounded calmer.

"Good to see you, man," Skeets said as they shook hands and embraced.

"Here, this is for Iris." Roberts handed him Mama's diary.

The front door closed, and the next thing I knew, Skeets slipped the diary through the crack of the closet door. I caught a glimpse of his smile.

"Good night, my Wild Iris Rose."

Chapter 11

How much fire of desire must be in my Lord?

A BEAUTIFUL SUMMER morning coaxed me out of numbness and sorrow. I took a blanket to the hammock at first light and listened for the mourning dove's plaintive woo-hoo-hoo-hoo. He usually perched on the telephone pole like a dutiful sentry, silhouetted against the dawning sky. Sunbeams emerged, multiplying their power on the dew until every grass tip twinkled with light.

I rolled to my back, hanging one leg over the side to create some swing. No trace of clouds in sight. A red-tailed hawk floated on an updraft. Scanning the horizon, I wondered why God had made the sky blue instead of pink or some other color. Blue was the right choice—not that God would have asked me.

Skeets stayed with us an extra week after the funeral, because Nana's disease had flared up. We exchanged long hugs with our grandparents—a sadder goodbye than usual. They drove off in their maroon Skylark.

Afterwards, my uncle mentioned he'd spoken with our dad. A snake-like feeling coiled around my neck. His voice was solemn. In a matter of days, our father would be in charge of our world. My thoughts took off on a hundred-yard dash.

Though Nana and Pops lived an hour away in Akron, I didn't realize then that Father would eventually isolate us from them.

Estrangement was not yet a word in my collection.

For the time remaining with Skeets, we lived in full-on adventure, showing him our favorite haunts. We spent long afternoons in the Middle Strip, which he renamed *The Lost World*. Wy and I ran ahead, jumping over ankle-breaking burrows to find the hollow log where a porcupine lived. I believed unwaveringly it crouched inside, studying us with beady eyes. Soon Skeets and Tuck caught up to scavenge for quills.

Then we detoured along the creek, searching for raccoon, muskrat, and possum footprints. Like scientists, digging out the clay imprints with sturdy sticks, we placed them in the sun to dry. Some impressions looked the same to me. Only Skeets could tell which was which.

Heading upstream, I came upon the best find of the day—a school of tadpoles. Skeets helped me capture a dozen or so in a mayonnaise jar. I called them swimming apostrophes.

When the afternoon heat peaked, we loaded up our modest treasures and headed back to civilization. I was intent on making a small habitat for my frogs in disguise. Skeets found Tuck's old baby bath. I scattered sand and pebbles in the bottom and placed a flat lichen-covered rock in the middle. It served as a perfect island, sloping down on one side. I added moss and grass clumps and poured in creek water from a jar. The tadpoles slid happily into their marshy home-away-from home. We fed them tiny pinches of frozen spinach, because they weren't ready for insects. After a week, seven of them formed stubby little legs.

Another morning, Wyeth seemed gloomy at breakfast. Resting his head on one arm, he stared at nothing. His soggy Lucky Charms floated in pink-tinted milk. Tuck was trying to hang a spoon on his nose, and I was busy making hot chocolate, when Skeets whirled into the kitchen. Surveying the scene, he leaned toward Wyeth, pointing his finger like a pistol.

"Hey, cowboy!" he said, in a backwoods drawl. "Let's shoot some cans and swap some lies!" Skeets had morphed into a hillbillyish character with slits for eyes and a strange looking grin.

My brother straightened up with sparkler eyes. "I'm in!"

"Lies?" I said, half-scolding.

"You know darlin'!" He winked. "Exaggerated tall tales to make us better shots and handsomer men."

"I'll fetch my slingshot," said Wy. "What we got for ammo?"

"Hold yer water boy! I bought us some B-B's—*and* guns to match."

"No way!" Wyeth jumped up from his chair.

"Sure as shootin'! Now let's git some targets, and move on outta here." He pretended to spit on the ground.

We headed toward the trashcans to find target-worthy objects. An empty sweet corn can, a plastic margarine container, and an egg carton would do. Then Skeets found a Frosted Flakes box featuring Tony the Tiger.

"Whoo-hoo! Now we're talkin' big game! C'mon Petticoat Junction. You too Scallywag." He smiled at Tuck. "We ain't leaving no stragglers."

I skipped inside to get ready.

Down on Rocky Cliffs River, Skeets lined up the containers on a piece of driftwood. Tony the Tiger got killed countless times. Pellet holes peppered the box. After awhile, Tuck and I waded along the shore to cool our feet, leaving the "men" to have a showdown.

"Aw, I can whack that a mile away with one eye closed!" Wy spouted.

"You can't hit your butt with both hands!" Skeets laughed. They were play fighting like animals do when they feel safe.

To settle it, they put a donut-sized rock on the log to shoot from five feet away. If they both hit it, they moved back another five feet, and so on, until somebody missed. Loud whoops echoed off the cliffs with each successful hit.

At twenty-five feet, Skeets hit the log instead of the rock. He collapsed on the ground as if struck by a stray bullet and pretended to sob. Wyeth gloated, lifting his BB gun high in the air. I giggled, and Tuck was bent over with laughter.

After a bit, we gathered our things and turned toward home. A small black snake slithered across the path. Wyeth trapped it lightening-quick, stepping on its 'neck' to grab its head. The snake spiraled around his arm.

"Well I'll be—a black rat snake!" said Skeets. "It's young'un, but it'll get three times as big."

"Whoo-eee!" Wy was jacked. "A six footer?"

Skeets nodded. "Got a name for it?"

Wyeth paused. "Elvis," he said, finally.

"Elvis?" I asked.

"Yeah. His shiny black skin is something Elvis would wear."

"That's assuming it's a boy," I said, feeling outnumbered.

At the house, Wyeth cleaned dirt and cobwebs out of a large dairy crock that Mama had used to plant geraniums. Its sides were smooth and deep, making a perfect snake pit.

Skeets covered the bottom with newspaper. "Snakes gotta pee just like us," he explained, though I wasn't sure how.

"And how do they hear without ears or scratch their noses without hands?" I asked. "Birds probably have the same problem." I should've kept my questions to myself.

My uncle smiled.

"You're always wonderin' bout things that don't matter," Wyeth said.

"And *you* don't?" I countered. "I remember a speech about dandelions!"

Wyeth ignored me as he lowered a half-round slab of bark in the bottom. "There...now he can hide if he wants."

"That is—if he is really a he, and not a *she*." I lifted my nose in a huff.

Skeets found an old window screen in the garage for a make-shift lid. He told Wyeth to put a heavy rock on top.

I fingered my black smooth stone, still hidden in my pocket.

Skeets said we'd need to find crickets or little voles to feed Elvis. I didn't want anything to do with rodents or their allies. Wyeth and Tuck eagerly set mousetraps by the woodpile, using cardboard tubes left from Christmas wrapping paper. They stapled the tubes at one end and dropped a small piece of Velveeta inside. Then came the waiting.

Though eager to help Wyeth, Tuck wasn't terribly interested in having one of nature's pets after the skunk incident, unless you count lightning bugs. He was far too busy learning how to whistle. Watching his attempts, I wondered how whistling came into existence. It wasn't involuntary like a sneeze, but definitely a *bird* skill—not *muffin* or *horse*.

Tuck blew lots of soundless air and gave up. "It doesn't work for me-ee," he wailed, facedown in the grass. "It just doesn't!"

"I know why!" said Skeets. "Everyone knows that winking comes before whistling?"

"What?" I asked, slow to catch on.

"C'mon, buddy," he said. "Don't jump ahead. First you have to learn to wink."

Tuck's face brightened. Skeets showed him how, but Tuck practiced in secret.

"Somethin' in your eye?" Wyeth asked Tuck after supper one night. I scowled at my older brother as Tuck fled from the room.

A day or so later, Tuck had mastered the skill and winked at the gas station man, the pet store lady, and all the shoppers at the grocery. Most everyone smiled or winked in return. He even winked at some local dogs, but they only stared back with tipped heads.

One night in the car, Tuck made an announcement. "The moon is my friend."

"Were you winking at him?" I asked.

"No, silly."

"Then how do you know?" I looked out the window.

"Because, he's following me."

The moon appeared to travel with us as trees and telephone poles passed by. The bright globe hung as a constant in the darkened sky, while the car gently coasted up and down over the rolling countryside. I closed my eyes and pretended we were flying. A week with Skeets felt like a magic carpet ride, floating us far above realities that would soon return.

Chapter 12

ON THE DAY Father would return, we had to clean the entire house including the garage. Skeets strolled out to the living room. "Okay, guys!" he shouted, with hands on hips. Tuck came running. Wy showed up after a minute, taking his good ol' time. "Here's the plan." My uncle sounded firmer than usual. "Your dad doesn't like clutter. So every afternoon, say 'round three, before you even think about watching a TV show, collect your stuff and take it to your room. If you wait till he turns in the driveway, you're hosed."

"What, like some ritual?" snapped my almost-thirteen-year-old brother.

Skeets inhaled. "C'mon pal, I'm giving you a clue here. You'll dig your own hole with that act, yeah?" He put a gentle hand on Wyeth's shoulder.

My brother's jaw tightened. He lowered his head.

"Okay, get crackin'." Skeets said, following Tuck. Wyeth groaned about every thirty seconds.

It was true. We'd scattered our junk everywhere—shoes and squirt guns had piled by the back door and beach towels draped the railings. Comic books and an empty bag of chips were strewn across the couch. Unfolded laundry had been stacked high on the swivel chair. Mama used to keep us in line, watching out for things that made our father edgy—things that never occurred to me. Now it'd be up to us.

Maybe it would be up to me.

My body felt cumbersome. It was too early to be tired. We all carried a load upstairs. Skeets picked up whatever fell out of Tuck's arms.

After that I stripped my parents' bed, dumping dirty sheets in the laundry chute. I checked on the boys to see if they were dillydallying. Wy was sweeping the garage with a push broom. Tuck shelved odds and ends. He paused to wiggle his hand into Wy's first baseball mitt.

I returned with clean linen and stretched a fitted sheet over the mattress. I had to look for the pistol. Skeets was busy vacuuming the living room. My thoughts went crazy. I quickly peeked under. It was still there. My stomach knotted. I quickly ran through all the things I could do, but decided it was best to leave it alone. I didn't feel any better.

When Skeets finished, I heard a great sigh. I tiptoed to the doorway. He stood in the hall, staring at old family pictures. I came from behind, wrapping my arms around his waist. His body swelled with labored breathing. A warm tear splattered on my forearm.

"What's wrong?" My throat tightened.

He seemed focused on a picture of Mama as a girl. To my surprise, he reached up and unhooked a faded portrait of Father's family.

"What is it?" I whispered.

He angled the frame so I could see. My father's parents looked like stone statues. Their perfectly combed hair framed pale faces—always without expression. My dad was their only child, other than his sister who died at birth. "Hanky," as they called him, looked about five years old. His short hair had one unruly cowlick that no dollop of Vitalis could tame.

Skeets pointed to my father. "His eyes..." my uncle stammered. "What are his eyes...saying?"

"His eyes?" I stalled. I'd never thought much about my dad as a little boy. He rarely mentioned his childhood. "Well, I don't know...'cept Tuck looks over the top of his eyes like that when he's in trouble."

"What do you think his dad said right before the camera clicked?"

I checked my grandfather's expression. "Shut up and stand still, or I'll beat the tar outta ya!"

Skeets peered at me. "How'd you come up with that?"

"Grandfather said that to Wy once."

My uncle nodded. "See his hand on your dad's shoulder?"

We examined the photo.

"He's gripping him!" I said. The boy's shirt showed shadows where his father's fingers dug in. I glanced up at my uncle's face. A small muscle near his jawbone swelled when he clenched his teeth. His eyelashes were still moist. "What makes you so sad?"

Skeets wiped his eyes. "I don't know." He hung the picture back on its nail. "I don't think your dad got much love."

My heartbeat quickened. *Didn't get loved?* I blinked hard. It was easy to only see Father as a grownup—the one in charge. He never cried or said anything if he felt sad. He just carried on, day after day, as if life was a never-ending chore. If Father carried pain it only made him angry, and I for one didn't want to be around that.

I ambled back to the bedroom, heavy in thought. After cornering the ends of the top sheet, I straightened the bedspread and put a clean pillowcase on Father's pillow. When it came to covering the second pillow, I hesitated.

Skeets rolled the sweeper into the bedroom.

"What about Mama's pillow?" I asked.

"Either way the bed will feel empty." He plugged in the cord. "Just do it out of respect, I guess." He switched on the sweeper.

I put the pillowcase on and hugged her pillow. My sadness welled. It was no substitute for my mother's soft body.

Finally the house looked pretty clean. I dashed upstairs to change my shirt. When I returned, Wy had stretched out on Mama's side of the bed. It was annoying—him wrinkling my perfect work and all. But tears dripped down his left temple. I kept moving, acting unaware. He sat up anyway.

Skeets hollered for everyone to gather under the sycamore tree out back. He brought out an aluminum ice tray, covered in cellophane. We'd made grape juice cubes that morning. Toothpicks worked well enough as popsicle sticks. Waiting for the liquid to freeze was the hard part. Waiting was always difficult. Now we were waiting to start a different life altogether.

My hair felt damp with perspiration. A light breeze brought some relief. Tuck's eyelids became heavy, and he dosed off on the cool grass. Wyeth seized his melting cube before the ants got to it.

No one spoke for a while.

Skeets' eyes were half-closed. He stared hard at the ground. I figured he was trying to say goodbye, but didn't want to.

"Don't say it," I said, breaking the silence.

He gazed up at me.

I raised my eyebrows like it was obvious. "Don't say goodbye." Tears gathered in the corners of my eyes. "Too sad."

He lowered his head again.

I wiped my eyes. Skeets had become the sun, moon, and Milky Way to us. Without him everything would be... empty... dreary... joyless. No single word in my collection described it. His absence would be as real as Mama's. But as we sat there, an edgy restlessness took over. Father would be coming any time now.

The remaining sliver of my cube slipped off the stick. I let it melt away.

"This totally sucks!" Wyeth said, spearing ants with his toothpick. "What the heck are we going to do?"

"Well," Skeets sighed, "You're going to honor your father." He spoke with certainty, as if he'd thought out every possible move in a chess game.

"Yeah, right." Wyeth forced a mocking laugh.

"I'm serious." Skeets paused until Wyeth's eyes met his.

"Why? He doesn't deserve our respect." Spit flew from my brother's mouth.

"Maybe not, but it's how God set things up."

That did not fly with my brother. Might as well offer him a straightjacket.

I wondered about the word—*honor*—picturing a dramatic curtsy of some kind. "But I *don't* respect him." I covered my mouth immediately.

Skeets smiled sadly. "That's honest—but it's not okay."

"What if he gets mean and ugly with us?" I asked.

Skeets squinted and exhaled slowly. "You have to ask God. I know that sounds weird, but it's what I do. You probably don't believe this yet, but God *will* talk to you."

Wy gave him a blank look. I sat perfectly still. Tuck stayed in dreamland.

"Take the clock, for instance," Skeets said. "Since I've been here, I've seen 8:38 a bunch. And sometimes it turns to 8:39 right when I look."

I leaned forward, curious but confused.

"It's a promise for me—in Romans—so I can leave you kids and not worry if I did right by you or not."

Chills surged over me head to toe. The thought was too fantastic—words rising off a Bible page as a direct answer from God? In Anna's 8-Ball game, messages like "Without a doubt" or "Don't count on it" floated up into view. But that was all fake. Anyway, Mama had put a kibosh on that toy. Still, I was crazy enough to believe God spoke to me at school that terrible day.

Tuck turned over. Skeets stroked the soft curls on his head.

"I can't promise your dad won't hurt you," my uncle said. "But know this—your dad is sad too and probably worried sick about raising you by himself."

Our uncle didn't know how much Father had changed in the last six months. I cringed inside.

Wy twisted away, pinching clover heads off their stems in the grass.

Skeets rolled to his feet to stand. He arched his back and stretched before walking to the side yard to glance down the road. "Pssst," he said, motioning Wyeth to follow.

I stayed with Tuck, brushing ants off his pudgy legs.

They stood by the hedge, nearly out of earshot.

"I *hate* him!" Wyeth said to Skeets with scrunched eyebrows.

"Shh." Skeets glanced my way.

I pretended to be oblivious.

Skeets leaned forward toward Wyeth. "If you get on the wrong side of your dad, he'll get on the wrong side of you and round it goes." He spoke in a dope-slap way, as if what he said was obvious. Still he pulled Wyeth close, holding the back of his neck in a manly sort of affection. If Father had tried that, Wyeth would've immediately spun out of his grip. Then again, Father wouldn't do that.

"Listen to me, Wy." His voice had softened. "Later that poisonous hatred will make you *just like him.* That's how it works."

Wyeth's lips thinned. I imagined a war inside his head.

"I believe..." My uncle's voice broke up. "...That's *exactly* what happened to him."

It was too much. Wyeth broke loose and paced around the yard.

Skeets wearily shook his head. After a minute, he strolled over to Elvis's den and stooped down to remove the screen. "Hey! You gotta see this!"

Wy sprinted over. I struggled to my feet, pulling Tuck awake. We huddled around the clay pot. Weeping willow branches swayed around us like soft arms. Wyeth had dropped a vole in the den that morning. The frantic rodent scurried around the perimeter hoping to escape. But Elvis wasn't hungry then and eyed the poor critter from his bark hideout. Now, the snake unhinged his jaw to swallow it alive, tail and all. The boys gawked in wonder.

Bile rose in my throat. The creature was doomed. Any struggle was useless. Gradually, the snake would suck its squirming body into a tunnel of death. I looked away. It was too sickening.

Then, I heard it—a rumble in the distance. Father turned onto our road in his dingy yellow Buick with a broken grill. Wy had called it the scary-movie-car. Soon it would be a sound I'd hear every day and every night. And my heart would beat hard every time.

Chapter 13

SKEETS AMBLED TOWARDS the car when it rolled to a stop. Wyeth didn't look up, but his face flushed. Father stepped out, removing his sunglasses. His eyes looked swollen, his face unshaven. Soiled rings of under-arm sweat darkened his white shirt. Skeets extended his hand first. They shook and spoke for a short time.

"*Remember...*" I said sternly to Wyeth.

"Remember *what?*" he said.

"What Skeets said."

"Oh shut up." He spat on the ground. "Quit trying to be the mom."

Skeets carried his suitcase. Father followed holding two bags of groceries, one with a big box of Cheerios sticking out the top. My father caught the screen door with his foot so it wouldn't slam.

Wyeth, Tuck and I remained like small soldiers at attention, waiting to greet our commander-in-chief. Soon, they returned. Wyeth shook hands with Father but didn't make eye contact. He would've rather shaken a fist. I stepped forward to embrace my father. We exchanged a brief, formal hug. His shirt reeked. He let go before I did. I stepped back. Tuck leaned into him. Father patted his head. I couldn't help but wonder if we weren't all missing Mama something terrible. I was.

Skeets broke up the stifling moment. "Hey! Your dad bought steaks! C'mon buddy." He tapped Wy's shoulder. "Let's start the charcoal." My brother bolted toward the garage.

"Daddy, come! We have a new pet!" Tuck tugged on Father's shirtsleeve. For a split second Father hesitated. I heard the faintest sigh. But he trailed wearily after Tuck and then squatted by the snake house to get a closer look.

"He's eatin' dinner," Tuck explained.

"A real humdinger!" Father's enthusiasm seemed unnatural, but at least he was trying. His shoulders remained slumped. Tucker beamed. I didn't know *humdinger* was another word for snake.

Father stood and rolled his shirtsleeves. He glanced toward my tadpole aquarium near the bushes and raised his eyebrows. "And what we got goin' on over here?"

I rushed toward him in awkward strides. Would he let me keep them? I pointed to a cluster of half-formed frogs hiding under a fern.

"Now that's a happy little family," he said in monotone, wiping sweat off his forehead.

I looked up at him with big eyes.

He forced a smile.

Dinner came together eventually. Skeets let Tuck peel five potatoes. They didn't have to be perfect, but Tuck insisted he wasn't done after twenty-nine minutes. With the rest of our preparations stalled, we moved about the house like actors at their first rehearsal. No one knew his or her part except for Skeets. He whistled a few notes out by the grill.

Finally, we gathered at the table. "Please pass the salt"...and... "Any more mashed potatoes?"...was the gist of the conversation. Skeets could've eased the tension, but he didn't. The fluorescent light over the sink flickered like the bulb was about to go.

I stood to clear the dishes, but Father motioned me to stay. I slid down in my chair.

"Kids..." He paused, finishing a giant bite of steak.

My uneasiness grew the longer it took him to swallow.

"With your mom gone, well, I hope we can start over," he said.

Tuck was trying to balance peas on his knife. I tapped his leg and gave him the stink eye.

"It won't be easy," Father's voice faltered, "but...we can try...to be a family again." He pulled a shopping bag out from under the table. "I brought some things to get us off on the right foot."

With a stiff arm, he handed Wyeth a Rubik's Cube. "This will be a challenge for you, son." Their fingers did not touch.

Wyeth's jaw opened. He flashed an angry sideways glance, but quickly resumed a blank expression.

Tuck got an Etch-A-Sketch. Father gave him a short lesson on making a "stairway." Skeets helped him erase the screen, shaking it upside down.

After that, Father pulled a long thin box from the pantry. "And for you, little Flutterby—a pair of stilts." He screwed the top and bottom pieces together and locked the footholds in place about ten inches off the floor. "Now wrap your skinny arms around the poles and step up." He held my waist with strong hands, keeping me in balance. It boosted my confidence.

After turning with his help, I stepped forward on my own. I started out fine, but got going too fast and crashed into the winged-back chair. The stilts went flying, as the chair tipped over backwards. I winced. Had I busted the chair? I peered up over the cushion to check Father's expression, and everyone broke out with laughter. Laughing felt good.

Tuck and Skeets cleared the table while I started some dish-water. Father searched the utility cupboard for a new fluorescent bulb. Skeets asked Wyeth to dry dishes and whispered, "Don't you dare complain." Wyeth snorted like a horse but complied. Tuck fed Kibbs—his daily chore. Then the two men carried garbage cans out to the curb.

"Wyeth! Keep up!" I said. The clean dishes were heaped dangerously high.

"Okay, okay." He snapped the end of his towel at Tuck, who giggled with delight.

Wyeth grabbed the next plate. Tuck struggled to get behind him as part of the game. Wyeth tricked him and spun around the other way. They collided and the plate went flying, exploding into a hundred pieces when it hit the floor. We stood utterly paralyzed. All air escaped my lungs.

After a few frightful seconds, we raced around to hide our mistake. It was automatic. Tuck's face was flushed as he fetched a paper bag from the broom closet. I picked up the big pieces as fast as possible, not caring that one had cut my palm. *Hurry, hurry.* Wyeth bit his lip as he swept up all the shards. Quiet and swift. No one would know. It was our way.

Somberly, we finished the dishes. I wrapped a paper towel around my hand to stop the bleeding. I felt chilled from perspiration.

Wyeth toyed with the Rubik's cube. "He must think I'm an idiot."

"Who, Father?"

"Yeah. He said it would be a *challenge* for me—like I'm stupid."

"That's not what he meant." I sounded like Mama.

"How would *you* know?"

"He was simply trying to say it would be interesting...or maybe exciting for you." I too was uncertain of Father's intention.

"You don't get it. He doesn't jab at you!" His voice trembled with hurt. "You're his little Flutterby, remember?"

I fumed. "You always make him sound mean. What if he was trying to be *nice*?"

"Trying to be nice?" His voice cracked. He pitched the cube hard into the couch. If Wyeth already felt exasperated over a comment, how would we survive one hour with our father, let alone weeks or years?

My legs went limp. "What do you *want* from him?"

Wyeth's temper flared. "I want him off my back! I want him to say sorry! But he can't, he just can't. He's gotta have a dog to kick, and it's always gonna be me!"

Skeets and Father came up the front steps and entered the house. Had they heard us? I hid my hand behind my back.

Our uncle glanced around. "Everything okay?"

None of us could speak. My whole body stiffened. I slowly backed against the counter to steady the towering pile of dishes and pans with one arm. Wyeth folded his arms and looked at the floor. The men waited for an answer. I could hear the clock ticking like a bomb.

Tuck traced lines on the linoleum with his big toe. He started squirming and finally caved. "We broke a dish, Daddy. But we didn't mean to."

Chapter 14

IN THE LUCID hour of sleep, right before waking, I found myself in a scene with familiar people hiking up a mountain trail. The well-marked path meandered through shaded woodlands of red oaks and sugar maples. Pincushion moss carpeted the forest floor, and in certain places, tree roots formed little stair steps.

After a while, the trail zigzagged up a steep hillside until we came upon a large clearing filled with wildflowers. I picked a few and lifted them to my nose. It was good to take a break. I peeled off my windbreaker. Canteens of water were shared.

Eventually we gathered, ready to press on. I glanced around to locate the path, but it seemed to end in the clearing. A woman shouted, "Here it is!" But it was only a dark rotting log.

Right then, another set of hikers reached the same meadow. The newcomers milled in all directions, searching for the path as well.

"We're befuddled too," I said to one of them, using a word from my collection. But without a path, they turned like scared sheep and funneled down the way they'd come.

"Don't you want to see what's up ahead?" a man near me hollered.

The last one to leave waved his hand down sharply.

We prepared to move on. I placed a deflated inner tube on a tall bush as a marker, in case we got lost. Dreams are weird like that. We combed the alpine meadow for hours on end, searching for the trail. I gave up and trudged along like a foot soldier, not knowing who was in charge or where we were headed.

Then, after all that tramping, I came upon my inner tube! Had we been going in circles? I stepped closer. Something was different—the tube was inflated. It made no sense at all. I picked it up to bring it along and yet, what for? No lake or river in sight.

A moment later, a lady yelled, "Over here!" We all hiked toward the sound of her voice. On the edge of the clearing, she'd found a brand new solid-looking boardwalk. It smelled of fresh cut cedar and appeared well built with sturdy railings on each side. Smiles spread from face to face. It was the way to go.

Though still uphill, the boardwalk made our journey far easier. By nightfall, we reached the timberline and came upon a great lodge. I caught a whiff of—oh, the smell of roasting turkey! Light glowed from the windows. Pressing my nose against the cold glass, I saw a fire crackling in the hearth. And music, yes—a mandolin, a flute, and maybe a fiddle. It felt like coming home to a great family gathering, though it wasn't anything like my real home.

I heard a man's voice. "I want to be there when they arrive."

My eyes slowly opened. I sighed softly, not wanting to wake up in my room.

Someone was using the hall phone. I leaned forward to hear. Skeets spoke quietly. "Yeah, I miss them too. Tell Musa to mind the maamas." He paused. "No, no. Ask them to wait. I get to Entebbe at 10 p.m. Okay, see you that side in 36 hours."

I swung my legs over the mattress edge and rubbed my eyes. The mountain lodge had been so real. Most of my sleep scenes seemed cartoonish or bizarre like the Twilight Zone. This one felt different. Since Mama's startling appearance in my dream the night she died, I believed heaven was nearby—mostly invisible—but next to earth. Some dreams felt like traveling between them, as if someone accidentally left a door open. I jotted down several details in my notebook.

A quiet knock interrupted my thoughts.

"I'm up," I said.

"Hey Pupcake." My uncle's cheerful voice didn't agree with his eyes. I always noticed mouths, but eyes gave away secrets too.

He sat at the end of my bed, balancing his coffee. "My plane leaves for Amsterdam in a few hours. Thought you'd be asleep."

"Not me. I'm usually in the hammock by now."

"Of course. I knew that." The table lamp cast dark circles under his eyes. "Writing down a new word for the collection?"

"No, I had a dream."

"Yeah?" Lifting one leg onto my bed, he leaned against the bedpost. "Tell me."

I described the whole adventure—inner tube, boardwalk, and all. He paid close attention. Afterwards, we sat silently for a moment.

"So," I asked, "is God talking to me?"

His smile revealed his beautiful teeth. "You *know* it!"

"But what does it mean?"

Skeets stared straight ahead in thought. "Well, you're on a journey, in a wilderness of sorts, but you're not alone. That's good." He paused to sip his coffee. "You had a path, then it disappeared."

"Yeah, and we were lost for hours!" I squared my chest.

"I know. It will feel that way at times."

"Will? I don't understand."

"You get that this is about *now*."

"Now?"

"You lost the path when your mama died."

A tingle rolled across the back of my neck. *Now.* My thoughts spun out.

Skeets continued. "With all that wandering—something unseen is happening."

I couldn't keep up. He lost me.

"Think about it, girl." He put his mug on the floor to use both hands. "The inner tube gets filled with air. It's the Spirit, yeah? Coming like a life ring."

A memory flashed through my mind. A life ring had kept that man afloat in the frozen river till help arrived. "But what good is an inner tube on top of a mountain?"

"Think symbolically," he said. "Life ring—a ring of life surrounding you."

"First of all, this whole 'spirit' thing sounds scary," I said. "At church they say, 'Holy Ghost.'" I lifted the sheet over my head.

Skeets moved over closer. "He's good, not creepy." He pulled the sheet down. "What's going on in that head of yours?" He calmed the static in my hair.

"I think the Holy Ghost spies on me and tattles everything to God. You know, all the bad stuff." I folded my lips in.

Skeets let out a lively laugh. "What bad stuff?"

"Like last May. I found a bunch of jelly beans that Wy missed in his Easter basket, and I ate 'em all."

Skeets covered his mouth and raised his eyebrows, but I knew he was pretending.

"Or the time I accidentally poked a hole in the sofa cushion with Mama's scissors. I couldn't bear to tell her, much less Father. Can you imagine?"

"Rissy." His eyes danced. "The Spirit isn't nitpicky." He cleared his throat. "Tell me something. Do you think God's like that too?"

"Probably," I whispered.

"Why?"

"Because when someone doesn't know about church, God's nice and all because He wants you to come," I explained. "When you're a member for a while, it changes. He gets stricter. You have to do everything right, 'cause now *you know better.*"

"I see. So once you start coming to church, He turns into a mean guy?"

"Well sure, if you're bad."

"What if you're good?"

"He's probably nice to those people." I stopped to think. "See! That's the problem—I never know if I'm good enough."

My uncle nodded. "And what about Jesus?"

"Well, He's different." I doodled a flowery heart on my paper.

"How so?"

"He was one of us."

"Girl, would you believe me if I said that God and His Spirit are just like Jesus?" He waited for me to look up. "Think about ice, water, and steam."

"What about them?"

"They're all made of water, yeah?"

"Of course," I said, rolling my eyes. "I'm no dimwit."

He shifted my notebook to his knee and scribbled something: *Same in substance—different in form.*

I thought about it. No one had ever explained it like that.

He continued. "What you really need to know is they're all like Jesus."

I wanted to believe that.

He placed the pen in my palm, closing my fingers around it. "Write everything down, Wild Iris Rose. God is going to show you things." He echoed what Mama had said.

My thoughts returned to the dream. "What about the board-walk?"

"You take a guess."

"We won't wander around forever?"

He nodded. "*And...*"

"Somehow, we'll find the way to go?"

"And the lodge at the end sure seems like heaven, yeah?" Skeets made things simpler.

"Explain it, though." I waved a circle in the air with my right hand. "I mean the whole dream, in one sentence—so I can write something down."

Skeets looked at me with soft eyes, tilting his head slightly. "It's all about trust."

"No, no. I need more than that."

He took a deep breath. "To go on with God...you have to be willing..."

"Have...to...be...willing..." I repeated, writing each word.

"To walk in days of mystery." He stood up, straightening his shirt.

Mystery. The other hikers wouldn't risk going any further without a path. The dream story seemed clearer now. Still, a sinking feeling weighed on my shoulders. What would our world be like? Why did Mama have to die? I remembered the broken plate.

"Oh Skeets!" I rushed over and wedged under his arm.

"Promise me something, Iris. Out loud. Right now." He stooped down to see my face. "Say you won't give up on God."

My eyes filled up fast. I cried hard, and he simply held me for a while.

"C'mon now, I want to hear you promise." He waited.

Words formed, muffled by his shirt. "I won't...give up," I said.

"On God." He squeezed me. "Say that part."

"On God." The words felt empty.

He gave me a tight hug. "I'm going to miss your amazing little mind." He sighed. "You understand far more than a ten-year-old."

"Ten and a half," I said.

A gray taxi pulled into the driveway at 7:10 a.m., and my favorite person in the world left for the other side of the planet. Tuck sat down and cried for all three of us. Father bent over to console him. Wyeth disappeared to the backyard, and I ran to my room to hide. My notebook lay open on the bed. I held it tightly.

Soon his airplane would become a tiny mosquito in the sky and disappear through the clouds. It felt like treading water, out of my depth—a heavy rock tied to my ankle, pulling me under... losing strength fast.

Chapter 15

NO MATTER HOW often I straightened our family portrait, it always hung crooked.

It must've been strung wrong. With my index finger, I traced Mama's profile from the top of her head, through her curls, and over her shoulder. The glass pane felt hard. My eyes watered. Ducking my chin, I slipped out the front door, but there was nowhere to go. I raced to the end of the driveway, tears lining my cheeks. Wherever I went, there I was.

Far away in Africa, Skeets was as good as dead to us. I ambled toward the backyard and leaned against the garage wall. Like a hollow tree, I stood for no apparent reason other than habit.

The patio surface felt rough under my right foot. I glanced down. Years ago, Wyeth and I had made handprints there in wet cement. Mama begged Father to let us. Next to our imprints, he scrawled, "1972." I was only four that summer.

I pressed my hand inside the small print. My fingertips extended far beyond the impression. It was hard to believe I'd grown so much. I longed to be her again...that little girl whose happiness was as simple as a bowl of crisp Cheerios in fresh cold milk. That girl who loved the barefooted feel of moss and the sound of wind in the trees. The one who whispered things to God in the dark, after Mama kissed her forehead and switched off the light. My heart lifted a little.

"Iris! Where *are* you?" Father called. "Come and set the table!"

"On my way!" I tried to sound chipper, though my voice cracked. Sunday mornings were anything but restful until church was over.

I raked my bangs over my puffy eyes before entering the kitchen, hoping to be invisible. Father didn't say a word. Tuck busily colored a drawing at the table. The tip of his tongue stuck out when he was concentrating.

Father focused on the frying pan. In our family, burning bacon was an unforgiveable sin. Mama had learned that the hard way. Father's rant at her was still branded in my mind—chilling in its unpredictability.

Still, I had to admit—no one cooked bacon like my father. As a little girl, I stood on a short stool to watch. It didn't feel strange to be physically close to him then. I'd hold his belt loops for balance. He smelled of Brylcreem.

First he'd dump the entire package in the skillet, separating the slices with two forks. They looked like wide slippery noodles as he swirled them around. When a shallow layer of sizzling grease formed, he'd stretch out four or five strips at a time, piling the rest to the side. They fried more evenly that way, thus eliminating the revolting problem of chewy bacon fat. Father had it down.

He used to be animated on weekends, singing songs like *Take Me Out To The Ball Game*. Sometimes he'd click on the transistor radio. The announcer would cheerfully broadcast an up-and-doing world...the Fourth of July parade, a sale at Higbee's, or a fiddle contest at Farmer's Market.

Now, the kitchen felt unnervingly silent, except for the sound of spitting grease. I studied his face through the spaces in my hair. His eyes unblinking, his lips pursed. I'd taken for granted that life would move forward after Mama's death. Instead it had stalled and somehow depended on how Father did without her.

In some ways, I didn't really want to grow up yet. I pulled the silverware drawer open and considered the word—*grownup*. It wasn't an accurate description. Adults should be called grown-outs or grown-olders, as they certainly weren't getting any taller. And if teens were teenagers, why weren't children called childagers or the elderly, oldagers? Someone needed to fix that at the dictionary office.

I turned with utensils in hand to set the table but stopped cold.

Father had removed Mama's chair. Without thinking, I'd counted out five of everything. A lump rose in my throat. I quietly returned one set.

Wy made his grand entrance, scuffing his shoes across the floor. He dragged his chair out from the table, which made a screechy sound, and sat down in a huff. He just wouldn't be quiet or go along with things. He couldn't be tamed. My stomach tightened.

Soon we gathered at our places with food as our main reason to be a family. Not much was said, though everyone made sure the bacon got divvied up fairly. I knew Father's toast routine by heart. He always saved it for last. First, he spread butter on his toast for a whole minute, carefully smoothing the pale yellow pat out to the crust. Not a smidgen of bread remained butterless.

"Iris, pass the jam," he said.

I handed him the jar. His hand trembled. My jaw fell open a little, but he acted like nothing was wrong. I glanced at my brothers, but they were busy chowing down. Father's hands kept shaking as he opened the lid. Still, he spread the jam out to the edges with equal determination as though it was a work of art.

All of a sudden, he lost control of the knife. It clattered on his plate. At the same time, the toast flipped over upside down on the floor. He cursed, pounding his fist on the table.

The boys stopped eating. My entire body froze.

With a look of disgust, he stood up abruptly, accidentally jarring the table with his thighs. I grabbed my orange juice, but Tuck's glass tipped over. Father flung the toast in the trash and headed toward his bedroom. "Church is in an hour. I want everyone in the car at 9:45," he said.

Before the bedroom door shut, Wyeth mocked Father with an exaggerated salute. My face got hot. I glared at my brother, but he only mimicked me.

"What's your problem? It's your turn for dishes," he said tersely.

"Not so fast! I did 'em last night!" All I had to do was raise my eyebrows and gaze in Father's direction. The last thing Wyeth wanted was Father as our referee.

"Okay, okay." He rose from his seat and pointed his butter knife in my face. "But you'd better decide who you're with—me or him—'cause it might come down to that." Father had been home less than a week, and Wyeth had already drawn a line.

I was speechless.

Tuck picked up some colored pencils to finish his picture. I watched him while drying dishes. He'd drawn our family in stick-figure style with Mama much larger. She flew over us in what appeared to be a wedding dress. Wyeth had to be the one with a red ball cap, and I recognized myself as the one with long straight hair. Tuck's own image was the smallest figure on the page, but more detailed. He drew himself holding the moon on a string like a balloon. Tuck even included Kibbs in the scene. But a fourth kid in the drawing had no eyes, a straight line for a mouth and very large hands.

"That doesn't look like Billy," I said. "You should draw his teeth—they're always showing."

"No, Rissy." He shook his head. "It's just *our* family."

Apparently, the extra person was Father.

After wiping the counters, I laid a frozen package of meat out to thaw. Tuck and I scrambled up the stairs to change into Sunday clothes. Wyeth retrieved the Plain Dealer from the driveway, hiding the cartoon section for first dibs later. I watched out the window. No matter. I knew most of his secret spots. Tuck filled Kibbs' bowl, but the cat was nowhere to be found. Eventually we discovered him under the couch.

Tuck tried coaxing him out with a dab of bacon grease on his finger. "He never hides under here, Rissy."

"He'll come out when he's hungry," I said. "C'mon, it's time to go."

Tuck insisted on sliding a saucer of milk under the couch. Father would have my head if he knew.

At 9:44, we climbed into the backseat of the car with only a minute to spare. No one wanted Mama's place in front. I untangled the seatbelts in the back. For many years, we never wore them and nothing happened. Now it was a rule. We also weren't allowed to smudge the windows with our noses or hands, so I made Tuck sit in the middle. Father climbed in. We backed out slowly and eventually turned on Lake Road heading east toward the bridge.

Tuck pressed my nose. He wanted to play a game we'd invented called, *Yes, Sir—Yes, Sir,* but it wasn't exactly a car game.

"Not now." I brushed his hand away.

The game was actually a short play where I pretended to be a robot. I'd fold myself into a ball inside a large cardboard box from the basement. Our couch served as a shelf in a toy store. Playing his role, Tuck came to the so-called shop to make a purchase. "Oh, what's this?" He'd say in a loud deliberate voice. "Maybe I should turn it on!" Then he'd giggle. Of course I'd taught him his lines with appropriate theatrics.

He'd open the box flaps and push the START button—which was my nose. I'd come alive, wide-eyed with power, rising like a towering giant. With short mechanical movements, I'd systematically scan the room until my eyes fixated on Tuck. With fear and delight, he'd make a mad dash. I'd follow in a relentless march, shouting, "Yes sir! Yes sir!" All through the house you could hear his high-pitched screams followed by laughter. When he got cornered, I'd purposely fold up, fetal and motionless. He'd calm down, and then we'd start all over again.

I gazed fondly at my little brother. We'd made up over twenty games that only the two of us played. Mama had written their titles.

Our car sped along past Kensington School and then Bearden's hamburger joint. Right away we came to the bridge. Father was driving rather fast, though we weren't late. I looked through the windshield. Up ahead an elderly couple strolled alongside the road. The woman clutched the man's arm, though he steadied himself with a cane.

All at once, I noticed our car drifting right, away from the centerline. Until that moment, I'd never thought much about driving. My neck muscles grew taut.

Father was checking out the lake to the left. "The wind's sure kickin' up white caps," he said, as the car veered straight toward the pedestrians.

Everything went into slow motion. My legs pushed down, as I leaned left. With great effort, I raised an arm. My eyes squinted and a sound rose in my throat: "Faaa-therrr!" I screamed. The man and woman turned. Their eyes widened. Mouths opened. I buried my face in my arm, bracing for the impact.

Father jerked the wheel hard to the left. The brakes screeched as our car slid sideways. I looked up and saw another car, swerving wildly to avoid ours. We barely missed the old people. Inches at best. Finally, the Buick lurched to a stop. The man and woman had collapsed on the ground. Grimacing, the old lady held her knee, and one of her shoes lay upside down in the middle of the road.

"Iris!" He released a huge breath. "Don't *ever* shout at me!" Father was nonplused. "Did you see what almost happened?" He clung to the steering wheel.

"Yes sir," I mumbled. "Sorry."

"Man alive!" He turned to face me. "Just keep quiet, for Pete's sake!"

"Yes sir." I whispered. Shivers coursed through my body.

"What happened? What happened?" my little brother whined.

"And you hush up too!" Father pointed a shaky finger at Tuck as he backed the car off the road. Then he climbed out to speak with the couple.

I scrunched down in my seat, wondering if he'd bring them over to force my apology. I lowered my head into my hands. Tuck hid his face in my side.

"Unbe-leee-vably stupid!" Wyeth said, punching the back of Father's headrest.

"You calling me stupid?" I flashed an angry look.

"No, you dumb muffin! It wasn't your fault at all!" Wyeth unbuckled his seatbelt to get a better view out the window. "Why do you take his crap?"

"I don't know!" My heart thumped hard.

We watched Father help the man and woman to their feet.

"Why are we here?" Tuck started to whimper.

I had to keep him from crying. "We've just stopped for a minute. Father is seeing if those old people are all right. They fell down."

"There ya go!" Wyeth rolled his eyes. "Makin' it all nice."

"But, Daddy's maaaad again." Tuck gripped my dress with both hands.

"Everything's okay, buddy. I promise." I put my arm around Tuck and pulled him close. "Quiet, now! He's coming,"

Father strode briskly back to our car and slid into his seat. "She only skinned her knee," he reported. "They live nearby." He didn't sound relieved. His face shone with sweat. As we drove on toward church, he fumed silently.

"Stay clear," Wyeth whispered. "It's Bone Cat City today."

To make matters worse, our near-accident had made us late.

We hustled to a side entrance of the church, falling in line like little ducklings until Father found an empty pew near the back of the sanctuary. I sat between Father and Wyeth, unable to focus on anything in the service. My mind replayed the scene on the road. Invisible arrows of disgust shot from Wyeth toward Father, passing through my body, ripping up my insides. I wanted to jump out of my skin and tear away.

After the benediction, my Sunday school teacher worked her way through the crowd. She tried to engage me with her eyes, but I stared past her. Fortunately, another parent snagged her in conversation. I pulled Tuck out the side door and we bolted to the Buick. Polite church talk was such an exhausting duty. This time I hunkered down in the seat behind Father, out of his line of vision.

The ride home was somber. A cloudburst of rain beat on the roof. Father turned the wipers on high. With closed windows, we were all breathing each other's air. It was a stomach-turning thought. We didn't stop at McDonald's, which was Wyeth's chief reason for going to church. Father drove right past the Golden Arches without blinking. He stayed in the right lane going slowly, while other cars went by on the left. I thought we'd never get home.

A red car cruised by. The license plate said, "BBLE 403." Right after that, a second red car followed. Two identical cars. That seemed odd. I straightened up. Its license read "AVEC 389." Something fluttered in my chest. In sixth grade French Lab, the teacher said *avec* meant "with." I don't know why I'd even remember that.

As soon as we pulled in the driveway, I busted out of the car, stormed in the front door, and ran up the stairs. Grabbing my Bible and a flashlight, I wriggled under my bed. It was only a hunch, but maybe God was speaking to me in code.

"BBLE" could be short for Bible. Or bubble. Or babble. Still, if God was going to say anything to me, it had to start there. But 403 could be anything. I turned to page 403. Smack dab in the middle of Job, the text expounded on "the prosperity of the wicked." Maybe the number meant chapter and verse. It had to be 40:3, because 4:03 had an unnecessary zero.

Only certain books had 40 plus chapters. In Genesis, I read how the Pharaoh was hopping mad at his butler and the baker. In Jeremiah, the sins of God's people had made Him livid. I sighed and adjusted the flashlight under my chin. Maybe the whole idea was crazy.

I turned to Isaiah 40:3. My heart rate finally slowed. I tracked the numbers on the page to verse 3 and read every word, despite what they taught me in Reading Lab. The second time through, something like a weighty blanket came down on me. It felt like the x-ray cape they place over your body at the dentist office.

> *In the wilderness prepare the way of the Lord,*
> *Make straight in the desert a highway for our God.*

Wilderness. Skeets had told me I'd be wandering in one for a while—or at least it would feel that way. And a highway in a desert? A road in the middle of nowhere? It seemed like the boardwalk from my dream.

I flipped back to find 38:9 but went too far and ended up in Psalms. No matter. I knew for a fact there were at least a hundred chapters there. I turned to Psalms 38:9.

> *Lord, all my longing is known to thee,*
> *My sighing is not hidden from thee.*

Avec. With. In a way, God had rolled under the bed next to me—*with* me. I rested my head on the pages and wondered if that was really possible.

Chapter 16

MAMA LEFT US when the roses were in full bloom. For some odd reason I remembered that. Along the road toward the Middle Strip, day lilies flourished. Hydrangeas came next, puffing out like giant popcorn balls, while daisies showed up here and there with sunny faces. And finally, the purple shoots of Russian sage opened their tiny buds as the grand finale of summer beauty.

But fall arrived too soon, bringing the dreariness of winter on its heels. Flowers shriveled up overnight, fatally singed by the first hard frost. I wondered if plants had feelings when I saw their drooping heads. The trees became colorless, as leaves turned brown during an early cold snap. The glory of fall had been stolen, and the fragrance of summer went with it.

Then one day, I couldn't remember Mama's scent. In the months after her death, it soothed me to whirl around in a shroud of her hanging blouses and dresses. Her clothes smelled like talcum powder and lavender, but there was something more. I could smell Mama.

That day, I hurried home from school heading straight for her closet. I shrieked when I saw a row of empty hangers. It was too hard. I crumpled face down on the floor and bawled until there were no more tears.

Turns out Father had hauled her things to the Salvation Army for strangers to buy. *Strangers!* He saved a few nicer sweaters for me, storing them in the cedar trunk with mothballs. *Mothballs!*

Little by little, other traces of her slipped away. Mama's answering machine greeting remained for a while, but Father eventually changed the message. Had he no heart? That time, I almost started screaming at him. Instead, I ran to the end of the driveway and sat in the pouring rain to cry.

Still, if I closed my eyes, I could imagine her laugh and the way she said, "*There's my girl...*" But even that was fading. Then, one bleak November afternoon, something I'd long forgotten came to mind.

"Wyeth!" I shouted. "Wyyy-eeeth! Where are you?"

"Up here! In my room!"

I clambered up the stairs and burst through his open door.

Lying prone on a giant beanbag chair, he seemed detached. "Don't go monkey on me now." He flipped a page of his comic book and didn't look up.

"Remember the Thanksgiving play when you were one of the Indians, and you wore that headdress, and I had to be the turkey, and we used all those pillows to make me fat, and I was so..." I stopped to inhale.

"Slow down, motor mouth. How could I forget?" He blew a big bubble of Bazooka gum.

"Mama was the narrator!"

He popped the bubble. "What's that have to do with the price of eggs?" He tossed his comic book abruptly, like I had bothered him.

"We recorded her part so we could practice at school with the other kids. Remember?"

"I'm not following." He rolled over and sat up to face me. "Cut to the chase."

I let out a deep sigh. "I want to hear her voice again." It was hard to say openly what I really wanted. My chin began to tremble.

Wyeth blinked hard. His wheels were turning now. For once, he didn't put me off. Separately, we searched the upper shelves of our bedroom closets. I pulled down a beach towel still rolled around my damp bathing suit. It had a nasty case of mildew. A few art projects had been shoved behind it, but nothing more.

"Any luck?" I yelled.

"Nothing 'cept some baseball cards I lost."

"Drat. How 'bout under your bed?"

I heard him rustling around. "Nah, just dirty clothes."

"Come over here then." We pulled out a musty hatbox of school papers stored under my bed. Mama had kept Wyeth's A+ science report on his ant farm and a stack of word lists we used for Kensington's Spelling Bee. Report cards, a ruler and a pink eraser. Not what I'd hoped.

The linen closet came next. Only a battered shoebox seemed like a possibility. Inside was an empty, amber-colored bottle that smelled faintly of vinegar.

"Weird," I said quietly, shaking my head.

From there we groped through every drawer in the house, rifling through assorted files, old calendars and sympathy cards stacked in Mama's roll top desk. The cassette was nowhere to be found.

"I know," said Wyeth. "The fruit closet!"

We stampeded down the basement steps, heading toward the cellar pantry. The door into the pantry always scraped the cement floor. We had to muscle it open. Inside were shelves of canned food and jugs of distilled water. Father also kept a first aid kit, a radio, matches, candles, and other emergency items. We lived in the shadow of the dreaded atom bomb, though decades had passed since the war.

"The fruit closet," as it was known, was a small inner chamber of the cellar pantry. Father had stacked storage boxes in front of its entrance. Wyeth shoved them to the side and accidentally tipped one over. Father's papers spilled out, but we paid no attention in our excitement.

The fruit closet kept its name for no obvious reason. The door was a large piece of plywood, cut to fit the opening. Wy pried its simple latch open, and we peered into the dark space. As expected, no canned peaches or pears in sight. Its title was simply illogical, like Wyeth saying "May Day! May Day!" when Father pulled in the driveway. What could be lovelier than a day in May? The English language was full of such oddities, and I found that annoying or fascinating depending on the day.

Instead of fruit, Mama had used the closet to stash miscellaneous things—broken Christmas decorations, old coats that needed mending, and our winter boots. A small trunk on the floor contained dress-up clothes and costumes.

"We should call this the Mishmash Closet," I announced.

"What are you talking about?" Clearly Wyeth did not share my passion for words. "Stay focused, Rissy. This might be the jackpot."

The trunk wedged under the bottom shelf seemed like our best bet. Mama kept the Indian costume in there, along with the colorful feather headdress. Wy pulled out rumpled hats, a pair of long white gloves and a sequined skirt, which he held between two fingers as if it had cooties. I found the large rabbit facemask Father wore one Easter that scared me half to death. We pulled everything out, hoping to find the cassette at the bottom.

Nothing. My heart sank.

"It's probably long gone, Rissy." His voice quivered with sorrow.

"I can't give up, I *just can't*."

"Father will be home soon. You know it'll upset him. He acts as if Mama never existed." He tilted his head and gave me a gentle look. "We've gotta let it go."

Tears welled on my lower lids. He rested his hand on my right shoulder and in that moment, his kindness meant more than the tape itself. I gave in.

That evening everyone left the table after dinner except Tuck, the slowest eater on the planet. He hummed quietly, dipping his last fry in catsup. Then he coaxed a few peas on his fork as if they were little green aliens. "Better jump on my spaceship," he whispered.

Hot water formed rising suds around the dirty dishes. Breakfast, lunch and dinner plates were stacked high in the sink, because Wyeth was lazy or ornery—take your pick.

Luckily Father hadn't noticed the pile. He was banging around in the cellar adding to his supply of distilled water. All at once, it became eerily quiet. In a split second, I thought of the box we tipped over in our dogged search. A moment later, angry words spewed up the stairwell. "Someone's been screwing around with my boxes!"

My heart jumped.

Father started up the stairs. At the sound, Tuck stopped humming. He ran on tiptoes to the coat closet. As he left, his fork fell, launching several peas into the air.

I stood stiff as a flagpole at the kitchen sink. "Hurry, hurry!" I whispered to the soapy foam. Suds covered a multitude of sins.

The clump-clump of heavy shoes reached the top step. I shut off the faucet and slowly turned around, bracing against the counter. I faced mean dogs that way too. Sometimes you have to act like you're not afraid.

"For the love of Pete! What's *wrong* with you kids?" He said. "My boxes were all shifted around." His red face was a scary face. "What the hell's goin' on?"

"I...I lost something." My voice sounded munchkin-like.

"Speak up!"

Clearing my throat didn't help. "I was looking for...something," I said, trying to sound normal.

Three flies circled the dollop of catsup left on Tuck's plate. Father picked up the newspaper and slowly rolled it.

"Lookin' for *what*?" he said, with the quiet sizzle of a lit dynamite wick. The paper became a rigid rod in his hands. He scanned my face without blinking.

"An old cassette tape—" my voice faltered, "that's all."

"You'll have the devil to pay if you're lying!" The newspaper came down with a loud whack, killing one of the flies. It spattered ketchup all over the table. He hated flies.

I flinched at the sound.

"Stay out of the cellar pantry!" he barked. "I don't want to tell you again!" He threw the paper in the trash. "*Got it?*"

"Got it," I echoed right away.

He took a step toward me. "You mouthing off at me?" His low tone grew with intensity. "Don't you have any respect?"

"No, sir—I mean, yes sir." I could feel his glare. My skin bristled.

He inspected the pile of dishes for a moment. "All right then. Clean up this mess. And where's that brother of yours? Why isn't he drying for you?"

I shrugged. Any truthful answer would bring trouble.

"That kid needs a swift kick in the pants!" Father trudged back down the stairs, carrying a jug of distilled water. "He's a damn ghost, slinking 'round here half the time."

Waiting for my heartbeat to slow, I pulled on Mama's yellow rubber gloves and submerged them in the dishwater. They were still too big for me.

Right then the phone rang. "I'll get it!" I grabbed a towel. "Somerset residence. Iris speaking." Suds dribbled down my arm.

"*Iris?*" Nana's voice sounded feeble.

"We can't talk now!" I whispered vehemently. "He's here!"

"*What? Not at church? But it's Thursday.*"

"I know, I know! For some reason, he stayed home tonight." I glanced over my shoulder and froze.

Father stood in the doorway. "Who's on the phone, Iris?" He said, narrowing his eyes. He'd come soundlessly on purpose.

The yellow glove slipped off my arm onto the floor.

"*Iris? Are you there?*" asked Nana. I buried the receiver in my sweatshirt.

"Who is it?" Father started moving toward me. "Don't make me ask again!"

I recoiled as he snatched the phone from my hand taking the other yellow glove with it. He spoke with his mouth on the receiver, but angled the earpiece away from his ear. It was going to be a monologue. Then the shouting began.

"I told you already! I don't want any contact! We're doin' *just fine!*" His tone made me feel faint. "When the kids talk to you, they get all stirred up about their mother. It makes a mess of everything, so LEAVE US ALONE!" he bellowed, before slamming the phone on its base. Throwing the glove at me, he returned to the basement moaning to himself.

Nana and Pops had been careful to call in the afternoons after school or on Thursday nights. I felt safe just hearing their voices. Still, Father was mostly right. In the early months without Mama, Tuck would sob on the phone, pleading for them to come get us. Wyeth seemed downright grumpy afterwards, which only provoked Father. I felt overjoyed at first, but afterwards, I'd hang up and cry, missing Mama more than ever. And hearing their voices made me wonder why Skeets hadn't written. My grandparents said he'd sent a blue airmail letter to us every week. Father had probably pitched them. He had the only key to the box.

Something inside me was growing cold. I didn't want to stay hopeful. I didn't want to feel that familiar ache. I didn't want to cry anymore. I turned and washed the dishes without a single tear.

Then one evening, a few days before Thanksgiving, I took a bag of garbage out to the garage as usual. We had an old refrigerator out there for extra storage. It was smaller than our Frigidaire and came up to my chin in height. I'd passed it a thousand times and always noticed how dusty things got in the garage. But that night, on top of that little fridge sat the missing cassette tape—*all by itself.*

I gasped. For the first time in my life, I truly wondered about angels.

Chapter 17

THE MORNING AFTER I found the cassette, I slipped a note under Wyeth's door that said, "FC4P." It was code to meet in the fruit closet after school at 4:00 p.m. Tuck would be at the Peate's house.

That afternoon, we met at the appointed time. I'd borrowed my teacher's cassette player and surprised Wyeth with the tape.

"What! Where'd you find this?" He snatched it from my hands.

"On top of the fridge in the garage."

"No way!" He turned the tape over and over.

"I think an angel put it there," I said.

"Right, psycho."

"It was there—all by itself—I swear."

"You're telling me it sat on top of the fridge for two whole years—and you happened to notice it yesterday? C'mon!"

I wanted to believe God cared about my small prayers. I shook off my brother's predictable doubt. "Who cares? It's here now."

The fruit closet had recently become our bunker in the war to preserve life apart from Father. It was risky, but I didn't care. Now and then Father entered the general storage area of the cellar pantry, but we left that part undisturbed. As far as we could tell, he never opened the inner fruit closet. Given the cobwebs and dust, no one had for quite some time. We claimed it as our own.

Once emptied, the space measured roughly four by eight feet. With a terrycloth towel and a bucket of soapy water, I had washed the shelves and then the floor, getting the worst of it. Then Wy spread out an old sleeping bag on the cement. We'd found an orange crate for a small table and used battery-powered candlesticks for light.

Father's boxes remained neatly stacked in front of the entrance. To avoid messing with them, my brother had removed the door pins from the fruit closet door. Unhinged, the door easily slid to one side, and that way, we left no trace of our comings and goings.

We climbed over the boxes into our secret foxhole. I placed the tape into the recorder and looked straight into Wyeth's eyes. "Are you ready?" I asked.

He nodded. Our mood turned solemn as we lay head-to-head, our knees bunched against the closet wall. Wyeth twisted the candlestick lights off. As soon as I pushed PLAY, it was as though we entered another realm. The sound of Mama's voice filled the hidden chamber.

"In September, 1620, a hundred and two souls boarded the Mayflower and set sail on open ocean..."

In the dark I listened, captivated by each word. Our Mama seemed as real as ever. My entire body prickled with wave after wave of goose bumps.

"Nearly half of them died the first winter. They suffered loss of family, friends, and the comforts of home. The New World was full of danger and uncertainty."

My vision blurred as tears pooled in the corners of my eyes. The words seemed alarmingly true. True for *now*. My lungs heaved. I swallowed down my rising pain to not miss a word.

"Those who survived gave thanks to Almighty God. He brought them Indian friends who showed them how to catch fish, plant corn, and extract maple sap for syrup..."

There were silent spaces on the tape where the narration stopped for various scenes. I remembered how mortified I felt after being assigned the turkey role. Mama had softened my embarrassment, taking a brown stocking cap and cutting three holes so I could see and breathe. She sewed feathers on it and made a cardboard beak. It blended in with the rest of the costume, and I felt disguised enough.

"Friends and countrymen, Indians and Pilgrims, traders and hunters, women and children...let the feast of gratitude begin..."

My chest ached. The tape brought to life all that seemed good. I'd been numb for so long. Wyeth's breathing also changed.

"They shared a grand meal that day, in hopes that it represented a future of peace and prosperity, knowing they would survive if they worked together, but perish if divided against each other."

Survive. Divided. Perish. The words hung in the air, heavy with meaning. Tears pulsed down my temples as I stared at the dark ceiling. Wyeth placed one arm over his eyes. His left elbow rested on my shoulder. I could feel his body quaking.

"In the words of their Governor, William Bradford, 'They knew they were pilgrims, and looked not much on those things, but lifted up their eyes to the heavens, their dearest country.'"

I tried to picture Mama in her radiant white dress, the one she wore in my dream. Oh that heaven would touch earth again. The sound of her voice surrounded us, tender with love and bold in confidence.

"Beyond all their losses, their future held the promise of adventure, of freedom, of new lands, and so they were carried forward by faith and hope."

The tape ended. I automatically rewound it to play again. We listened to it three times. Then we were silent, waiting for the click of the recorder going off. I knew Wy was weeping. Neither of us spoke for a long time. In some way I can't explain, it bound us together, and I loved my brother at that moment more than ever before.

After a bit, Wyeth slowly rolled over. Sitting up, he took the tape out of the player and held it in both hands. With a bowed head, he wiped his cheeks on his shirtsleeves.

"Don't tell Tuck," he said in a quieted voice.

I nodded in the dark. "It would wreck him."

"Agreed then?"

"Agreed."

Father hollered from the top of the basement stairs.

"Hey you kids! Are ya down there?" He'd come home early.

Our bodies turned to stone.

"Hey! You hear me? How come dinner's not started?"

I glanced out a crack in the fruit closet door to see if the pantry door was completely shut. It was, but we'd left the light on accidentally. All we could do was wait. And hope. The floor creaked under his weight. He moved across the kitchen floor and went out the backdoor.

Chapter 18

DURING THE NEXT weeks, Wy and I listened to the tape over and over. I wanted Mama to magically break in and say something new. She didn't. Even the wonder of hearing her voice became familiar. It felt like another wrenching goodbye, as we returned to our New World.

Most days when Father was at work, my brother and I resumed our snappy ways, mildly annoyed and exchanging our usual banter. Wyeth said I was bossy, and his laziness exasperated me to no end.

When Tuck wasn't at the Peates, he clung to me like a shadow unless I distracted him with a picture book or cartoon. It didn't seem possible to forget Mama, yet now and then we'd all crack up over a show like *The Little Rascals*, as if nothing had changed.

At 5:00 p.m. I'd start tidying up the living room. Everything shifted into high gear when the squeal of faulty brakes signaled the scary movie car was home. Off went the TV. Wyeth would streak out the backdoor in a flash. Tuck usually scurried to his room, and I'd head to the kitchen. Lickety-split, thawed meat began to sizzle in the frying pan when I turned the burner on high. Father would mount the front steps, pausing to check the mail. I'd hear his mail key turn. His profile shadowed the small windows in the door with silent force. By the time he walked into the kitchen, I'd be peeling potatoes or measuring water for rice, as if dinner prep was well underway. My heart pounded every time.

In the months since he'd been in charge, we learned to cover for each other, saying as little as possible. White lies and half-truths became acceptable, because what Father didn't know made life easier. I avoided trouble by being quiet and invisible. Father hung the yoke of housework on us in our mother's absence. I became the family cook with a limited number of recipes. Hamburgers, baked potatoes and peas were our standard fare. Father assigned us different rooms to clean once a week, and to keep the peace, I redid some of the boys' work. Kibbs threw up right on the line between rooms one afternoon. Of course Wyeth and I got in a scrap about who had to clean it up. I wiped up my half in protest. He waited till he heard Father's car to do his half.

Once on TV, a sitcom mom said, "Placation had risen to an art form," regarding the TV dad. The word echoed in my mind. I searched my dictionary. *Placation—to make somebody less angry.* That pretty much summed up my life. I added it to my collection.

Noise and confusion easily riled Father, and so Tuck had to be managed. I'd give my little brother a small bowl of Cheerios at 4 p.m. so he wouldn't be whiney before dinner. It curbed his appetite but didn't spoil his meal. Father was all about The Clean Plate Club.

At bedtime, I'd place a surprise under Tuck's pillow from the Sleep Fairy, if he went to bed without fussing—a marshmallow, shiny nickel, or a bubble gum comic.

I became a quick study of what kept Father calm. He liked an orderly house, meals on time, and a chance to read the newspaper without interruption. One time, I stole the neighbor's paper because ours had gone missing.

Fortunately, he didn't ride me as hard. He needed me to carry on Mama's work as best I could. Yet Wyeth's anger toward Father remained an unsettling wild card.

Trouble always started with little things. One time Wyeth forgot his manners and reached across the table for butter, instead of asking Tuck to pass it. Father marched him straightaway to the garage to eat his dinner alone.

Another night, Wyeth snuck down to the basement to watch TV on the old black and white Zenith after bedtime. He lost his television privileges for a week. The second time it happened, he wasn't allowed to watch TV for an entire month. He was still bitter about that.

"I just couldn't sleep. TV calmed me down," he said. Fortunately, he complained to me in private and not to Father's face.

"I'm sorry, Wy, but if you disobey him, he's gonna blow his top. You're being a crick in the neck!" I scrunched my eyebrows. "Why can't you just get along?"

"I know, I *know*. But a whole month...it's just plain mean!" Wyeth kicked his sneakers under the bed.

With Mama gone, Father made other changes. For instance, he announced that we would no longer celebrate Halloween. Being in the tooth business, he denied us hoards of free candy. Sugar was already rationed. He said it was all for our good, because demented people put razor blades in candy bars. "Besides," he added, "costumes are a waste of money." Hope drained out of my veins, as if anything fun would be taken away by yet another rule. Tuck whimpered in the pantry. Wy went out back and hit the tetherball extra hard.

November came, and I turned eleven. I had asked for a Skipper doll, because I wasn't allowed to own a full-bosomed Barbie. According to Father, they were too adult for young girls. Mama had said "It's just romance, Hank. Nothing more." But Father insisted it would cause inappropriate imaginings. Skipper remained their compromise. He bought me the blond-headed doll, not realizing that the newest version sprouted tiny breasts with one rotation of her arm. She also grew in height and fit into Barbie's wedding dress—which was all that mattered to me.

The next Saturday, I searched the house for my new Skipper. No luck. Anna had expected me around 1 o'clock, and it was already half past the hour. I left without the doll. We converted her bedroom into a miniature church for weddings. The Barbie with the worst case of ratty hair became the evil queen or all-around troublemaker depending on the storyline. Bad Barbie always tried to stop weddings. The bride and groom had to flee on a white horse—a breathtaking ride to Lovers' Peak. Anna made snow-covered mountains by stacking six pillows in pyramid style, placing a clean sheet over the top. A box fan made a perfect windstorm to heighten the drama. Anna Rae pulled the shades, and we took turns flicking the light switch for lightening.

Usually Bad Barbie got stuck in an avalanche or fell in a lake, but today she had a tantrum, pounding the ground and wailing over her lost love. Anna Rae took the amorous couple to the summit, where they dismounted and shared a straight-arm hug.

The glorious tale always remained the same, with an occasional subplot or different staging. Anna Rae and I were discussing the props for a Hawaiian Barbie wedding when she brought out a Skipper doll, still in the box. I knew it was mine. My cheeks grew red-hot. Then a real girl fight lashed out as we both struggled to lay hold of the box.

Her mom heard our squawking and marched upstairs to cool things down. Finally the truth came out. Wyeth had sold my brand new Skipper to Anna Rae for a few dollars, saying he found it at a garage sale. He swindled the deal to buy Jawbreakers and Slow Pokes at Mike's Delicatessen. I huffed a deep sigh and said sorry to my friend.

After dinner, Anna's family came over to talk it out. The whole thing felt acutely uncomfortable. I never meant to involve any parents. Wyeth sat rigidly on the kitchen stool. He mumbled a forced apology in the faintest voice ever heard, and looked at his feet as if he'd never seen them before.

Father seemed to inhale more than exhale, building up steam like a pressure cooker. Perspiration beaded across his forehead as he listened to Anna's mom. I could feel a dark mood brewing, hidden by the polite and calm discussion. I should've just given the doll to my friend. Father would let Wyeth have it soon enough, but we'd all be miserable for days, even weeks. I twisted a rubber band around my index finger and watched my fingertip turn blue.

Father said, "It won't happen again," and gave a quick nod to the dad.

The band snapped as their family rose to leave. We stood too. Father managed a tight smile as he ushered them out the door. Anna, the last to go, let the screen door slam. It was a sound that really annoyed my father under the best of circumstances. My knees turned liquid.

Father signaled to Wyeth.

"Outside. *Now.*" His words felt like blunt jabs with a pointy stick, even though I wasn't in trouble. Wyeth glared at me. I looked at him with my best basset-hound eyes. He squinted at me and followed Father out the back door toward the sycamore tree. I didn't hear what went on, but knew it would be far worse than usual. Stirring up any kind of public shame was unforgivable.

I scrunched up my legs, muffling my ears with my knees in case things got ugly. Running my thumb back and forth over the teeth of a comb, I made a tick-tick-tick sound. Tuck dashed upstairs to his bedroom while the coast was clear.

When Father came inside, his face looked pale and clammy. He seemed more like a stranger than a dad. He asked me if I'd memorized my verses for the day. His voice sounded eerily flat. I guess I took too long to answer. He told me to go to my room.

The evening ended, and everyone but Wyeth had gone to bed. In the dark silence, I heard him plodding up the steps. I thought for sure he'd spend the night in the old Chevy truck out back. Then again, it was November. A cotton sleeping bag wouldn't cut it, though Wyeth was stubborn enough to try.

I pulled the covers up to my nose and laid one arm over my eyes. My body felt encased in cement. Wyeth was mad at the whole universe, which now included me. My door creaked open. I froze, waiting for him to say something mean. Instead, a small hand touched my arm.

"Oh!" I said, sitting upright.

"Ris-is-sy?" Tuck whispered. His voice broke up with shivers.

"You scared me! Why are you outta bed?"

"I'm afraid. It's so dark." It was a moonless night.

"C'mon...climb in here." I pulled his arm. His skin was nubby with goose bumps.

"Something came in the hou-se-se. It might come to m-y ro-om."

"It's just Wyeth going to bed late. He's upset with Daddy."

"Dad-dy's...maa-ad...at me-ee, too." His body trembled with chills.

"No he's not. He's just mad—it's not your fault." I put my arms around him. It didn't seem to matter what I said. Lately, his tears triggered easily. My heart felt weighted down for him. "Buddy, listen now. Let's say a prayer. I'll start things off, okay?"

"Mm-hmm." He sniffed a few times.

"Dear God..." I paused, having a momentary loss for words. My throat constricted. "Where... *are*... You?" I whispered. Strong feelings surged. My honest question came as a surprise. I didn't

SUSAN D. HILL

want Tuck to know I was upset, but the rising pain in my heart was in charge. I curled away from his small body.

"Rissy? You still praying?" he asked, trying to look at me in the dark.

"No..." I wiped my eyes and nose on my nightgown. "Go ahead."

"Okay." He pulled the covers under his chin. "Dear God, I thank you for God." He paused a moment. "Please ask Him to br-ing the hap-py again—in all these rooms. Amen."

Tuck laid in my arms the rest of the night. I could feel his lungs rising and falling. The longing in his prayer for "the happy" was a tall order. Tears flooded the corners of my eyes. Drops left my cheeks, making a tap-tap sound on the pillow. I stayed awake long into the night, wondering what would happen the next day, and the day after that.

In the end, Wyeth had to find odd jobs like walking dogs, carrying groceries, or sweeping out a basement or two until he could buy new dolls for both Anna and me. We celebrated with a double wedding.

The incident was over, yet Wyeth had changed. Anna Rae and I watched him shoveling snow in the driveway through the kitchen window. His face had no expression at all, even when he lifted a big shovelful. His eyes seemed puffy.

"I think he's giving up," I said.

"Giving up what?" asked Anna Rae. She looked at me through her bangs.

"I don't know."

She waited, bowing her chin.

"He might go silent on me." I said.

"What?" She brushed her hair to one side.

"Or he might run away." I didn't really know what to say.

"What makes you think that?" said Anna Rae.

"He has shark eyes, again. Like when Mama first died."

Chapter 19

"THERE!" I SAID. The marshmallow began to form a foamy cloud in my hot chocolate. I licked the sticky froth off the spoon. "Just right."

Wyeth had already chugged a Mountain Dew, the showoff. Father called that soda "sugar oblivion" and would not buy it. Wy had been sneaking it, using his snow-shoveling money. Cocoa was still permitted.

It had taken twenty-five minutes to make a perfect cup. First the milk boiled over. I poured it through a fine sieve to remove any scalded "skin." An ice cube made it too watery. I added powdered milk and some heaping spoonfuls of *Quik*, reheating the mixture over blue flames. The marshmallow gave the crowning touch.

Wyeth eyed me when he saw the mess. Pans, spoons, and ingredients covered the countertop.

"What," I said.

"All this for one cup of cocoa?"

"I want perfection."

"Chauney, if you ask me," he said. "You'd better clean up. He could come anytime." Time had wiped away the tension. Wy was back to being his snippy old self.

It was Christmas Eve day, and Father planned to quit work mid-afternoon to do some errands. Mrs. Peate took care of Tuck for several hours each day now, so Wy and I were on our own.

Just as Wyeth turned to leave the kitchen, a mischievous thought flitted through my mind. Using my spoon, I flicked my gooey marshmallow at him. It made a nice splat on the back of his head. A direct hit! I had declared war.

He whirled around. Eyes big, mouth ajar, he fingered the warm spot and realized what I'd done. Then he charged me. For a while, I successfully dodged him, skirting around the breakfast table. Noticing his bare feet, I escaped out the back door, thinking he wouldn't follow me in the snow. Weak with laughter, I slowed down to glance over my shoulder and was promptly tackled. I got what I deserved—a snow sandwich. But seeing his astonished face was worth it. He'd been so glum.

"Sheesh Rissy!" He pulled me up. I laughed when he tiptoed shoeless across the snowy yard as if walking on hot coals. He slammed the door for effect.

The shower water came on upstairs. I dropped another marshmallow in my cup and went down to our bunker. Hidden away in the fruit closet, we stored Mama's diary in an aluminum cookie tin. I steadied my cocoa on the orange crate to leaf through the pages of her journal.

On Christmas Day, a year ago, she'd written a curious sentence: "Ephraim means fruitful, for God had made him fruitful in the land of his affliction."

Fruitful. Here I was in the fruitless fruit closet thinking about fruitfulness. It was funny or mystical, depending on how you looked at it.

On the opposite page of the diary, Mama had taped a section from one of Skeets' letters. I recognized his handwriting. It said, "God calls you 'Ephraim.' Read Zechariah 10. Some promises there for you."

I planned to check it out when Wyeth yelled down the basement stairs.

"Father just called. He's on his way, and he's bringin' a tree!"

"Comin!" I'd have to read it later. After sealing our secret place, I hurried upstairs to get the kitchen shipshape. Wy entered as I finished wiping the sticky counters.

"Father wants you to go get Tuck," he said.

"He probably asked *you*," I countered.

"Naw. He gave me other things to do."

"Like what?"

"Like unraveling Christmas lights, for your information," he snarled.

"Too bad!" We both hated that job worse than untangling coat hangers, which Mama had said were "ridiculously tenacious." She used words like that for my benefit, knowing I'd go to the dictionary. I grabbed a coat and my bunny fur muff, pausing in front of Wyeth to exaggerate my smile.

"Get out, Bone Cat!" he said, shoving me away.

A cold wind blew in when I opened the door. There was something exhilarating about being the first one to step out in new fallen snow. Lacey snowflakes had been coming down thick. Like a clean white canvas, it inspired me to create something. Dragging one foot at a time, I carved half-circles with each step, forming a long wiggly snake in the snow. I looked back to see the pattern as I crossed the road. A peach and plum sunset colored the sky. Christmas lights blinked on around the neighborhood. Some homes glowed with electric candles on their windowsills. My nose felt cold, but my hands and feet were warm.

Tuck was already bundled in his winter coat when I got to the Peate's home. He wore a Santa stocking cap and red rubber boots. In his arms, he grasped a green paper bag with a white ribbon at the top.

"What's in there?" I asked, stepping inside the their front door.

"Snickerdoodles." He made a dopey grin. Brown curls framed his pink cheeks. He could have passed for an elf if his ears were pointier.

"Iris, there's a letter here for you." Mrs. Peate handed me a blue mailer and furled her eyebrows.

"Oh!" I rushed over to take it.

"Everything okay?" she asked.

"Yes ma'am." My voice had risen in pitch. "Thank you so much!" I folded the mailer and carefully wiggled it into my coat pocket. We said our goodbyes.

"One of Tuck's gloves is missing!" she hollered after us. "But we'll search for it!"

I waved back to acknowledge.

Following the snow snake home, I held Tuck's bare hand inside my muff. My other hand clutched the treasured letter from Skeets. It felt a little dusty. I thought about how it had come from a hot dry place on the other side of the world.

"Rissy, where does the sun go at night?" Lately, my little brother had been asking the strangest questions.

"Maybe it gets tired and goes to bed like us."

"But why does the sun wake up at the other end of our street?" Tuck pressed.

"Hmm," I said. *Pretty smart for a four-year-old.* "Well, before the sun goes to bed, it rolls around the earth to visit Uncle Skeets. Then it comes back up the other side." I motioned a circle.

"So Skeets lives underneath us?"

This was getting complicated. "Not really. He's just faraway, buddy." I didn't know how to explain that we were the ones moving around the sun or that we could stand sideways on a round earth because of gravity. It would have prompted a hundred new questions.

"Mmm. I see." He skip-hopped to keep up. "Is the sun a boy?"

I smiled in the darkness. "The sun is a *thing*—not a he or a she. It's an it!"

"What's an 'it'?" He was persistent.

"Tucky! Stop!" I moaned. "Race you to the house!"

By the time we reached the back door, Father and Wyeth were already wrangling a giant Douglas fir inside, stump first. Tuck ran ahead to hold the door. Once erected, it became clear the tree was too tall. Father sawed off at least a foot and a half before anchoring it in the base. Then he strung the lights.

I gave the tree a drink, filling the base to the brim. The bushy thing felt like something wild we'd brought inside to tame. We dressed its branches with small angels of all shapes and styles, shiny red and green balls, fake candy canes, and many keepsake ornaments Mama had collected over the years. In a shoebox labeled "Oh Tannenbaum," I found hand-crocheted snowflakes that had been starched stiff—Nana's handiwork. There were also miniature nutcrackers that looked like mean little men. We hung them, using a stepladder. Finally, we draped tinsel on each branch, making long silvery icicles. The decorated tree shimmered like a prince in royal garments.

I skipped into the kitchen and noticed two large grocery sacks stuffed full. It was my job to put groceries away, but Father lurched forward to stop me.

"No, no! Those are for Christmas! Don't you peek now, Honey." I stepped away, stunned at the good humor in his voice. I couldn't remember the last time he had called me "Honey."

He dusted off a Nat King Cole LP and placed it on the turntable. "The Christmas Song" changed the atmosphere. The singer serenaded us about roasting chestnuts with his warm silky voice, and violins sighed like girls in love. I walked around dazed and cheerful, my skin tingling.

"Deck the Halls" came next—the lively song had peppy brass horns. Tuck frolicked through the living room, circling the tree and the couch in a figure-eight pattern. Then he paused to ask me yet another question.

"Do trees have teeth, Rissy?"

"Teeth?" I twirled by him, half-listening.

"Well how do they eat?"

"They don't! They're just big drinkers." I pulled him down to check the water level in the base. "See, silly pony, I filled the base plumb full, and it's already taken a giant sip." The water had dropped half an inch.

"So it drinks through its leg, instead of a mouth?"

"Well, kinda. Plants are different from us."

He ran his fingers through the tinsel. His eyes sparkled. "When I drink water, does my tummy come after my throat?"

"Of course!" I grabbed his hand and spun him around.

"Then where does it go?"

"In the toilet! And don't ask me if trees pee, 'cause I don't know!" I tickled him until he begged me to stop.

A few days earlier, Mrs. Peate had driven us kids to the old Kresge's department store to shop for presents with our allowances. Now, squirreled away in separate rooms, we wrapped our gifts in white tissue paper and thin red ribbons. I bought a magnifying glass for Wyeth, a bug box for Tuck, and a bag of black licorice for Father. One by one, we placed our small offerings under the lighted tree. I stretched out on the floor to marvel at the spectacle.

Father hummed along with the music when, "Frosty the Snowman" came on. He added bites of ham to a family-sized can of bean soup already heating in a saucepan. "Mmm-mm—doo-doo, doot, doot, doot, doo-doo."

Tuck started skipping around the tree again.

Finally, Father ladled steaming soup into four bowls all in a row. I sliced the bread. Dinner would be early, so we could attend the candlelight service.

"Boys? Supper's on!" he hollered.

I set the breadbasket on the table and carried the soup bowls to each place. My brothers appeared, and we scooted in.

"Tucker James? Why don't you say grace tonight," said Father.

Tuck folded his hands with great ceremony and bowed his head so low his curls almost skimmed the surface of his soup.

"Dear God. Thank you for Daddy, Wy, Rissy—*and* Kibbs," he shifted to a whisper, "Could you please kiss Mama?"

A long pause followed.

"And thank you that I can wink," he said. "But remember, I don't know how to whistle yet. A-men."

"A-men," we joined in unison.

"No white flags on the table now." Father referred to our constant failure to place our napkins on our laps. We devoured our soup as if we hadn't eaten all day.

"With all this snow, we outta go sledding on Old Peet's Hill," said Wyeth.

"Yeah! Daddy, you come too!" Tuck added.

"My sledding days are over. Can't risk it." Father wiped his mouth.

"How come?" I asked.

"When I was in college, my dorm sat on top of a knoll." Father laid his spoon down to take some bread. "One night, me and my pals got a hose and iced that hill real slick." He made a sly grin. "Then, we borrowed some cafeteria trays."

Wyeth rarely made eye contact with Father, but now he stared at him.

"We looked down that hill, half-scared to death," Father continued. "At the bottom was a parking lot. My buddy Fritz agreed to go first."

I stopped eating.

"Well, he flew down that hill, screaming like a girl, draggin' all four limbs to slow himself down."

I chuckled at the thought. The corners of Wyeth's mouth curved up.

"Did he die? Did he die?" asked Tuck, his mouth stuffed with bread.

"No, but he slid under a pickup and immediately slammed into a car tire."

"Ooh," I groaned.

"Fritz had a bloody nose. It was pretty bad—in fact, he probably broke it—but that didn't stop us. We all took a turn or two anyway."

Wyeth's eyes grew big. I didn't know our Father had such a wild streak.

"But Daddy, you coulda been kilt," said Tuck in a soft pouty voice.

"It's 'killed,' son, not 'kilt.' We were okay, really. Three guys stayed at the bottom to tackle. I cracked my kneecap though, and it's never been the same."

Wyeth shook his head. "Hey Tucky, pass the bread?"

Tuck didn't respond. Wyeth might reach across the table again. I clenched my teeth.

"Tuck! The bread!" I spoke with quiet urgency. "*Give it to Wy.*" He pushed the breadbasket over, and the moment passed without incident.

"If the snow isn't packed, we'll need a toboggan," said Wyeth.

"Tubes are fun." I said.

"Yeah—super fun to watch you flip and face plant." Wyeth was ever so faithful to bring up embarrassing things.

"At least I didn't fall off the T-bar lift and knock a dozen skiers down like a bowling ball!"

Tuck started giggling and snorted accidentally, bringing laughter all around. I couldn't take my eyes off my dad. His smile changed his entire face.

Temperatures had dropped. Frigid air stung my cheeks as we walked in from the church parking lot. The chapel's only light came from flickering candles. The tall organ pipes filled the room with voluminous sound that vibrated the floor. Soon we were singing familiar carols.

Long lay the world...in sin and error pining,

Till He appeared and the soul felt its worth...

I inched over toward Father and slowly leaned into his side.

The thrill of hope, the weary world rejoices
For yonder breaks a new and glorious morn...

I slid my left hand around his elbow. He didn't seem to mind.

Fall on your knees...Oh hear the angel voices
Oh, nigh-ight divine, Oh-oh night, when Christ was born...

With my other hand I found Skeets' letter, still concealed in my coat pocket. I looked up. Curved beams in the ceiling seemed like great arms over and around us. Two men and God had replaced one mama, but I didn't feel better, not in the deep places.

My father offered my brothers and me some semblance of family, a shared history understood by no one else. Yet my uncle gave me something I could barely describe. Safety? Not exactly. He lived in Africa, after all. Kindness? Maybe. It was something that kept me alive. It lifted me above a bottomless sorrow that came at night and calmed the fear that could easily swallow me whole.

Wyeth and I shared our grief in unspoken ways. Somehow it joined us together. I guess we were old enough to know our lives would never be the same, but not old enough to go out on our own. I knew when he was awake in the late hours. I believed he had a tear-streaked face, just like me. I could hear his night sounds, though we never talked about it. But Mama was gone now, and no matter how often our longing for her surfaced, she'd never come back.

The organist started the prelude for "Joy to the World," and the congregation rose to their feet. I joined in, singing quietly at first. With each verse, the music mounted with the emotion of triumph. It moved me. I stood on my tiptoes and sang in my loudest voice.

Let ev-ev-every heart, prepare-er-er Him roo-oo-oom...
And heav'n and nature sing, and heav'n and nature sing...
And heaven, and hea-a-ven, and nature sing.

126

The silence that followed seemed quieter than usual. Vibrations from the last chord sent tingles over my entire body. I felt hushed with awe. But it was more than that. I closed my eyes. The air rippled with an invisible current coursing through the room. I stayed as still as possible.

Then as was our tradition, we sang "Silent Night" without the help of the organ. A bouquet of worship filled the sanctuary. And Father cupped his hand around mine.

Chapter 20

O N THE DRIVE home, I searched the sky in earnest for the Christmas star. Wyeth blew smoke rings with moist air, and Father seemed pleasantly distracted. Tuck complained of having bugs in his nose. I told him his nostril hairs were frozen, which only alarmed him that his nose was growing hair in the first place.

By tradition, our family opened presents on Christmas Eve. As soon as we pulled to a stop, the boys rolled out from the backseat and dashed straight upstairs to change into their pjs. I waited to walk in with Father.

I passed Wyeth as he thundered down the stairs. "C'mon pokey," he said. "No namby-pambying around. Get your nighty on so we can start!"

Tuck followed, hopping a step at a time. I hurried. As soon as Father came out in his bathrobe, the frenzy of pulling ribbons and tearing paper began.

I opened some bubble bath powder from Tuck, and Wyeth gave me his old 45 of "Yellow Submarine" with "Eleanor Rigby" on the flip side. I had broken the tenth commandment for years by coveting that record. Nana and Pops had sent us red envelopes with Christmas tree stickers on the front. Inside was a crisp ten-dollar bill.

At last, the time came for Father's gifts. He rumbled around in the kitchen. "Don't come in yet—it's not ready!" he said happily.

"How soooon?" asked Tuck, shifting his weight from one foot to the other.

"No peeking now. It's almost time." Father re-entered the living room and tied dishtowels around each of our heads to cover our eyes. He had us hold hands and steered us into the kitchen.

"On the count of three, remove your blindfolds. One, two...three!" Father leaned against the sink with one foot crossed over the other. He lifted his arms in a Vanna White way over the bounty of grocery store treasures. The counters were stacked with all kinds of treats rarely allowed in our family.

I couldn't believe my eyes. There were Pop Tarts, Twinkies, caramel apples, Alpha-bits cereal, Frito Corn Chips, Coca-Colas, Hershey's chocolate bars, Cheetos, Peanut M & M's, chocolate Necco wafers, Jujubes, Lemon Heads, popcorn balls, ice cream sandwiches, Bit 'O Honeys, and a giant box of Captain Crunch. In addition, Father gave Tuck a large box of Cheerios all to himself. I received a candy necklace, and Wyeth got a pile of bubblegum cigars.

"Well, c'mon now—what-cha waitin' for?" Father motioned us to come. It was a Willy Wonka dream to be sure. He chuckled in a high voice and retired to his chair with the newspaper, while we gorged. Sugar took effect immediately, making us silly and hyper for a good hour before we wiggled around in our beds.

Tuck wanted to sleep with me. He'd been wary of Santa ever since he accidentally peed on Santa's lap in the toy department at Higbee's. Jolly St. Nick turned into an angry old man that day, spouting cuss words and wrecking his act. Tuck bolted to the ladies lingerie section, hiding behind a rack of slips, until Mama and I coaxed him out.

After my little brother nodded off, I was still wide-awake. I pictured Skeets' letter and decided to save it for Christmas Day. Then I remembered Mama's diary and the verses in Zechariah. My curiosity stirred. The house seemed dead quiet. I felt for my slippers and tiptoed downstairs.

Father had fallen asleep on the living room couch. A half-empty jug of distilled water sat on the floor next to him. The Christmas tree lights illuminated the room, enough for me to step over the wrapping paper still littering the floor. As soundless as a deer in a winter forest, I passed through the room.

The basement stairway had one creaky step. I remembered that when it groaned. A flash of chills swept across my body. Father moved a little. I continued, putting weight on the next step gradually.

Once in the fruit closet, I turned a candlestick light on and opened Mama's diary to where I'd left off. She'd already written down various phrases from chapter ten:

ZECHARIAH 10: (NASB)
"Ephraim _will_ be like a mighty man...
Indeed, their children _will_ see it and be glad,
Their heart _will_ rejoice in the Lord...
They _will_ remember Me in far countries,
And they with their children _will_ live and come back.
I _will_ bring them back from the land of Egypt...
And they _will_ pass through the sea of distress...
And I _will_ strengthen them in the Lord,
And in His name they _will_ walk," declares the Lord.

According to Skeets, God had called Mama, "Ephraim." What an odd statement. First off, she was a woman, not a mighty man. But how exactly did he know these things?

Within the verses a curious pattern had emerged: every single line had the word "will" in it. That struck me. What were the chances of that? Mama had seen it too because she'd underlined each one. She wrote at the bottom,

"These things _will_ happen, because God holds the future."

Little did I realize just how prophetic those words would become in our lives.

I snuck back upstairs, avoiding the tattletale step. Father lay on his front with his face turned sideways. He snored with his mouth open. I dipped my hand in the base of the tree to check the water level. It had dropped considerably. *What a drinker!* Silently, I poured the distilled water down the base of the trunk to keep from making a sound. I glanced repeatedly at Father. When his snoring stopped, I froze. When it rumbled again, I continued until liquid reached the top.

It had been such a cheerful day. Perhaps Father wouldn't mind if he caught me out of bed. After all, I was keeping "Oh Tannenbaum" alive. A faint aroma lingered by the tree. Something like fingernail polish remover.

In the dim light, I looked closely at my dad. The skin around his eyes appeared red. Near the bridge of his nose, a small pool of tears had not drained from the corner of his eye. My father must've been crying. He never cried! A hundred questions whirred through my mind until a single thought formed.

He must be missing her. I covered my mouth and quickly stepped away. My eyes filled up fast. Once in the kitchen, I whimpered into a tissue. I didn't know how he felt about Mama after their big fight. For all I knew, he hated her for taking Wyeth's side. Most of the time, he just seemed angry or withdrawn.

I blotted my eyes. Now I felt something entirely different. This time, my tears were for him—for them—and for things that could never be.

I sank down on my chair at the kitchen table and rested my head. Something strange and sad and wonderful was happening all at once. I felt the rush of a Ferris wheel rise, weightless and giddy. Maybe Father *had* loved Mama. And if he did, we were a true family. It wasn't all a lie.

But after reaching the crest, the Ferris wheel feeling dropped down. My stomach rose up in my throat. Nothing would ever be the same without her.

I remembered sneaking glimpses of their kisses in the hallway. Or how she ran her fingers through his hair, soothing him at the end of a long day. Yet I twisted with memories of angry faces, slamming doors, and fearful arguments. Then came the silence—plenty of wrenching, uncertain silence.

But all that didn't matter now. There was no wife, nor any need of a husband. Just a father and a man—but a man who had loved his wife. To me, that somehow mattered. I soared to the top of the wheel again.

Scooping a handful of Alpha-bits, I made a pile on the table. Sad memories faded. Light-heartedness remained. I wanted to linger in it. For one crazy minute, I thought about kissing him on the cheek. No. Probably not smart. Instead I simply smiled at the thought and nibbled on cereal, absentmindedly laying out sugary letters on the table.

Soon sleep began to pull on my eyelids. A giant yawn followed. I stood and stretched, glancing back at the table. Carefully placed in a neat row, I had spelled the word, "D-A-D-D-Y."

Chapter 21

A DOOR BANGED shut, jarring me awake. It sounded like the front door. What was going on? It was still dark out. Tuck didn't stir. He must've been in sugar-plum-fairy-land.

Someone crossed the living room. My pulse quickened. It had to be Father. He grumbled out loud, as if arguing about something. I only made out the swear words. Then his creaky bedroom door closed.

My bedside digital alarm clock said 3:33. I sighed. On Christmas morning, we had to stay in bed till first light. It had become a new rule when Tuck tried to rouse everyone at 5 a.m. last year. Snow flurries swirled outside the window in the moonlight. The furnace rumbled on. Warm air purred through the register next to my bed.

I thought about Skeets' letter. It was still in my coat pocket downstairs. I hesitated. Father might hear me. Ten minutes flipped by on the clock, before I made up my mind. I slipped out of bed.

After silently working each step on the staircase, I slowly heel-toed to the front hall closet. In the dark, I felt the envelope's dusty texture and jiggled it free from the pocket. With letter in hand, I returned. An overwhelming urge to hurry surged in my chest.

Once back in my room, I searched for fingernail scissors. I kept them in a basket on my dresser. Mama had taught me to cut international mailers. Tearing them open often damaged the words.

Tuck whimpered a little. I waited. He stretched out his legs. I listened for his rhythmic breathing to return.

Prying open my top drawer, I groped around for a flashlight. Of course it was buried under a thousand things. I pulled it out inch-by-inch, watching Tuck. Then, clutching my tools and the letter, I rolled underneath my bed.

Three sides of the mailer had to be cut in order to lay it flat. I trimmed the edges carefully. After adjusting the light, I spread out the thin blue paper with both hands. Five months had passed since our uncle had left.

To Mr. Wy Coyote, Wild Iris Rose, and Little Tommy Tucker...

My eyes welled, blurring my vision. I wiped tears on the sleeves of my flannel nightgown.

It seems you are not getting my letters. The Peates don't mind playing postman, and I think that's okay. I'm sad your dad will not let you see Nana and Pops. Over here they say, "The teeth of a man serve as a fence." Apparently your dad has shown his teeth.

I want to know how you are doing? Oli Otya? That's how we say it in Uganda: Oh-lee-OAT-tee-yah. Practice that so you can greet me properly when I return next summer.

The orphanage here has four new children. Some were living on the streets, selling stolen mangoes and jackfruit to get by. Rissy, there's a girl named Sanyu here who reminds me of you. She's my Sacajawea. And Wy, I want you to meet Musa, a boy about your age. He's our official bat catcher.

Those furry, flying creatures have a colony in a huge canopy tree near the compound. We like them because they eat insects—a thousand mosquitoes an hour! We only eat an average of two bugs in an entire day, so as you can see, their help is indispensable. (A new word for the collection, Iris).

However, if a bat gets inside, Musa whacks it with a broom. Don't worry. It only stuns the critter long enough to return it to the night sky. His BATTING average is .333

(Ha!)—Better than Pete Rose, that ballplayer from Cincy!

Anyway, I think about you three all the time. And I mean—all the time. We see the same sun and the same moon, but not at the same time. And that means we're far away from each other. Yeah.

But my heart is yours. You are indispensable to me.

I know you miss your Mama something terrible. So do I. Still, remember our talk on the day your father came home. You'd agree with me if I said it's foolish for a blind man to pick a fight with his guide. In the same way, you must get along with the dad God has given you as a guide for now. Write me soon, and give your letters to Mrs. Peate.

All my love,
Skeets
P.S. Can Tuck whistle yet?

I lowered my chin and cried my eyes out. In a few short paragraphs, my uncle felt alive to me again. The words carried his whimsical spirit across zillions of miles, because he wrote the same as he talked. I longed to rest my head on his chest, to feel the thump-thump of his wild and wonderful heart.

After a few minutes, I calmed down and tried to imagine his sunny world of mango trees and bats. I'd seen some Polaroid photos he'd sent to Mama. Closing my eyes, I envisioned beautiful children with shining faces and white teeth. They had lovely brown eyes and dark skin. I saw them in tattered clothes, running barefoot on rust-colored dirt, older kids carrying younger ones on their backs. In my mind, they were all very thin. So thin that Skeets' long arms encircled the entire group. I wanted to be there—with him, with them. Gradually, I drifted back to sleep.

THE BOX SPRINGS squeaked like mice chattering around my head. It took me a moment to remember where I was.

Tuck squirmed around again. "Rissy?"

I crawled out. "I'm here."

"Is it time? He asked.

I looked at the clock. Hours had passed. It was nearly 7:30. "Yes! The sun should be back any minute from Africa."

We put on robes and slippers. I crossed the hall to nudge Wyeth and noticed one foot sticking out of his covers. Wrapping my arm around the exposed ankle, I quickly scraped my fingernails across the sole of his foot. He jerked and kicked like a bucking horse, but it did the trick. He climbed out of bed to join us.

Pale gray light bathed the living room. I peered out between the curtains. The morning sun would soon inch up over the horizon. Fresh snow had made all things new, erasing my snake lines as waves remove footprints in the sand. My teacher said the earth as a living planet continually renewed its scars. We were more like the moon. Our damage showed.

The boys seemed unusually serious for Christmas Day. They perched on the bottom step with long faces. I plugged in the tree lights to perk things up. No one wanted to knock on Father's door, so the waiting began.

"Be right back." I slipped away to the fruit closet to hide Skeets' letter. I'd tell Wyeth later. Before placing the blue mailer in the aluminum tin, I read it one more time.

"That's strange," I whispered. Skeets said Musa's batting average was .333, the same number I'd seen on the clock. Was it a coincidence? Maybe God had something to say. Skeets always acted as if these things were normal.

I opened my Bible. Genesis 3 didn't even have 33 verses. I went on to Chapter 33 to find a story about Jacob apologizing to his brother. Maybe God wanted me to be nicer to Wyeth. I pressed on.

In Exodus 33:3 God said He wouldn't go on with his people anymore, because they were stubborn. In fact, if He was in a bad mood, He might even kill them. *Great. That sounded too much like Father.* Leviticus had nothing, and Numbers talked about the Mushite family.

"Mish mash mush," I muttered to myself.

"What are you doing down there?" Wyeth whisper-yelled from the top step.

I knew for certain he'd think I was nuts.

"Coming!" I shut my eyes and prayed. "God, are you trying to say something?" Before I continued, the word "Jeremiah" flashed through my mind. I coughed a tight laugh. What if I was making up the whole blooming thing?

"Rissy! We want *you* to knock on Father's door." I heard Tuck's tiny scared voice.

"One second!" I tried to not sound irritated, though I was.

Jeremiah 3 only went to verse 25. I flicked pages forward as fast as possible. My finger traced the numbers in the printed columns. Finally, Jeremiah 33:3...

Call to me and I will answer you, and will tell you great and hidden things which you have not known.

My body went limp. *God?* A faint rushing sound filled my ears. It was a quiet roar, like a faraway ocean, the noise you hear in conch shells.

"Rissy?" Tuck called out, tromping down the basement stairs.

I quickly slipped out the fruit closet door.

He'd already made it to the bottom step. "Ri-i-ssssy!" he whined.

Grabbing a can of stewed tomatoes, I leapt out of the pantry in the nick of time.

"What you doin'?" he asked, gazing past me.

"Lookin' for this." I showed him the shiny red can.

"Ew. For breakfast?" he asked.

"No! No! Puddin' 'N' Tame! Ask me again, and I tell you the same!" We marched back up to the main floor. Tuck still didn't know about our secret bunker. He might innocently blurt something to Father. It was too risky.

Wyeth had returned to the bottom step of the stairway near the living room. He sat slouched over—chin on hands, elbows on knees, and feet, pigeon-toed. His giddiness from the night before had completely crashed. "I checked the stockings," he said in monotone. "Father stuffed 'em with more junk food. He didn't even try..."

I flashed angry eyes at him. Tuck didn't know about Santa yet. Mama had always put special gifts in our stockings.

"Just tell him!" Wyeth said. "It's time he knew a thing or two."

My eyes got big.

"What?" asked Tuck.

"Don't!" I said, pointing a menacing finger and standing as tall as I could.

He marched over to Father's door and glared, his arms crossed. Then he whirled around with fists in the air. "Santa Claus is really just our father, Tucky boy," he announced, wincing a fake smile at me. "There! I said it!"

Tuck's face went blank. I couldn't read his expression. I turned on Wyeth. "You're a first-class jerk, you know!" Heat rushed into my face. "Don't listen to him, Tuck."

"What about Santa at the mall?" Tuck's chin quivered a little.

"They're all fakes. Guys wearing beards and costumes," Wyeth said without a care.

I could've burst out of my skin. I wanted to pounce on him, but any commotion might stir up the wrong mood in Father.

I whispered in Tuck's ear. "I'll explain it to you later. Everything's okay."

The floor was still strewn with torn wrapping paper and ribbons. Still fuming, I needed to do something. Grabbing handfuls, I jammed the waste into the trash.

"Angry-cleaning, again?" asked Wyeth.

"Shut up," I snapped.

We three sat, staring at the floor.

I'd become someone I didn't know anymore. It wasn't just anger toward Wyeth, or dread about Father. It wasn't even sadness about losing Mama. My whole body felt heavier, though I hadn't grown much. I was tired. Yes. That was it. Not needing-sleep kind of tired. Nor bored-tired. It was a weary tired, like I didn't want to fight anymore. But I couldn't quit—for Tuck's sake.

"*You* do it Rissy. *You* get him." My little brother broke the silence.

I blinked hard several times. Standing by Father's bedroom door I knocked gently. Nothing happened. I tapped a little harder, using pointy knuckles. Not a sound from the other side. I pressed my lips together. Lifting my fist, I made two loud thumps.

"For the love of Pete!" Father bellowed. "I'm sleeping!"

His tone hit me forcefully. I stepped back. No jolly happy soul from the night before.

"*Great*," said Wyeth. "Back to normal." He plodded upstairs.

Tuck ran to Father's door before I could stop him. "It's Christmas, Daddy!"

I pulled Tuck into my arms, hauling him away from the entrance. "He'll come...you'll see...be patient now," I said.

After a minute, Father appeared at the door with disheveled hair, rubbing his swollen eyes. "You're right." He cleared his throat. "Merry Christmas to all!"

I was old enough to hear the sarcasm in his voice, but knew it was really pain. I'd seen the tears on his sleeping face.

"Daddy?" Tuck held his chin down and looked up with big eyes. "Are *you* really Santa?"

His question seemed to hang in the air.

Father frowned at me, and I offered a sad-eyed shrug. The moment felt painfully quiet. Finally, after a long awkward pause, he answered. "Yes, I am."

"I don't understand." Tuck said, his eyes wide with wonder.

"It's okay, buddy," I chimed in. "You don't have to."

"No! I wanna know!" Tuck insisted. "How do you get to all the houses in one night?"

I covered my mouth with one hand.

Father stroked his unshaven jaw. "Well, it's a miracle, sonny boy. One helluva miracle!"

That seemed to do it for my little brother. "Now can we open our stockings?"

"Have at it!" Father grunted, heading toward the bathroom. I heard the familiar plop-fizz. He took Alka-Seltzer for headaches. He had headaches all the time now.

Tuck opened a box of Lemon Heads and popped one in his mouth. I folded up on the wingback chair, pulling my knees to my chin. Christmas joy had vanished like a startled bird, flying away through the trees, leaving only the tiniest footprints of its presence. And all our decorations, presents and treats seemed ridiculous. Sickening. My eyes stung.

Chapter 22

THE FIRST CHRISTMAS without Mama seemed like the longest day of my life. Father remained on the couch, sweating profusely. The TV blared for hours. He acted grouchy as all get out, wearing his headache face—tight lips and creased brow—a clear signal to leave him alone. To use his phrase, "even a moron could get that."

Tuck whined for more Christmas treats, and I caved. He wouldn't quit jumping off the ottoman pretending to be Superman. I had to do something. Wyeth was barricaded in his room. He didn't answer my knocks, so I slid a note under his door:

Going NUTS out here! Want to sled at Peet's Hill?

A few seconds later the lock turned. Electric guitars screamed a tinny sound from his headphones. My jaw opened. Father believed hard rock was "The Devil's Doorway."

"I can hear that, you know!" I mouthed the words with breathy vehemence.

He hit *Stop* on his Walkman. "So what?"

"So you're going to be a deaf old man."

"Right-on." He pried the headphones off.

"Father would've heard it too, except for the TV." I added the real reason.

"Buzz off! It's my life!" he said, shoving me away and shutting

139

the door in my face. Fortunately, the toe of my shoe stopped it from slamming.

"*Come* with us," I pleaded softly through the door.

After a moment, the door cracked open a few inches.

He appeared surprisingly meek. "Aw, okay," he said. His eyes met mine for a millisecond, and I knew not to ask anything.

Father had nodded off. We left him a note. I guaranteed Tuck a whole quarter if he could get his snow pants on without a word. As soon as we stepped out in the crisp sunny air, some of the heaviness lifted.

"You know the tittle-tattle about old Peety," Wyeth piped up, turning toward Tuck as we strolled along toward Peet's Hill.

I ran around to protect my little brother. "Wyeth!" I said firmly.

"He killed a deputy sheriff at the bottom of the sledding hill..."

"Stop it, Wy!" I pulled Tuck close, but he pushed me away.

"Really?" said Tuck, eyes aglow.

"Yeah! Put a bullet through his heart. They found him face down in the creek."

I couldn't stop them.

Peabody Hill bordered the east side of the Middle Strip. Back in Prohibition days "Old Peet," as he was known, ran a whisky still in those foothills. He claimed self-defense for the murder and never went to jail. In the end, his moonshine killed him anyway. Some called it poetic justice. I never saw any poetry in it.

The story had become creepier in the telling.

"The old coot never cut his hair, his beard or his fingernails. He ate squirrels and slept in a pup tent with his feet sticking straight out." Wy let out a belly laugh.

"Ew-ew." Tuck puckered his lips and then snickered at the thought.

I didn't want to imagine the toenail part. His exaggerations were getting ridiculous. Before long Wy would have him growing vampire fangs. Still Tuck wanted all the ghastly details. There were definitely a few things I didn't get about boys.

The hill swarmed with kids. My brothers dragged the toboggan to the top, but I opted for the inner tube. Bouncing was funner. Mama had said "funner" wasn't a word but every kid I knew used it.

From the top, I took in the scene. Kids in different colored coats looked like sprinkles on vanilla ice cream. Some chased each other with snowballs. Others squealed as they sledded down steeper places. A few moms waited at the bottom, clutching bundled babies. The dads seemed more apt to join in the scramble. I would've made it fun if Tuck had been riding with me. Left to myself, I didn't pretend.

After a few tube runs, I wasn't laughing or even smiling. The happy sounds of others made me feel ghostly—there, but not really there. Gray corduroy clouds had moved in from the west, edging out the blue sky. I trudged back up the slope.

Pushing off once again, I threw my body over the tube's hole but landed unevenly. The tube spun around, taking me down the hill backwards. I hit a powdery ledge and suddenly, momentum took me—tube and all—into the sky.

Time slowed...a burst of white...weightlessness...the tube falling...a scream. Then, smash...my head and shoulder. *Crap! ...Oh-oh-oh*...tumbling down, down, down. *My wrist, oh my-yy wrist.* Fuzzy trees, spinning.

Focus returned gradually. Too stunned to move, I stayed on my back. My cheeks burned, icy hot. A warm wetness dripped from my nose. I tasted blood.

Somewhere above me, a little girl was crying. "Paaa-pa!" she called out. I wondered if my tube had flattened her.

Soon a man spoke. "Let me see, baby doll." He sounded kind. I pictured him wiping her tears. "That tube really decked you!"

She sniffed between sobs but soon calmed down.

"I see you lost a boot," he said. "Looks like you still have your foot."

She whimpered a little laugh.

"Let's check for missing toes." He had her squealing now.

I covered my face with my right arm. Bright red blood stained the sleeve of my coat. My heart hurt. Maybe no one would find me.

"She went down over there!" someone shouted. My wrist throbbed. Footsteps came close, crunching through icy snow. A man picked me up. His moist breath smelled of cigarettes. The urge to throw-up curled in my gut. I blanked out and never saw his face.

The next thing I knew, they'd wrapped me in some kind of blanket. The wool fringe itched my face. I heard voices.

"Yeah, I'm her brother..." It was Wyeth.

My heart lifted. I wanted to speak but couldn't.

"Someone should look at that wrist—her left one," said a man. "She winced when I touched it."

"She might have a concussion too," added a woman.

"Okay. C'mon Tuck."

They lifted me onto the toboggan, and the sound of the sled, scraping snow underneath my body calmed my nerves.

My vision came clear. It seemed like hours had passed. Luckily I was in my own bed. Tuck leaned against the footboard, his eyes fixed on me.

"Hey," I managed, before clearing my throat. "How long have I been out?"

"A very, very, very long time." His sweet face looked furrowed with concern.

"How many Pink Panthers?" Half-hour cartoons measured time for Tuck.

"At least three. Maybe more." He fiddled with a Nerf rocket I'd found at a garage sale for ten cents.

"Don't worry. I'll be okay."

"Daddy won't answer my questions... he's all ma-ad again." Tuck's voice quivered.

"Yeah, I figured." My head pounded with pain, and my left wrist had gone numb under a bag of ice. I scooted back to sit up a little.

"Tuck! Dinner!" Father yelled.

He left the room, making motor sounds as he flew the rocket over the banister.

I glanced out the window. Darkness would soon follow twilight. Cold already seeped through the glass panes.

Wyeth entered, carrying a tray. He'd brought me a steaming bowl of macaroni chili, a stack of saltines, and a glass of milk. Two Bayer tablets rolled to the side of the tray.

"Here ya go, cripple." He wouldn't make a very good nurse.

"What's going on downstairs?" I meant *with Father*. He understood. We used the spy language of siblings—talking without really saying things outright.

"Still cranky."

"Who made the chili?" I asked.

"Chef Boyardee."

"Is my arm broken?"

"Don't think so. Time will tell," Wyeth lowered his head. "But he won't pay for an x-ray." Mama would have insisted on an x-ray. He turned to leave. "I have to eat with them. You know how it goes."

I nodded.

He left silently.

I nibbled chipmunk-sized bites off a saltine. The aspirin went down with a sip of milk. If I sat up straight, the room spun around, so I used the extra pillow to prop myself halfway. My eyes felt drowsy. Not meaning to, I dozed off and let my dinner go cold.

I came to when the door swung open, and Father entered. I flinched in surprise.

He seemed at a loss for words. Seeing my uneaten food, he frowned. "Well, you're alive, I see," he said.

I barely moved. For some reason, he stayed about ten feet away. Was he joking or irritated?

"We'll see if you're still around in the morning." He didn't offer the slightest smile. Did he care?

"Okay." I sunk down in my bedding.

He headed toward Tuck's room.

"Goodnight," I said, but Father had walked out of earshot. "Merry Christmas," I whispered. I wanted him to count my fingers to make sure all ten were there.

I must've fallen asleep again. My dinner tray had disappeared and the whole house seemed dark and quiet. I didn't dare get up on my own. No need to brush my teeth. I reached for *The Living Bible* on the shelves next to my bed. Nana once told me to read a Psalm if I needed cheering up. I landed on chapter 15.

> *Lord, who may go and find refuge and shelter*
> *In your tabernacle up on your holy hill?*
> *Anyone who leads a blameless life and is truly sincere.*
> *Anyone who refuses to slander others,*
> *Does not listen to gossip,*
> *Never harms his neighbor...*
> *Keeps a promise even if it ruins him...*
> *Such a man shall stand firm forever.*

I slouched against the headboard and thought about the keeps-a-promise part.

Mama had lived her promises. She never left Father, despite his fussy rules and angry moods. He could be intensely *birdish*. But she'd touch his shoulder gently or smile at him across the room. It wasn't easy. I found her crying at the kitchen sink once. Her teardrops poked holes in the sudsy water. Still, she pressed on.

When Wyeth acted like a big stubborn mule, she'd wrap her arms around him from behind and kiss his head. He'd squirm free and walk off without looking back. That must've hurt.

Tuck could be ornery, when tired or hungry. And I had the gall to argue with her over dumb old flip-flops on the last day of her life. But she hugged me that morning. She kept loving and giving, *no matter what*—her love bubbling up like a spring.

I had promised Skeets that I would not give up on God.

"I hope I can keep that promise." I whispered to myself. And God, if He was listening.

Leaning forward, I placed the Bible on the table. At the same time, I noticed movement in my peripheral vision. I turned to see. Goose bumps radiated up my neck, tickling the back of my ears. The motion had startled me, until I realized it was my own reflection.

Over to the side of the room on my desk was a small round mirror. The china stand holding it was white with pink roses. It had been Mama's. Nana thought it should be mine now, even though I didn't care much about my appearance.

But something strange had happened. The small eight-inch mirror was precisely positioned to frame my head. And I mean *precisely*. The image of my flushed face filled the looking glass and stared back at me.

Right then a phrase floated through my mind: *You don't see yourself, do you?*

I heard it clearly, but couldn't make sense of it. I *did* see myself in the mirror. It made me shudder. I turned off the lamp and stretched the covers up to my nose.

In the dark, I thought some more about it. I didn't actually hear a voice. Not like the day in the school parking lot. The words came like small autumn leaves floating on the surface of a brook. I simply plucked them up. I imagined my hand in the cool water. The soft wet leaves like little rafts, coming one-by-one. I smiled a little. It felt like an unexpected present. Something gentle. But I didn't understand it. Not yet.

Chapter 23

OUR CHRISTMAS TREE turned brown surprisingly fast. Father made us remove the decorations before he shoved it out the door. A trail of pine needles remained as he dragged the once beautiful fir down the driveway, dumping it on the curb like road-kill.

It was just as well. Christmas had ended for me on Christmas morning. My left wrist healed gradually with the help of an ace bandage. Father returned to work, and in a matter of days school started.

In the New Year, Lake Erie didn't freeze because of milder weather. Father told us that meant more humidity and overcast clouds. How long can one survive under endless grey skies and sloshy snow? Still, temperatures dropped enough at night to keep the ice-yard frozen at Billy's. Anna Rae and I skated there after school before gathering Tuck at the Peate's house by dark. Skeets' letters came about every three weeks, reminding me to smile.

More often than not, Father had to work late leaving dinner in my hands. I also scrubbed Tuck in the bath, read him a chapter of *Charlotte's Web*, and settled him in bed before our dad even pulled in the driveway.

One Saturday in late March, I asked Father if Anna Rae could spend the night. It was Spring Break, so he couldn't use the "school night" excuse. Father didn't like other people in our house, especially kids. He squinted and tapped his crossword pencil on the kitchen table. I continued to clear the dishes.

"Is the laundry done?" he asked in a low voice.

"Yes."

"Have you memorized your verses for Sunday?" He didn't look up from the paper.

"Un-huh."

Wyeth stood in the hallway miming our conversation out of Father's view. He shook a scolding finger each time Father said anything. I glared at him for a few seconds and mouthed the words, "*Shut up!*"

"Anna can only come on Thursday," I tried to sound pleasant.

It wasn't fair. Wyeth had frequent sleepovers, though always at other kids' homes. I couldn't because I had to put Tuck to bed. In a way, it was easier with Wyeth gone. He could barely stand to be in the same room with our dad. Father probably felt the same. They never touched or kidded around and only exchanged words when necessary. Still, I didn't enjoy the same freedom. I took a stiff stance. Father *had* to say yes.

"Okay. This *one* time."

Wyeth put his hands on the sides of his cheeks, opening his mouth as a mockery of shock. My blood boiled. I stuck out my tongue at him.

Thursday morning finally arrived. Tuck had recently discovered *Mister Rogers' Neighborhood*. Spellbound, he stood four feet from the TV, watching the friendly man zip up his sweater and tie his sneakers.

My little brother glanced around the room, then back at the screen several times. I dropped an armload of bedding on the living room couch.

Mr. Rogers had just finished his opening song. "*Hi Neighbor!*"

"Something wrong, Tucky?"

He cupped his mouth. "*Who* is he talking to?" Tuck blurted in a hushed voice.

I smiled. Tuck needed a fatherly person around. I played along.

"*You*, of course." I said. "He wants to be your neighbor."

With big eyes, Tuck faced the TV again.

"*I'm glad we're together again...*" said Mr. Rogers, as if he'd been listening to our conversation.

Tucks lips parted. "He lives on *our* street?"

"No, he lives in the TV, right here in our living room." I struggled not to laugh.

Tuck cautiously made eye contact with Mr. Rogers.

"It gives me a good feeling when you like to be with me..."

He darted over to whisper in my ear. "How'd he get in there?"

That would be like trying to explain Santa coming down the chimney. "I don't really know, but you should answer someone when they speak to you," I said. "It's the polite thing to do."

"Would you like to be my neighbor?" Mr. Rogers asked, with perfect timing.

Tuck bobbed his head immediately, and from that time on, he had a TV daddy. He never wanted to miss a single show, and somehow that comforted me.

I prepared a Princess Bed for Anna Rae and me. Mama had invented it. Pushing the loveseat face-to-face with the couch, I placed a broom vertically between them as a tent pole. Sleeping bags helped cover the crack between the two sofas. A large sheet canopied the bed. I secured the sheet to the broom tip, looping a rubber band around it. Then I tucked the sheet's edges under the cushions. We'd enter where the couch extended beyond the loveseat. Mama said guests should always have the couch side. I didn't mind the smaller space.

I planned Cheese Rarebit for dinner, which amounted to chunks of Velveeta cheese melted in a little milk and spooned over saltine crackers. Tuck could peel some carrots. For dessert, we'd have grape juice popsicles made in ice trays like Skeets had taught us. I pulled out the game of LIFE and placed three plastic cars on START.

The doorbell rang. I sprinted to the door. Anna had crammed all her stuff on a small red wagon. She'd brought our favorite Jigsaw Puzzle—*Princess of Treasure Island*. It featured a beautiful female pirate, which we both agreed was odd. A real girl in short shorts wouldn't be caught dead in the company of old men with salty beards and missing teeth. Anna Rae also brought Burry, her stuffed-animal lion. She managed to squeeze in a box of Captain Crunch and her favorite pillow, not to mention a small overnight bag. It was all roped to the wagon Beverly-Hillbilly style.

We organized everything, hiding the cereal under the couch. Father had banned sugar again after our Christmas splurge. Anna laid out puzzle pieces, while I started the cheese sauce.

Meanwhile, King Friday from the Neighborhood informed my brother that people could do anything in The Land of Make-Believe. Tuck wanted to fly. With wild abandon, he jumped off Father's chair, again and again, until the front door opened.

Father scanned the scene.

We all stopped, as if caught red-handed. Tuck slowly balled up on the ground. I felt an adrenaline rush. Father grumbled while hanging up his jacket. After shutting the closet door, he pulled himself together and gave Anna Rae a thimbleful of nice-ness.

"Well hello there, Anna." He wasn't *really* glad to see her.

She stood wide-eyed and frozen.

"What's for dinner, and why is Tuck jumping off my chair?" He tried to sound normal through clenched teeth.

"Cheese Rarebit, and he wants to fly," I said.

"What?" He wrinkled his forehead. Answering both questions together seemed to annoy him, even though he'd asked two questions.

I opened my mouth to explain.

"Never mind," he said, barreling into the kitchen. Flinging open the freezer door, Father pulled out a Jeno's Pizza. He shoved the frozen slab in the oven before the stove had a chance to pre-heat. Then retreating to his bedroom, he shut the door a little too quickly.

Anna stood completely still. Her face had flushed bright pink. "I think...I...well, maybe I should go," she muttered.

"It's different now, I know." My heart pounded. "But listen—we won't see much of him." Our eyes met. She didn't look convinced, but nodded. Usually Anna was chirpy and soft—a true *muffin-bird*.

Anna, Tuck and I quietly ate our cheesy crackers and carrot sticks. Father wolfed his pizza at the counter. Wyeth never showed up for dinner, and Father didn't ask where he was. That was altogether strange.

He finished eating and wiped his mouth on the kitchen sink rag. "I'm going out. Get Tuck in bed on time." He didn't say where he was headed and briskly closed the front door. A haunting silence filled the room, as if he'd intentionally left his shadow behind. His reading glasses watched us from the kitchen counter.

Someone had to break the spell. I crossed my eyes and puckered my lips, waiting for them to notice. Tuck started to giggle. Anna finally grinned. I brought out the homemade popsicles, and soon our grape-stained mouths added color to the sport of making wacky faces. Anna pinched her lips into a flat line and croaked a high-pitched reptilian sound. She flashed her purple tongue. My whole body felt lighter.

We played LIFE until our cars were loaded and we all had piles of money. I forgot the time until Tuck yawned. After bedtime stories and a potty stop, I settled him in his bed for the night, using a box fan for white noise. I returned downstairs, stopping by the front door to peer at the empty driveway. Where was Wyeth? Or Father for that matter?

In the dark, Anna and I climbed into our Princess Bed and snuggled under afghan blankets. We used flashlights to pretend we were camping and nibbled on the forbidden sweet cereal. All the while I listened for the rumble of our old Buick. The hall clock chimed eleven times.

"Maybe we should go to bed." My eyelids felt heavy.

"But, your dad..."

"I know. He's never this late."

"Shouldn't we lock the door?"

Was she afraid of strangers, because Father wasn't home? Or worse, afraid of his return? Probably both. I knew that feeling all too well.

Her question troubled me as we brushed our teeth. *What should I do?* She wriggled into our makeshift bed. I looked outside for approaching headlights. It was dark and still. I turned the dead bolt lock on the front door but left the outside light on.

Anna's lay motionless. She'd fallen asleep, but my thoughts spiraled into full-blown alarm. *Had Wyeth finally run away? Did something happen to Father? Should I call Nana and Pops to tell them we were alone? Or dial 911? Would the police come and find the gun under Father's bed?* My mind roiled with questions.

Finally after midnight everything faded to black. As sleep came, I entered a dream:

I am standing at a stove, frying an egg sunny-side up. I season it as it quivers and crackles on the hot pan. It is a cheerful sound, and I feel happy inside.

Father strolls into the scene, stopping short to see what I am up to. "You're doing it all wrong!" he shouts, snatching the spatula and budging in front of me. I withdraw in anticipation—our movements like a familiar dance. He cracks two more eggs over mine, chopping up my sunny yolk. My jaw opens, but I'm unable to speak. Then he adds extra salt and pepper. Too much, I think. When fully cooked, he promptly eats all three eggs.

I am stunned. I want to yell at him, but my voice doesn't work!

He leaves the scene. My body starts shaking in disbelief. "That was my egg!" I can only mouth the words. A loud groan follows, but he never hears me. So I beat the wall with my fist, striking it over and over and...

What? Oh-oh! All at once I awoke to a real thumping sound. Louder! Now violent! My pulse soared. A rush of wind brought a sudden clatter of rain. Was it just the storm? Lightening lit the window by the front door. Someone was there. My whole body still shaking...too frightened to answer, but terrified not to.

Chapter 24

Perspiration fanned across my skin. I could see the dark shape of a man. It had to be Father. He leaned heavily on the door. I mustered all my strength to crank the lock. My heart pounded forcefully. When the bolt finally released, Father burst into the room and fell flat on his face. His left arm caught my shoulder and knocked me down next to him in a heap.

Anna released an earsplitting scream.

"Shut up ya lil' brat!" he yelled, as loud as I'd ever heard him. He reeked of body odor and smoke.

Quiet as possible, I scuttled backwards on all fours to hide behind the couch.

"Irisss! Where'd the hell d'ya go?" Stinging mad, he struggled to stand.

The push-pull of wild thoughts took over. I nearly darted out the backdoor. *But Anna—oh, and Tuck!* I couldn't swallow.

Father scanned the room.

Oh God, help me, help me, help me!

"I can't seee yooo!" He bellowed.

There was no choice. "Here." I panted shallow breaths. "I'm here." Slowly I rose, my legs as weak as noodles.

He staggered toward me.

I stepped back, but he lunged and landed a hard slap on my cheek. I reeled helplessly into the wall. The floor rose up. Tiny floating lights. My face numb and stinging. The room turning.

I focused and gasped. A threatening finger right in my face.

"Don't-choo *ever* lock meeout, girl! Thisss *my* house!" The air smelled sickeningly sour. "You got thaat?"

My apology didn't come fast enough. I tried moving my jaw left and right.

"Answer me! Where's yer ressspect?" he roared, stomping his foot.

My stomach heaved. I felt unable to speak. Anna's muffled cries got louder.

With the full brunt of his heel, he kicked the lampstand across the room. Glass shattered, sending splinters in all directions. He turned and kicked the wall next to my folded body. The sound made me dizzy with fear.

"Stooo-pid kid! You had *no right!!*"

I didn't move. *Oh God, oh God.* My cheek felt lava hot.

Finally, he stumbled away toward his bedroom. The springs moaned under the dead weight as his body collapsed on the bed. I prayed God would make him forget about his gun. What if Wy came home at this hour?

My whole body trembled uncontrollably. I clambered back into the Princess Bed and put my arm over Anna's back. Her body felt rigid. Buried under layers of blankets and pillows, she smothered her sobs.

"It's okay now." I felt for her hands in the dark. "He's gone." We locked onto each other. It took awhile for the shaking to stop.

In the black silence, she spoke in the tiniest voice. "I'm gonna run home."

"You can't. It's pitch dark. Besides, if you do, your parents will think something's wrong."

She threw off the covers. "Something *is* wrong!" Her voice, bolder now.

The words stabbed. They spoke of what I feared most after coping with Father for so long. I didn't want to believe that. A stubborn bone in me resisted. "He's just moody."

"*Moody?* Has he ever hit you that hard?"

"I got spanked. Every kid does."

"Nah. I mean *beat up.*"

Kids like me didn't get beat up. That kind of thing happened downtown in back alleys. "I made a mistake, Anna." My voice broke up. "I locked him out."

She faced me upright. "What is *wrong* with you?"

"He's doing the best he can." I echoed Mama's appeasements.

"I'm so scared." Her voice quivered. She started to sob again. "I wanna go home!"

"Wait! I've got a hiding place. Grab your pillow." I pulled an afghan blanket out and took the flashlight.

She calmed down and hooked her hand inside my elbow. As soundless as ghosts in white nightgowns, we moved through the minefield of glass shards. I glanced at Father's bedroom door. A dim light suggested he might be awake. We tiptoed past it and headed down the basement stairs.

Once inside the cellar pantry, we were out of earshot. "Here it is—the fruit closet. He doesn't know about it." While she held the flashlight, I slid the inner door to one side. "You can't tell anyone. Wyeth'll kill me."

We climbed over the storage boxes. I pushed the orange crate to one side to arrange our bedding on the floor. She spotlighted the ceiling, searching for spiders.

"Don't worry. I cleaned them out already."

She offered a feeble smile.

I jiggled the door back in place and covered the flashlight with a Styrofoam cup. It made a perfect nightlight. We settled in, spooning with bent knees.

"I'm still afraid," Anna Rae whispered.

"Wait until first light. He'll sleep late." I pushed the blanket under her chin. "You can pack up then."

"I don't think I can sleep."

"We can try. We're safe down here."

Two floors above us, Tuck seemed far away. Good thing I'd turned on his box fan. White noise helped him sleep through almost anything.

"I'm thirsty, Rissy." Her body shivered.

Anna didn't deserve to be scared or cold or even thirsty. I'd risk almost anything to make things okay for her.

"You stay put." I grabbed the cup over the flashlight and paused to listen. The house seemed quiet. *Could I make it to the kitchen without stirring Father?* I wiggled out through the opening.

Then it dawned on me—gallons of distilled water were right there on the pantry shelf.

I unscrewed the lid from one and poured the cup half full. Angling my shoulder back through the closet door, I handed her the drink. She gulped a huge swallow and immediately spewed the rest. The cup fell from her hands.

"What's the matter?"

"It's poisoned!" She spat and choked, fighting for air.

The water did smell weird. "Maybe it's old." It had been down here for years.

"Am I gonna die?" Her eyes filled.

"You spit it all out."

"No, no! I swallowed some!"

The floor above us creaked. Someone crossed the kitchen. Adrenaline surged. I slipped in the rest of the way and pulled the door shut.

"Be quiet!" I said, turning off the flashlight.

The movement overhead stopped. Father had probably heard us. The basement door opened. My stomach jumped with fright. Someone stood at the top of the stairs. I could feel his presence. Anna concealed her face in a pillow, muting her coughs. It didn't help. He started down the stairs anyway.

"Shhh. Don't even breathe!"

The pressure in my lungs became excruciating. He entered the cellar pantry, pulling the chain on the overhead light bulb. It made a grinding-chink sound. I grit my teeth. Through the bottom slit of the fruit closet door, shadows moved inches from our bodies on the other side of the plywood. I saw the soles of his shoes. The silence of his listening was dreadful. Any sound, any movement, any slip up and we were had. Every muscle in my body braced for the blows I imagined would come in a matter of seconds.

"Rissy? Are you down here?" It was Wyeth.

My heart burst. "For crying out loud! You scared us to death!"

He moved the door to one side. "What are you ding-dongs doin'?"

"Never mind! Turn off the light!"

He pulled the chain, and our eyes adjusted to the nightlight.

"Where have you been?" I felt drenched with sweat.

"I've been *out*, but then it started raining. I don't have a

154

curfew, see, 'cause as far as he's concerned, it's good riddance!"

"What do you mean?" I asked.

"Don't be a *bird* brain. You know we butt heads." He gnawed on a Pop Tart. "The less we see of each other, the better. It's sort of an unspoken truce." Wyeth licked his lips. "I just came home to eat."

"Don't you *dare* leave me and Tuck alone anymore!" I clenched his sweatshirt in my fists.

"Hey now. Settle down." He turned away to break free. "What's going on anyhow? The living room's a mess."

"Father didn't come home till after 2:00. I didn't know what to do. I thought he'd have a key. He went crazy on me 'cause I locked him out."

"What happened to the lamp?"

"He kicked it."

"*And* he slapped her real hard," Anna added.

"What?" Wyeth seemed alarmed.

Anna and I sat in the shadowy closet. He leaned in to take a closer look. "Have you guys been crying?"

I didn't answer.

"He also poisoned the water," she continued.

"Now, hold on!" he said.

I rambled all the facts in short order. "Anna freaked, and I didn't want her running home in the dark. We came here to hide. She got thirsty, so I opened this jug of water, but it's gone bad."

"Slow down! Distilled water doesn't go bad. Let me see it." He grabbed the plastic gallon and smelled the opening. Shaking his head, he winced. "It's booze, you fools. Straight-up alcohol." Wyeth took a drink. "Probably vodka."

"So, I'm *not* gonna die." Anna slumped with relief.

"I wondered where the old geezer kept his stash. He's been drinking hard since Mama died." Wyeth smirked. "Ain't a secret no more!"

My mind swelled with realization. No wonder he stayed out late most nights. On Christmas Eve, he'd had a whole gallon next to him on the couch. And that explained his grumpiness on Christmas, the Alka-Seltzer, and..."Oh no," I stammered.

"What now?" Wy screwed the lid back on, wiping his mouth on his sleeve.

"I killed the Christmas tree."

"What does that have to do with anything?" He tilted his head.

"I watered it with vodka."

"So I *am* gonna die!" Anna shrieked.

"NO!" we said in unison.

Then we all hushed—still as death. Upstairs, a toilet flushed.

Chapter 25

Nothing more happened that night. We packed Anna's
things, and she hightailed it home just before daybreak.
Sluggish from lack of sleep, I moved by sheer will. My legs felt
heavy. The shag carpet seemed thicker. I swept up broken glass on
the wood floor and handpicked slivers out of the rug using a
flashlight to find their glint. With Father still asleep, vacuuming
was out of the question. After folding our bedding, I dragged the
furniture back in place and even screwed in new light bulbs. For
Tuck's sake, I erased any trace of trouble.

Through the front windows, a pickup truck splash through
patches of melting slush. Its headlights flashed in my eyes as it
turned. Overcast clouds made the day feel like night, but blue sky
was coming. Our house remained quiet. It was only 7:45. I trudged
upstairs and crawled into bed. The pillow felt cool on my cheek.

Soon, a small hand jiggled my arm. The clock read 8:11. I'd
just fallen asleep. Groaning, I turned away.

Tuck shuffled to the other side. "Rissy?" His blinking eyes and
freckled face emerged inches from mine. His nose-breath smelled
sweet. "Why'd you paint your face red and purple?"

Longing for more sleep, I wasn't really listening. "Sure." I said,
hoping he'd go away.

He edged up on the bed's sideboard to examine me closer.
"*Your cheek has colors.*"

I checked his expression. You'd have thought I was a big hairy spider. He stared at me with narrowed eyes, and his mouth formed a tiny little hole.

Your cheek has colors. His words rolled around in my mind until they registered. I jolted upright, hiding my cheek with a few locks of hair. "Oh that!" My skin felt puffy and hot. "It must be a bruise, yes—I bumped into something."

"Into what?"

"Well see, that's the thing..." I fake laughed. "I'm not exactly sure because it was dark. I couldn't see where I was going." Moving my jaw brought sharp pains.

"That's a berr-ry baaad owhee." He glanced away. "I'm hungry."

The phone rang. I swung my feet out. "Hold on." I hurried to the hall phone and lifted the receiver. "Hello?"

"Yes, is this Dr. Somerset's number?"

I cleared my voice. "Yes, Ma'am."

"Well, I'm waiting at his office with my boy, Charlie. We came right on the dot at 8:00 to get that new night brace thingy, and the door's locked—meaning he ain't here. And now I'm gonna be late to..."

"Sorry to interrupt—but—my father's sick." It was all I could think of to say.

"Why didn't he call?"

"I guess he didn't know he'd be sick." I sounded a bit snippy.

"Well somebody better make some calls, or there'll be a load of angry folks down here before you can say snap-crackle-pop!"

She hung up abruptly.

Fatigue draped over me like a heavy coat. I pulled on some jeans and then carefully stretched the t-shirt hole over my sore face.

"C'mon," I said to Tuck. "Let's go have us a big ol' bowl of Cheerios." I motioned him to follow, trying to act cheerful. Once settled at the breakfast table, Tuck spooned clumps of Os into his mouth and studied the back of the cereal box.

I sprayed PAM oil on the hinges of Father's bedroom door. Pops had taught me that trick. I opened it silently and eyed his room through the crack. A slice of sun cut through the drapes, crossing Father's back in a blazing line. He laid diagonally in bed, clothes on—shoes and all. If not for his snoring, I'd have thought he was dead.

I leaned in to get a better look. The entire room smelled of what I now recognized as alcohol. He rustled a little. My heart jumped. Should I tell him about the phone call? I backed away from the door. Writing a note had its risks too. I imagined his re-action—"*Why didn't you wake me up!*" It was a pay-it-now-or-later choice. But after last night, I couldn't face him.

I found a lined notepad. It took several minutes to get it right—urgency without scolding. A PATIENT CALLED. Not specific enough. CHARLIES'S MOM TELEPHONED. No. Would he know them without their last name? I turned the paper over. IMPATIENT PATIENTS! I shook my head. Too sassy. I needed a new piece of paper. CHARLIE AND MOM AT OFFICE FOR NIGHT BRACE. It would have to do.

I tiptoed into his room, holding my breath. After setting his alarm for 8:30, I laid the note next to it and slipped out quick as a rabbit. It was 8:27.

"C'mon Buddy. Let's get some air."

"I haven't finished my Cheerios."

"Just come." I sounded firm.

The phone rang again. I ran to catch it before the second ring.

"Somersets," I said, sounding vexed.

"*Yes, this is Mr. Thomlin. Is Dr. Somerset there?*"

"He's sick."

"*I see. My daughter had an 8:15 appointment. Can you reschedule?*"

"No, but I'll tell him." I shrugged, trying to shake off the heaviness. I jotted another note. PLEASE CALL MR. TOM LYNN. It was 8:28. No sooner had I hung up, when the phone rang again.

I pressed my lips together and blinked hard. "Yes?"

"*Hello, honey. How's everything?*" A lady's voice tweeted happily.

"Just swell." I had no idea who she was.

"*I'm calling from the church to remind Dr. Somerset about the committee meeting at 7:00 tonight.*"

"Okay." I couldn't stand it. She twittered away, as I quietly put the receiver on the base. It was rude, but we had to get out of there. The kitchen clock said 8:29. I scribbled: COMEDY MEETING

AT SEVEN and shoved both messages under Father's door right when his alarm went off.

Pulling Tuck by the shoulder, I steered him toward the backdoor. He clutched his bowl as I grabbed our jackets and a rain poncho. We paused only to slip on our shoes before heading around the corner of the garage.

I made a place for us, laying the poncho on heavily dewed grass. The cloud cover had broken up, but the air carried a morning chill. I zipped up Tuck's coat. Fortunately, the sunny east side of the garage captured enough warmth. Mr. Kibbs often stretched out along the same wall to bask in winter sunshine. Still, I was shivering.

The phone rang again. My heart beat hard and fast. Father finally answered by the thirteenth ring. I should've turned on the answering machine. Though muted by walls, his tone sounded gruff.

We couldn't avoid facing him forever. I looked at my little brother. His shining eyes and perfect skin looked beautiful in the sunlight. He had no idea what was really going on. I wiped his milky mouth with my sleeve.

"You stay right here and watch for Kibby." I said. "He didn't show up last night. If we don't get him home, he might go wild on us." A weird feeling moved through my stomach. *Go wild on us.*

"Kitty likes this spot," I said. "I'll be back in a minute."

"Where you going?" Tuck asked.

"To get some baloney—we'll lure him in."

"Oh-kaaay. But I'm co-old." He didn't sound happy about the assignment.

I slinked around the corner to eavesdrop. No sounds. I stuck my head inside the door. Shower water was running. I snuck to the fridge and pulled out a round slice of meat. Father probably wondered where we were. I quickly penciled another note: TUCK AND I WALKING ANNA HOME. Lying had become so easy.

Back outside, I placed tiny pieces of baloney a foot apart, making a Hansel-and-Gretel trail that led to Tuck. He stooped with his jacket pulled over his knees, waiting for Kibbs. I waited for the sound of Father's car.

At last the front door slammed. He slowly backed out the driveway. It took forever. Finally, the muffler gurgled when he stepped on the gas. I leaned against the garage wall, exhausted. A tear crept down my cheek. The sun darted in and out of the clouds.

Within minutes, our kitty showed up. Tuck pounced on him, startling the poor thing. He scolded Kibbs for wanting to run away. Of course the cat didn't grasp why he was in trouble, when in fact he really wasn't. I felt the same. I thought about Father's shaky finger pointed in my face. What would the day bring?

Tuck was expected at the Peate's around 9:30. I found fresh clothes for him, though the shirt and pants didn't match. While he dressed, I packed his favorite books, some Old Maid cards, a box of raisins, and a warmer jacket in his small Bugs Bunny backpack. They'd feed him lunch. Hand in hand, we strolled to the end of our driveway and glanced both ways. He stepped into the street, but I hesitated, remembering my bruised face.

"C'mon." He glanced back at me. "There aren't any cars."

"You're big enough to go on your own."

"I am?" His face became animated with surprise.

"Yes. I'll watch till you get there."

He crossed the street with a skip in his stride and a hopped up on the other curb. Then he turned and winked. I winked back and waved. He spun happily with arms up high and trotted the rest of the way. When Mrs. Peate opened the front door, I turned my back.

Tuck's pure *muffin*-ness had lifted my spirits. I smiled briefly, though I wanted to hide in a closet and cry my eyes out. Tears gathered. I wandered back to the house. *What's going to happen to us? If only Skeets would come.*

I'd been clenching my teeth and now my jaw pulsed with pain. I knew where to find aspirin, but didn't bother. Only parents could distribute medicine—one of Father's rules. Any resolve to keep everything together was fading. I buried my face in my arms at the breakfast table and eventually fell sound asleep.

Wyeth stumbled into the kitchen. He flicked my head. "What's happening, Big Pony?"

I heard him pour something in a glass, but didn't look up.

"Short on sleep, I see." He slid into the chair across from me, guzzling his drink. "Cheerios for breakfast—*again*?" He laughed. His solution to father was avoidance, and clearly it was working for him. He seemed chipper as a finch in a birdbath on a spring day.

I raised my head, wincing from the crick in my neck. I'd been slumped over for hours. The clock showed it was almost noon! Crusty particles itched the corners of my eyes.

As I met Wyeth's gaze, his eyes widened. "Holy Cow, Iris!" He jumped to his feet. "Have you looked in the mirror?"

"N-no."

He came around the table to get a closer view, and then marched me to the hall mirror. I stood in shock. My left eye was totally bloodshot. A fat lip jutted out and deep red and purple splotches covered my cheek.

"*He* did *this?*" Wyeth asked, in a loud voice that made my head throb.

I stared at my reflection and nodded. Tears watered my eyes. *Who was this girl looking back at me?* I'd had my share of scrapes and tumbles, but nothing like this.

"That's it!" He stomped in a war dance around the room. "Never mind that he ran off on Mama and she died! It doesn't matter that he makes you do everything. Does he even care? *No!*" He shoved a chair. "All he cares about are his ridiculous rules! And now, he comes home stinking drunk and slaps you *that* hard? He can go to hell for all I care!"

"Stop it Wyeth!" I covered my ears and ran to my bed.

His rant continued as he followed me up the stairs. "I'll fight him if I have to! I will, *I swear it!*"

I rolled under the covers toward the foot of my bed.

He found my head and yanked back the comforter. "We're running away, Rissy," he said in a low voice that didn't sound like my brother. He slid off the bed, still muttering about his plan.

A hopeful thought formed. *What would it be like to leave? Was it crazy talk? Could we find a way to live apart from Father?* I imagined the possibility.

Chapter 26

GRADUALLY, I OPENED my eyes. Who knew where Wyeth had gone? The afternoon sun had overheated my room. I peeled back the sheet. It was almost 4 p.m. Tuck would return in half an hour and soon after that, Father.

I peered into the bathroom mirror. My bruises felt tender. Blood vessels streaked my left eye, but my lips seemed a little less swollen. I lifted cool water to my face.

Wearily, I headed to my chair. My Bible lay open on the seat. I picked it up. God had said He knew about my deep sighing. I think He meant all the time and anywhere, not just under my bed. If there was ever a moment to hear from God, it was now. I didn't have time to wait for something magical to happen. My uncle's words came back to me. *Write down anything that stirs you as you read, when you feel a flutter inside.* I scanned the open text on page 547. My eyes jumped around the page. Some words came alive with meaning. How could God know?

> *My soul yearns for thee in the night,*
> *My spirit within me earnestly seeks thee...*
> *For thou hast been...a stronghold to the needy in his distress,*
> *A shelter from the storm and a shade from the heat;*
> *For the blast of the ruthless is like a storm against a wall...*
> *And the Lord God will wipe away tears from all faces...*

Thou dost keep him in perfect peace,
Whose mind is stayed on thee,
Because he trusts in thee."

I sifted out those particular phrases, skipping other ones with terms like "scorched" or "languishing"—believing God wanted to comfort me. Maybe that was cheating.

The chapter was called, "Song of Trust." A quiet calm settled on me. Thoughts about our broken family started to lose their terrifying power. I closed my eyes. *Perfect peace*, like lying in a field of flowers.

Then, unexpectedly, I envisioned a vast scene. The picture appeared blurry except near the center where a small circle formed a magnifying lens. Everything in the circle was perfectly clear—lush grass, mossy tree trunks, and pussy willows. It reminded me of the Middle Strip. The image lasted only a few seconds. I felt intrigued. A clear circle...a magnifying glass...*focus*! In an instant, the verse and the vision merged. *Perfect peace, whose mind is stayed on thee, because he trusts in thee.*

"It's over now. No more of this crap!" Wyeth shouted downstairs. Even at a distance, his rage rattled me. I made my way down the steps.

Empty distilled water jugs were scattered all over the kitchen floor.

"What are you doing?" I yelled.

"We're exposing him!" he shouted, dumping another gallon of vodka down the sink. "It's the only way!"

"He'll get you for this—he'll get *us*!" Terror shot through my body.

"No he won't, 'cause we won't be here! Besides, this is the last one." He threw the empty container against the wall. "What's done is done."

"He's coming in less than hour—what then?" My voice cracked.

"I don't know." He paused for a moment. "We'll stay the first night in the Middle Strip. I'll grab sleeping bags. You find a couple cans of baked beans and deviled ham—anything we don't have to cook," he said.

"And where will that get us?" Spit flew from my mouth as I shouted. Had he forgotten it was March?

"All three of us missing?" Wyeth laughed with contempt. "It'll shock him good!"

"No, no!" I put my hands over my ears.

"*What* don't you get?" He pulled my arms down. "You're the one with the bruises!"

"We can't leave!" I shrieked back. "We're children! We have no money!"

"We'll walk to Akron—to see Nana and Pops. I'm calling them right now." He tried to sound calm and logical. "It'll take us a week—enough time to get the cops off our trail."

At that point I sank to the floor, completely dissolved in tears.

"Oh, c'mon! Don't be a sissy!" He shook me hard. "Crap!" he said, kicking a few empty jugs across the room in frustration.

The walls closed in like quicksand. Images of Tuck, hungry and cold, wandering in darkness, no place to sleep, I couldn't take it.

Wyeth finally knelt down next to me. "Rissy," he said, gently. "Talk to me."

It took awhile for me to speak. I hadn't felt that raw since Mama died. I wiped my eyes with the neckline of my shirt. My words staggered out.

"We—*need*—to be a family..."

He listened, waiting for me to finish.

"For Tuck."

"But you, me, and Tucky will always be a family," he said, searching for a Kleenex.

"But Nana—and Pops—can't take us!" I cried.

"I *know* that. It'd be temporary." He handed me a paper napkin.

I couldn't breathe through my nose at all. The peace I'd experienced upstairs had vanished. Yet, at that precise moment, I heard a voice—clear and serene. *Iris Rose...* It felt as if Skeets had entered the room and placed a hand on my shoulder. I blew my nose and suddenly felt brave enough to resist Wyeth's wild plans.

My brother sat cross-legged, lost in thought.

"Wy, listen to me." I took his arm. "If we lose Father—we'll lose each other too." I shook my head left and right. "Don't you see? It happened to Mama."

"Mama? What are you talking about?"

"When her real parents died—she also lost her sister." I dried my cheeks.

"*Sister!*" Wyeth's eyes crunched into slits. "What sister?"

"Nana told me the sister went to a different family. Mama never knew her." I faced him squarely. "Don't you get it? Kids don't have a say. We could lose each other!"

My words visibly settled on Wyeth like a weight around his neck. He stared at me with parted lips. Just then, the front door opened. *Father.* My heart catapulted in my chest. Surrounded by empty plastic jugs, there was no time to run. How would we explain?

Tuck toddled into the kitchen. "I'm home." He said the obvious, but it got me thinking. *Home*—yes. Dorothy learned that the hard way in Oz.

"Yes, we are all home now," I echoed back, staring at my big brother.

Wyeth lowered his chin.

"Not yet. Daddy's not here." Tuck's inclusive love pained me. Wyeth and I sat in sheepish silence.

"You look scary," Tuck said to me. "What's this?" He pointed to the containers.

"We're—spring-cleaning, that's all," I said.

Wyeth huffed. "Right."

"When's Daddy comin' home?" Tuck asked.

His simple question grabbed me by the collar and shook the living daylights out of me. Wy and I jumped into high gear, throwing empty jugs out the back door.

"Soon Tucky, real soon," I said. "You help Wy."

I pulled Banquet Chicken from the freezer and turned the oven to the highest setting. After quickly arranging the strips on a cookie sheet, I slid them into the cold oven. The little white timer wasn't on the spice shelf. A frenzied search brought no results.

Next, I vacuumed any remaining glass splinters from the carpet, until the crackling sound stopped. Then I windexed muddy cat prints off the table and set out some silverware.

Out back, the boys were pouncing on the containers to collapse them. They made such a racket I could barely stand it. Father could pull up any second.

"Hey, keep it down!" I shouted to Wyeth. "Where you gonna hide 'em?"

"In the old Chevy. He won't look there!"

It would have to do. I dumped frozen lima beans and corn in a saucepan, adding some water. The burner wouldn't light. I used a match. Meanwhile, I buttered some stale rolls and surveyed the room. Everything was almost ready.

A small bouquet of plastic daisies on the bookshelf caught my eye. I used it as a centerpiece. Digging around in the linen drawer I found three candles. One was half-used, yet it matched the other two and fit nicely in a ceramic candle base I'd made for Mama at school. She often lit three candles when praying for us.

The clock said 5:18. It was a miracle Father had not yet walked through the door.

I glanced in the hall mirror to check my face. My heart dropped. I ran to find Mama's makeup in her bathroom drawer. Father had thrown it all away. I had to improvise. Calamine lotion might work. I blended it into my skin. When it dried, I took a cotton ball and patted talcum powder on my face. Hoping to hide the bruises, the cover-up made me appear deathly ill. Not sure what was worse.

I scrambled to the front door, listening for the muffler. Nothing. I stepped outside to check. Only a few kids on bikes circling a yapping dog. Back in the kitchen, Wyeth and Tuck sat at the table with their hungry faces on. Wyeth's expression turned blank when he saw my face.

"You guys are a mess! Go wash first," I said. They left for the bathroom.

The matchbook had one match left. I lit the three candles. "Mama, if you can see us, please pray." My voice quivered. I steeled myself, fighting back tears. The last thing I needed were wet lines down my powdered cheeks. "The chicken!" I opened a smoking oven to rescue the singed chicken strips.

Wyeth coached Tuck in the hallway. "Whatever happens, don't say anything about her face. She's using makeup now. Girls are touchy about stuff like that."

The boys settled in. I served up our plates. Tuck lowered his chin and stared at me on the sly. Wyeth nudged him, but he didn't quit. It was 5:35.

"Are we gonna eat or what?" Wyeth asked.

"I think we should wait a bit." Everything had to be perfect when Father walked in. "Just a few more minutes."

The boys moaned.

"Chicken's too hot anyways." I added.

Wy watched the clock. The second hand ticked its way around the dial three times. Then he lifted his fork and started eating. Tuck did too. I had no appetite.

SIX O'CLOCK CAME, then seven. The smaller candle burned out. The boys had finished supper long ago and were watching a rerun of *Happy Days.* Fonzie was my older brother's idol. Wyeth always acted like a greaser afterwards. Normally I would've teased him.

"Exactamundo!" said The Fonz, followed by phony audience laughter. I rested my head on the table, staring past my cold food.

The distant rumble of Father's car grew louder.

I bolted straight up in my chair. "*He's here*," I said, breathlessly.

Wyeth flipped off the TV. "C'mon Tucky. Lets go read comic books. I got a new *Human Fly.*" They hurried up to Wyeth's room.

I didn't know if it was better or harder to face Father alone. Maybe less complicated, but still frightening. I tried to take slow deep breaths as I microwaved his dinner. The steaming food looked shriveled and unappetizing. The sound of heavy shoes on the front steps told me I didn't have time to reheat my dinner. I quickly returned to my place, sitting with my back to the front entrance. With one elbow on the table, I covered the bruises with my left hand.

He entered and closed the door quietly. I bowed my head, picturing his movements from the sounds. *God help me.* After hanging up his coat, he strolled toward the table. I felt his eyes looking over the dinner table scene. The two remaining candles had melted down to stubs. I sensed him standing right behind me, a few feet away. Was he remembering the night before? My thoughts galloped out of control.

He stepped over to examine his dinner plate and let out a faint groan. I felt his disappointment. He sat down and picked up his fork, poking at his food. I took fleeting glances to check his mood. His face looked sickeningly pale. Finally he cut a bite of chicken but stopped chewing after a moment. He gaped at me.

I couldn't swallow, blink, or move, wondering what might happen next. He laid down his fork and reached for me. I leaned back slightly. He waited for me to relax. Then tenderly, he pulled my hand from my face. I looked down. Blood rushed in all my veins. How could the man who did this, touch me now so softly? I felt a different kind of pain. A love and hate so strong I thought my heart would rupture.

He studied my face. Some of the talcum powder came off on his fingers. He rubbed them together. Slumping back in his chair, he lowered his head, covered his face, and wept with deep sobs. His lungs heaved for air.

Until that moment, I'd never actually seen my father cry out loud.

My tears came too. The dam had burst, probably from relief. I don't really know how much time went by. Eventually he stood and went to his bedroom without a single word. That was the hardest part for me. I wanted him to say something—anything. I needed him to tell me everything would be all right. I longed for his gentle touch. Instead, he shut his door.

I blew out the two remaining candles and dumped our food in the trash.

Chapter 27

IN THE FOLLOWING days and weeks, I told teachers, neighbors and friends that I'd been in a bike wreck. My fib became quite elaborate. I described how Kibby had jumped out of the bushes in front of me. Swerving to miss him, I smacked into a tree. The force chucked me over the handlebars into the hammock, which helped break my fall. That part was miraculous, I knew. Still in motion, I flipped out of the hammock, and that's when my face met an Adirondack chair in a most unpleasant way. It all happened very fast, I explained. Tuck gave me a squinty look—aware that I had changed my story.

Father discovered his vodka was missing. To our surprise, no hot molten tirade came down on us—no blaming or threatening. Instead he silently went to work and came home day after day. But his eyes seemed like dark empty holes.

The next few months, I felt strapped into a Tilt-a-Whirl. At times, Father went to bed and didn't get up for several days. Sometimes it lasted a week. I could see it coming. Usually the day before, he'd forget to shave or comb his hair. He'd also get grouchy about little things like the TV volume. Sometimes he'd panic over misplaced glasses and accuse us of hiding them. My stomach felt full of rocks.

When he stayed in bed, he didn't want to be bothered. I fielded phone calls, keeping a tidy list. Some of them hung up on me, though I did my best to sound secretarial. Any food or drink I left inside his bedroom door went untouched.

Tuck didn't believe my lame excuse that Father was ill again. "He can't be sick *all* the time!" He'd plop down on the floor next to Father's door to listen, angling his small body this way and that. Sometime he'd lay flat to peer under the door. He should've been kicking a ball in the yard or catching beetles. Instead he fidgeted there like a bird scavenging for picnic table scraps.

Wyeth stayed out of the way. He could barely conceal his mounting hatred. They rarely crossed paths. When Father asked him to do an extra chore, he'd snarl under his breath or kick a wall when our dad walked out of earshot. Once Father told him to "Shape up!" My brother got so livid his eyes bulged and his nostrils flared. I knew in that moment that Wyeth had become all *horse*, or maybe *mule*, if such variations existed in Nana's game. There was no *muffin* left in him.

When things were tense, Father retreated to his room. After a time, the heaviness would pass. The sound of running water in Father's shower signaled the first sign of normal life. My heart would rise. He'd come out of seclusion with a shiny scrubbed face, smelling like aftershave.

In anticipation, I'd prepare anything in the cupboards I could find. Instant Folgers was better than no coffee, and Tang substituted for orange juice. Toasted English muffins with jam spread to perfection worked fine as long as I checked for bread mold. He'd scarf it all down in a matter of minutes. I'd watch him, pretending to be busy. Afterwards, Father would pat my head as he went out the door.

That pat meant everything. My whole day felt sunnier. I'd hum at the sink while scrubbing breakfast dishes. But crazy times soon returned.

Father came home one day with three large boxes of Jockey underwear. He said he got a "remarkable deal." I wondered how on earth he'd stuff them in his dresser. He'd never wear them all out, even if he lived to be a hundred.

Another time after supper, he jabbered away on the phone using phrases like "high rate of return" or "small initial investment," selling something to unknown people. He had a whole speech memorized that included funny jokes, important statistics and a sales pitch at the end.

"Hey, that guy liked my *spiel!*" he said after hanging up. I nodded and ran upstairs to look up the word spiel. Before I returned, he'd already placed another call, gesturing wildly with his free hand. Some nights he droned on and on. I'd have to plug in the box fan upstairs. Otherwise, I couldn't sleep. What on earth was he selling? It couldn't be underwear.

During what seemed like better times, Father would do other strange things like jogging late at night. One time I waited in the dark hall, wondering what would happen. Where was he going? The night was pitch black. It replayed dreadful memories. I didn't dare lock the door. Hours ticked by. My eyelids grew heavy.

Later, his footsteps startled me. I darted behind a chair, trying hard to be calm. He entered quietly and locked the door. The clock said 1:13. He'd been gone for over three hours.

In other phases, he'd eat and drink weird things like Swiss cheese and grape jelly sandwiches. The worst was peanut butter and baloney on raisin bread. For a while he became a complete vegetarian, but later added raw eggs to milkshakes and swallowed a pile of vitamins every day.

Wyeth summed it up. "Hank gits some harebrained idea and goes ballistic wid it." It bothered me that Wy had started to call our dad by his first name. Of course he didn't say it to his face, but it still felt testy, even reckless.

One Saturday, Father was chatting away on the phone. He marched back and forth as far as the cord would allow, talking too loud and laughing at the same old jokes. Any patience I'd mustered day in day out had dried up, and my whole body fumed with anger. I wanted to yell, "Stop it! Just *stop* it and *be—our—dad!*" But if he asked me to explain myself, what would I say? I pictured his hawk-like eyes darting to and fro, waiting for my answer.

Leaving the house was the only way to avoid blurting something I'd regret. I grabbed the dusty library book under my bed and a few dollars to pay the fine.

TAKING TUCK TO LIBRARY. I left the note on the kitchen table. Once outside, the fresh air felt soft. Tuck had to take extra steps to keep up with my death march. After a few blocks, my temper melted away.

Tomorrow was the beginning of June. I felt numb thinking about the anniversary of Mama's death—still a month away.

Maybe after this long year of sorrow, I could finally enjoy the 4th of July holiday.

We happened to see Anna Rae on the way. She waved us down and ran over. "I have good news!" She bent over to catch her breath. "Huntington Beach is opening soon. My parents said I'm old enough to ride my bike there!"

"Great," I said, not really caring.

She checked my expression. "Well, what do *you* want to do this summer?"

I looked down at Tuck, who'd found a cupcake in the grass. It still had a birthday candle stuck in the frosting.

"I want to have a normal day." I paused, biting my lower lip. "You know," I continued. "Like people who go on picnics."

"Who's having a picnic?"

"No one I know." I looked up at the sky.

A few awkward seconds passed.

"My daddy's taking me to get the brakes fixed on my bike. He's gonna get me a horn so I can warn people I'm comin..." She jabbered on and on, but I only half-listened. "...And he's even buying me streamers for my handle bars!"

I felt stuck on an island far away. My lips stiffened, as I tried to hold in my feelings. "Swell."

Tuck had picked up the cupcake.

I grabbed his little mitt. "Leave it buddy. The ants got it first." I turned to Anna. "Gotta go."

She stood in the same spot until we turned on Elmwood Road toward the library.

As we entered the building, I lifted my index finger to my lips, reminding Tuck to be quiet. We passed the Resource Desk and climbed the stairs to the second floor where they stacked picture books in bins. We first came to a large birdcage by the reading room where a half dozen finches happily tittered and fussed about. They were building nests in tiny hanging baskets, fighting over strips of cotton. We watched them for a little while, and then Tuck ran to throw himself on a giant beanbag chair. I searched the bins for some new bedtime stories.

Flipping through the choices, I came to a book with a teddy bear on the cover. Tuck would be all about that. I skimmed the pages. The story told of a little girl who went to bed without her favorite bear. She thought about calling her mom but remembered she had a flashlight. On each page, she scanned different places in her room searching for her bear. Everything in her bedroom looked fuzzy, except where she pointed her light. The beam formed a perfect circle of light.

All at once, I remembered the blurry landscape and the magnifying lens I'd seen in a daydream, months ago. Electricity zinged through my body. Was God speaking to me in the library? I leafed through the pages to the end where the girl finally found her teddy. For the longest time, I stared at her bear in the lighted circle.

Focus on Me. The word floated down serenely like feathers landing on my head and shoulders. My skin rippled with tiny pinpricks. I blinked a few times and glanced around the room, moving only my eyes. Curiously, all the birds in the cage were completely still, and their heads pointed in my direction. Did they see something I couldn't see? Was God actually in the room? No one else seemed to notice. But I felt it. Something was there. Someone. I stayed motionless.

Eyes on Me...perfect peace.

On the way home, we played Waterbaby. Tuck wanted to skip ahead.

"Hey, hold up Spanky." I stopped and knelt down. Tuck traipsed back, and I showed him the place where a triple "W" had been carved in the slate sidewalk. "Wyeth *always* forgets this one. You can really score if you remember."

Tuck grinned ear to ear. We continued on, slower now, watching for more W's.

A twisted knot inside my gut had unraveled. I felt lighter and walked along in a blissful way. The feeling grew and pulsed out to my fingers and toes. I started to sing.

"Swing low, sweet chariot-ot...Comin' for to carry me home."

Tuck, still looking for W's, padded behind.

"Sw-ing low, sweet chariot-ot...Comin' for to carry me home." I wagged my finger at him. "I-I looked over Jordan, and what did I see-ee?"

"Comin' for to carry me home." Tuck caught up, singing the only part he knew.

Flapping my arms like wings, I circled him. "A band of angels comin' after me-ee." I swooped in and planted a kiss on his head.

He pushed me away, giggling. "Comin' for to carry me home."

Then I whistled the refrain. We strolled along happily, until I noticed the faintest one-note sound coming from Tuck. At first I thought he was humming. He'd lowered his chin, but I could see his puckered lips. I squatted down on eye level.

"Hey!" I said.

He was trying so hard. Out came an airy sounding note. With shrugged shoulders, he offered a shy smile.

I clapped for joy. "You're whistling!"

Chapter 28

Tuck practiced whistling in the coat closet. I cringed, thinking Wy had teased him. Then again, Father's grimaces could put a kibosh on just about anything. I suggested he go outside to work on it.

Warm weather finally arrived and lemonade stands popped up overnight. Anna Rae and I sold flavored ice cubes on toothpicks. We started with grape juice ones and added Tang to our selection. A & W Root Beer cubes became a surprise hit, but the Mountain Dew ones were wildly popular with Wy's friends. June had been unusually hot, and sales were hopping.

Beaconsfield's Fourth of July Parade always had a theme, and this year it was "Honoring Our Heritage." As a tribute to our ancestors, Anna Rae and I thought it best to look, dress and walk like old women. I pulled a box of cornstarch from the cupboard.

"This'll do," I said to Anna. Tuck joined us as we rummaged around the house, thinking up our costumes. We told Wyeth we'd concede and let him be an outlaw instead of an old farmer. He refused unless we agreed to hand over half the prize money. First place guaranteed the winner twenty-five bucks.

"Otherwise, you fools," he said, "It's embarrassing! I'm a teenager now."

"No way! You only get a fourth," I countered. "Fair is fair."

He ditched us.

I drew wrinkle lines on Anna's face with a magic marker, and she drew mine. We made long skirts from old ruffled curtains and added shawls to look like prairie grannies. As a finishing touch, we massaged cornstarch into our hair over the kitchen sink and then used bobby pins to shape our dusted locks into small buns. It proved to be a messy ordeal.

I wanted Tuck to be Johnny Appleseed, but he stuck out his lower lip. Action figures had taken over boy-world. Some kind of *Gunsmoke* getup would have to do. After all, Ohio in earlier times was considered the West. I gave him Wy's cap gun and strapped the holster around his slim waist. He let me whiten his hair.

"You're the town sheriff now," I said, duct-taping an aluminum foil star to his shirt. "You gotta protect us from wild critters—especially snakes and coyotes." I topped him off with a straw cowboy hat. "No shootin' people, okay?" He squinted at me.

Outside, we fitted our red Radio Flyers with TV tray tables, forming the basic structure for a covered wagon. An old twin sheet previously used as a ghost costume worked perfectly for the covers. We cut the material in half. My wagon cover had two eyeholes, which we thought was rather funny, but it proved useful for spying on coyotes. Any dog would do. Tuck had his cap gun ready.

Our baby dolls wore bonnets and dresses. Anna couldn't resist outfitting her poor old guinea pig as well. Kibbs would have none of it. We swaddled the dolls to cushion their ride in my wagon and placed the guinea pig in an Easter Basket up front. Anna's wagon carried all our supplies—a canteen of water, Ritz crackers, and some unshelled peanuts. We also packed a toy doctor kit with loads of Band-Aids. She roped the wagon handles to our bikes, while I made cardboard horse heads for the handlebars. Finally we pinned signs on the wagon covers. In bright blue letters they said, "Beaconfield's Golden Agers." Anna's mom had come up with the title.

Mrs. Peate crossed the street to check our progress. At first, her eyes didn't blink at all. Then she covered her mouth. I looked at Anna. Perhaps we looked like resurrected ancestors.

At the beginning of the parade, Tuck strutted out in front of us. Anna and I rode sidesaddle, pushing our "horses" forward with our left legs. It was no small feat. We had to stop several times to pull our skirts out of the spokes or switch sides.

Wyeth stood on the curb, mouthing the word "chauney." I stuck out my tongue. He raised his eyebrows in a Groucho Marks way, but I refused to give him the laugh he wanted and stuck my nose in the air. Billy waved from the corner by Mike's Deli. I scanned the crowd, hoping to see Father.

After twenty minutes, Tuck had run out of caps and climbed in with the guinea pig. Anna and I eventually walked our "ponies" to save our skirts. In the end, we won fourth place and got two coupons for free ice cream at Baskin-Robbins. Anna tucked her coupon in her shoe. We sat in the shade to eat crackers and peanuts.

Father never came to the parade. He'd left the house early to do errands and wasn't there to see us receive our award ribbon. He didn't clap for us or snap a picture. He probably wouldn't take us for ice cream either. It was hard feeling invisible. My excitement quickly dwindled as we trailed home.

"You're quiet." Anna Rae noticed. "What's the matter?"

"Nothing." I muttered.

The mess in the kitchen suddenly came to mind. Cornstarch had likely left a film all over the sink. We'd also forgotten to put away markers, scissors, and tape.

"Oh no!" I picked up the pace.

"What's the rush?" Anna hurried along. The wagons bounced hard on the sidewalk cracks, and the wagon cover collapsed on Tuck.

"Whatcha doin' Rissy?" His head poked out from the sheet.

"Hang on, Tucky!" I glanced back to see if everything else was holding together. The guinea pig's bonnet had fallen over its eyes and it started squealing. That frightened my brother, the sheriff. He rolled out of the wagon. One of the dolls jiggled out with him, but Anna scooped it up.

As soon as we turned on our street, a weak, sickening feeling swept over me. Father's Buick sat in our driveway. Anna slowed down too. She grabbed her guinea pig and doll, and turned to go home. Tuck and I pressed on until we reached the house. Dropping my horse-bike on the lawn, I gathered my skirt, mounted the steps, and shoved through the door.

"I'm home! Don't worry!" I shouted. "I'm here to clean up!"

Right in the midst of our clutter, Father sat at the kitchen table reading the paper with his back to me. He didn't reply. My throat tightened. For a moment I stood still, just trying to breathe. Tuck ran in on my heels and collided with me. I gave him a stern look.

As soundless as caterpillars, we crawled around the floor, picking up markers, scissors, and stray bobby pins. Then I stood to wipe the dusty sink.

I heard a chuckle.

"Iris." Father laid down his paper. "Let me see you."

I curved around slowly.

"Hoo-whee, girl! You're lookin' a bit witchy today!" Father was actually amused. No fake sales-call laughs.

I sighed with relief.

"What the heck have you done to yourself?" he said, laughing freely.

I whisked my skirt side to side. "I'm an old-fashioned lady, see? A Golden Ager!" I felt my head for the bun. Wisps of hair had fallen loose. I'm sure I was a dreadful sight.

"And I'm the sheriff, Daddy!" Tuck pulled off his cowboy hat, and a puff of cornstarch plumed in the air.

"Well, I guess you're going to be oldsters for awhile." He fingered the black marker. "It's permanent you know."

I fled to the mirror.

"Don't worry," he hollered, breaking up with laughter. "It'll fade by the time school starts in the fall!"

I tore up the stairs to start a shower. After much shampooing and scrubbing, I had a bright red face with faint gray lines. At least my hair looked normal again. Tuck reluctantly got in the tub.

When we came downstairs, Wyeth stood at the stove frying a thick piece of baloney. My mouth watered.

"It tastes just like a hotdog if you eat it with ketchup and Wonder Bread," he said.

"Where's Father?" I asked.

He pointed to the table. A note said: PERFECT DAY FOR A SAIL. MEET ME AT THE DRY DOCK LIFT AT 3:00.

"I'm not going." Wyeth stated.

"C'mon Wy, you *have* to. Ple-e-ase?" I wondered if the memory of Mama's death would draw us closer as a family or lock us in solitary cells. Wyeth made his sandwich. I added more baloney to the empty pan and laid out two bread slices. He still didn't commit. Using ketchup, I made polka dots on each slice. Then we sat in silence, eating our flat hotdogs.

A whole year had passed. Mama had been at the very same table eating pecan pie—her last meal on earth. I wanted to tell my brothers what God had told me in the school parking lot...and my dream of Mama in her white dress. Would they think I was crazy?

What if I showed them the verses in Zechariah 10, the ones where Ephraim's family passed through a difficult time? How could I explain it? And what about the miracle of finding the cassette tape or the library book? Somehow it all gave me reason to believe God existed. But Tuck was too young to get it. And Wyeth? Well—telling him was entirely unnerving. I couldn't face his mockery.

I missed Mama. Most days I shook off my longing. Today, it flared. But Father had laughed. Tuck whistled, and Wyeth hadn't run away from home—yet. We were still a family.

I smiled a little.

Wyeth stood up and spoke in his friendliest voice. "Allow me to clear the table. Anyone for dessert?" I knew he was angling for ice cream.

I remained silent long enough to make him fidget. His eyebrows curved up, pleading with me. I caved. "You better be nice, *all day.*"

He beamed back.

"It's only one o'clock. Let's go to the pool afterwards," I said, turning toward Tuck. "I'll teach you to sleep on a cloud." I said, referring to a back float. "We'll practice in the shallow end of the pool."

His eyes sparkled.

I quickly scraped our bread crusts into the garbage. At the bottom of the pail was an empty vodka bottle.

Chapter 29

W HEN THE MANAGER of Baskin-Robbins saw my prize-winning coupon and three kids, he brought out one giant bowl with six scoops. Mint chocolate chip for me, rainbow sherbet for Tuck, and Rocky Road for Wy. Cool Whip and maraschino cherries crowned our creamy dreamy dessert. We gorged. I let each spoonful melt slowly on my tongue.

Afterwards, we rode our bikes to the city pool. Wyeth sped ahead, but I glided along with Tuck. His bike still had training wheels. The pool was jammed with kids, but we found an open corner in the shallow end.

"C'mon buddy," I said. "Let's have a try. We don't have much time." I glanced at the pool clock, calculating the time it would take to meet Father at the marina.

Puffing his chest like a baby robin, my little brother held his breath and leaned backwards. I supported him underneath. It took a minute or two, but he finally relaxed. My arms felt the shift in his body. Slowly, I let go and presto! He bobbed on the surface.

"See? It's easy!"

Tuck chuckled and accidentally gulped a swig of water. He crunched into a ball, grabbing me as he sank. I waited for him to get some air. Pool water glittered light across his face. His wet eyelashes were clumped in groups. Still flushed from the bike ride, his skin was as rosy as a freshly picked apple. His lungs filled with air and he arched back, wanting to try once more. I held him, and like magic he floated again.

Wyeth seemed doggedly determined to stand up out of the water on a kickboard. But he was too tall, and the board too small. In some mathematical way, it simply wasn't possible. Tuck imitated him, and with my help, managed to get up for a few seconds. He raised his arms and squealed, "I'm happy as a flea!" as he spun off the foam base.

Wyeth scowled.

We splashed each other, did underwater handstands, and played tag until the lifeguard's whistle signaled Rest Period. Wrapped in towels, we headed for the snack bar. I sprang for fries with money from my ice cube sales. Crisp potato strips came to the counter sizzling hot. I sprinkled them with salt. Wyeth squirted a pool of catsup in each corner of the paper holder, and then we sat on a picnic bench to share them. Something about swimming made me ravenous.

The clock inside the food stand showed it was already 2:30. "We'd better get cracking," I said. Wyeth gave no clue as to whether he'd come sailing or not. Tuck and I dressed, rolling our suits in our towels. I strapped them under the bicycle seats with bungee cords, stalling for my big brother. He didn't come out of the changing room. I dilly-dallied for two extra minutes. Still, no Wyeth. Tuck and I pushed off for the marina without him.

Father had already stepped the mast on our small boat. The fore and backstays were fastened and taut. He must've had help tilting the tall wooden beam into its hole on the deck. The mast was at least two stories high. When we arrived, he was busy attaching two shrouds to each side. All six thick wires kept the mast in place.

Like other dry-dock sailors, we stored our 19-footer on a trailer and used an electric hoist to put it in the calm water of the cove. Renting waterfront space was "outrageously expensive," according to Father. *Outrageous...outrage...rage out.* It was a troubling word. I imagined a cartoon character, spewing out angry words like fiery flames.

Cobwebs veiled the front section of the hull. It had been more than a year since we'd been out for a sail. Father placed a thermos, three Cokes and a bag of pretzels in the cockpit. When I climbed aboard, he tossed me the jib sail bag.

"Remember your figure-eights?" He meant the knot tied at the end of the sheet lines.

"Aye, Captain." I played along.

"Alrighty then," he said. He licked his index finger and held it up to check the wind's direction. He always waited for me to do the same.

I wetted my finger. Our eyes met. We both said, "South" at the same time. An offshore southern breeze offered the smoothest kind of sail. We smiled at each other. As I'd hoped, Father seemed cheerful. On the sailboat he shed his seriousness. Fresh air and rolling waves released him from being the orthodontist, the solemn churchgoer and the strict parent. I loved my father the sailor.

I connected the top of the jib sail to the rope that would raise it up and then latched the bottom corner by the tip of the bow. Both sheet lines had to be worked through the pulleys on each side of the boat. I tied the special knot at their ends. Who in the world decided that a rope should be called a "sheet" in the first place? Probably someone like Wyeth—a person who made things confusing just to be annoying. It was his brand of *bird-horse* trickery.

Father threaded the mainsail into the track on the mast and tightened the outrigger. I wiggled flat wooden battens into their pockets on the sail. Finally ready, Father used the control box with red buttons to hoist our baby-blue boat into the air. Tuck and I rolled the trailer back to its shady spot as our dad lowered the hull into the water. The hot sun beat down on us. I couldn't wait to get out in the cool lake air.

Right then Wy rode up on his Huffy, sliding his wheels sideways in the dirt. I paid no attention, though I smiled inside.

Father didn't notice Wyeth's late arrival—or at least he didn't let on. He was sprawled across the transom, attaching the rudder and tiller. My brothers stepped off the dock into the cockpit. I stood on the deck, ready to raise the jib.

Father waved me down. "Not enough breeze in the cove," he said. "We'll need a tow."

Power boaters and sailors were two different breeds. Sailors always had the right of way, but our zigzag tacking frustrated their straight-line courses. Still, they gave us rides out to open water in the same way that horses tolerate birds on their backs.

A guy who'd named his boat "SEA CHANGE" took our

bowline. The title was printed in big letters across the stern of his cabin cruiser. We tugged along, past all the luxury yachts docked in rows near the clubhouse. A few pelicans stood on wooden posts, surveying the possibilities for lunch near a man cleaning some fish. At last we reached the mouth of the cove.

Before the boat driver dropped our towrope, Father had me put up the jib. The smaller sail luffed in the wind, making the happiest sound. It reminded me of pendant flags, waving excitedly at the beginning of a race. As soon as Father raised the mainsail to the top of the mast, the boat driver prepared to turn us loose. Wyeth coiled the bowline. The wind filled the sails and off we went. Father grabbed the tiller just in time.

The rumble of large motorboats and their exhaust fumes were behind us now. We entered a world of quieter sounds and natural smells. Traveling with wind power felt like flying, in the same way that seagulls coast over glassy lake water. The gentle flap-flap of the sail's edge was soothing. I pictured Mama sitting with us.

Everything felt different out on the lake. I could be myself. No dishes to worry about, no scary jitters in the night—just the lively sound of moving water and soft breezes combing through my hair. An offshore wind blew steadily from the southwest. We sliced through the water past the lighthouse with both sails pulled in tight. This was called "beating." The word made me uneasy. I thought the sailing term should be changed.

Soon, Father let the mainsail out, almost perpendicular to the boat. The wind pushed us from behind, and we were "running." That term made no sense at all, because sailboats didn't have legs or motors. In no time, we'd traveled a few miles out from shore.

"Ready about," Father gave the signal. "Hard-a-lee." He pushed the tiller away from himself. It was sailing jargon for turning the bow of the boat into the wind to take a different tack.

The other way to change directions was called a jibe, which brought the stern of the boat into the airstream. Father didn't like to jibe, because the mainsail often swung sharply when it caught the wind. If you weren't watching, the wooden rail along the sail's bottom edge could really conk you on the head. The rail was called the *boom*—a perfect word for it.

A puff of wind came, and the boat lurched forward. Father had taught me to read the water. Stronger breezes came in patches that

184

looked like corduroy. He steered toward the dark rippled water, and soon we were clipping along at a good pace. I leaned out, fully extended, playing teeter-totter with the wind. Over my left shoulder, I could see the centerboard, knifing through the water like a dolphin's fin. It kept us in balance.

Skeets once said that sailing was like faith. God was the boat, with Jesus as the centerboard, and the Holy Spirit moved us forward like the wind. I asked him if I was just along for the ride. *No,* he had said. *You have to raise your sails. That's the faith part.*

We sailed several long stretches, crisscrossing our way further out from shore. After a while, the air slowed. Then it all but petered out. We waited and waited. Father stood to study the water, checking the slant of other boats and searching for telltales. Our sails billowed lazily, back and forth.

"For crying out loud, he said. "We got us a real Chinese laundry here!" Without the wind, the sun felt blistering hot, and several pesky flies showed up. "Okay." He sighed. "Everybody overboard." He lowered both sails.

Wy cannonballed off the bow, making a dramatic splash. Father made Tuck put on his life jacket, and then we jumped in together—clothes and all. The water felt velvety soft.

"You seadogs may have to tow us to shore!" Father filled his thermos cup and took a long drink.

"Look Rissy," said Tuck. He practiced his back float, but his life-jacket did all the work. "It's so easy!" He clasped his hands behind his head, pretending to nap.

"That doesn't count!" I said.

"I'll show you cracker jacks how it's done!" Wy grabbed his life vest but made the mistake of trying to put it on in the water. Threading his arms through the holes, he managed to buckle two straps, but couldn't cinch it tight. All I could see was two flailing arms in a floating vest without a head. We laughed ourselves silly. Even Father grinned.

Eventually our fingertips had wrinkles. Father lifted us aboard, extending a hand to Tuck first and then me. Wyeth squirmed up on the transom, avoiding his help.

Father opened a Coke for each of us, and we passed around the bag of pretzels. He poured another cupful from his thermos and scanned the skyline.

I stretched out on the deck's flat surface. It felt toasty on my skin. Gentle waves rocked the boat. Tuck inched over to nap with me in the warm sun. I felt happier than ever. That is, ever since Mama had left us.

Chapter 30

"WAKE UP SAILORS!" Father spoke abruptly. "Wind's pickin' up." He chugged what was left in his cup.

I sat up to get my bearings as Father prepared to raise the mainsail. Wyeth opened the thermos looking for a drink and made a sour face.

"Wyeth, get the jib up!" Father barked.

The breeze had shifted, blowing in from the northwest now. Large swells rolled across the lake, gently lifting and lowering our little boat. But all that changed as soon as the sails went up. We surged forward, moving fast. Now the bow had to plow through the waves, making it a rougher ride. We all held on. Father let out the sheets, spilling wind from the sails when stronger bursts came. I clenched my teeth. Gusts roamed across the waves, casting purple-black shadows on the water.

"Oh boy! Now we're flying," shouted Wyeth. He leaned out further than any of us, hooking his ankles under the hiking strap for leverage. Father, Wy and I sat on the high side, but it wasn't safe for Tuck. He held onto my ankle down in the cockpit.

I glanced toward the west. A cloud front had formed on the horizon.

We came about, changing direction. The sails shook violently as the boat curved around. I rushed to the other side. In my haste, I slipped, landing hard on the mainsail cleat. My thigh stung.

"Stop hanging on the shrouds, Wyeth!" Father sounded harsh. I checked my brother's expression. His lips were tight. One time he did pull on the mast wires and they broke loose. In a strong wind, that would've been dangerous. I understood why Father said it, but he could've been nicer.

The waves grew wider and higher. We were beating fast enough to make a wake.

"I could waterski at this pace!" Wy yelled. He loved the thrill of speed.

Apparently Father did too. "Ready about...Hard-a-lee." To my shock, he shifted our tack away from the cove.

I cringed. "Aren't we going in?" I glanced at Tuck who gripped my leg with both hands.

"Perfect day for a sail!" Father winked at me. I blinked hard several times in disbelief. We had a long way to go, and it would take a while with choppy water. If Mama had been there, she'd have said much more. But I wasn't Mama.

The threatening cloudbank had tripled in size and looked heavy with rain. I glanced around the lake. Other boats neared the cove's entrance. Fear passed through my body like an eerie ghost.

I bent down to speak in my little brother's ear. "Tucky, put on your lifejacket."

"But it's wet and cold," he said in a baby voice. His face was colorless.

"You *have* to, and I will too." I buckled his first and then secured mine.

Our boat heaved over another swell. Bile seeped into my throat. I focused on the horizon, but it didn't help. My stomach cringed with nausea.

"Father! I'm scared!" I cried.

"Nonsenssse!" he said, "It s'all right!"

The dark front pressed closer. Wyeth held the jib sheet, ready to uncleat the line if any blast of wind got too strong. But he wasn't having fun anymore. His other hand clasped the edge of the cockpit. His flushed cheeks meant he was either embarrassed or angry. I could only assume the latter. My eyes begged him to do something, but he looked away.

"Whoo-hoo!" Father hollered. "Let's see what thisss ol' girl can do!"

How could he play chicken with an oncoming storm? Had he lost his mind? My whole body started shaking. I rose up, holding the boom for balance and faced him squarely. For once I didn't care.

"*What* are you doing?" I screamed. "Take us in!"

"Sit down!" he roared back, steamrolling my courage. I shrank back to my place. Tuck's cheeks were wet with tears. I pulled his body close.

"Oh, yeah! Feel the power!" Father seemed completely unconcerned.

Vomit rose in my mouth, burning my throat. I swallowed it down. Minutes dragged on. I simply couldn't take anymore. Enough was enough! I glared at Father.

But his face had fallen with dread. His eyes were fixed on the water. What was happening? I quickly looked over my left shoulder. A giant swell less than twenty yards away roared toward us.

"It's a rogue wave! We'll have to turn into it!" Father yelled.

A spray of wind and water blinded me temporarily. I quickly wiped my eyes. The huge wave rolled in, cresting with white water. There was no escape. We braced for it.

"Ready about!" Father yelled. But he didn't point up fast enough. The wave sucked us into its roll. To prevent going over with it, Father turned the other way, hoping to ride out the wave like a surfboard.

Abruptly the mainsail jibed. The boom swung hard and fast. We barely ducked it. Father and Wy scrambled to high side. I straddled in the middle, reaching for Tuck. Rushing water threatened to swamp the low side where he sat balled up.

"Tuck! Tuck! Come up here!" I didn't have the strength to lift him. He'd let go of my ankle but refused to budge.

The hull leaned at such an extreme angle that the boom dragged in the water. Wyeth tried yanking in the sheet to get it out of the drink. But the more he pulled, the more we tipped.

"What the hell are you doing?" Father sounded completely frantic. "Let it go!"

Wy released the rope and thrashed about, trying to free the jib sheet as well. Tuck started to wail. If I went down to get him, my weight might've tipped the balance.

Then everything slowed in my mind.

In one terrible moment, another wave crashed over the

transom. Tuck opened his mouth to scream. The terror in his beautiful eyes made my heart stop. The wave overwhelmed him, and he disappeared with it.

The boat capsized, throwing Wyeth backwards into the mast. The flood of water smacked me down hard into the lake. Not knowing which way was up, I gasped for air when I reached the surface.

Father had flung his entire weight over the high side of the boat to hunker on the centerboard. "It's going to turn turtle! Wyeth! Get a life jacket for the mast!" The top of the sail had gone underwater. Father leaned counter to the tipping boat, but he could not right it in the storm.

"Tuck!" I shrieked. "Where's Tuck! I don't see him!" The relentless waves pounded us. "Tuck! Where are you?"

Wyeth swam to the cockpit, searching for a lifejacket.

"Faster, Wyeth! She'll go over! Get it under the tip!" Father screamed. The squall bore down on us in full fury. Rain drops stung like hail.

"Father!" I yelled. "Tuck's gone!" I took panicky short breaths.

"He's got his lifejacket on!" Father seemed entirely focused on saving the boat.

I swam around the back of the hull toward the cockpit. "Tuck! Where are you? Answer me!" I became completely hysterical. "Wy-yeth! I can't find Tuck!"

"What?" Wyeth stopped hunting for the extra lifejacket. Father started cussing him out. My brother ignored him.

"Tuck!" Wyeth yelled. "Tuck!"

I pulled myself up on the stern for a better view. But everywhere I looked, sheets of rain made an endless gray world. I started to wail. "Where are you! Where..." My weight popped the rudder off. I grabbed it with my right arm. Waves battered me. I bawled uncontrollably. *Tuck, oh God! My little Tucky!* If he was gone, I wanted to go with him. Nothing else mattered. My chest heaved with pain again and again.

Both Father and Wyeth were shouting Tuck's name now. They sounded far away, drowned out by the storm. *Oh God, oh God... where is he?* My soul reached toward heaven as though I had to press through some kind of wall. *Jesus... please come. Please, please come...* Warm tears streamed down my cold cheeks. Rain drummed my head... *please God*... wind sprayed water up my nose... choking... gasping... shivering... *please, please, please.*

I HAD BLACKED out. In a dream-like trance, I saw a great expanse of water above me, as though I stood at the bottom of the lake—maybe fifty feet down. All was serene, away from the storm above. Overhead, a dazzling light filtered through the depths, tinting the water in beautiful turquoise hues. And somehow, I could breathe. Perhaps I had died.

As the light increased in brilliance, three figures took shape. They appeared as people in flowing robes, descending toward me though they weren't really swimming. The water around them glowed as if they carried light inside their bodies. They drifted closer. Gradually their features became distinct. What wondrous eyes and lovely smiles.

Then I heard a childlike voice.

"Mmm—this'll be fun," said Tuck.

Startled, I turned sharply to my right. "Tuck?"

He acted as if he hadn't heard me and stretched his hands toward the shining people.

"Oh buddy!" I lifted my arms to hug him. "You're okay!"

But like a dream, he didn't see or hear me. My whole body strained to touch him, but he remained just out of reach. He seemed calm and his eyes twinkled.

Soon I realized that the lighted beings had come to meet him. Not me. They surrounded him, and one gently caressed the side of his face. It was something Mama would've done. And slowly, Tuck's skin started to glow.

Chapter 31

"SHE DRIFTED OVER a hundred yards away," said a man. Hushed voices came from my right, but I could not move.

"Good thing she wore a life jacket, though that didn't help her little..." His voice trailed off. "The water could've taken her."

"My God." Nana said, sounding hoarse.

My heart leapt! She seemed so near. Maybe I was dreaming.

"Where are the others?" my grandmother asked.

"Upstairs in Room 33. Third floor."

Something beeped quietly every few seconds. Sheets surrounded me. *I'm...in bed.*

"Why aren't they together?" It was Pops. His voice quivered, but the sound made me warm inside.

"Well, this little gal almost left us," said a woman with a southern accent. "Hypothermia. We just released her from intensive care."

I'm...in a hospital... others... Room 33, third floor. Three, three, three...familiar, somehow. I had forgotten why. My mind clouded over, and I faded away.

Later, someone sniffled. Next to me. On the left side. My eyelids felt sewn shut. I moved my left fingers slightly.

"Rissy!" It was Wyeth. He took my hand. "I almost...thought..." His raspy voice broke into quiet sobs.

Every inch of me felt weighted down by sandbags. Sleep returned.

A swishing sound moved about the room. Someone there again. Soft hands wrapped something around my upper arm. Short pumps of air...squeezing tight...then hissing. A cool palm on my forehead. It felt like Mama. I so wanted it to be Mama. The corners of my eyes filled. I could move again. I licked my dry lips, squinting in the bright lights. The room looked fuzzy around the edges.

"Well now, there you are little miss!" the nurse said. "I brought you some apple juice, darlin'. Your family will be coming in soon." She placed the straw in my mouth. I took a small sip. The sweetness trickled down my parched throat. I wanted a longer drink.

"That's it...easy does it," she said.

A tear escaped, rolling down my cheek. I felt her eyes on me. She couldn't see my heart burning up for Mama.

"Oh darlin'...I know." She touched my forearm and laid a tissue in my palm. "It's going to be a hard day."

Approaching footsteps echoed in the hallway. The nurse raised the back half of my bed. The motor purred as it lifted my upper body.

"Now remember," she said offering me another sip. "God's got this." She blotted my eyes and then checked the drip line attached to my arm.

What is she talking about?

Nana, Pops and Wyeth entered the room. They all had big eyes, which meant something. Maybe I was an awful sight. Where was Father and Tuck?

"How you feeling honey?" Nana asked. She leaned forward to kiss me, and I placed my arm around her neck. She smelled fresh like soap, her cheeks warm and soft. I sighed from deep inside. I didn't want to let go.

I cleared my throat. "A little weak."

Pops reached over to pull on my pinky. He offered a sad smile, his watery eyes blinking hard. I took Pops' hand in mine. I wanted to hold my grandparents forever. Father had kept them away for such a long time.

Gradually my thoughts gathered, forming a memory. Out of nowhere, fear flattened me.

"Does Father know you're here?" I asked, feeling jumpy inside.

They both nodded gently.

"But where is he?"

A long pause followed. Nana gazed downward. Pops geared up to say something. He glanced at the ceiling, stuttering for the right words.

"Well...hmm...he went with some officers."

"Officers?"

"Yes. The police." Pops straightened his posture.

"Police?" I gasped. Chills instantly covered my body.

"That's right. They took him to the station...to ask him some questions."

My mind ran wild with patchy images...the storm, the capsized boat, Father yelling, the raging wind and rain, and unending waves.

My heart pounded hard in my ears. "What about Tuck?" I sat straight up. "Where is Tuck?"

Nana leaned forward, her eyes flooding with tears. A deafening stillness filled the room. Her lips were trembling.

"What's going on?" I looked at their faces one by one.

Nana just shook her head.

"He's with your Mama now," Pops finally said.

My hands flailed in the air. "No-oh!" I screamed. "It's not true! I put a lifejacket on him!" I fought, as if I'd been attacked by a swarm of wasps.

"Honey, *hon-ey.*" Nana tried to calm me, but I pulled away.

Wy rushed to my side. "Rissy, listen!"

"But you were looking for him!" I yelled.

"I know, I know! Listen to me! He got caught under the main-sail. That big wave swamped him under. I couldn't get to him!" Wy wailed into my bed sheets. "I tried, Rissy! I tried *so hard!*"

In that moment, it felt as though the building had collapsed on me, crushing everything. "No...oh-h...no!" I rolled into a ball, screaming into my pillow. "Oh God, oh God! Why? Wh-yyy Tuck?"

Chapter 32

How much anger is the wrath on injustice?

ALFWAY UP THE STEPS to our front porch, I stopped cold. It
was a shell of a house—no Mama in the kitchen, no Tuck by
the TV chatting with Mr. Rogers. Just lifeless rooms. Our house
was not a home anymore. I didn't want to be there or anywhere.
Pops placed his hand on the small of my back.

My grandparents said Father had been arrested but was out
on bail. Still, he didn't show up at the house—just like when Mama
died. Three days had passed since the accident. It didn't feel like
three days—or an accident, for that matter.

Stretched out on Tuck's bed, I cried late into the afternoon.
Hours went by, measured only by tissues piling up near me. I
vaguely recalled Nana sitting next to me, stroking my hair.

Hushed and serious voices followed the ding of the doorbell.
The phone wouldn't stop ringing. Pops asked me to come down
for dinner. Casseroles and cakes crammed the counter, but the
smell of food made me gag. Nana forced me to drink liquids, a sip
of ginger ale here and there. A bowl of mint chocolate chip ice
cream melted into mint chocolate soup in front of me. Anna Rae
came by and briefly hugged me. She seemed like someone I only
once knew.

Everything good or happy had died in the hospital—the day I

knew Tuck was really gone. It is strange to move around as a living person when you've completely lost your heart. Many times I felt outside my body, numb to everything. Other times my weeping went on and on.

The night brought terrifying dreams. They always started with the sound and feel of pounding waves. I'd be shrieking for Tuck or see Father's angry face shouting at me. Sometimes Wyeth would swim so far away looking for our baby brother that he'd disappear too. In one dream, snakes surrounded the boat and took bites out of the hull. It would jar me awake. In the mornings, my sheets and blankets were all tangled and askew.

Now I lay awake in the dark after a particularly dreadful dream. I listened to the tick-tick-tick of my Timex, trying to clear my thoughts. The look of terror on my baby brother's face seemed stained in my memory forever.

I remembered holding his thin body in the pool as he arched into a back float. He was happy and peaceful then. He trusted me. I pressed in, trying to remember every detail—the texture of his perfect skin, the weightlessness of his body, his tiny baby teeth, and the clear blue sky reflected in his eyes. But as with Mama, everything would eventually fade. Her soothing voice, her fresh-clothes smell, the way she laughed and all her chauney ways had all diminished into faint memories. I could only expect the same.

Time is a stealer.

I turned to lie on my front and count tick-ticks. When I got to 113, a phrase slithered into my mind.

You killed him.

My lungs emptied.

You made him wear his life jacket. It trapped him under the mainsail.

"No! I tried... I tried to help!" I argued anxiously.

Wyeth could've pulled him out. He didn't stand a chance because of you.

The realization roared around me now. I pulled my pillow over my ears, and tossed from side to side. Was it my fault? I felt upside down and inside out.

"Oh Tucky," I whispered in the darkness. "I didn't know...I didn't know." I started to cry. He'd been so frightened that day. He didn't want to wear his cold, wet life jacket.

He's dead, because of you. The voice inside my mind wouldn't let up.

I had told him to wear it. I failed him. It wasn't right. Not right at all. I deserved to drown, not him. It *was* me. I wept into the night.

In the morning my pillow was still damp.

The front door opened and closed. I dozed a few more minutes. Then I heard angry shouting. I stumbled out of bed, making my way to the stairs, whirling around with dizziness. I grabbed the railing.

"Pipe down, boy!" My father's voice sounded deeper than usual.

Where were my grandparents?

"You wreck everything!" Wyeth yelled so loud his voice cracked. My brother absolutely hated being called a boy.

They were having it out in the kitchen, a real showdown. I'd lived in fear of that ever since Mama died. Immediately, I thought of the pistol. I staggered down the stairs to Father's bedroom and sprawled on the floor to get under the bed. I rolled over to look up. Duct tape hung in shreds. The gun was missing! Adrenaline flashed through my body with lightening speed.

"Give it here!" Father demanded. "Don't be an idiot!"

I pushed out from the bed but stood up too fast. The room turned again. After steadying myself on the edge of the bed, I ran to the kitchen.

"You were plastered that day!" Wyeth held the pistol with both hands, pointing it at Father's face. My brother trembled all over.

"Wyeth!" I screamed. "What are you doing?"

"Stay back! I mean it! I'm going to end this nightmare!" he shouted.

"Iris, go away!" Father emphatically motioned me to leave with his left hand and raised a scolding right finger at Wy. "Now listen here! You want to rot in jail? You want to make your life miserable?"

"My life *is* miserable!" Wyeth's face contorted with rage. "Don't you *get* that?"

"That's a bunch of crap. You have no idea how good you got it!"

197

"Everything *good* died with Mama!"

That gave my father pause. He swallowed hard.

I couldn't swallow at all much less breathe.

"You're going to give me that gun—*right now*!" Father took a step forward.

"Back off, old man!" Wyeth hopped out of reach and waved the gun. "I'm the one in charge!"

Father stood his ground. "It's terrible. Don't you think I feel it?" His tone had softened. "Nobody wanted Tuck to die, least of all me. C'mon now, son."

"You didn't go in when you knew the storm was coming!" Wyeth's bold words rang true.

Father raised both arms in the air. "We were having high adventure! You talked about skiing behind the wake!"

Wyeth shook his head hard. "You cared more... about the boat... *than your own son!*" He choked with great sobs. Tears dripped down his red cheeks. Still he aimed at Father.

"Without the boat, we'd been sunk." Father tried to sound calm but his face dripped with sweat. "All of us, not just Tuck. Don't you see?" He slowly reached toward my brother with his palms up.

But Father's pleas did not sway Wyeth one bit.

"You weren't paying attention! You made the boat jibe!"

Father shook his head and looked down. "I didn't mean any harm."

"How 'bout being a *drunken lunatic*, Hank! How 'bout slapping Rissy so hard her whole face got black and blue!" Wyeth spit the words out.

Father was undone. His neck muscles corded like tight ropes as he lunged at my brother. Wyeth bared his teeth and squinted, as if squeezing the trigger.

"Stop!" I shrieked.

Father shoved me hard to the side as he dove for Wyeth. I collapsed in fright.

A shot went off. The kitchen light shattered overhead, and glass hailed down on us. The deafening blast numbed my hearing. For a second no one moved.

Wyeth had actually fired the gun.

Father grabbed Wy's wrist, trying to shake the gun loose. He was much stronger, but Wyeth hung onto that pistol with wiry grit. They crashed to the floor in the struggle, flipping chairs as they went. Inevitably, Father overpowered Wyeth.

Then he stood up, looming over both of us and turned the gun on my brother. I couldn't believe my eyes. "That's it! It's over! You pull that kind of stunt again and you're off to a detention place, a lockdown, see? Now *I* have something on *you*, pal!" He stomped out of the house, letting the back door slam good and loud.

Wyeth stayed on the floor, crumpled and broken, heaving great sighs. He clenched and unclenched his fists. I laid in a heap a few feet away. We bawled our eyes out until our grandparents' Skylark pulled up in the driveway ten minutes later.

Chapter 33

NEWSPAPERS PILED UP on the backdoor bench. They reported our tragedy, showing a large photo of Tuck in his *Gunsmoke* outfit. The bold-print headline said, "MAN LOSES SON IN BOAT ACCIDENT — CHARGES FILED." A second article showed Father in handcuffs. My face burned.

Nana and Pops apologized repeatedly to the authorities for leaving us alone at the house. They'd only stepped out to fill a prescription and get some groceries. It's not like we weren't old enough. Rather, they never imagined what took place in our kitchen.

Apparently, Father had been waiting for an opportunity. He probably wanted to get rid of his gun. Detective Roberts said he didn't have paperwork for it, whatever that meant. Still it felt creepy to think he'd been parked nearby, watching us in his scary movie car.

At Tuck's funeral, I felt empty inside. My tears had all but dried up. A fog settled over my mind, and I didn't sing a single song. Afterwards, too many people I didn't know touched me. I tossed and turned through a jumble of blurred faces. The air stunk with body odor. It might've been the hottest day of summer. Like Mama's funeral, it sure felt like hell to me.

Visitors showed up at the house later. I hid in the fruit closet for hours, pretending to be Helen Keller. Her world seemed better than mine. Nana let me be. Who knows where Wyeth went. He had secret places too.

Skeets couldn't come. That part was unbearable. Nana explained that if Father went to jail, he couldn't be our legalardian—a word I didn't know. It sounded very reptilian. Skeets would take care of us, she explained, but he couldn't make the long trip twice so he waited for the court's decision. I pulled out my blue Webster's to look up "legalardian." It wasn't in the dictionary.

The next morning, Skeets phoned. After visiting with my grandparents, he asked for me. My chest ballooned.

"Iris," he said. "My beautiful one." Deep sighs followed. I knew he was crying. "You must feel really lost right now." He paused again.

My eyes filled.

"You don't have to say anything," he said, tenderly. "In my heart, you are in my arms, and we are swinging in that hammock out back. And Wy will climb in at the other end and put his legs next to mine." His voice cracked with emotion. "We're going to get through this. You, and me, and Wy."

I nodded but still couldn't speak. My chin quivered as I winced.

"I know you're listening, my girl," he said. "Picture Jesus holding Tucky—yeah, I'm seeing it. Can you? That boy is happier now than he's ever been. *Right this minute.*" He cleared his throat. "And, he's completely safe."

Safe. That was a word I needed to hear.

"God knew he was coming," Skeets continued. "I betcha that kid has already winked and whistled for everybody there."

I coughed up a tight little laugh. Still my body roiled with pain.

"I'll be with you soon, my girl."

"Mm-hmm." My voice sounded feeble, like the only place still alive in me had shrunk to nothing. I handed the phone to Nana and ran out the backdoor.

Wyeth laid in the hammock, looking at the sky in a dead stare. He let me crawl in next to him. My tears would not stop.

EACH DAY BROUGHT more changes, slamming our world like a wrecking ball. Blow after blow, we had no time to recover. My father's orthodontic practice had already withered. On the phone, Nana referred clients to a Baytown orthodontist. Several people spoke harshly to my kind grandma, in tones I could hear. After that, a plump lady in a pink suit showed up to pound a FOR SALE sign in our front yard.

"Hey!" I said, marching toward the door. "*We still live here!*" Pops grabbed my arm just in time and explained that Father needed money to pay his lawyer. It never occurred to me that he'd sell our house.

Within ten days, it was a done deal. Father took the first pro-posal—"an absurdly lowball offer," according to Nana. On the last morning before the realtor took the keys, I laid on the floor of every room for ten minutes. Flat on my back, I tried to store away memories, at least good ones. Next, I rushed around, sipping water from each tap. After that, I headed outside to the patio, placing my right palm over my four-year-old handprint. Mama had been alive that day—the day I'd pressed my tiny hand into the squidgy ce-ment. My fingers didn't fit in the space anymore.

Then, I turned to hug the sycamore tree, and a blinding sad-ness rained down. Mrs. Peate found me slumped at the base of the trunk with my head between my knees. Sitting quietly, she took my hand and waited till I was ready. Sunshine filtered through the leaves, dappling our legs and shoulders with light. A gentle breeze kept the flies away. I used to pray there, but now I had nothing to say.

Eventually we sauntered down the driveway. Before crossing the street, I stepped on a "W" in the sidewalk. I didn't care any-more.

WYETH AND I lived with the Peates for the last part of July to be near the courthouse for Father's trial. Nana and Pops stayed too but checked on their home in Akron on Saturdays.

It was weird to see our old house through our neighbor's windows. Kibby seemed utterly confused. During the day, he'd trail home to curl up in a window well on a bed of dry leaves. I knew his haunts. Sometimes he'd hide in the vinca plants in the shade of the house. Though the plants were lush with periwinkle flowers, I didn't feel free to pick even one.

Over the next few weeks, lawyers threw around horrible sounding words like manslaughter and homicide. They called Father abusive and reckless. A psychologist used complicated terms that surely branded him a nut case. I had no desire to look up their definitions.

When the trial started, Wyeth had to testify. The lawyer asked him about Hank's behavior since Mama died. A shiny sweat formed on his brow and upper lip.

I took a deep breath and sat on my hands.

My brother went into great detail, including the fact that Hank had wacked me across the face in a drunken rage. He described the horrible bruises and my bloodshot eye.

I wanted to disappear. I could feel people looking at me.

After that, he had to tell the jury about our sailing disaster. It was pure torture. Tears flowed when he recounted our search for Tuck. He wiped his eyes on his shirtsleeves. His inflamed cheeks deepened in color as he ranted about the gun scene. He exaggerated a little, but to his credit, he did not lie.

I buried my face in my hands.

Father never spoke for himself in the courtroom. A lady with black-rimmed glasses told about the strain of grief and single parenting. A ruddy-faced man in a coast guard uniform discussed "unintended mishaps" with sudden storms and rogue waves. Father watched the floor.

On the final day of the trial, a woman with heavy eye makeup stood as the jury's leader. When the judge read the charge— "Negligent Homicide"—she said, "Guilty!" practically hissing the last syllable. Nana nodded and whispered, "He's unfit to be your dad."

Still, he *was* my dad. He seemed to like my tadpole family last summer. I remembered holding his warm hand at the Christmas Eve service. He laughed seeing our parade costumes and permanent-marker wrinkles. He was a man who loved our Mama.

But now, Hank Somerset was a criminal. He would be in prison for several years because of Tuck's death, and we'd live in Uganda with our uncle till Christmas. At that time, the judge said we could visit our father under supervision.

Wyeth looked up at the ceiling and huffed. "Like we'd *want* to!"

Father refused to make eye contact as he left the courtroom in handcuffs. His face looked boney and gray. The judge stacked his papers, and people filed out. I pressed my lips together. The room seemed to be shrinking. Pops took my arm when I stood up to steady me. And just like that, my family life came to an end.

Chapter 34

I HOBBLED OUT the Peate's front door, dragging my suitcase. Our neighbors promised to care for our wandering orange tabby. They'd need a ton of baloney. I handed Mrs. Peate $11.45 to help cover the cost. It was all I had. But she folded my fingers around the cash and shook her head no. We said our goodbyes, and Pops shook Mr. Peate's hand. As we headed for Akron, I gazed down the street at our house until it went out of view.

Wy didn't look back at all.

I reached into my pocket to be sure my black smooth stone was there. It had become a piece of my life, something to remember the day with Skeets down at the river.

So much of my life had been stripped away. When I wasn't beat up by anger and sorrow, I felt nothing. Nothing at all. For instance, a baby went missing from a campsite in Australia. Mr. Cronkite said a wild dingo dog got it. Normally, I'd want to know everything, but I didn't even sigh. I stood in Nana's kitchen watching the TV, calmly stirring a saucepan of sloppy joes. When the commercial came, I switched channels to see what else was on.

I felt separated from the world, as if encased in a giant glass ball filled with yellow Jell-O. I only came out of the goop if Wyeth talked to me, and he only said three or four words once in a blue moon. There wasn't any teasing or tickling. He stopped giving me horse-bites. No snarky comments, either. Something cold and hard grew soundlessly inside me, and I didn't know how to stop it.

When Skeets arrived on U.S. soil, his evening flight from Chicago was delayed several hours and finally cancelled. We'd gone to the airport for nothing. Wy and I sat solemnly in the backseat of the Skylark on the 45-minute drive home.

I was still asleep when Skeets' morning flight landed. My bedroom door creaked open. I sensed my uncle watching me. A small tear pooled in the corner of my eye. I felt broken in pieces. He stroked my hair to the side of my face and said nothing. He seemed to understand the yellow Jell-O me.

I GAZED OUT the oval window of the plane, leaving it all behind. Skeets, Wy and I took off in a rainstorm but soared upwards into bright blue sky. The sun was always shining up high, even though it remained dark and wet below. I thought about that for a while.

On the second flight, the landmass disappeared and the plane flew over endless ocean. Clouds erased the horizon, making a swirl of blue and white space.

I dozed off and later woke to find a tray with miniature food servings. Only the saltines appealed to me. I nibbled like a mouse and pushed the rest away. Night had fallen outside.

The next time I came out of sleep, I smelled coffee. The stewardess said, "Good morning!" and handed me a small can of apple juice and a muffin. Hours had passed. Sunlight peeked in below the window shades. People started to stir. I gobbled the muffin and drained the juice can. Eventually the seatbelt light came on, and our plane coasted through clouds back down to a gray and gloomy earth.

Inside the airport, people of all colors, shapes, and sizes moved in steady streams. I caused a few pedestrian collisions, because naturally I veered to the right. In England, right was wrong, and left was right—the right side to pass. Skeets clutched my hand.

Wy and I sipped on orange Fantas and shared a basket of fish and chips. The chips were really fries, but I didn't have the nerve to tell the waitress. Afterwards Skeets picked up a newspaper and bought us bubble gum. We lollygagged at the gate until they announced our boarding time. The last thing I wanted was another long airplane ride. But now, life consisted of many things I didn't like.

A minute after takeoff, I pressed my nose against the double-paned window. What was happening in those small houses below? Were kids under their beds crying? What arguments went on in tiny cars winding along spaghetti-like roads?

I remembered telling Mama that people looked like ants from an airplane. Alarmed by my statement, Tuck had asked "Then what do the ants look like?" Of course he misunderstood, but that was Tuck's amazingly curious mind.

Skeets dozed next to me under a thin airplane blanket. Wyeth sat in front of him. A hefty military man more than filled the window seat, crowding my brother's space. Wy leaned hard to the left. His shoulder stuck out in the aisle. Maybe the man reminded him of Hank.

I knew I didn't want to remember. Father would be "Hank" now—just a guy in jail. His name rhymed with crank, drank, and rank. Other words cropped up as I went through the alphabet. "Sank, spank, stank, tanked and yank," I whispered. Not a single positive one.

The plane rattled through a patch of rough air. I tightened my seatbelt and gripped the armrests. My mind wandered to the gun showdown. I'd visualized it in slow motion countless times. Who was right? Wyeth had spewed such hateful words—all riled up like a wild pony. And he shot a *loaded pistol*!

Hank didn't cause the storm on the lake or the giant wave. Then again, he had guzzled a thermos of vodka. But he never meant for Tuck to die. Still the worst part—what seemed so completely unforgivable—was that he didn't search for Tuck right away. I shook my head, fighting tears. I released a long slow exhale. Deep down I didn't want to believe my father was a thoroughly rotten human being. He had brought Cokes and a bag of pretzels on the boat. He wanted our Fourth of July to be fun.

The stewardess came by. "How're you doing, sweetheart?" she asked.

Do you mean the part about my Mama and brother dying—or my father in jail? Emotions blazed over my entire body. "Fine," I said, with my head lowered like a reined horse.

She chirped something in response, handing me some soda

and a shiny bag of peanuts. Her hair was jelly-rolled in a tight French twist, and she wore frosty orange lipstick. Her winged-tipped eyeliner gave her a flirty look. She was mostly *bird*, I decided.

A sip of Coke fizzed on my upper lip. I emptied the bag of nuts on my square napkin and watched tiny bubbles rise in my drink—anything to stop the rip-and-tear going on in my mind.

Skeets sat up straight. "We should try to stay awake," he said, tapping Wy's shoulder. Then he turned toward me. "It'll be night when we get there, yeah?" His glassy eyes stared at me. I knew he wanted to talk about things, but for some reason, he held off.

No matter. I didn't care to think, much less talk. I shrugged and gave him a whatever-you-say look.

Chapter 35

WE ARRIVED IN Entebbe late at night. Every part of my body ached for a bed. Ugandan authorities examined our passports and papers. A female official peered over the court documents at Wy and me. She had skinny legs and a round torso. A white slip flashed its ruffled edge along the hemline of her dark uniform. Altogether, she looked extremely *bird* in an ostrich kind of way.

"Why you bring children to Uganda?" She pecked at Skeets, tapping her pen on the counter.

"They have no parents," he said. It wasn't the whole truth, but the paperwork told the rest. "I'm their closest relative, and I work here," he added.

"Dis is no place for dem," she scolded.

That made me breathe a little faster. Our uncle hadn't explained much about the world we were entering. He'd only summed things up with an old African proverb: "When elephants fight, the grass suffers." Beats me why anyone worried about a lawn.

Finally, she waved us through. We collected our luggage and entered the damp warm air of a moonless night. One lamppost lit the entire gravel parking lot. Everything felt darker in Africa.

I sat on my suitcase, waiting for our ride. One of Skeets' duffle bags was partly unzipped. In the opening, I noticed a plastic bag full of paper money. The currency wasn't American. I bent over to read the small print. It said "MONOPOLY."

"The beast lives!" Skeets said.

I jumped to my feet.

Smiling at my distress, he tipped his head toward the approaching car. "I meant that jalopy coming over yonder." The brakes squealed as it came to a stop.

"Oli oyta, my brotha!" Skeets said, and then introduced Okello, our driver. His teeth beamed with Cheshire-cat brilliance against his brown skin. His name sounded like a cross between "okay" and "hello," which fit his friendly manner.

"You are welcome please," the man said to me, repeating the same words to Wyeth. Had we forgotten to say thank you?

Okello towered over us, standing at least six feet high. He wore camo pants and a t-shirt that said in small bold letters, "THERE'S NO PLACE LIKE HOME." My throat tightened. He helped Skeets load our bags. In the dim light, I spotted a rifle strapped between his shoulder blades. It gave me a start.

"Betcha it's a machine gun," Wyeth whispered in my ear. That didn't help.

Wy and I climbed into the backseat of The Beast. Okello slid in front on the right side to drive and laid his weapon against the gearshift.

Was he protecting us from animals, or people?

The car lurched through every rut in the road. Okello swerved to avoid some of the worst potholes, making me more than a little queasy. Driving on the wrong side felt completely strange, but it would be the least of my worries. Up ahead, a group of men with guns partially blocked the road. Okello rested a hand on his rifle.

Skeets immediately told us to crouch on the floor. "It's a checkpoint. We have to stop." He sounded stern. "Don't move or say a thing." He covered us with a large burlap coffee bag. The itchy cloth smelled foul, but there was no time to object.

Fear clutched my throat as the car slowed.

"Muzungu!" a man shouted. "What have you brought us?"

"Well hello, gentlemen!" Skeets sounded jolly. "Are you working hard—or hardly working?"

Several of them snickered. "Papa Nsiri!" One seemed to know my uncle.

"Yeah, it's me. How is the night?" asked Skeets.

"It is—somehow," one said.

I'd soon learn that *somehow* was an all-purpose word for many non-answers.

"We are needing some chai," said another.

"But you have not improved the road since I left!" Skeets teased.

That time they really laughed.

Skeets unclicked his seatbelt and shifted his weight. "Here's a hundred, ssebo."

I figured out then that chai was money, but $100 seemed like a lot of dough! Maybe he used the Monopoly money. In that case, we'd be rich here. Our car edged forward.

"Muzungu. We know dat you are good for more!"

"Not tonight, fellas. Sula bulungi!"

We pulled away. They protested loudly. My heartbeat ramped up. *Would they shoot our tires? What if they found us?* But soon, their rant faded away.

Half a minute later, Skeets lifted the musty bags. "You stowaways are home free." I knew he'd make light of it, though his tone had been serious.

"Good grief." I calmed the static in my hair with trembling hands.

"That was pricey," said Wyeth.

"Ah, but you are so worth it!" Skeets winked.

Okello kept a wide grin, glancing back at us. "It be a hundred *shillings*, not dollars," he said.

"About thirteen bucks," Skeets said. "They'll get some goat on a stick and a few Nile Beers."

I grimaced. Goat meat sounded horrid. I pictured the whole animal on a stake over a fire. Okello wove through another section of crumbling pavement.

Wy scooted forward to lean against the front seat. "Are checkpoints like toll booths?"

My uncle chuckled. "That'll be the day! God knows they need new roads."

"Then it *was* a bribe. I knew it!" Wy spoke as if he'd been reading spy novels.

"Yeah. I usually joke my way through. Not taking any chances tonight," he said, clearing his throat. "These are rough times. Some people haven't had a decent meal in days." His voice had softened. "Sometimes a little kindness brings favor."

The situation seemed complicated—like you had to be caring and polite, but also tricky and sly.

"Why'd they call you Papa Na-zeer-ree?" Wyeth seemed surprisingly gabby.

Skeets turned around. "Nsiri means 'mosquito.' I explained to them how I got my nickname."

"So you're Father Mosquito here?" My brother jabbed Skeets in the shoulder.

"At first they called me 'katimba ka nsiri' which means—mosquito net. In their view, I'm netting their 'pesky nsiri,' or the orphans who beg along the road. But they're not pests to me."

That settled Wy down.

I looked out the dust-covered window. Silhouetted by a streetlight, several women wearing long skirts stooped over flickering fires. The smoky air reeked like burning leaves and left a bitter taste in my mouth. Countless figures in ragged clothes mingled along the road's edge.

"Why's everyone up so late?" Wy asked.

"Night-time is market time. Too hot in the day," said Skeets.

A small child with bony legs and sad eyes watched my face as we rolled by. I wondered if he had a mama.

As we neared Lake Victoria, the air cleared out. I finally relaxed when Okello pulled into a hotel parking lot. At last, a place to rest. We climbed concrete stairs in the dark. The elevator, Skeets said, had not worked for years. He unlocked the door to our room with an old-fashioned skeleton key.

My eyelids were heavy with sleep.

"You're awful quiet." Skeets pulled me close.

I didn't know where I was, or where I was going. And in truth, I didn't have much to say. My arms went limp when he hugged my tired body.

Okello handed me a small jar of water. "Dis water okay. It be boiled." Then, he pointed to the sink. "Don't drink from dere."

Chapter 36

THE NEXT MORNING, I awoke to the rhythmic sound of sweeping. Twisting free of the sheets, I peered out the half-opened window. A woman cleared a dirt walkway with a broom made from long grasses bundled together. Our second floor room had a view of the hotel's empty swimming pool. A large crocodile had been painted on the bottom. In the deep end, greenish-brown water and dead leaves hid the tail.

A few flies buzzed along the window. I brushed them toward the opening, but they whizzed to the top. "There's no way out up there," I whispered. The window curtain hung on three hooks. I counted nine holes where hooks had gone missing. The fabric dipped in those places, spilling light into the room. I took in the scene over my shoulder.

Wyeth and I had shared the only bed. Okello lay stretched out on a grimy looking couch, too short for his lanky body. Skeets made do on the floor with several blankets and a pillow. I nestled in the arc of his legs, waiting for him to wake up. His legs felt strong against my back. We were on the other side of the world. It didn't seem possible.

We'd slept in our clothes. I quickly felt the outside of my pocket to be sure my stone hadn't fallen out on the trip. It was still there.

A clinking noise came from some pipes. Skeets smiled when he opened his eyes. "It's our turn for water."

213

I gave him a puzzled look.

"To shower." He stretched his arms. "Running water comes once a day. You go first." He'd been here before.

"Me?"

"Yeah, but I'll warn you—it's a bit nippy."

He was right. The rinse-off felt good, but my teeth chattered the whole time. The guys took turns, and soon we headed to the dining room.

"I need kaaaa-waa!" Skeets said, pretending to be desperate. "It means coffee."

The strangest food had been set out on a long counter. My lip curled when I noticed baked tomatoes. My uncle showed me "ma-tooke"—a cooked banana-like fruit served with peanut sauce. I backed away, opting for plain white toast and a slice of pineapple. We sat in a booth with a wooden table. The vinyl seats had split in several places, and foam stuffing bulged from the cracks. I was glad to get out of there after Skeets paid the bill.

Once on the road, he explained the war-torn scenes that filled my wondering eyes. A ruthless dictator named Idi Amin Dada had caused devastating conflict and bloodshed. His name sounded like "A Mean Daddy," which is how I'd remember it. Wyeth asked thousands of questions, but Skeets resisted giving too many details. "You don't want to know," he'd say. Still, the wrecked buildings stirred a sense of horror.

The Ugandans kicked Amin out with the help of the Tanzanian army, but normal life was slow to return. New leadership proved shaky, and violent skirmishes broke out randomly. The Church of Uganda had temporarily adopted Skeets' orphanage in the chaos. "Together," he said, "we've been working hard. But it's tough to restore a place so beat down." He used the word *despondency*. I'd need to look it up.

We drove further west, out of Entebbe toward Masaka. A few bombed out buildings had been claimed by tall leggy birds that looked like old men in judicial robes. "Marabou storks," Skeets said, when I pointed. Rotting garbage was piled up everywhere, and its stench filled the air. I tried breathing through my mouth.

"Why aren't we hiding today?" Wyeth asked.

"Night is a dangerous time," said Skeets. "Some would kill for your car radio."

My eyes widened.

"But those guys *knew* you," Wyeth said.

"Yeah. They respect most Westerners 'cause we're here to help. Violence is more about tribal hatred." Skeets rubbed his whiskered chin. "Still at night, things happen. Anyone can be easy-pickings."

I caught a glimpse of Lake Victoria before the road veered inland toward Masaka. Skeets prepared us for what we'd see ahead. The city had been virtually destroyed. "Between war and disease, the medical center is basically a place to die," he explained. "These days, most Africans never see the backside of fifty."

Masaka seemed like an endless slum. A man in soiled clothing stood in front of what remained of the Bank of Uganda. Animal carcasses hung in the hot sun gathering flies. It was enough to make you sick. Still, fruit and vegetable stands added splashes of color—a hopeful sign of progress. Small booth owners lined every inch of their limited wall space with assorted products from cigarettes and Cokes, to Band-Aids and handmade crafts. Chickens ran free, but small goats were tethered in grassy places.

"Many of our kids have come from here," said Skeets.

We slowed to give a few coins to three boys with shovels. They'd been filling potholes with gravel and dirt.

"Gyebale emirimu gy'okola!" Okello said, leaning out the window to high-five them. The boys ran to our car with big toothy grins. He patted their dusty shoulders.

"Thank... you... for... da... work... you... are... doing!" Skeets said. Then he turned toward us. "Say... every... word... separately—so they can understand your English."

The little guys shouted, "Weebale! Thank you!" Our Land Cruiser rolled on. Okello said it was best to keep moving through Masaka. I didn't dare ask about a bathroom.

Once out of the city, the countryside thrived with lush beauty. You couldn't drive ten seconds without seeing something in bloom. A few mud huts dotted the scenery, but many lay in ruin. Sometimes a small plot of crops appeared along the road. Naked toddlers played in the reddish brown dirt. An older boy herded a few cows on the road's edge with a long stick.

After traveling eighty some miles to the outskirts of Mbarara, we finally pulled up to a large metal gate. Skeets said the church had built a compound wall around the property. "You'll be safe here, Rissy."

Okello lightly tooted the horn. A few seconds later, the gate opened and a young man in long brown pants and a bright orange t-shirt came through to greet us. "Papa! Oly otya!" He had beautiful teeth.

"Bulungi," said Skeets. Then he turned to us. "This is Waiswa—WHY-soo-wah. Now you say, 'Oli otya.'" Wy and I made our first attempt at the language.

Waiswa let out a bighearted laugh. "You are most welcome."

"Don't worry. Everyone also speaks English." Skeets added, stepping out of the vehicle. He walked up to Waiswa. "Ssebo, how are you *really*?"

"I am paining in my lungs, Papa." His smile faded.

Skeets laid a hand on his breastbone and prayed for healing as if it was something he did every day. No one ever did that at our church. People hardly even touched each other, except for funerals when they touched too much.

A moment later, more than a hundred kids came running and shouting. Older kids carried babies or had small children in tow. Little ones leaped and waved, squealing with excitement. I leaned back as they surrounded our vehicle.

"Ah, look! They have dressed up for you!" said my uncle.

Young girls wore frilly Easter dresses in all colors and sizes. Up close though, I saw missing buttons, broken zippers and jagged rips. The boys dressed in badly matched shirts and pants and a few tromped along in oversized shoes. Most wore flip-flops.

Okello brought the Land Cruiser through the gate, driving slowly through the compound. Countless arms reached through the open windows. Bright faces and gleaming teeth—I'd never seen so much happiness. You'd have thought someone won the lottery. My uncle ambled behind the car. A dozen kids flitted near him like bees around a hive.

We coasted up to a lime green building. The sign read, "Guest Quarters." Okello parked in the shade and carried our bags in. Skeets announced that Wy and I would greet them after resting. Sighs and moans went up as I passed directly into the building with my chin down.

Wy didn't seem to care. He jumped out of the car and joined

some boys who'd tossed him a soccer ball. From the window, I watched Skeets embrace child after child like a father returning home.

It was too much. I turned away and laid face down on one of the bunks. Something pulled hard at my heart. I hid my face.

Skeets entered. "Is there any water?" he asked in almost a whisper.

"Yes, in dere. I get it." Her voice sounded sweet.

"Weebale, Sanyu."

Skeets came to the edge of my bed. At first he sat silently, laying his hand on my back. Maybe he was praying. I turned my head toward him. A light breeze brought relief from the hot afternoon sun.

"It's okay, my girl." He pulled out his bandana to dab my wet cheeks. "You've been on a very long journey." His touch was so kind. "But now we can look at the sun and the moon at the same time."

Chapter 37

CLINGING TO A TRAPEZE bar, I swung forward. Skeets stood on a platform across from me, thrusting the other bar in sync with my movements. Back and forth, back and forth. He nodded in time, sweeping one hand like an orchestra conductor. I saw no ready-set-go in his expression. Instead, he waited with believing eyes.

I didn't dare look down. My arms already pricked with numbness. It became harder to hang on. Panic rushed through my mind. I had to do something. Lifting my legs, I tried swinging a littler harder, building higher and higher. Drums sounded. Could I do it? Would I? Anticipation peaked. I let go in midair. *The bar, the bar! Where was it?*

It popped me awake.

Outside the window, drumbeats echoed my pounding heart. I glanced around to get my bearings. Our suitcases lay on the cement floor, still labeled with airline tags. My breathing slowed. The soft bed underneath me was not a platform.

"Just a dream." I sighed.

What would happen next in this strange and unfamiliar place? Twilight fell as cool evening air poured through the open window. How long had I slept? A bowl of mushy-looking food sat on the rickety bedside table. A tiny note in Wyeth's handwriting leaned against the dish. It said:

Posho and beans. P.S. I didn't spit on it.

I braved a bite. It didn't taste so bad. I ate a few more spoonfuls, and my hunger pains began to fade. A canteen labeled "SAFE WA-TER" hung on the bedpost. I splashed some on my face and neck, and then took a good long swig.

The drumming ramped up. What was going on? After putting on a fresh shirt, I tied my hair in a ponytail and leaned out the door.

An African girl about my age sat by the entrance. She hopped up to greet me. Startled, I stepped back. Her hair formed two stubby braids. She wore a shirt that pictured a beautiful white horse.

"I am called Sanyu." She had a soft smile.

I mirrored her. "I am Iris."

She seemed a bit taller than me. "I wait for you, Iris Rose." She knew my middle name. "Papa wants you to put on the off," she said.

"On the off?" I asked, thinking about light switches.

"So dey won't bite you." With her hand, she imitated a buzzing insect.

"Oh, the 'OFF.' You mean bug repellent?"

Sanyu nodded once and simultaneously raised her eyebrows with one rapid up-down motion.

"Da wind be good tonight. Mostly keep dem away," she added.

I pulled out some OFF from my toiletry pack.

Sanyu waited while I smeared bug dope on my face, arms, and legs. "Come, now," she said gently. "Is time to worship."

I felt a hole inside when it came to God. We hadn't gone to church since Tuck's funeral. I didn't let on.

She offered her hand. Her palm had white skin like mine. I'd never noticed that, because I didn't know any black people at home. We strolled under the dusky sky toward the sound of singing and drums.

"One time," Sanyu said, "I didn't want to go when worship start. I told Papa I need to make short call."

"You have a telephone?"

"No, no." She giggled. "It means I go to latrine."

"Oh." I puckered my lips.

"Instead I go to borehole to cool my feet, yes?"

I nodded, though I didn't have a clue about what a boar hole was exactly and imagined the worst.

She stopped walking and faced me. "Dere by borehole, a very tall angel stop me."

I glanced around. The mention of angels was only slightly less scary than ghosts.

"Yes. Do not fear. Dere are may-nee."

"Many?"

"Is okay." Sanyu touched my arm with both hands. "I call him Tall One. He say to me, 'Where are you going, little daughter?' And I feel badness about my lie and bow to ground. Tall One touch my head, like dis." She spread her palm over the top of my forehead. "And den, warm—like glow of candle—went through my body."

I couldn't believe my ears.

"He say, 'Sanyu, you *need* to worship your God.'"

Her story threw me off. A worship service was another word for church—a weekly meeting. The angel made it sound like an action instead of an event and necessary, for her sake. I'd always believed the opposite. We attended church for God. It was all about keeping Him happy, so you could get on with life.

We started walking again until we entered a large dining hall. Crude tables and benches had been pushed to one side. Lit by two hanging light bulbs, the room contained well over a hundred people—mostly children. Their thin bodies danced in unison with hands up, reaching to the heavens. It looked like a field of wheat, swaying in the wind. They sang in a screechy kind of way, but their voices were joyful.

Come! See what the Lord has done!
...What the Lord has done for me-ee!

Wyeth slumped against the wall near the drummers. He had to be exhausted from our trip. I wondered what brooding thoughts rumbled in his mind. The atmosphere seemed thick. I felt a little woozy. The room trapped plenty of body heat, not to mention smells. Sanyu locked arms with me. I moved in tempo with her to be polite, but had no desire to sing. Yet, Tall One might discover me. Angels could easily zero in on a faker.

If God be for us, who can be against us?
He's never failed me yet...

He's never failed me...
No never ever...
Oh-oh, never failed me yet...

At one point, they sang the refrain over and over and over. It wore on like a skipping record. My body felt burning hot. Deep sighs kept rising in my lungs. The nonstop chanting got louder. High-pitched whoops put me over the edge. I wanted to explode.

Impulsively, I jumped up and tore out into the night, sprinting faster than ever. A couple of bats swooped by me. Their vibrations sent chills down my neck. Ducking my head, I ran on until I reached the compound wall.

"I can't take it!" I screamed. "I don't believe anymore!" With arms stretched out, I reeled around defensively, half expecting to see Sanyu or Skeets, or even that angel. But I was alone.

I lowered my chin. Tears formed. "It's too hard." I whispered to no one. "It's just *too hard!*" Under a starless sky, I wandered along the wall, rubbing away my tears. Bug repellant stung my eyes. I kicked patches of tall grass in frustration and lost my balance, landing hard on the ground.

Near me stood an old wooden cross, firm as a planted tree. Small smooth stones were scattered around its base. Some had letters on them. I picked up a larger one and turned it over in my hands. Scribbled in black, it said "Taata." I had no idea what that meant. Another said, "Mukulu." A third said, "Maama." Shivers crawled over my body.

Maybe the rocks were some kind of African gravestone.

Chapter 38

I'M NOT SURE how I made it back to my room that night. I vaguely remembered a woman muttering, "Poor chile," as she helped me into my pajamas. She must've unpacked my bag as well.

I rubbed my swollen eyes in the morning light. Sunbeams spotlighted the inflight magazine on the nightstand. I didn't steal it. The stewardess said I could have it. I flipped through the pages to one that showed a World War II pilot standing next to his plane. "7447" was painted on the small aircraft. The man looked like President Eisenhower.

Nana once said the former leader was very powerful, but also wise and kind. That made him hard to categorize in our game. Curious, I asked for her opinion on Eisenhower's *bird, horse, or muffin* status. She dried all the pots and pans in the drainer while considering my question. Finally, she faced me. "Well, I'd say he was predominantly *horse*. But in some ways," she added, with a far off look in her eyes, "he qualified for all three." That comment took the game's mystery to an entirely new level. It seemed like an impossible combination, because *horse* and *bird* were infinitely different from *muffin*.

I studied the photo in the inflight magazine. The airplane's number—7447—caught my eye. It belonged in my special collection of words like "civic" or "kayak"—words that remained the same, spelled backwards or forwards. Mama called them palindromes. The best ones were phrases like, "A Santa at NASA," or "a nut for a jar of tuna."

During the past year, a set of numbers sometimes pointed to a Scripture. With my BIC pen, I circled 7447. Skeets had told me airplanes were symbolic of seeing things from God's perspective, a bird's eye view of things. But if I didn't believe that God really cared about me, why did I watch for Him to speak? I dragged a pillow over my head and returned to sleep.

A tiny hand touched my arm. I surfaced from the covers to find Sanyu holding a baby. One glance at me, and the wide-eyed infant shrieked.

"Sorry," said Sanyu. "He not use to Muzungu face. You are like ghost."

I sat up and smiled. When I reached for the baby, he started to wail.

"Now you are lion!" said Sanyu, trying to calm him. She burst into a great smile. "He think you will eat him," she hollered, scuttling away.

Alone again, I surveyed the room. The canteen felt full. I drank a few sips. The airplane page was still lying open. Someone had drawn a line down the middle of the number so it looked like 74/47. Underneath the numbers, a certain someone had written the word, "Psalms." It had to be my uncle.

"A real mind reader." I said, closing the magazine.

The sound of footsteps brought Skeets and Sanyu into my room.

"Hey Diddle Diddle," he said. "You gotta quit scaring the babies." He tried to sound serious, but pressed his lips together to keep from grinning.

"I can't help it if my face is white." I said, wondering if he'd bring up the night before. He didn't seem upset. At home, if I'd left church that way, Hank would've hunted me down for a dreadful lecture.

Instead, my uncle took a long look at me. "I thought you ran off with the moon."

I glanced away.

"So, did you make any nocturnal friends?" he asked.

I shook my head slightly. He used a big word for my benefit, but I didn't know if he meant bats or angels.

"Well, don't let 'em follow you inside. We have a rule against shrieking, yeah?"

I returned a forced smile.

"Listen, some new kids are coming in from the streets today," he said. "I was hoping you'd help us greet them. Sanyu can show you what we do."

Sanyu took me to the girls' bathing place—a cement room with high windows. She carried a bucket of cold water. I brought my own towel, a bar of Dove soap, and a green tube of Prell. She told me to soap up and then dump the water over my head to rinse. I nodded and pulled a tattered curtain for privacy. Sanyu fetched a second bucket of water. How did she know I'd need it? Next time I'd use less shampoo.

Bathing was primitive, but the latrine was far worse than I imagined: a seven-by-ten inch hole swarming with a hundred flies. Fortunately Skeets put "a honey bucket" in my room for nighttime use.

Sanyu had saved me some fry bread and a little porridge. I ate while she combed out my stringy hair and began "plaiting."

"Your hair softer den horsetail," she noted. It was nice to have a friend.

She told me what to expect with the new kids. "At first dey be shy. It hard for dem to speak." Her able hands worked out a bad tangle. "Dey sometime cry."

"What do we do?" I asked.

"Gentle touch and kindness of words."

Most of the orphans had shaved heads. Sanyu's hair was long enough for little braids. She unwound them and fluffed her hair with a fork-like comb.

"Want me to do yours?" I asked. "I know how to French-braid."

Her smile brightened. We traded spots.

"Your hair is like a muffin," I said in wonder of its springy texture.

"What dat?" she asked, checking my expression.

"Where I come from, *muffin* is all-things beautiful." Braiding her hair felt like weaving cotton candy.

"Will the new kids know any English?" I asked.

"Not much, but dey learn, somehow."

We swept the bath water toward the drain. Sanyu handed me a

woven basket to carry my stuff. As we left the bathhouse, she stopped and faced me. "We give deese kids posho and beans, clothes-ses, and a place for sleeping. We touch nice." She paused, holding my arm. "But only God can heal... how you say... dere heartsick?"

I swallowed. I too belonged to the motherless tribe.

I dropped off my toiletries at the guest quarters and hung the towel to dry. Then we strolled through the compound toward the gate. No one hurried in this place except the chickens. A large milk cow chewed a mouthful of grass and watched me pass. Even the animals stared at Muzungus.

A bunch of kids staggered up a path carrying large plastic jugs. They were surprisingly strong. Water splashed from the openings. An older girl balanced a yellow container on her head. I wanted to try that. Sanyu watched where my eyes went. "Dey prepare for washing."

We came to a large garden area where a dozen boys were hoeing the moist soil. I recognized banana trees and pineapple plants by their fruit. Sanyu pointed out maize, cassava, pumpkins and sweet potato crops. She showed me where the mangoes grew, and we found a giant jackfruit. Its outer skin looked like a thousand peas crammed together.

"Da HOPE family work in garden today," she said.

"Who are they?" I asked.

"Papa build four homes here. Two for girls, two for boys. Dey called LOVE, JOY, PEACE, and HOPE. Each group work as families, taking turns."

"Which is yours?"

"Da JOY house. Is our day to burn garbage." She crinkled her nose.

Some chickens scurried in front of us as we reached the gate.

Waiswa stood in the shade. He wore dark navy pants and a loose t-shirt with a Cleveland Indians logo. As we approached, he laid his long gun against a tree.

"Oly otya!" said Waiswa, beautiful teeth and all.

Sanyu elbowed me. "Say, 'Otulo tunnuma!'"

I shouted the phrase. Waiswa released a great laugh.

"Zuukuka!" he said, shaking a finger at me.

"What just happened?" I turned to Sanyu.

She covered her mouth. "You say 'I am feeling sleepy,' and he say, 'Den wake up!' We not understand how your night is our day, because we live here always."

I returned his smile. "Oly otya?" I laid my hand on my breast-bone. "Are you paining still?"

"It be all *gone!*" He sucked in his lips and shut his eyes, raising one hand straight into the sky. It seemed like he was about to cry. I glanced at Sanyu.

"He giving thanks," she whispered.

Sanyu and I sat cross-legged on the ground, waiting for the new kids to arrive. Next to me, a group of ants worked their way through the grass jungle. Several carried crumb-sized particles. They were having a tough time. Open dirt was only six inches to their right. It would be easier going, if I could steer them that direction. Yet if I frightened babies, I could only imagine how the ants felt. A human smile might terrify them in a T-Rex kind of way. Still, I walled off their path, hoping to drive them out of their jungle. They didn't seem to want my help.

Three honks signaled the van had arrived.

"It's Papa," said Sanyu. Waiswa checked through a small open-ing at eye-level in the gate. No crowd of kids came running this time.

"Why isn't everyone greeting them?" I asked.

"New ones ashamed of dere rags. Dere be greeting for dem later."

Three scrawny children climbed out—a girl about our age and two little boys who clung to her. They would not look at us and ap-peared scared to death. Skeets came around the vehicle and got down on bended knee. He spoke softly in their native tongue.

Skeets pointed to me and gently placed the smaller boy's hand in mine. He couldn't have been more than four years old. How did he survive without parents?

"This is Boy Sunday," said Skeets.

I stared at my uncle, wondering if I'd heard right. "Boy Sunday?" I silently mouthed the words.

"It's a street name," he said.

I felt nervous. "Oly otya, Boy Sunday."

"I am fine," he murmured in a weak voice.

"You are welcome here," said Sanyu.

"I am fine," he repeated. It must've been the only English phrase he knew.

The other boy was called Jonan and the girl, Binti Doris. They were siblings. Sanyu took their hands, and we headed toward the supply container to pick out some new-used clothes. Jonan chose a red t-shirt that said NIKE, and Binti found a flowery sundress. Boy Sunday picked a pair of blue shorts and dug through a pile of shirts. You'd have thought it was Christmas morning.

Sanyu brought the electric razor out to shave their heads. After that, Binti undressed the boys and heaped their filthy clothes out on the dirt. "No washing dere rags," Sanyu explained. "We burn dem. Dey be da old life."

We scrubbed the boys head-to-toe with a special soap for lice, while Binti Doris washed alone in the girls' bathing room. Sanyu brought ointment from the clinic for the red spots on their skin. "Scabies," she said, using Q-tips to swab their blistering sores.

Binti returned in her pink and orange dress. Her freshly scrubbed skin gleamed in the sunlight. We gave the little guys brand new underwear, still in plastic wrap. Boy Sunday pulled on his blue shorts, pogoing on one leg until both feet found the right places. He turned to me for help with his shirt.

The t-shirt he'd picked showed a small boy holding a pale yellow balloon on a string. I caught my breath. Across the top it said "KENSINGTON SCHOOL." My heart sped up—*could it be?* I searched for the tag. It had curled with repeated washings. When I spread it flat between my fingers, three faded initials appeared—*TJS.*

Mama had donated Tuck's shirt.

And here it was—his very shirt in my hands. Everything stopped. I buried my face in the fabric, longing to catch a whiff of Johnson's baby shampoo or the earthy scent of fresh grass stains. But it only smelled like a musty storehouse. Tears made wet spots on the dry cloth.

Tuck had worn the shirt the day he climbed the jungle gym at Kensington for the first time. Mama's forehead had wrinkled with concern. *I'll hold him!* I shouted, scrambling up to steady Tuck at the top. His face was bright pink with excitement. I hooked my arm around his body and felt the thump of his beating heart.

Tuck had once colored a picture of himself holding the moon like a balloon on a string. *The moon is my friend,* Tuck had said.

How do you know? I'd asked, as we drove through the countryside in my grandparent's car.

Because he's following me.

Sanyu, Binti, and the boys stood motionless with unblinking eyes. Time had stalled. It took me a while to notice two thin arms around my waist. Boy Sunday held onto me, pulling me back from the sinkhole of memories. I lowered the treasured shirt and found his soft brown eyes. Brushing away my tears, I helped him put it on.

How had it followed me to this faraway place? It had traveled for months across two oceans in a shipping container. And now a boy had handpicked it from piles of used clothes, choosing it out of hundreds to start his new life. And this beautiful, brown-skinned boy would fill the space inside that shirt.

Boy Sunday stepped back and held out his arms, proud of his new clothes.

I let go of the shirt—and something else too.

God created two lights, it says: the greater one to govern the day, and a lesser one to watch over the night—the time of bats and nightmares and tears that would never end. But Tuck's friend—his heavenly nightlight—had found me, and it glowed in the darkness of my heart.

Chapter 39

BOY SUNDAY SHADOWED me for the next three weeks. At his first meal, he ate way too much, far too fast, and got a whopping bellyache. Skeets explained he wasn't used to eating daily. Not having food each day was a new thought to me.

He didn't mingle with other kids, though he watched with interest when the big boys played soccer—or football, as they called it. The hardest part came at bedtime, when he had to sleep without me. They put him next to Wyeth in the boys' quarters, but it wasn't the same. The first few nights, Skeets let me tuck him in.

Tuck him in... The words floated by like a heavenly whisper.

At first, Boy crawled under the bed. He seemed to think it was his tent. Maybe he'd never had a bed, and without language, it was hard to explain. I coaxed him up to the mattress, and he rolled around in the cool cottony sheets. When he finally settled in, I sang him the Happy Birthday song. His eyes widened when he heard his name and he patted my leg, urging me to sing it again. I did, slower and quieter, stroking his arm out to each fingertip. His eyes closed. When the song ended I sat very still and studied his curled eyelashes, until slumber rolled over him like a soft fog. There's nothing so *muffin* as a sleeping child.

But Boy Sunday was restless inside. The first week, he woke up every two hours, frantic as a toddler lost in a department store. Wy tried to calm him, but usually had to get our uncle.

That routine went on night after night, until one morning Skeets announced that Boy Sunday had slept five hours and twenty-two minutes! Two nights later he slept nearly seven hours, and after that he even missed breakfast one morning. I found him sound asleep under his mosquito netting.

Jonan and Binti Doris got used to things quicker, probably because they had each other. She knew more English and helped interpret, even though Wy completely messed with them saying guys were "cats," girls were "chicks," and "bad" meant cool.

One afternoon, Binti and I played Mancala in the shade of a large canopy tree. We used an old egg carton and forty-eight dried beans for the pieces. Boy Sunday leaned against my back, watching a vulture adding sticks to its nest in the branches above. From time to time he'd flap both of his thin arms, spreading them wide like a bird coasting on rising air.

The creepy bird looked prehistoric with its hooked beak. It had a pink face and a gray skullcap, which strangely matched its choir robe of feathers. Skeets called it the neighborhood rubbish collector.

That day a black-faced monkey with whitish fur showed up to steal her egg. The bird's cry sounded like "Mama! Mama!" She fought fiercely. The monkey, full of tricks, easily maneuvered through the treetops. We all watched the skirmish until the monkey backed down.

The mama bird, however, didn't ease up until her enemy was completely out of the tree. It took some doing. Boy popped up to help. He grabbed a stick to chase the monkey over the high wall, yelling, "Genda! Genda!" which meant 'Go away!'" The wiry chimp disappeared, and the mother vulture nestled over her egg. My eyes came to rest on that small gentle boy trying so hard to sound big and fierce.

"Binti," I said. "What do you know about Boy Sunday?"

She shrugged. "He live on da street."

I was certain she knew things. "How'd he get his name?"

Her face fell. She shook the beans in her hand like a pair of dice. "He stay by da church in Masaka. Next to dat...was place of bad tings. He live in middle of two buildings."

"Like an alley?" I formed a narrow space between my hands.

She eyebrow-nodded which either meant, *yes* or *I don't under-*

stand, but I'll go along with it. "He so hungry, he beg da church lady. She give him banana, or sometimes little dry fish."

"So what about his name?

"Da bad place people see da boy is good for using. They say to him, 'Beg from church peoples for shilling or be beat—okukuba!'" She backslapped her hand for emphasis. "Boy go on Sundays and sit by church door. He say 'Nyabo, Ssebo, mpolayo ssente?' It mean Madam, Sir, borrow me some money? 'Nja kuzireeta mangu'—I pay you soon."

"Did they care, I mean—did they help him?" I covered my heart with one hand.

"Yes. Dey gives coin and touch Boy head. We watch dis." Binti's brow twisted up with pain. "But bad place people take money. They *take it all* and beat Boy too." She shook her head hard.

"Is there more?" I paused, breathless.

"I too sad to tell." She lowered her face.

"You can tell me." I reached over to hold her hand. We both checked to see if Boy was still out of earshot. He stood guard, watching for the egg-stealer.

"Boy *had* mama," Binti said in hushed tones. "She be sick and leave him *dere* saying, 'Nkomawo'...meaning 'I return.' She go to hos-pee-tal. If she meet death, she hope for church...to be mercy...for son." Her voice broke up.

"So—she *died*?" It was hard to say.

"No. Da mama got well and came for Boy." She winced.

"It's okay." I said, waiting for her to come around.

"Bad place people beat her to die because her son is now dere 'Boy Sunday.' He get da money for dem."

White-hot fury burned my face.

A tear traveled down Binti's cheek. "Worse about it," she said. "Boy saw da beating and stay with mama till she gone to God. Even days after—he not leave."

Boy Sunday started skipping toward us.

My heart dropped. I stood up abruptly. "I have to go!" I started to run. "Will you...keep him?" I didn't wait for her reply.

I stormed into the guest quarters and paced back and forth. Deep wordless groans filled my chest. I kicked and threw anything in range. Toilet paper rolls shot across the room like comets.

Books and shoes went flying. Seizing the inflight magazine, I shredded page after page. *The cruelty!* I hurled the canteen. *Why?* I flung myself on the bunk and screamed into my pillow. The heat of the day felt sticky hot. My body twitched with agitation.

All at once, I heard loud squawking and fluttering wings. The chickens were making a racket right outside my window. I knew what that meant. I'd seen it before. Grabbing a broom, I plunged it through the window, swatting at them to break up the fight. It was always the same story—picking on the weakest. They moved on.

Sinking down on the bed again, I laid back and folded my arms over my eyes. A haunting stillness followed, and I remained there for the longest time. Gradually, I inhaled deeply as my thoughts began to clear.

The numbers 74/47 came to mind. I bit my lip. I didn't have a Bible. Before we left, I'd shoved mine in a storage box at my grandparents' house, packing only my dictionary instead. Glancing around the room, I noticed another one on the shelf. I opened it, half-heartedly flipping past Nehemiah and Job to Psalm 74. I translated the verses out loud using my own words—the only way it made sense to me.

> *You disappeared like you're angry!*
> *Have you forgotten us?*
> *The bad guys are in control here!*
> *They're monsters wrecking everything!*
> *Why aren't you doing anything about it, God?*
> *Are you leaving us here to rot?*
> *Don't you see that people will blame You?*

I couldn't believe someone as mad as me had written something like that in the Bible. I stared at the phrases on the page. My curiosity grew. I turned to Psalm 47. Again, I paraphrased. This time I didn't like the message.

> *Clap your hands, everyone...*
> *Sing your loudest song of joy to God...*
> *For He is the greatest God ever.*
> *He crushes people who are against us.*
> *Sing your best song, all the time...*

For God is totally in control...
And He is king over all the earth.

Right. Two Psalms saying exactly the opposite, just like their numbers. It was troubling. I didn't feel one bit better. A fly droned around the right side of my head. I whacked my ear pretty hard and watched the fly buzz away.

"Hmm." It was a man's voice.

I glanced over my shoulder.

Skeets stood in the doorway, leaning against the frame with his arms folded. It startled me. How long had he been there? He scanned the room. "I heard some hollering," he said, raising one eyebrow. "Thought there might be a bat problem."

I was in no mood to laugh.

"Looks like you might need Musa's broom anyway."

"Already got one," I said.

He came near, stepping over the debris. "So you finally checked it out?" He pointed to the open Bible.

I slammed it shut.

"Both Psalms *can't* be true at the same time, can they?" he said. "Is that what you're thinking?"

If he had been Wyeth, I would have said *shut up.*

He squatted down to my level. "Hey, there..." He tugged at my arm tenderly.

I jerked my elbow out of his hand and faced him squarely. "Why Mama?" I yelled. Why Tuck? Why Boy Sunday?"

His eyes softened. "And why *Iris?*" he said. "You feel it too, don't you?"

It finally occurred to me. I'd spent so much energy worrying about others, it was tough to admit that I felt deserted by God. I blinked hard. "Why haven't you talked to me about Tuck?"

His lips tightened with hesitation. "Believe me, I've thought about it a hundred times. I cooked up a thousand explanations."

"But *why?*" I stood up.

"Because the truth is—we'll never make sense of his death, Rissy. We can't stop tragic things from happening."

I marched to the window on the other side of the room. "Do you *know* how Boy Sunday got his name?" My voice trembled.

He gave a slight nod. "My girl," he said sadly. "Listen now."

233

His eyes became glassy.

"It's not right!" I shouted.

"Yes, I know. But I'd rather believe God's in this mess, than think we're just floundering here." He understood what I was really asking.

"How can you trust?"

Skeets' head was bowed. "I argued with God too—for years, in fact. But eventually, I stopped putting His heart on trial."

"What does that mean?"

"It's easy to think God doesn't care." He rubbed his temples. "But He came here. He *knows* what it's like...the hunger and thirst, the pain of it all."

I examined Skeets' face—his honest eyes, his flushed skin.

"All I know is something happened when I chose to believe God's heart is good in spite of everything. I started to look beyond the brokenness. What's unseen became more real to me than what I saw with my natural eyes." He spoke of mysteries that felt out of reach to me.

Stooping over, he picked up a roll of toilet paper and began rewinding it. "At times, I feel like Psalm 74, but I always return to the promises in 47. Trusting God is a choice." He paused for a moment and then faced me. "Because here's the thing, Rissy. Trust matters."

"Trust?" I wanted to understand.

"Because you can't get close to someone you don't trust."

Sunlight poured into the room, illuminating the pale turquoise walls. I turned to gaze out the window. The land glowed with that particular splendor of late afternoon light when colors come alive again.

Skeets joined me at the window, his shoulder pressing against mine. "And when I'm close to God, He tells me things—and that makes all the difference."

"But, I don't know how to get there," I said. "Where *you* are."

"I know," Skeet said. "But you will."

"*Somehow.*" I said with uncertainty, like an African.

"Yeah. Somehow..." Skeets ambled over to the chair by the desk.

I sank down against the wall and didn't say anything for a while. I thought about Tuck's radiant face when the angelic beings came to take him. I'd felt left behind at the bottom of the lake. Was it a hallucination? Or had God showed me something I couldn't see with my eyes? A gentle breeze played with the ripped magazine pages.

"You know, I actually came by to tell you about a dream I had last night." He paused. I didn't respond. He went on anyway. "You were wearing a lacey white dress."

I scrunched my knees up to rest my chin on them.

"You were in a dark cave," he continued. "But here's the weird part: you had pushed so hard against the back wall, your body made an impression in the rock."

I glanced at him. "That's impossible."

"It's dream language, Rissy. Think of it like a handprint in cement—a sign that you lived there."

I felt nothing.

"A man stood at the entrance," said Skeets. "He knew exactly where you were and was determined to get you."

Get me? That was disturbing.

"He had to work his way through endless tunnels and crevasses." Skeets made a rollercoaster motion with his arm. "It took several months."

"What was I doing?" I asked.

Skeets hunched forward and clasped his hands. "Hiding."

I shifted my weight.

"At first, you didn't know he was coming. When he finally got there, you pushed even harder into the rock."

The thought of being in any small space with my father felt suffocating.

"The strange thing was—he didn't say a thing." My uncle shook his head. "He simply stood there, taking in your situation."

I shrugged. Hank often had trouble with words.

"After a few minutes, the man simply offered his hand. You thought about it for the longest time—maybe as long as a year."

I huffed. "So."

"Yeah—so what," Skeets sighed. He stood to leave, nudging my shoes to one side with his foot.

"Wait." I said. "Please, finish."

After a moment, he went on. "Well, you reached out with one finger—testing to see if the man was just an illusion. But he was real." Skeets moved toward me. "Then the man wrapped his hand around your finger and waited for you to take the first step. No use dragging you out of there, yeah?"

That didn't seem like my father at all. He wasn't patient or kind. I'm not sure he would've even looked for me. He didn't search for Tuck. I rolled to my feet. "Well, I don't care about Hank anymore!"

"Hank?" Skeets chuckled. "No, no, little bird." His countenance lifted as he reached for my hand. "It was Jesus."

I didn't see that coming. Moisture formed in my eyes. "Did I go with Him?"

"Well." Skeets leaned in to kiss my head. "I guess only you know."

Chapter 40

"Hey Muzungu!" Wyeth came from behind.

"Hey yourself." I didn't feel up to his shenanigans. Binti had taken the boys to the garden so I could have some time to myself.

Wy strolled along as I headed toward the borehole. "Ya know, I had a sister once...a scrawny Bone-Cat girl who made a mean fried baloney sandwich." He waited for my response.

I gave none.

"You see...I kinda miss having someone to mess with." He jabbed me.

In a way, we'd grown apart. I wasn't sure why, except that we reminded each other of our old life—that other place and time where Hank had blown things to smithereens.

"C'mon, I'm *actually* being nice!" He flashed a goofy smile and bumped me out of my zombie march.

I dropped my yellow water jug and chased him, which was exactly what he wanted. In fact, he ran backwards just to taunt me with his ability to stay out of reach. I slowed when I realized he was heading right for the cows' watering trough. I didn't warn him. Sure enough, he plunged in butt first.

"You twerp!" He looked pitiful. "Why didn't you stop me?"

Everything went in full reverse. He raced after me. I dashed back for my empty plastic jug, using it as a weapon to conk him left and right. He fended off my blows. I grew faint with laughter, until he flung his dripping wet t-shirt on my face.

"Okay, okay!" I said. "Truce!" It was hard to not think about cow saliva.

We rinsed off at the well, and I filled my yellow canister. On the way back he carried it for me. That was unusually kind for Wyeth. We walked in silence for a while.

"So-o, how are..." he started.

"Not so good." I knew he'd have questions.

"Wanna..."

"Talk?" I interrupted.

"Well, *yeah*. We're on the other side of the planet, and other than Skeets, you're the only family I got," he said.

"Sorry. I'm a mess."

"I see that. I'm not an idiot." He jump-switched his feet so his left foot stepped forward when my right foot did. Usually, I'd counter-move to keep us walking in unison—left feet together, then right. It was our childhood game. He wanted to play, but I ignored it.

"How do you just go on?" I asked.

"I try not to think too much." His tone was practical.

"Cool." I didn't sound enthused.

"Look Rissy, all we got is *now*. Skeets told me that."

"What's the point? Everything I love gets taken away or wrecked."

"I'm still here. What about me?"

"I just tolerate you," I said rather dryly. Our eyes met. He knew I didn't mean it. The corners of my mouth gave me away.

He ran a few steps ahead and turned to face me. "C'mon! Argue with me, you Big Pony. Get it out! It's like you're mad all the time!"

I put my hands up sharply. "What don't you get?"

"I know, I know. But there's something else going on." He wouldn't relent.

"Don't you ever wonder about God?" I half-shouted my question. "I mean, where is He when all the bad things happen?"

"I don't go there. Why bother yourself?" He faced forward, to walk side-by-side. "Besides, I don't need all that sin and salvation stuff. I'm not bad anymore."

"You're kidding, right?"

"I was just miserable at home," he said. "That was a lot of it."

The path turned to the left to avoid a large anthill.

"The point is, I'm not a killer or a drunk," he continued. "Why would God have to die for me?"

His words stunned me.

"This is how I see it, Rissy." He cleared his throat. "It's like I'm standing on a curb, minding my own business, when someone yells 'Watch out! There's a truck coming!' And then Jesus runs right past me into the street and gets hit by the truck. I feel bad about it, but not in a personal way." He shrugged. "Why do I have to thank Him for dying or give Him my life?" Wyeth kicked a stone off the path. "It not like I'm driving the truck."

His reasoning made sense.

"And as far as bad things happening—*bad people* are mostly to blame. That's what jails are for." He picked up the heavy container. "These African kids have gone through worse crap than us, and they still go on."

We continued along the path in our own thoughts. A dove flew over us and landed in a mango tree. Its peaceful song was—krrrr, oo-OO, oo—which sounded different from the ones back home. But the noise in my head refused to be quiet.

"Do you know about Boy Sunday?" I broke in.

"Not yet. I know some of their stories."

"Like whose?" I asked.

"Musa, for starters."

"What happened to him?"

"Forget about it." He set down the container. "You're already whacked."

"No, tell me. I want to understand."

"Okay, but you'll be sorry." He rolled his eyes and then stared at me for a moment. "Musa's family shacked up near Jinja town, by the big lake."

"Where the airplane landed?" I asked.

"No, further east. His mama sewed dresses, and his father raised cows. He had a little sister, too."

I sat down on the container. *Had?*

"So one day, Amin's army was out looking for recruits. Musa and his dad were moving cows on a back road, not botherin' nobody, when these soldier guys—two of 'em—pulled up on a boda-boda.

"What's that?" I asked.

"A motorcycle. The men told his father to come with them, but his dad refused. He said, 'Ndeka!' meaning 'Leave me alone!'" Wyeth glanced around to see if we were by ourselves. He lowered his voice anyway. "So one soldier said, 'Do you want to be happy or sad?' His dad stalled. It was a trick question. Finally he said, 'Happy.'" Wyeth lowered his face. "Turns out it was the wrong answer, 'cause they shot him dead."

I gasped.

Wy struggled to not lose it. After a minute he continued.

"Then they turned on Musa. Course he's going ballistic, watching his dad bleed out on the ground. And what do those jerks do? They asked him the same question!" Wyeth's eyes became slits. He spoke through tight lips. "Musa begged them, saying, 'Please let me pass. I have Mama and sister to care for.' The soldiers put their guns to his head. 'Happy or sad,' they yelled. He got so scared he peed himself, but they just mocked him, saying 'Da bay-bay sheet!' Finally Musa said, 'I am sad.' And they took him to be a soldier, away from everything he knew."

I looked at my brother in disbelief. "Oh my God," I whispered.

"He was only ten, Rissy. They wanted him all along, 'cause it's easier to brainwash kids into killers. He won't talk about what they made him do."

At that moment, we heard animated voices. Musa and Sanyu ambled down the path with their water jugs in tow.

"Kulikayo!" Musa's friendly greeting made it hard to believe he had been that ten-year-old boy. I tried not to stare. How could he seem okay? He had no downcast eyes, no trace of sorrow, no flicker of shame like Binti and the boys when they first arrived. Wy and I stood as stone pillars and failed to return his greeting.

"Have you taken lunch yet?" asked Sanyu, covering the awkwardness.

"No...we're just going...now." Wy spoke for us.

"Dey have cooked cassava and brought tilapia from da pond." Her eyes danced. To eat anything other than posho and beans was a treat.

I ran toward the village, too upset to say anything at all.

"We find you later?" Musa shouted, as if saying—*is everything okay?*

I heard Wyeth whispering to them.

He finally caught up with me. "Hold on!" Lugging the water

made him huff and puff. "See, I shouldn't have told you."

When we got to the guest quarters, I had a stomachache. He left my water jug by the door. I went in to change my clothes.

"You go on." I shooed him away. "I'm not hungry."

Questions tapped on my head all over again. How did these kids not die of fright? What happened to Musa's Mama and his sister? And Binti and Jonan—what was their story? I roamed around the room, restless as a caged animal. Wy was right. I had to stop thinking so much.

I changed out of my wet shirt and brushed out my hair. At least a half hour passed before I simmered down. A stack of typing paper sat on a small desk next to a old Royal typewriter. I thought it might be good to draw something. I searched for crayons or a pencil but there weren't any. Even my BIC pen had gone missing. I opened several drawers and found scissors, some paperclips, and a ball of twine.

The idea of making paper snowflakes came to me. I squared one sheet, cutting off the longer end and folded it three times to form eight sections. Trimming the corners, I shaped the square into a circle and then cut different patterns in from each edge to make it extra lacy. White snippings fell to the floor, scattered about my feet. I took my time, working carefully. Finally I laid down my scissors and opened the snowflake.

There was something magical about symmetry.

Symmetry was a word I liked. The dictionary definition didn't make sense, but Mama had explained the general idea by pointing to butterfly wings and the design of most flowers. I saw it in the reflection of trees on smooth water. I found it on playing cards—hearts, diamonds, spades and clubs—anything folded in half that looked the same on each side. It felt pleasing to my eyes.

A commotion outside my window brought four faces into view.

"Yeah, the House Troll is still in there." It was Wyeth.

Musa, Sanyu and Wy bounded into the room, squishing through the door like the Three Stooges. Binti followed. I knew my brother had rallied them to cheer me up.

"What're you doing?" asked Wyeth. I feared his teasing, but when he saw my snowflake, he seemed genuinely interested.

Binti touched the delicate paper, examining its patterns. "You teach me?"

"Me too!" chimed Sanyu.

I pointed to the paper supply and stood up to get more scissors. Wy and I both squared and folded a clean sheet to demonstrate.

"If you cut too big, it won't hold together," I explained.

The others eagerly started.

The day wore on as we quietly made snowflakes. I needed their company, but I didn't want to talk. Somehow they seemed to know. Toward the end of the afternoon, Wy and Musa stapled a piece of twine to each paper flake. Then they took turns standing on a wicker chair to tape the dangling snowflakes to the ceiling. Soon it became a contest as they scuffled over the chair.

"Stop!" said Sanyu. "You break it!"

A bell sounded. Binti jumped up and grabbed Sanyu's hand. "We be late for cooking."

"Webale," I said to them. Sanyu paused to smile.

The boys finished hanging up the last snowflakes. There must have been over four-dozen in various shapes and sizes.

"Race you to the front gate!" Wyeth taunted, heading out the door.

Musa whooped and followed in hot pursuit.

I swept the confetti-like scraps into a dustpan. I liked the quiet sound of the broom. I liked the clean floor. Afterwards, I spread a comforter across the cement and laid face up, extending my limbs in a cat stretch. I wanted to remember happier times.

The paper flakes swayed and turned in the late afternoon breeze like the dance of cottonwood seeds bringing "snow" in summer. Snow made everything fresh and lovely again. Shutting my eyes, I imagined catching them on my tongue with Tuck. He had asked me if snow was a milk-product. After all, both were white and cold. It was a brilliant question.

Soon, I heard the sound of bare feet padding across the floor. I kept my eyes shut but knew it was Boy Sunday. He crawled in next to me, placing his head in the crook of my shoulder. He wiggled close to find a comfortable position. I'd come to know his funky smell. He didn't bathe everyday. All at once, his little body became perfectly still. I sensed him taking in the beauty of our snowfall.

"Ooh..." he cooed. "Dis be happy-nest."

Chapter 41

THE COOK HAD made a thick soup with leftover tilapia and rice. "Greens" that looked like kale had been added, along with chopped peppers and tomatoes. In my old life I would've gagged, but I was hungry enough to eat dead grasshoppers.

I took my bowl and settled near Jonan. He was such a solemn kid—worse than me. His jaw appeared crooked, but I didn't know if his deformity came from birth or injury. A closer look revealed a thin jagged scar that stretched from his chin to his ear where the corner of his jawbone should've been.

Boy found us and began scarfing down his supper. Binti carried two bowls to our table, giving one to Jonan. Her blue cooking smock amounted to a piece of torn sheet. "Is mighty fine?" she asked, sounding very Wyeth.

I eyebrow nodded.

She beamed. "Deese two bin talkin' bout worship tonight," she said, glancing at the boys. "Dey wants to drum."

Boy tapped his spoon on his thigh. He understood more than he let on.

"It'd be past their bedtime," I said.

"Papa say it okay."

If Boy went, he'd want me to go. I hadn't been to worship since that first night. Skeet had given me freedom to choose. Fortunately, Tall One had not materialized out of thin air. Yet.

243

Sanyu set up tubs of warm soapy water. I helped her wash and dry 155 metal plates. We stacked them in the cooking hut and hung our towels under the eaves.

Clouds had gathered, giving cool relief from the sweltering day. I strolled back through the compound toward my room. Some bottle-cap checker games were underway, drawing a small crowd. A few kids played hacky-sack tag. Several girls sang in tempo while twirling a jump rope. Once inside, I stood at my window, taking in the scene: happy children with full bellies in a land of eternal summer.

I wondered what Hank saw out his prison window.

The call to worship sounded. Drums worked better than any loudspeaker. Boy entered the room and grabbed my hand. "You come dis night." It wasn't a question.

I gave a clap. "A whole sentence in English!"

Sanyu stood at the door, clearly amused. "I practicing him to speak."

He pulled my elbow. "Jjangu olabe!"

"He say, 'Come and see.' And I say, if you be sadfull dere, I return you here."

"Okay. I come." Somewhere along the way, I began switching to African English, dropping some words and saying the rest separately. I took a light sweatshirt. The humid wind brought hope of rain.

Drumbeats vibrated the ground under my feet. You'd have thought we were going to a rock concert. Shouting, singing and dancing...whoops and hollers too. It felt free, but not in a braless-woman kind of way. Boy Sunday straddled the end of a long wooden bench, drumming with two sticks. Everyone from old to young knew how to dance, even the smallest toddlers. I felt like the nerd at the party.

The King is coming from on high...He is the light!
He touches us with pow'r and might...He is the light! Oh Je-sus...

Sanyu clutched my hand. I copied her moves. She nodded, assuring me that I'd get it. Their hops and turns and claps were in sync. Like a flock of flying starlings, they shifted their movements without any wrecks.

He lifts our chins to rise again...He is the light!
It doesn't matter where we've been...He is the light! Oh Je-sus...

The dance marathon lasted nearly an hour. Exhausted, I sank down on the bench. At least I had overcome my tendency to be a bystander.

Skeets told a story about King David, saying he would not give something to God that cost him nothing. I gave that a thought. The kids pulled wads of colorful paper money from their pockets. Musa and Wyeth passed baskets up and down the rows. I soon realized the offering was Monopoly money! No prank like that could happen in our church.

"Oh! I forget." Sanyu handed me some bills. "Dis be payday, and I da banker." She handed me a stack. Each miniature bill had my name written across the back.

"But it's fake!"

"You work in garden. You help Boy. You do washing chores. You worthy of pay. Quick now, give some to God." She was firm.

I dropped a mint-green $20 bill in the basket and noticed one smooth rock at the bottom. Some poor kid probably didn't get paid. Maybe it was all he had, but I was pretty sure it didn't cost anything.

"Tomorrow, we pay da rent, and food bill, and den..." Sanyu sighed happily, "We go to village store!" Her smile stretched across her face. I could see every tooth in her mouth.

"Rent?" I asked.

"Yes. Papa call it playing, 'Our Town.'"

The wind had picked up, blowing leaves and dirt through the open-air pavilion. The building offered little more than a roof and a few half-walls. The worship time ended with a slower, soothing song. Everyone swayed like mothers rocking babies.

With softer music, I heard the sound of weeping. I scanned the row for Boy Sunday. He stood in front of Binti. She'd draped her arms around his shoulders and he sang with closed eyes. His cheeks appeared dry.

Still, somewhere, someone was crying.

I squatted down to see if I could hear any better. Across the aisle, Jonan lay sprawled on the concrete floor. His shoulders moved up and down with great sobs.

Just then lightning flashed, and a great crack of thunder followed. A wind gust engulfed the room as the storm front hit. Rain roared down on the metal roof. My uncle motioned everyone to head for bed, and kids scattered in all directions. Wyeth signaled that he would take Boy Sunday. When the room cleared, Binti was crouched over Jonan, but he continued to wail.

"Skeets!" I shouted. "Something's wrong!" I pointed emphatically at Jonan.

"Let's take him to the staff house!" Skeets had to yell over the noise. He carried Jonan while Binti and I ran ahead. Once inside, we dried off and huddled around the brokenhearted little boy. I put my hand on his head. Skeets spoke a simple prayer.

"Father, You know all about Jonan. You've been with him from the beginning. Hold him and comfort him like no other. He is too young to be so sad." Skeets looked up at me. "Get my sleeping bag for the couch."

"I stay by him?" asked Binti. Skeets nodded. We found an extra pillow and blanket. Then my uncle walked me to the guest quarters with an umbrella.

"You okay?" he asked.

"I know that kind of sorrow."

"Yes...you do." He paused at the door to embrace me.

I went inside and crawled into my dry warm bed. The downpour had lost its fury, but rain pattered steadily on the roof. In the dark, I replayed the evening in my mind...the dancing, the singing, and drummers tapping their hearts out. Maybe our worship released the rain, refreshing the earth. The storm had arrived like a stampede of horses. I pictured Jesus riding a white one.

Then I thought of Jonan's small body, weak with sorrow. He was "sadfull" to use Sanyu's word. It was a feeling I understood. Someone, somewhere, was always weeping...and it usually happened at night.

Chapter 42

IN THE MORNING hours, I drifted in and out of a light sleep. Mist and sunshine filled my mind like the dawn after a rainstorm. I sensed the presence of a kind man kneeling by my bed. I didn't look at him. Slowly, he leaned in close. Would he kiss my cheek? Perhaps he had a secret to tell. I could almost feel his breath on my skin.

I am sovereign over the tiniest things, he whispered.

Immediately, I opened my eyes. No one was there. I glanced around the room. It had seemed so real, but I didn't understand.

Thoughts of Jonan popped me into action. I found my flip-flops and pulled on a fresh shirt. My head poked through the neck hole just in time to find the doorway. I ran smack into Skeets.

"Whoa there, pony-tail!"

"How is he?"

"He slept some. Binti and I, less. And yes—he's still crying."

My thongs were on the wrong feet. I switched them and turned to go.

"Hold on." Skeets took my hand. "Walk with me." We headed out the entrance.

"I don't get it. Jonan's been here almost two months." I looked into my uncle's eyes. "Is he really *that* unhappy?"

"It's hard to say," he said. "If you ask these kids about their maamas or taatas, they cry hard tears."

"Wait a minute. What's a *taata*?" I'd seen it written on a black stone—the ones piled under the wooden cross out back.

"It means 'father.' They hardly speak of them."

"Why?" I rubbed sleep sand out of my eyes.

"Many fathers desert their kids here. It's one thing to lose a parent because of war or sickness. It's much harder to feel discarded."

I stopped walking.

Skeets looked at me. "Unthinkable, I know. Sanyu was abandoned as a baby. We found her at the dump." He put his arm around my shoulders. "But Jonan's sadness is different, I think."

We continued a little slower.

"Grief has its own rhythm," he continued. "Much sorrow is about loss. Or maybe remorse." We went around the building's corner. "Still, other weeping means a change is going on."

"Change?" I squinted, shielding my eyes from the bright sun.

Skeets had that faraway look. "You know," he said. "Like a caterpillar to a butterfly." He took a swig from his water bottle.

I stepped up on a long bench by the schoolrooms, keeping a hand on his shoulder as we strolled along. "But that doesn't happen to people," I said. "We are the same from beginning to end, except we get fatter and older when we stop getting taller."

Skeets laughed. "Do you think I'm fat or just old?"

"Neither really." I smiled and hopped back down.

He tipped the black water jug near the boy's latrine. The large container sat on a tree stump and had a small spigot at the bottom. Kids washed their hands there, since they didn't have toilet paper.

"The boys need to fill this," he noted.

My curiosity piqued. "What exactly is this 'change' kind of sorrow."

"It's like a transformation. Now there's a hundred-dollar word. Look that up in your Webster's."

We neared the staff house entrance.

"But what does that have to do with a little kid who can't stop crying?" I felt irritated and thoroughly helpless.

Skeets turned to face me, blocking the door. He wanted my full attention. "Think of Jonan like that empty black jug. Whatever happened to him drained his soul dry." He pushed my bangs to one side. "Transformation is like getting a refill with something better."

"A refill? Like a Coke?" I was being pesky.

"No, Rissy." His clear green eyes waited for mine. "Like a fountain."

Jonan was still sleeping on the couch. His eyelashes were moist. Binti squatted on a stool, holding a bowl of porridge for him. The corners of her mouth turned down and she shrugged.

"I stay now," I said. "You do what you need."

She rose and handed me a tattered pillowcase she'd been using as a Kleenex. It was damp and soiled. I rinsed it out in the washbasin and hung it in the sunniest window. Then I returned to Jonan's side.

Initially, he had seemed as *muffin* as every other kid here. But the scar along his jawline told a different story. Sometimes he had a bird-like restlessness, picking at his food with thin fingers. Once I saw him kicking small stones, stirring up dust like an angry mule. There wasn't really a category in our game for the heartsick.

Sunlight crept across the floor as I silently read several children's books stacked by the couch. One told a story about a boy who wanted a pet alligator. But the cute little lizard grew up to be a scary monster.

Maybe we needed a category for monsters. Bird, Horse, Muffin, and *Alligators*. Like taatas who left babies on garbage heaps.

Jonan rolled to his side, licking his cracked lips. I held a glass of water near his cheek and tried to lift his head.

"Saagala," he said.

Sanyu came in and knelt down next to me.

"He said, 'Saagala.'"

"It mean, 'I don't want.'" She stroked his head. "Okunywa, Jonan."

Whatever she said worked. He leaned forward and took a sip. Tears slipped down his cheeks again. It didn't seem possible that a child could cry for hours on end. Sanyu brought a clean terrycloth rag to dry his face.

"Why he so sad?" I silently mouthed the words.

She raised her eyebrows and shook her head. "Not yet time to ask."

Boy Sunday peeked in the doorway. I motioned him to come. He carried a homemade slingshot, which consisted of a small forked branch with a thick rubber band. In his other hand he held five bottle caps.

"Who give to you?" I asked, pointing to it.

"Muzungu." It had to be Wyeth. The duct tape handle gave it away.

I was certain it involved some horse-trading. "Did you carry his water?"

Boy nodded. He held it close, like a prized possession.

Sanyu shut her eyes. Her lips started to move. I figured she was praying. I blotted Jonan's tears and bowed my head too. But that meant talking to God. And if I did that, I had to believe in Him. I pursed my lips but said nothing out loud.

God? What about Jonan here? He's just a little kid who has nothing. No mama or taata. Something happened. I've seen his scar. If you could...well, I know you're busy with presidents and wars and car accidents, but if you would only take a second...and...

My throat swelled. Would God answer me? I listened in the stillness as Sanyu continued her prayers. Boy fiddled with his slingshot. Soon, Jonan began sobbing again. I had to get out of there. Binti came in as I left.

The sun had risen high in the sky. A few maamas sorted dry beans in the shade of the Hope House. I looked the other way. I didn't feel like talking.

Sanyu caught up with me. "You have da payday?"

I felt in my pocket. The Monopoly money was still there.

"Come." She took my arm. "We pay bills and shop."

Sanyu handed a fake hundred-dollar bill to the Joy House mama. She told me to put my rent money in Skeets' mailbox. Then we stopped by the cook's hut, and paid fifty each.

"Now da fun!" Her eyelids fluttered with delight. At one end of the storage container stood a small wooden shack. Inside, every shelf was stuffed with a myriad of goods. You could buy head-scarves, old watches, bubblegum, Frisbees, or sodas to mention a few. Musa was the storekeeper that day. I wondered at the smiles on their faces.

Skeets pulled up in the Land Cruiser.

Wy swung the door open. "Wanna go to town?"

"Why not," I said. Sanyu remained, still trying on scarves.

At the gate, Okello joined us with his AK-47. We swerved

around large puddles and pulled out on the main road. The car's gutsy engine roared like a roused lion.

Traveling on the roads felt harrowing. Trucks passed us with inches to spare. Skeets veered right and left to avoid potholes. It made me sick as a dog. We nearly hit a woman carrying a giant bundle of bananas on her head. She stepped off the road's edge with perfect timing. Skeets didn't seem nervous at all.

Finally, we stopped in front of a small dingy store and waited for Okello to give the okay. An Indian man with a turban looked up as we entered his grocery. He nodded excitedly and brought out four Cokes with straws. The sweet fizzy drinks were warm, but brought the comfort of home. Wy and I sat on some boxes near the counter. Skeets and Okello sat on tall stools.

"Okay!" Skeets said in a gruff voice. "Hand over the chocolate!"

The Indian chuckled as he went to the back room and returned with a bag of Hershey's kisses. I couldn't believe my eyes! We hadn't had candy in so long.

At the same time the shop door opened. The storeowner quickly tucked the bag under the counter. A large African man in uniform strutted up to the counter and barged into the conversation. I leaned back.

"I am your customer!" he announced. His forearm had a snake tattoo.

"When we borrowed you last, you didn't pay back!" said the owner.

The big man puffed up his chest. "What have you for eating?"

The shelves were half empty, displaying an odd assortment of packaged foods.

"We have remained with fish only," he replied.

"Sirya Byennyanja! Ndya nnyama yokka!" The man scoffed with disgust, pounding his fist on the counter.

I jumped in my seat.

"English, please!" said the Indian.

Skeets translated. "He says he doesn't eat fish. Only meat."

The storekeeper stared at the proud man who would not look at him. The African grew more impatient by the second. Finally he flashed a knife.

Skeets stood up and stepped forward. Okello gripped his gun, ready for action.

The Indian turned and marched to the back room. He argued with a woman in another language. It sounded like a fight. Then it got quiet. He returned with a slab of raw red meat and wrapped it in a piece of newspaper.

"Away now!" he said, handing the package to the rude man.

The man gloated over winning the standoff. He waved his blade as he left.

"*Alligator*," I said under my breath. "Definitely, *alligator*."

The storeowner adjusted his turban. "We barely survive with all the looters."

"You have gun?" Okello asked him.

He sighed. "No, but as they say, 'a bone in a dog's mouth keeps him from biting you.'"

"Only for a while," said Skeets.

The man pulled out the hidden candy. My uncle stacked real bills on the counter.

"You are overpaid!" said the Indian.

Skeets winked at him. "Cokes and chocolate are hard to find, ssebo."

I knew he was paying for the meat as well.

Back on the road, Skeets spoke up. "Tonight we're having an overnight for the new kids. I need your help."

"Our help?" I echoed.

"Yeah. See the white tag on each kiss?" He held up the bag. "I want you to replace it with a strip of paper the same size and write a name on it. One for each kid."

"Only one kiss? That's worse than one Lay's potato chip," Wyeth said.

"It's not about the candy." Skeets glanced over his shoulder at us. "Street kids either work like dogs or steal to eat. I want them to understand what a gift is."

"But you make them pay for rent and food," I added.

"As they should. But, this is different."

We drove along a back road to avoid foot traffic. I noticed a pair of shoes placed perfectly together on the side of the road. It was the second time I'd seen shoes left behind. I elbowed Wyeth and pointed.

"People disappear in this country," he whispered.

I let out a nervous laugh. "Right."

He cupped his mouth by my ear so no one else could hear.

"I'm serious Rissy. Musa told me. When the government kills somebody, shoes are the sign. Causing fear gives them power over the people. They're workin' it, see?"

We turned into the compound, and Waiswa locked the gate behind us.

Chapter 43

THE JALOPY SPUTTERED to a stop by the staff quarters. I jumped out to check on Jonan, only to find an empty couch. My heartbeat sped up. I ran out to call Binti but she was nowhere in sight. Musa stood in the doorway of the Love House.

"Where's Jonan?"

"At borehole. Binti take..."

I took off before he finished.

As I came near, a high-pitched squeal stopped me short. Then I heard giggling. Binti tickled her brother as she scrubbed him clean. The kid rarely even smiled.

I skipped the rest of the way. "What happened?" I asked.

Binti gave me the eyebrow nod and smiled. She dried Jonan off. As soon as he was dressed, he ran off to play.

"Tell me, tell me! I can't stand it!" I cried out.

Binti's grin revealed her crooked teeth. She automatically covered her mouth. "My brotha be paining in heart long time. Tears and tears. Many."

My hands rose up. "I know! I was there!"

"No, I meaning long time *before* Papa take us from street. I tink he cry bout Taata again."

"You have a father?" I asked.

"Two years back, our fa-tha became Amin soldier. My brotha angry den cuz Taata prepare to leave us. He fight Taata for gun

254

and shot go off. It cut through Jonan face." Binti pointed to her jawbone. "He not talk to fa-tha after dat."

"Where is your father now?"

"He die in war. Den sickness take our mum too. In my mind, I tink...Jonan still sadfull bout dat."

I felt stricken by the thought. My mind reeled with images.

But Binti wasn't a wreck. "It okay, Rissy. Dere be good to tell." She spoke calmly and made me sit on a wooden bench by the hand pump.

"Today, when he git quiet a bit, I say, 'My brotha...you pain-ing for Mummy?'" She dumped dirty water from the basin. "But he say, 'I *not* sad Binny.' Den I ask, 'You angry at Taata?' but he shake da head no."

"So why all the tears?" I asked.

"Jonan say 'Heaven be *kilungi*. It mean *wonderness.*'" She hugged herself, imitating his strong feelings.

Heaven?

Her face brightened like she'd saved the best part for last. She plopped down on the bench and pulled me close. "Den, when we walk here Jonan use da tiny voice..." She meant he whispered. Her face clouded up like she was about to cry.

"He say to me, '*I never know'd a love like dis.*'"

"Like what?" I asked, lifting my shoulders.

"He feel God wid him so powderful, it make him cry."

Pressure mounted in my lungs. "So, he cried his eyes out, be-cause of God?"

"Yes! Dat it!" She jumped to her feet. "God come down to us at worship time last night." She laughed and clapped once. "I know—cuz I feeled it den too! Jonan have tears, cuz it be so good, he fraid it go away like Taata and mummy."

I felt bewildered. Things were not as they seemed. Never in my world had a child wept for joy or love. Kids cried over paper cuts, broken toys, or sad goodbyes. The closest I'd come to happy tears was Christmas Eve, leaning into my father's side with Skeets' letter in my pocket. I believed then that God would hold my broken world together.

Jonan was far too young to pretend. And why would he? Something happened to him that I could not explain.

I never know'd a love like dis. Maybe it was the fountain.

SANYU AND I scribbled names on thin strips of paper for each chocolate kiss. We stored them in the mini-fridge in Skeets' simple kitchen. Wyeth and Musa set up the main area of the staff quarters like a huge secret fort. Skeets had given them an old blue spinnaker. The boys rigged the giant curved sail to create a tent, attaching different points to the ceiling. Then they strung up white Christmas lights, making a starlit sky like a small planetarium. Blankets covered the floor, and we arranged pillows and couch cushions around the edge to form a circle.

"Every ting ready!" said Sanyu. Drumbeats signaled the call to worship as twilight fell. Most kids would go to the evening service. I waited for the new kids to arrive.

Boy skipped in and swung on my arm as if it were a jungle vine. We fell into the pillows. A new little girl entered the room, wearing a lime green smock. She held hands with Sanyu but trailed behind on tiptoes.

Jonan rushed in ahead of Binti.

"Hey Jo-jo," I grabbed his wrist. "Tears all gone?"

He grinned. "Greens" from the evening meal were still stuck in his teeth. He hopped around on one foot, no longer that serious shy boy moping in the shadows.

My heart swelled.

Excitement sparkled in the air like lightning bugs. I could see white toothy grins in the dim room. Skeets lit a candle and placed it on a wooden stool in the center of the circle. He motioned everyone to sit down. Boy burrowed under my arm.

"Let's give thanks," my uncle said. "Everyone say one thing. Sanyu, you start."

"I say, rain!" she shouted.

The small girl next to her in the green dress tucked her chin—too shy to speak.

Skeets pointed to my brother. "Now you."

"Warm Cokes!" Wyeth said.

The turns would go clockwise and come full circle to me.

"Matooke," said Jonan.

"Dancing!" said another.

Tension was building in my head. I didn't know what to say.

Binti went next. "I thanking God to love us."

Skeets agreed, giving an emphatic nod.

"No more rags," said Musa, sporting a Superman t-shirt.

"Nseka!" shouted a girl. It meant, "laughter." Some giggled in response.

Boy Sunday didn't say anything, but held up his slingshot.

"Ah, yes!" Skeets winked at Boy. "Our watchman."

Then, all eyes turned to me. I wet my lips. Why was this so hard? Sure, I felt thankful for things...for Skeets and Nana and Pops.

"So Rissy, you're last," Skeets filled in the silence. "What are you thankful for?"

I exhaled deeply. "I guess...fountains."

Skeets gave a knowing smile. "And I'm thankful that God, who is sovereign over all things—is first and foremost a father."

"But what is—sovereign?" I had to ask.

"Like *kabaka*, meaning a king that rules over a land. Of course that can be bad or good."

"Yeah, like Idi Amin," Musa said quietly.

"And that's my point—God, who is in charge of everything, could be a mean and punishing ruler," said my uncle. "But He's not. He's a father!"

Any talk about fathers was like listening to someone sing out of tune.

Skeets continued. "And not only that...He wants us to call him Taata, Papa or Daddy. Think of *it*! But here's the thing." Skeets opened his Bible. "He's *not* like your earthly fathers."

The room became still as a graveyard.

"God is not angry. He's not the drunk father who beat you or left you behind."

I crossed my arms. *But He did nothing while our real fathers did.*

Skeets had bookmarked two pages. "It says here, when you were lost and helpless, 'the Lord your God bore you, as a man bears his son, in all the way that you went until you came to this place.' That means God has always been with you."

He wasn't there for Tuck. I couldn't stop arguing inside.

Skeets flipped over to the second marker. "Your maamas are also gone now."

A few kids lowered their heads. Boy covered his eyes.

Skeets read a different passage: "God says, 'Can a woman forget her sucking child, that she should have no compassion on the son of her womb? Even these may forget...'" His voice trembled a little. "But...the Lord says, 'I will *not* forget you.'"

How could anyone really know? Those sentences were thousands of years old. Maybe things got so bad, God gave up on us.

Skeets closed the Bible. "A long time ago in America, there lived a man and his wife who were unable to have children of their own. They became very rich selling candy." He opened his hand, revealing a Hershey's kiss. "You know, a *switi* like this."

The kids perked up.

"The man sold many of these, calling them chocolate kisses. He earned billions of shillings *and* gave it all to care for children like you." Skeets lifted his arms. "That is what your Taata in Heaven is like."

My uncle motioned for me to stand. Reluctantly, I rolled to my feet.

Then he said to all the kids, "Do you know how God feels about you?"

No one said anything or moved.

Skeets drew me close, holding my face in his hands. "When you see God, face to face, you will know what love is. His tenderness for you is not something you can fully understand on earth." Suddenly, he wrapped his arms around me and whirled around making a complete circle. My feet landed feather light. Then he kissed my forehead.

I wanted that love.

"God has a father's kiss for you," he said to all the children. "You are no longer orphans. You are now sons and daughters."

I returned to my place next to Boy. Sanyu brought out the tray.

"And His love cannot be earned or stolen. It is a gift," Skeets said, ending his talk.

The kids jumped up and crowded around Sanyu as she handed out chocolates to each one by name. Skeets watched happily and put one arm over Wy's shoulders.

"Heck no!" Wyeth pushed him away. "You ain't kissing me!" Skeets puckered up and tried anyway. A happy scuffle followed.

Sanyu led the singing. "Oh see, what the Lord has done!"

The kids echoed the refrain, and soon they all were clapping in rhythm.

I laid back on the pillows, wishing the overnight would end.

Chapter 44

THE HOUR GREW late. Skeets gathered bedding from a storage closet, and we nested together under the parasail sky. Though our starry night was electric, at least we didn't have to worry about disease-carrying mosquitoes. I placed a cotton blanket over my legs.

Binti slid in. "Can I share da cover?" Her breath smelled faintly of chocolate.

"Of course, you Big Pony." I lifted it to share.

"Tell me, if I be pony, does dat make me *horse*?" she asked.

Wyeth and I had used our game terms without thinking.

"Well, not really," I said. "No, you are mostly *muffin*. Only a pinch of *horse*."

Sanyu came over to join us.

"What be *muffin*?" asked Binti.

"I know dis game," Sanyu interrupted. "*Muffin* is like sleeping baby."

"Yes, but to start off it's actually a small cake, sweet and spongy—about this big." I formed a circle with my hands to show them the size. "You eat it for breakfast."

"Den I not sure bout dat!" Binti retorted.

"But Sanyu is right." I touched Binti's arm so she'd look at me. "In our game, *muffin* means all things beautiful and soft and kind. You know—gentle old grandmas with smooth hands. People who

260

laugh easily, and babies too. *Muffin* is good."

Binti smiled. "I want to be all tings beautiness." She rolled her body toward me. "Den what a *horse*?"

Skeets dragged a chair over and sat down with a steaming cup of tea. It smelled of lemon and ginger. "Now Binti," he warned. "That's a complicated question—one that can only be understood by playing the game." He towed his teabag around the hot water.

"But I want Iris to explainate," she said.

I leaned forward, scanning the room for Wyeth. If he was in earshot, he'd be mad. We never explained the game. It was an unspoken rule. Still, that seemed unfair to kids in another culture. Nana had always given us little clues.

I spoke in hushed tones. "The whole game is a way of understanding what people are like—their personalities for starters, but that's not all." I tucked my hair behind my ears. "It's also the way they look and talk and move about. *Horse* is someone who's strong, powerful, and bossy."

"What you say, 'bossy'?" Binti's forehead wrinkled.

I realized this could come out all wrong.

My uncle chuckled. "She means someone who takes charge, runs things—a leader."

I'd never thought of it that way, but Skeets had played the game much longer.

Binti leaned back on one elbow. "Mmm."

"But a *horse* person can also be a bully," I turned to Skeets. "Remember that guy in the Indian man's grocery who stole the meat? He was *horse*, but worse. Actually, I thought he was an alligator."

Skeets jutted out his lower lip. "I didn't know we had a new category."

Sanyu tipped her head to one side. "What about *bird*?"

"It's someone who's scrupulous and persnickety." I used two magnificent adjectives from my collection.

"Girl..." Skeets shook his head. "You'd better speak plain English."

"*Bird* is someone who gets mad easily." I fluttered my hands to act it out. "They're restless, touchy, picky, fussy." I said, using a whiney tone, pecking at them with my fingers.

Binti started to laugh.

Sanyu looked at me with big eyes.

"So tell me Iris," my uncle said, staring at the ceiling. "What do you say I am?"

I thought for a moment. "You're *way* too complicated to figure."

"Why's that?" He sipped his tea.

"Well, you're nice like a *muffin*, but not a weakling." I sat up and crossed my legs. "You're strong. Yet not overpowering like *horse*. And you're never flustered in a birdy way, but you see a lot, like a wise old owl." I said. "It's confusing. You don't really fit."

"How about your father?" asked Skeets. "What's his category?"

The question dropped heavily on my chest. "The *worst* kind of *bird-horse*," I scowled.

My friends looked at me with wonderment.

"*Bird-horse* be very bad den?" Sanyu asked.

I knew if I got started, there'd be things I'd regret saying. My face grew warm. The chill of perspiration formed around my neck.

Skeets leaned in. "Tell us more, Iris. It might help everybody."

I took a sudden breath and began to rant. "If we did anything wrong—anything at all—he'd chase us down like a wild horse. Other times he'd jab and pick at us." My throat swelled. "One minute, everything was okay, but an hour later our world was wrecked!" I pulled the covers to my eyes.

Skeets set his mug on the floor.

"Somehow we were always in trouble..." I didn't want to cry, but it was too late. "But half the time I didn't know why."

"We?" Wyeth piped in from across the room. "He mostly picked on me."

"I know." Tears surged. "But I still felt everything." An embarrassing silence followed. Binti placed a hand on my shoulder. A few minutes passed as I cried hard tears. Skeets stroked my head. Then there was quiet.

Sanyu nestled in close. "What about God?"

I scrunched my eyebrows. At first, I didn't understand. "What about Him?"

"Is God *bird, horse* or *muffin*?" she probed gently.

"I don't know. I just don't...I can't talk about it." I pulled the blanket over my head and hid my face in the pillow. And that was that. No one pressed me further.

Sleep eventually refereed a time out.

SUNLIGHT PEEKED THROUGH openings in the parasail. I stepped out quietly and walked down the borehole path to freshen up at the well. My cheeks felt itchy from salty tears. A shadow crossed overhead. I shaded my eyes to look up. The hooded vulture soared above with a mouse dangling from her beak. She'd caught a nice breakfast for her baby bird. Not so nice for the mouse.

I continued on my way. Sanyu's question about God had rattled me. I almost said, *bird-horse*. How could that be? How could God be like Hank? Was it fair to put God in a category? Did He have a personality like people? I mulled it over.

Bird was more than a whiney or nitpicky person. A vulture could see a lot from the sky. I thought of the taxi driver crossing the bridge over Rocky Cliffs River. He noticed the man falling through the ice, and that saved the guy's life. Maybe God was *bird* in that way—One who sees.

And what would it be like to see all things? It'd be a lot of information for one thing. Things had to be complicated for God. What was He supposed to do when one farmer asked for rain and another pleaded for sunshine? I supposed He could do both if they lived far enough apart. Still, how did He know what to do in difficult situations?

It was hard to imagine God's predicament. I didn't even trust my own eyes. What looked like sorrow in Jonan was actually joy. God poured out pure love on that little boy. And what about that night long ago when Skeets talked with Detective Roberts about Jesus? I saw God's love change that man's face. Maybe God was *muffin* too.

I came upon a few pushy goats. They sniffed my shirt to see if it might pass for breakfast. I shooed them off. Those flea-bit critters ate just about anything. Fortunately Skeets had tethered them to the fence.

At the borehole, I pumped enough water to quickly splash my face and arms. Without a towel, I'd have to drip-dry in the warm sunshine. An old tree stump made a nice perch. Everything seemed new again in the mornings.

The banana trees were laden with fruit. Their leaves glimmered with morning dew. I reached up to pry off a banana. Like everything fresh-picked, it had no bruises, no brown spots. If God made everything good and beautiful from the start, how did things go so wrong? Was God mad about it too? In a scary way, God seemed more *horse* than anything else—strong, but not very safe.

On the way back, Sanyu saw me coming and sprinted over. "You nervousing me!"

I lowered my chin.

"You be gone." She wiped her forehead. "And you never answered da question. I upset you, yes?"

I took her hand. "I be needing a tink."

She smiled at my African English. We headed toward the guest quarters. Others were stirring. A few girls recited rhymes while clapping each other's hands. Smoke from the cooking shed fire floated through the air. A new day was underway.

"Rissy." Sanyu pulled my arm. "Talk at me."

I looked into her soft brown eyes. "I guess God is *muffin*, because of the love He gave to Jonan." I leaned in. "But I too have felt tings—tings that Binti calls 'wonderness'"

Sanyu listened intently.

"But maybe God is *bird*, 'cause He can see things from up high."

"And what about da *horse*?"

"That's the trouble," I said. "Horses are totally *unpredictable*."

"What you say?" She didn't know the word.

"If God is *horse*, I never know what will happen."

Boy Sunday called for me.

"What I know'd is dis." She sounded firm. "God is good. So if He be *horse*, den He be a good horse. You don't know what He do or don't do, but you know Him. You don't know where He go, but you know Him, and you want to follow and go dere wid Him."

Until that moment, I'd never thought of *horse* as something good. But what she said was exactly how I felt about Skeets.

Chapter 45

A PLEASANT BREEZE rustled the leaves on the canopy tree. We'd been in Africa for several months, but it didn't feel like November here. At first I had been glad to get away from everything that reminded me of Tuck. Still, I missed adventures in the Middle Strip and craved blueberry muffins. I thought of TV shows like *Happy Days* and wondered if Anna Rae liked any of the eighth grade boys. I couldn't dwell on it.

Several weeks had passed since the overnight. The evening had stirred up many questions and some new thoughts. Still, a curious peace had come over me as if Mama was singing a faint lullaby in the next room.

Worship time felt different too. I didn't worry if I made the right moves at the right times. On Sunday nights, Wy and Musa passed the offering basket. One Sunday, I pulled out my fake money and plucked a few tens to put in. Jonan donated a smooth gray rock instead. When the basket came to me, I saw the word "Taata" written on his stone.

Binti put her face close to mine. "He forgiving our fa-tha," she whispered.

A sudden coldness came over my body. I stared straight ahead.

"Papa say it greatish offering of all," she added.

All those rocks by the cross out back were not gravestones.

After the service, I hurried back to my room to find the jeans I'd worn on the airplane. It had been too hot for pants. They were under the bed inside my luggage. Sure enough, in one of the pockets I found my stone. I had taken it from Rocky Cliffs River the day Skeets and Wy caught crawdads—the day we buried Mama. I rolled it over and over in my hand. The current had worn it smooth. It was a piece of home. But maybe it was more. Maybe it wasn't coincidence that I carried a stone in my pocket.

The next morning, some of the girls invited me to join their jump rope game. First I swayed with the movement of the ropes to get in rhythm.

> One, two three, four...open up the closed door.
> Seven, eight, nine, ten...now it's time to run in!

I hopped to the middle, jumping in time.

> Maama in da back room...cookin' up da bread.
> Taata ate so much...he almost dead.
> Brotha take da last piece...he's a bum.
> Sista cries her eyes out...not a crumb.
> Baby in da cradle...cryin' for some food
> Maama always busy...cuz Taata so rude.
> She bake another one...bigger den da last.
> Grandpa come in quick...and steal it fast.
> Taata gots a bellyache...Grandpa too.
> Bread's all gone...dere's none for you.

The twirling sped up.

> One, two...whatcha gonna do?
> Three, four...dere's no more.
> Five, six...can't eat bricks
> Seven, eight...throw da plate.
> What-ya-gonna-eat? Oh—no!
> Livin'-in-da-street? Don't go!

I leaped out and darted away. Their singsong was probably true, but I didn't want to think about. I reached in my pocket. My rock was still there.

Sanyu crossed the yard, waving her hands over her head. "It's time, it's time!" she shouted, rushing to meet me.

"For what?" I asked.

"Da crane flower!" she said.

You'd have thought a miracle had taken place.

"Come," she said, pulling my belt-loop. "I show you."

We ran toward the front gate where Waiswa sat in the shade. Plants with long leathery leaves like banana trees had been planted in a row along the compound wall. They never seemed all that special to me.

She held up several fingers. "We wait *four* years!" She was beside herself. Sanyu's excitement got Waiswa's attention, and together we walked down the row. One of the stalks had opened, shooting five bright orange petals upwards like a fan. Two deep blue petals stuck out level with the ground. It was a spectacular flower.

"Bird of Paradise," said Waiswa. "A long time comin'...slower den baby elephant."

How could something so beautiful grow in such a war-torn place? But life inside these walls was different from the world out there. In here, flowers were watered, children were fed, and you could sleep without fear. Out there a mass of needy people swarmed the edge of the road in ragged clothes—pot-bellied children, haggard women, and men who could steal with the flash of a knife.

Skeets ran over and interrupted. "I've had a call from the diocese up north. There's an abandoned baby in a certain village about an hour's drive from here. The priest said to come right away." He shuffled his feet. "Wanna go?" He looked at me. "I need a mama-girl to hold the baby."

"Me?" I asked, remembering 'Muzungu was like ghost.'

"Yeah. Tribal leaders believe I'm legit when I have my family along."

"What about Sanyu?" It seemed awkward to leave her out.

"Wy and Okello are coming too. Not enough room in the car. I have to pick up some chicken feed on the way back."

The Land Cruiser sputtered like it had a bad cold. To my relief, Okello climbed in with his AK-47. I sat on top of the toolbox to see ahead and lessen my nausea from pothole swerving.

The road teemed with activity. Several motorcycle taxis carried a few nicer-dressed people. Everyone else had to "foot" his or her way, as Binti would say. A tall slim man walked next to a bike loaded down with sugar cane stalks. Close behind, a woman balanced at least fifty bananas on her head. She made it look easy. Our car idled as a herder prodded his narrow-faced cows to one side with a long stick.

We passed a small market. Vendors selling shish kabobs crowded around a public transport van. Skeets said he never took his chances on "them vittles." One man had arranged tomatoes in small pyramids on the counter of his shack store. Behind him a sign said, "CHEEP cigars."

We broke free from the town still heading north. Up ahead three bricks, stacked end to end, stood in the middle of the road.

"Why are we stopping?" I asked.

"Road block," Skeets said quietly over his shoulder. "See those guys, lying in the shade over there?"

"Are we in trouble?" asked Wyeth.

"Only if you don't stop," said my uncle. He leaned out the window, "Oli otya, gentlemen!" They did not readily respond.

I slid off the toolbox, trying to make myself as small as possible.

Finally one spoke. "Olinayo ekyokulya kyonna?"

"Dey want our food," said Okello.

"Okay, let's give them what we have." Skeets said. Inside a small cooler we'd brought a few mangoes, some flat bread, and half a bag of Hershey kisses.

"Jangu wano!" said one soldier, reaching for his gun.

Skeets briskly turned to Okello. "No!" He spoke with hushed intensity. "Don't get out of the car. It's too risky."

My stomach flipped.

"Ssebo!" Skeets yelled, "We are in a hurry! Do you understand? Otegeera?"

The one with the gun walked very slowly to the car as if to aggravate my uncle on purpose. He pointed his weapon right in Skeets' face. "Ogenda wa?"

Skeets understood their question. Okello moved his gun out in plain sight.

"We go north to rescue children, abaana," said Skeets, keeping his voice calm.

"Papers?" It was the first time the armed man spoke any English. The tip of his gun was only inches from my uncle's head. The air felt too thick to breathe.

Skeets reached deep into his pocket and pulled out a folded paper that had yellowed with age. The man studied it and threw it back.

"Muzungu. You are from where?"

"I work with Church of Uganda near Mbarara." Skeets said. Sweat beaded on the back of his neck. "Muwattu, please ssebo, let us get on."

The man bent down to see Wy and me. His hand came through the back window as if he wanted to touch my hair. Not knowing what else to do, I put the half-bag of kisses in his palm. He stepped back appearing surprised.

"Switi!" he said, lifting it so the others could see. Then he turned back, examining us for what felt like an eternity. Finally he said, "Genda eri! Go away!" and waved us forward with his gun.

The moment had passed without trouble, but I knew something could've happened.

Chapter 46

How much fear will come on the wicked man?

W E JOURNEYED ON.
"How much longer," I asked in a loud voice.

"Half a kilometer," Skeets said. A wisp of white steam curled up from the hood. He pulled to the side of the road, cuffing the steering wheel in frustration. "It's boiling over again."

Okello touched his shoulder. "I walk dere and find da baby. No Muzungu—no bribe," he said, leaving the gun in the car.

"Okay." Skeets lifted the hood. "We'll meet you later." The radiator sounded like a teakettle on a hot stove. He waited a few minutes for it to cool. Wy and I climbed out to stretch our legs. "Stand back," he warned, loosening the cap with a wrench. Steam billowed out like a genie from a bottle.

"Settle down you old crank." My uncle was known to talk to cars. Wyeth grabbed the water jug in the back. Skeets poured what little there was in the radiator. "We'll need more." He scanned the area. A boy tending some goats watched us nearby.

"Hey, Omulenzi! Do you have water, mazzi?" asked Skeets.

The kid pointed to a borehole about fifty yards up the road.

"Thank God." Skeet said. "Wyeth, you guard the car. Rissy, come with me." He sounded uptight.

We trekked up the road with the empty jug. Skeet slung the

270

AK-47 over his shoulder. It was midday and getting hot. No one was at the well. He glanced around before leaning the gun against a tree. We cooled down wetting our faces and arms. Skeets cleaned his sunglasses with a shirttail. I pumped again to fill the jug, but cupped my hands when the stream came. For a second, I thought about starting a water fight.

Right then, a woman staggered toward us. She'd come out to the road through a cluster of mud huts. Moaning loudly, she held her head with both hands. The baby swaddled to her back was crying. She veered left and right, trying to find her balance.

Water drained from my hands. I stepped closer to Skeets.

A man appeared to be after her. He stomped out, holding a thick hoe handle. She quickened her pace, as he yelled a string of threatening words.

Blood raced through my heart.

The man caught up to the woman. Lurching forward, he struck her with the heavy handle. She shrieked like a dying rabbit. The force of the blow caused her to stumble forward a few large steps before falling to all fours. The baby came loose in the struggle, hitting the dirt with a thud.

In that moment, something inside me took over. I ran to that baby.

"Iris! No!" Skeets yelled. It was too late. I'd lost my mind. The cry of that tiny child had a magnetic pull as strong as a hundred horses. I made my body its shield.

Skeets pleaded with the enraged man. "Ssebo! Ssebo! There is another way!"

"Ndeka! Genda, muzungu!" the man shouted. Every word sounded like cursing the way he sneered and flashed his teeth. I started to shake uncontrollably.

As Skeets approached the man, he turned and lunged at me, swinging his club. A blast of pain shot through my upper leg. I cried out. The baby wailed louder.

Skeets jumped on the guy, and it turned into an all out brawl to get the hoe handle. The man wrenched it free long enough to clobber the woman again. She screamed and collapsed on the ground. Skeets was determined to stop him. He tripped the man to wrestle him on the ground.

Oh, God, oh God! I felt my heart would give out.

The men grunted and moaned as both struggled to get the upper hand. Skeets' face had turned beet red. He was much stronger than I knew. They went back and forth until my uncle finally rolled the guy over on a small boulder. The rock was squarely under his back and weakened him long enough for Skeets to gain control.

"Yimirira! Stop it!" yelled my uncle. "Your violence has no eyes!"

The man kept a tenacious grip on his weapon.

"Speak with me. Is she your wife? Mukyala wange?" Skeets asked.

The man huffed in frustration. He clenched his jaw. His eyes shot arrows.

I lowered my cheek on the baby's forehead. "Shh, shh," I said, trying to calm the crying infant. My leg throbbed, but I kept my body wrapped tightly around that child. The woman whimpered in pain. Barely conscious, she lay only ten feet from me.

The husband spewed more angry words. His eyes looked vacant and crazed.

"Okukuba—you beat her for what reason? Why? Lwaki?" asked Skeets.

All of a sudden, the man pushed him off with one great shove and yanked the club from his hold. "Woman *not* refuse husband!" he shouted. He swung wildly and knocked Skeets out cold.

I sucked in air. Terrifying images passed rapidly through my mind—he meant to kill us all. *The rifle. I must...*

As I squirmed to stand, he struck his wife with what seemed to be a fatal blow. I flinched at the sound and lost all strength. She did not move after that. The world started to spin.

The baby! I hunkered over the child as the man weaved towards us. It was too late for the gun. He bent over, thrusting me aside to find the concealed baby. He reeked of alcohol.

In that moment I felt utterly alone. The meanness of the world was at my feet. I felt faint. Everything became dream-like. He steadied himself, raising his club. I winced. *Oh God!* I rolled back over the child. *Help us!*

A swoosh of air passed my ear as the wooden club dropped inches from my head.

The ground started to shake. A loud rumble filled my ears. Then all at once, the thunderous roar of ten trains came over me. I heard a thunk. Then there was nothing but blinding dust. I coughed hard.

What just happened? My thoughts swirled with confusion.

Finally the air started to clear. The sound of the motor was deafening. The baby was crying so hard it barely took a breath. I wiped dirt from my eyes. We were under the fender of a car, between the front wheels.

I glanced around. It was Wyeth! He'd rammed the guy. The blow knocked the man fifteen feet. He writhed on the ground, clutching his thigh, groaning in pain. And Wy stood over him pointing the gun.

Oh God! He's gonna shoot him... "No-o!" My voice was hoarse.

Wyeth's shoulders shook hard. I heard his weeping. I twisted out, struggling to my feet. Limping. Each step brought sharp pains. Any moment the man might rise up, or Wy could pull the trigger.

But it hurt too much. I sank to the ground, crawling with one knee, dragging my injured leg. "Wy, no-o-o!" At last I reached him and wrapped my arms around his knees. "Please, Wy! Please don't." My whole body trembled. "Don't be like him..." I started to sob. "It has to stop."

It seemed like forever, but Wy finally gave up and dropped down next to me.

The angry husband seized the moment to get away. He stumbled off and ran smack into a woman with a basket on her head. He growled at her, batting the air like a madman before disappearing into the thick brush.

The motor's engine stopped, and Okello's boots appeared. I looked up. He held the gun. It was over. I crawled back to the baby. The little one had passed out from exhaustion. Burying my face in the cloth wrap, I cried and cried and cried.

Chapter 47

How much shouting will be done, when a white horse comes through the clouds in splendor?

Soon a small crowd gathered. Okello had Skeets sitting up and sipping some water. My uncle looked pretty rough. One badly bruised eye had started to swell. A thin line of blood trickled down from his left ear. It took him a while to get his bearings. Wy remained on the ground with his head between his knees.

A woman knelt by the collapsed wife. She put her hand on the woman's body. An older man with short gray whiskers and a brown cylindrical hat worked his way through the onlookers to speak with Skeets and Okello. I figured he was the village leader. The man spoke to Okello in Lugandan.

"Dey not sure da wife will make it," said Okello. "It a pity."

The village leader crouched down by Skeets. "Tusonyiwe," he said placing a hand over his heart.

"He be sorry," Okello said, glancing at me as well.

The man continued in what seemed like a long explanation.

Skeets listened patiently, resting his chin on his knee as if his head felt heavy.

Finally, the leader paused.

"He say dat husband make da woman to cry every day. Dis not first time beating for her," said Okello. "Dat why dey lie, saying baby is abandon. The maama try to save her child." He looked at the battered woman. "Maybe orphan now."

My lips parted as I put it all together. The baby by my side was the one we actually came to get!

"He begging for our help." Okello conferred with Skeets.

"Ntegeera, I understand." said Skeets, sounding utterly spent. "We'll take the child."

The village leader stood, clasping his hands as one praying and briefly bowed to my uncle. With glassy eyes, he repeated, "Weebale, ssebo! Weebale."

Okello carried me to the car. His strength and kindness made me calm inside. He took extra care with my wounded leg. Then he helped Skeets. I'm sure my uncle's "paining" was worse than mine. A woman had rewrapped the baby in swaddling cloth and tucked it in a basket. Wy climbed in. Okello placed the sleeping child between us in the backseat. My brother looked sullen and didn't want to talk.

Clouds had moved in. A light rain sprinkled the windshield as we pulled out. Fortunately the radiator had recovered. Soon the downpour tapped like hail on the car's roof. Slick muddy roads made an uneasy ride. We fishtailed around curves in the road. My uncle tried to hold his battered head steady. He kept grimacing. Okello had to pull over so Skeets could throw up. After that, Okello stuffed his shirt in a plastic bag to give Skeets a temporary pillow. The trip home seemed endless, as the red dirt road stretched out for miles and miles.

As soon as we pulled in the front gate, Sanyu took the baby. Musa stared at Skeets. Binti covered her mouth with one hand. Wy slid out and ran off.

"You talk at me later?" Sanyu said. "We were fearing."

I nodded.

From there, Okello took us straight to the clinic in Mbarara. A nurse brought out a wheelchair for Skeets. Okello carried me in. "Dey see you quickly," he said. "Muzungus be paying customers."

The doctor turned out to be Australian. He asked my uncle a hundred questions, while a nurse checked his blood pressure. When she stuck a glass thermometer in his mouth, Okello spoke for him.

The doctor used a pencil thin flashlight to check Skeets' eyes and then a scope-like tool for his bleeding ear. "Looks like a bad concussion, mate," he said, hanging his stethoscope around his neck.

I showed him the large bruise on my upper leg. He pressed in places and asked me what hurt. I didn't like the prodding.

"At worst," he said, "you have a bruised bone, my girl, and a boatload of damaged tissue."

"How do you fix that?" I asked.

"You'll have to tough it out with aspirin and some ice—scarce as hen's teeth round here." The doctor turned to Okello. "Apples, she'll be." He tipped his head toward me. "But this bloke's got to stay."

I kissed my uncle goodbye as the nurse wheeled his cot away.

"What be da room?" Okello asked her.

"1018."

I wondered where the other 1017 rooms were.

SEVERAL NIGHTS LATER, Wy showed up kneeling by my bed. He shook my arm hard.

"Sheesh Wy! You scared me half to death!"

"I gotta talk to you." He hadn't said much since that awful day.

I leaned over to turned on the small lamp. "It's almost two a.m.—can't it wait?"

His face looked as pale as the moon. The skin around his eyes had pink splotches.

"I had a terrible dream," he began.

"Well go on. I'm up now." Shifting my legs made me wince.

He launched right in. "I was sitting on a bench in the dark and I saw this red being that was an animal that stood like a person and it started moving toward me."

"Slow down..."

He gulped. "The closer it got, I felt hot as hell, here, inside my chest. When the 'thing' got to me, my whole body was on fire—my hands, my head and all the way down to my feet. I was screaming!"

I tried to remember it was just a dream.

"It felt like I was dying, Rissy!" He trembled all over. "The red creature just stared me down. I couldn't speak! I couldn't run away!"

Fears plumed in my own heart. "What did it want?"

"I don't know. The thing just walked away, but I was still in agony. I thought God was punishing me for wanting to kill that guy."

I shuddered.

"But right then, a bright glowing man appeared in the distance. I know this sounds strange, but it was like my heart pleaded with him to help me."

"And did he?"

"Yes, he came slowly. And as he got nearer, the fire started to go out. First, my hands and feet. Then my arms and legs and my head." Big tears streamed down his cheeks. "And...when he got to me... only my heart...was still burning."

Wyeth broke down and wept, hiding his face in my sheets.

I'd never seen him so shook up. I barely recognized his voice. I put my hand on his shoulder and waited. After a bit, he lifted his head.

"Is there more?" I asked, softly.

He wiped his cheeks. "Yeah." He sniffed hard. "The glowing man reached in my chest...and took...the fire away." My brother paused to inhale through his mouth. "Then... the pain stopped."

My skin tingled all over. We sat silently for a while. I wanted to say something, but it felt afraid. I screwed up my courage.

"Wy."

"Yeah?"

"That was God." I bit my lip. "You know that, right?"

His slow nod was surprisingly calm, as if he was thinking it over still.

Then he rose off his knees to sit next to me on the bed. "What did you mean when you said, 'Don't be like him'?"

"When?"

"When you didn't want me to shoot that guy."

"Oh." I looked up at the ceiling. "I guess I meant...like Father."

"I figured." He stood up to go. "I've hated Hank as long as I can remember. But right now, for some strange reason—I don't."

SKEETS' RECOVERY WAS a slow process. Okello drove to the Mbarara hospital every few days and brought us news. Once a week, he took us along. It was troubling though. On bad days, Skeets simply couldn't remember things. He'd ask us to explain what happened. Other times he felt too dizzy to get out of bed. The doctor told us he was improving, but I wondered. Waiting was sheer misery. I took to biting my fingernails until a nurse mentioned what kinds of germs lived there.

Many of the orphans decided they would fast and pray. The maamas worried about it. Some of the little ones were too thin to miss a meal, yet they'd hide when posho and beans were served. That floored me. The worship service turned into long prayer vigils as the kids pleaded in unison for God to heal their Papa Nsiri.

I asked God to use his *horse* power.

Three weeks passed. Finally the doctor called, assuring us that Skeets would not die. The hospital was ready to release him. Still, he'd have to take it easy for another month. We left for Mbarara.

Okello filled out triplicate forms and took down the doctor's instructions. Wy and I headed to room 1018.

"Hey Junebutter." Skeets perked up as I entered. His happy-go-lucky spirit made me cheerful inside. Fully dressed, he sat on the edge of his cot.

"What's crackin' buddy?" He lifted a weak fist to bump knuckles with Wy.

I started gathering his stuff in a small duffle bag.

"Hey, I want to show you two something before we go," said Skeets.

We gathered close.

The Bible lay open on his lap. "Check this out." He read out loud. "God says...'*Do justice to the fatherless and the oppressed, so that man who is of the earth may strike terror no more.*' Psalm 10:18." Skeets looked up at my brother.

Wy stood motionless. His face reddened.

"That's what *you* did, Wyeth."

My brother shook his head. "Yeah...but I nearly ran over Rissy, not to mention a baby!" He wiped his forehead with the back of his hand. "*And* I almost killed a man."

"But you didn't," said Skeets. You stood up to that guy. He could've done a lot more harm. This is God's way of saying He's proud of you—and you too Iris. It was a brave move."

Wyeth straightened his shoulders a little. I don't think Father had ever said anything like that to my brother.

"You're both more *horse* than you realize."

We shared a laugh. Wy picked up the duffle bag, and Skeets took my arm.

"How did you dig up that particular verse?" I asked.

"I didn't really. Look at the number on my door."

Chapter 48

"I GOT MY GIDDY-UP back!" Skeets said.

We pulled up to the gate mid-afternoon. Skeets' homecoming was nothing short of a spectacle. The Birds of Paradise had erupted into full bloom. One hundred and forty-five orphans, twelve maamas, eight teachers, three garden keepers, and two cooks came as one flock, waving paper snowflakes attached to sticks. You'd have thought someone was getting married. I couldn't stop grinning.

Greetings would take a long time, because Skeets would insist on hugging every single person. And he knew each one by name. I still mixed up Okot with Okette, and Obua with Olaa. It wasn't a simple thing.

In anticipation, the maamas and the cooks had prepared a banquet. They made stuffed tomatoes, fried eggplant, fresh mango and pineapple bites, not to mention cassava, matooke and sweet potatoes. They even made fried chicken, which the kids called "Kentucky" for short. It was an all-day effort. The big boys had to kill and pluck over three dozen chickens. Tables placed end-to-end were covered with fern branches in lieu of tablecloths. At last, platters of colorful food were presented and the feasting began.

Later that evening, song and dance reached an entirely new level. The worship wasn't just lively—it was heartfelt. I sang myself hoarse. Something magical happened when God's people brimmed over with thanks and praise. It was hard to describe—even if you had a word collection.

The hour grew late. I walked Boy Sunday to his sleeping quarters. We held hands, swinging our arms in step with our feet. I hummed one of the refrains. At the door, I bent over to kiss his forehead. He gazed up at me with shining eyes, pointing to the spot where I'd planted the kiss. "God feeld dat 'bout Boy?" he asked.

"Buli kiseera," I said. It meant—*always*.

Boy peeled away with a smile that wouldn't end. As soon as he darted inside, I sprinted as fast as I could through the compound. My leg no longer hurt.

As I rounded the staff building, I noticed Wyeth, out by the back wall. I came to a dead stop. He paced in front of the wooden cross. I hid behind a tree trunk, my lungs still heaving from the run.

In the moonlight, I could see he was alone. He mumbled aloud, but I couldn't make out any words. Finally, he stood very still with his head bowed. I waited.

Then Wy gently added a rock to the pile.

Chapter 49

M Y SUITCASE LEANED against the gatehouse, full as a tick. I
lounged in Waiswa's plastic chair, all fresh and clean in my
traveling clothes. Waiswa raked green coffee beans in an open area,
spreading them thin to dry in the sun.

It was mid-December, and we were going to America for
Christmas. My uncle had promised Nana and Pops. Of course Wyeth
left his packing until the last minute. The drive to Entebbe would
take the better part of a day. Skeets chatted on the phone in the office, confirming our flights. He said we'd catch the "redeye,"
whatever that meant, but it would still take four planes and over
thirty-six hours to get home. I pressed my lips together. We didn't
really have a home in Beaconsfield anymore.

Sanyu and Binti strolled across the grass toward me.

Binti carried a bunch of bananas on her head. "Mukwano
gwange, my friend," she said, lowering the greenish-yellow fruit.
"You must try before da journey."

I had wanted to balance things on my head since I'd arrived.
My neatly brushed ponytail would get messed up, but I didn't care.

Sanyu lifted my chin. "Your hair too slipperish, somehow." She
tied a bandana over my head. "Dere," she said. That did the trick. I
made it to the mango trees and back without dropping the stack,
while they cheered me on.

With ease and grace, Musa maneuvered a soccer ball to where

we stood by the gate. Jonan and Boy tagged behind him, drawing continuous lines in the dirt with their sticks.

"See dis?" Boy tugged my arm. His eyes squinted with serious caution. "Is mark of s-s-snake." The edges of his mouth revealed mischief.

I played along. "A *snake* print?" My voice rose an octave.

"We be scaring da girls," explained Musa. "If dey stay inside because of feared snake, we don't have to share da ball." It was a Wyeth-like plan.

"I see."

A public transport van squealed to a stop by the entrance. We hadn't ordered any taxi service. Its engine idled high. Heat waves rose over the hood. Waiswa laid down his rake and jogged to the gate.

Bodies shifted inside the small bus crammed with people. Slowly and carefully, a thin woman squeezed out. She wore a tattered pink gomesi, a traditional outfit. Her sandals looked at least a century old. As soon as she shut the passenger door, the van sped off, leaving her in a cloud of fine red dust.

Seeing no danger, Waiswa opened the gate and greeted her. She carried a quilted sling bag. Her shoulders drooped. She kept looking at her clasped hands, giving only a nod to Waiswa's welcome. Her chin quivered.

Sanyu stepped forward, stretching out her hand. "Kale, nnyabo," she said, giving a little curtsy.

The woman acknowledged by touching Sanyu's hand. Rummaging through her bag, she pulled out an orange terrycloth rag, which she used to wipe her eyes and nose.

"May we help you?" I asked, sounding like a store clerk.

The woman appeared to be in her thirties, yet she moved with the weariness of an older woman. She didn't reply. Her face clouded up. Something was wrong.

Skeets pushed open the screen door with his shoulder, carrying a large suitcase. He waddled toward us, but immediately turned his attention to the visitor.

"Nnyabo, oli otya?" He set down the bag and strode over to extend his hand. "You are most welcome."

"I de maama," she said, as if guilty of something. She sank to her knees.

Skeets knelt down with her. "Yes, please—I don't understand."

"I come to offer *many* thanks," Her sling bag fell off her shoulder. After a great sigh, she continued. "You fight mwami wange," she cried. "My wicked husband. Otegeera?"

"Oh!" I gasped. "She's alive!"

Skeets recognized her at the same moment. "Nnyabo!" He pulled her to her feet and embraced the poor woman. She went limp in his arms.

"I'm sorry." He spoke tenderly. "You have suffered much."

Sanyu dashed off. I knew she ran to get the baby. I shot off after her. We burst into the nursery together, but then she turned to me. "You do! You da protector of child."

I swept the baby into my arms, disturbing his morning nap. Startled, the chubby-cheeked child began to cry.

"Maama has come!" I spoke gently with him as we hurried back. "Da *maama...*"

He sized up his tearful mother with big eyes. Then out came his pink lower lip. He seemed mad and happy altogether. The maama kissed and kissed her baby son, making shrill whoops as African women do.

Their joy became my joy—a moment that would stay in my mind for a long, long time. Maybe such reunions would come for me.

Chapter 50

As we soared across the vast ocean, clouds, water, and sky all blended together. We could've been flying upside down, and I wouldn't have known the difference. Shades of deep blue and turquoise swirled with cottony white strands of clouds. When the sun broke through, tiny waves reflected twinkles of light.

I thought about how my body was actually 30,000 feet off the ground. For a moment, it felt inconceivable to be so high above the planet. I wondered if people felt the same kind of terror and astonishment in leaving the earth at death. On the other hand, it might be rather peaceful. If clouds blurred the border between heaven and earth, maybe you wouldn't mind leaving one for the other. Maybe you'd hardly know.

What if, night after night, God used sleep as a rehearsal for heaven? By falling asleep, we let go of everything we know to enter the realm of dreams. Then, when the time was right—we'd enter the greatest dream of all. I wasn't being morbid. I wanted to believe that Mama and Tuck were not far away—that what was unseen was close to the seen. And as Skeets said, the unseen was greater. It was the real story.

The flight attendant came by. "Miss? Is your seat belt on?"

"Yes, ma'am."

"Good. We're about to land."

Chapter 51

How much love does it take to save a man?
It takes it all.

DAY AND NIGHT switched places. Nana brought warm milk to help, but I lay in bed wide awake, imagining our appointment at the prison. In a way, I didn't want Wyeth to go. His dream had changed things, but seeing Father again spelled all kinds of trouble.

When you're half asleep your mind can get stuck in a hamster wheel of crazy thoughts. Sometimes you just have to change the subject yourself. I pictured Boy Sunday—his slingshot and bottle caps in hand, guarding the compound from monkeys. I finally drifted off.

When morning came, I peered out the window. A winter storm had blown in from the west. The howling wind in the night had subsided, and now lacey snowflakes floated down outside. I dressed quickly, and pulled on a wool sweater.

The family had already gathered at the breakfast table.

"The highways are looking bad, honey," Nana said to Skeets.

"No worse than muddy roads in Africa," he said.

"Slick as snot," added Wyeth.

Nana gave my brother a look.

"You'd better leave earlier than planned," said Pops.

"Well, no offense," Wy said, respectfully. "But I'm not ready to go today."

Everyone paused. I looked up from my oatmeal.

"Another time?" Skeets asked.

"Yeah, another time."

The two-hour trip took an extra hour because of icy roads. On the way down, Skeets told me Hank was lucky they didn't lock him up in the Ohio Penitentiary in Columbus. I didn't see how there could be anything lucky about jail. My uncle reached for my hand as we entered the outskirts of Marion Ohio.

My chest grew taut. I conjured up images of dark prison cells with slimy walls and moldy food. What was it like to be in a limited space? You couldn't run. Someone else decided what you had for breakfast. What if no one smiled? What if you never saw another smile the rest of your life?

I focused on the small town scene out the window and repeatedly smoothed the flaps of my coat for no reason.

Skeets kept eyeing me. "You okay?"

"I guess." I puffed out my cheeks, and then released the air like a slow leak.

Skeets checked his handwritten directions. "I think we're here—"

"What should I say to him?" I interrupted.

We pulled into the parking lot. The sign said, "Marion Correctional Institution."

"Don't think too much about it." He patted my hand.

"I'm nervous as all get out." I eyed the facility grounds. "What if he's mean?"

My uncle pulled the car to a stop and turned off the motor. "Iris, take it easy. The truth is—he probably feels more awful than you do."

I flashed my eyes, revealing my doubts.

"Think about it, girl." Skeets pulled the keys from the ignition. "He's lost everything too—and he's had loads of time to think about it."

My throat felt dry.

"When I see Hank," Skeets continued, "I'm gonna picture Jesus standing in there with us." He laid his hand over mine. "Because, in fact, *He is.*"

My feet felt heavy as rocks when we left the car. I followed Skeets, stepping in his footprints. His strides were bigger than mine, and I almost lost my balance. We entered the first building. The thick door closed behind me with a loud click. It smelled stale inside, like a basement. We'd all be breathing the same air. I don't know why I thought about that. My stomach roiled.

All kinds of people crowded the waiting room. No children though. A few men came dressed in nice suits—probably lawyers. Others wore ordinary clothes like me. One woman had a tight-lipped frown. Either someone had yelled at her, or she was about to yell at someone. Or so it seemed to me.

The reception lady in police uniform looked far too muscular for a woman. Skeets showed her our passports, and she asked him to fill out a form. We both had to sign a log, noting the time of our arrival. There was also a space for our time of departure. It bothered me that she didn't smile at all. Skeets handed her the paperwork.

Then came the waiting. It was worse than waiting for a dentist appointment. We sat on hard plastic chairs. I swung my legs and tried to remember jump rope rhymes. I quickly ran out of those. Forty-five minutes went by.

"Don't they know how long we've been here?" I whispered to my uncle through clenched teeth.

The uniformed receptionist came toward us. "We're having a lot of visitors today. You'll have to see your inmate in the old section."

Our inmate?

She motioned us to follow.

"Here we go," Skeets said, placing a hand on my shoulder.

We went down a long corridor with several more loud clicking doors along the way. The floors were shiny. Our footsteps echoed. Finally she put us in front of a double-pane window that had something like chicken wire between the two sections of glass. There were two chairs and two telephone receivers. On the other side was a stool with another phone.

"He'll be right in," she said, leaving us.

Another ten minutes went by. My uncle read a brochure titled, "Visitation Rules."

Finally I heard the muted sound of a door opening and closing on the other side. I drew air into my lungs and froze to my chair. A gaunt man in a one-piece orange jumpsuit came and sat in the chair. I looked up but kept my chin down. He had dark circles under his eyes and a butch haircut. How could this be my father?

Skeets immediately picked up his receiver. Slowly, Hank took his. I knew a conversation was happening, but I'd checked out. My thoughts raced through random scenes...the fruit cupboard bunker, Mama's hidden diary, broken glass across our living room floor, Tuck skipping around the Christmas tree, Wyeth locked in his room, Father tapping his pencil at the breakfast table. My old life roared alive.

I lowered my head into my hands, trying to stop the rush of memories.

Still, more thoughts piled up...an empty vodka bottle in the trash, Mama tying her apron and waving goodbye, Anna Rae crying in our princess bed. My throat felt parched, as if it was closing up.

Skeets put his hand on my back. "She's a little jetlagged," he said into the phone.

"I need some water," I whispered. My head was still down.

"I'll go see about it." He laid down the receiver and leaned down to whisper. "Rissy, try to say something." He stood up to find the police lady.

Now it was just the two of us. I hadn't planned on that. With all I could muster, I looked up into my father's face. His cheeks drooped. Wrinkles formed on his forehead. His Adam's apple rose as he swallowed.

"Hello." He mouthed the word since I hadn't picked up the phone.

"Hey." My lips moved, but I made no sound.

We sat utterly still, with blinking sad eyes. I didn't know what would happen next. In a way, I didn't want him to speak or try to explain. After a moment, I raised my arm and placed my palm on the window. I made myself look at him again.

His eyes were glossy wet. He put his hand up to match mine on his side of the pane.

"I'm sorry," he said silently.

A weight dropped off me. Palm to palm. Warmth, in spite of glass and wire. An exchange of something deeper than words. And I knew down to my toes that he really was.

Then I licked my index finger and held it up—as if checking the direction of the wind. His face brightened. He did the same and smiled.

And Skeets returned with a paper cone of water.

Chapter 52

Nothing held back, nothing kept in reserve,
Nothing kept for another day.
Nothing spent on something else that we don't know about,
It's all been spent, and it was spent in a day.

It's all been done, it's all been said, it's all been spent...
And it was finished,
Yes, it was finished in a day.

"What happened in there?" Skeets paused to log our departure time.

I hurried past him, skipping out the door like a calf on a spring day.

"Rissy, what did you say to him?" He ran up to join me. "When I came back with the water, he seemed like an entirely different man."

"Just 'Hey,'" I said, sprinting off, inciting a race to the car. Skeets stood still for a moment but could easily catch up. I stopped long enough to hurl a snowball, which dinged off his shoulder.

"Oh so, that's how you want it!" Skeets hollered.

I squealed as a snowball flew past my ear. Another one nailed me squarely between the shoulder blades. I slammed against the car door and crouched down to hide.

He trudged up, out of breath. "You win," he said, pretending disappointment. "But honestly, girl, I'm kinda perplexed. Did he say anything to you?"

I bent down to form another snowball, but he took my arm.

"Tell me, Rissy."

How could I describe it? I shuffled my feet. "Well, we sort of touched hands at the window."

Skeets smiled with his eyes half closed. He didn't ask any more questions.

When we reached Mansfield, we pulled into a donut shop. I carried my Styrofoam cup of hot chocolate back to the car. After we buckled in, I leaned toward him to lock eyes. "Can we take the scenic way back?"

"You want to see the lake or something?" he said, biting into a chocolate éclair.

"No-o-o." I found a cup holder for my cocoa. It needed to cool down.

"You want to see *home*."

I could only nod. I felt torn up inside.

As we headed northwest on Route 250, I fell into silence and stared out the window. Skeets let me have my space. I wondered about things. Was Anna Rae still my friend? What kind of people actually lived in our house now? Did they have a girl? Did she get my room? That stirred up the weirdest feeling. All my life, I grew up in that room until everything went wrong. Mile after mile, I opened up memories as if they'd been locked in a trunk and hidden in the attic.

Suddenly, I remembered my stone. Its hard mound protruded from my pant pocket. I pictured God pointing at it with His great arm extending down from heaven. I ran my fingers over it. Only He knew it was there. I had carried it for a long time, over many miles. But the stone was more than just a memory of my old life.

Skeets finally turned on Lake Road. We passed the Golden Arches where our family got cheeseburgers after church. Then we crossed the bridge over Rocky Cliffs River. Kensington School looked much smaller. The neon "Open" light was on at Mike's Delicatessen.

I pointed left. "Can I?" I wanted to walk the Middle Strip.

"It's a cold day." Skeets lowered his brow. "Are you sure?"

"I'm sure. I'll be out the other end in twenty—tops." I held my breath.

He pulled to the side of the road and studied my face. His hesitation was killing me.

"Okay, button up. I'll get some groceries and meet you by the house."

I hopped out.

I entered the silence of a snowy wood in winter. It was a beautiful sort of calm, even without the sound of birds. A breeze hummed in the higher branches. I snapped a twig, rolled a stone, and shook heavy snow off a branch simply to hear the criccck, grunnch, and whumphh.

There were no other footprints. I relished having the forest all to myself. My heart was fuller than full, and it felt like worship—even though I wasn't in church or singing my heart out. For once I wasn't crying my eyes out either.

I jumped over a familiar log. The bare trees looked so different, but I didn't need them to find the path. I passed through the willows, grabbing their long branch arms first with my left hand, then my right as if we were square dancing. I do-si-doed with a maple tree, using the tips of my boots to flick snow in the air. That didn't last long. I slipped and ended up flat on my back. The blanket of snow felt fluffier than a mattress. I stayed there, motionless. The winds had blown away the gray clouds, and blue sky appeared in the west. I closed my eyelids and rested. I just wanted to be there.

Skeets' words echoed in my mind. *All you have is now...*

After awhile, I stood and brushed off my coat. It had to be about 2:30. I plodded to the edge of the Middle Strip. No school children were on their way home yet. I passed Billy Stebbins' house to check on their homemade rink. It looked exactly the same. My mouth watered for Mrs. Stebbins' fries. The sidewalks were too snowy to see any "Ws," but I thought about our game and imagined Anna Rae prancing along next to me.

Soon, I stood directly in front of our old house. I bit the inside of my cheek. Did I dare knock? I was the stranger now. My knees felt weak, but I straightened my shoulders and quietly made my way to the front porch. Recklessly, I rang the doorbell and then started squirming. My cheeks felt hot. What would I say? A minute passed. I stretched out my neck to peer in the windows. Rocking in place, I watched for any signs of life. Finally, I pushed the button again. Still, no one came.

Was it okay to go around and see the backyard? It felt rash, but I had to even if my footprints gave me away.

The new owners had shoveled the patio. In fact, they'd moved the entire woodpile there. The new spot was much closer to the backdoor. Mama would've scolded about that. Mice lived in wood-piles, and she didn't want them getting in the house.

I knelt down by the spot where we'd made our handprints in the cement. I found mine and brushed it clean with my mitten. Then I laid my warm bare hand in the stone cold imprint.

And that very instant, God spoke to me clear as day.

There was a little girl here once, He said in the softest whisper.

My breath hitched. I was startled, but not afraid like the time in the school parking lot. A rush of love engulfed me. God, it seemed, cared about that little girl whose hand had once fit that mold. She was the hopeful kind, before all the sorrow and pain.

"I *am* that girl," I said peacefully. Something had changed inside me. Something felt better. I knew, because I wanted to see my father happy again. I also believed that Wyeth wouldn't be in trouble like before. And I understood that God had a house with a room just for me. A place where Nana wouldn't be sick, and Pops wouldn't be old. And just outside that house, I'd find Tuck whist-ling to all the stray dogs.

Best of all, Mama would come and meet me at the gate. I was certain of it.

But until then, I wanted to make the journey with Skeets.

And Jesus.

I stood up and wandered over to the sycamore tree, the place where I'd whispered things to God. I reached in my pocket and pulled out my stone. I rolled it in my hand and thought about the day we buried Mama. For a moment, I was lost in thought, my vis-ion blurred.

I'd almost left my stone at the cross in Africa like Wy, but I wasn't ready then. I'd nearly tossed it at the prison after seeing Father. But to be honest, down in the hidden places—it wasn't really about him.

I knelt down to sit on my heels next to the great tree. If I had

had a pencil, I would've scratched out the letters "G-O-D" on it. That was the thing—my deep secret. I closed my eyes and tipped back my head. The sun felt warm and soft on my face. I took a deep breath. It was time. I loosened my fingers and let the stone roll from my hand.

After Notes

IN 1997, I MET KATHLEEN when she joined my women's group. One of those Wednesdays, she described her earliest experience of hearing God's voice: It was an ordinary day in a school parking lot. God spoke in an audible voice and told her something she would not have humanly known—*and it proved to be true.* She was ten years old. Kathleen's remarkable encounter essentially inspired this novel.

For the last twenty-five years, I've collected many true accounts like Kathleen's experience including some of my own. I fervently believe that God seeks out points of contact with us. When it happens, we often think, *that's amazing!* And yet, it's not so farfetched when you remember this same God chose to enter the human race.

Everywhere I go, I meet people who are faithfully living the Christian life but say they have no real experience of God. Like me, they may feel touched at a candlelit Christmas Eve service. They may find countless biblical truths relevant to their lives. Still they shrug when it comes to any authentic experience with God. They're leery of being called crackpots, yet they long for something real, beyond mere religious activity and rhetoric.

In my first book, *Closer Than Your Skin*, I tell my own unfolding discovery of a God who is accessible and wants to be known. In this second book, I've woven *true* God stories into a fictional storyline with fictional characters so readers can see the variety of ways God is moving, speaking, guiding, encouraging, warning, and loving ordinary people like you and me. It is my hope that these stories will inspire you to look for His fingerprints in your own world of divine happenstance—that you will take time to consider a dream, notice a seeming coincidence, look up that Scripture, ponder some song lyrics, and develop your understanding of symbolic, metaphorical language—believing that God wants to speak to you *personally*.

Of course the fresh "words" of God have to line up with the written Word—which naturally makes the Bible a great place to start. The more you know the Bible, the more "vocabulary" God has to work with.

I also want to clarify that Iris' father, Hank, is not a reflection of my father. Quite the contrary. I was given a stable, loving father (and mother), and in that I am fortunate.

Nonetheless, earthly fathers profoundly shape one's idea of a heavenly Father. For better or worse, there is an astonishing parallel there. If your father was mean, silent, abusive or absent, those experiences cast the same shadow on God. That said, it's difficult to get close to someone who's hurt you, someone you don't trust, and this is often the spiritual logjam for many when it comes to knowing God. To make matters worse, if you feel far away from God, it's easy to get stuck in the quagmire of condemnation and wonder if God is for or against you.

Even the best fathers obscure what God is really like. We must experience this all-important relationship with Father God directly. We must swim in the ocean of His love—the only thing that can heal the wounds from our original human relationships. And we must find this connection with God for a very broken world, because we can't give to others what we don't have ourselves. May you find in this story something that resonates in your own life and come to know the living God, who is indeed closer than your skin.

SUSAN D. HILL
AUGUST 2015

Acknowledgements

WRITING A BOOK feels like a long pregnancy, and then you finally give birth. It's all consuming, complex, and sometimes tedious in the process. Delivery is always traumatic! I remember thinking: *I'll never do that again!* Yet the results are rewarding, and one easily forgets the pain.

So it was for me as I pondered writing a second and far more challenging book—a novel, for crying out loud. What was I thinking? My editor, Mick Silva, suggested fiction. In a vivid dream, my writing mentor, Kathy (Tyers) Gillin, waved me onward. My friend Kathleen's encounter with God in a school parking lot, and Don Potter's spontaneous song inspired me deeply. And so, I started to envision a story about ten-year-old Iris Rose Somerset, and her snarky older brother Wyeth. I even pictured a beat up old 1970s yellow Buick—the "scary movie car" driven by their father, Hank.

But writing takes an enormous amount of time. And one day I completely stalled out. The story had gone cold, and I questioned God. *Is this _really_ what You want me to do?* Within a two-week period, I was given a few startling answers.

- First, I received a baby shower invitation from my friend April Brown. She'd given birth to a baby girl and had named her, *Iris.*

- Next, a company included in my IRA portfolio mailed me a prospectus. The company at that time was called *Wyeth.*

- A few days later I pulled into a parking lot to make a deposit at my bank. When I came out of the building, next to my Subaru was "the scary movie car" I'd pictured for the book. It was pale yellow and even had a broken grill. I stopped and stared. My heart pounded. It seemed as though God was saying, "Yes! These are the characters! Here is the car! Follow the story and I will write it with you!" Seven years later, it is now in your hands. And so first and foremost, I have God to thank.

I also have many people to acknowledge. My husband, Duncan, believed in the project from the start and recounted many times the revelation and confirmations from God when I battled self-doubt.

He is also behind the character of Skeets, helping me shape this beloved uncle's unique personality and voice.

Mick Silva, my editor, also walked this seven-year journey with me. His keen insights and guidance were absolutely essential. Sheri, his wife, also cheered me on. They have become treasured friends.

To Kathleen Rock, Mary Jean Gaskill, and Jenny Thornburg, thank you for allowing me to fictionalize some of your true encounters with God. My hope is that your stories will be a gift to countless people.

To my writers group: Kathy (Tyers) Gillin, Jenny Thornburg, Sharon Dunn, Jamie (Upschulte) Downer, Lynn Kinnaman, Suzee Branch, Claudia LeCoure, Wynn Gillis, Lisa Weaver, Kristine Price, and others in those circles—where would I be without you! Some of you grew up under the shadow of alcoholism and helped me create Iris' complex father, Hank. Also, Jamie Downer and Suzee and Steve Branch served as beta readers, taking their own precious time to give me important feedback.

To my parents, Richard and Carolyn Donaldson, I am eternally grateful to you for giving me a loving and stable family and for believing in me as a writer.

To my children, Katie (and John), Sarah, and Nate, thank you for listening and encouraging me. And a special thank you to my gifted son, Nate, for his patience and artistry in producing the cover. Thank you to Kenzie Hopkins, Maizy and Cody Dykstra, and Rocket Smith for their willingness to pose for the cover photo.

Thank you also to The Ladies Aid Society, my Home Group, and my extended family for standing with me in this long, long process.

About The Author

SUSAN D. HILL graduated from Ohio Wesleyan University and worked in human resource management for ten years. She served as a leader with Bible Study Fellowship and Young Life, and currently works with Uganda Orphans Fund, a non-profit NGO founded by her husband, Duncan Hill. Since 2002, UOF has built over thirty orphanages or schools for AIDS and war orphans, and other vulnerable children in Uganda. She writes for the Fund, administrates a sponsorship program, and serves on the Board. For more information, visit **www.ugandaorphans.com**.

> "My husband's work with children at risk in Uganda has provided a dramatic backdrop for **Bird, Horse, and Muffin**—a context for hard spiritual questions and the presence of a mighty God."

Susan started writing for publication in 2003 through magazine articles with *Light & Life, War Cry, AWE, Christian Educators Journal*, and *World* magazine. WaterBrook Press/Random House released her spiritual memoir in February 2008:

Closer Than Your Skin:
Unwrapping the Mystery of Intimacy with God.

She has been the keynote speaker at numerous women's retreats, conferences and college gatherings, and facilitates an interdenominational women's study group that started in 1997. Susan writes a blog post every other week on her website and can be contacted online: **www.susandhill.com**.

The American Christian Fiction Writers' 2012 Genesis Contest for new authors recognized **Bird, Horse, and Muffin** as one of the top three novels in Women's Fiction.

Susan has been married to Duncan since 1978. They have three grown children, along with two granddaughters, and live in Montana.